PUFFIN CANADA

THE HIDDEN WORLD

Alison Baird is the author of *The Wolves of Woden*; *The Dragon's Egg*, which was nominated for the Ontario Library Association Silver Birch Award and designated a regional winner by the participating children; *White as the Waves*, which was shortlisted for the IODE Violet Downey Book Award; and *The Witches of Willowmere*. She lives in Oakville, Ontario.

Other Books by Alison Baird

The Dragon's Egg

White as the Waves

The Wolves of Woden

The Witches of Willowmere

THE HIDDEN WORLD

ALISON BAIRD

PUFFIN
CANADA

PUFFIN CANADA

Published by the Penguin Group

Penguin Books, a division of Pearson Canada, 10 Alcorn Avenue, Toronto, Ontario,
Canada M4V 3B2

Penguin Books Ltd, 80 Strand, London WC2R 0RL, England

Penguin Putnam Inc., 375 Hudson Street, New York, New York 10014, U.S.A.

Penguin Books Australia Ltd, 250 Camberwell Road, Camberwell, Victoria 3124, Australia

Penguin Books India (P) Ltd, 11, Community Centre, Panchsheel Park,
New Delhi – 110 017, India

Penguin Books (NZ) Ltd, cnr Rosedale and Airborne Roads, Albany, Auckland 1310,
New Zealand

Penguin Books (South Africa) (Pty) Ltd, 24 Sturdee Avenue, Rosebank 2196, South Africa

Penguin Books Ltd, Registered Offices: 80 Strand, London WC2R 0RL, England

First published in Viking by Penguin Books Canada Limited, 1999

Published in Puffin Books, 2000

5   7   9   10   8   6

Copyright © Alison Baird, 1999

Manufactured in Canada.

CANADIAN CATALOGUING IN PUBLICATION DATA

Baird, Alison, 1963–
The hidden world

ISBN 0-14-130293-3

I. Title.

PS8553.A367H52 2000   jC813'.54   C99-932517-5
PZ7.B34Hi 2000

Visit Penguin Books' website at **www.penguin.ca**

For my aunts and uncles in Newfoundland:
George and Bernice Morgan
and
Don and Sue Morgan

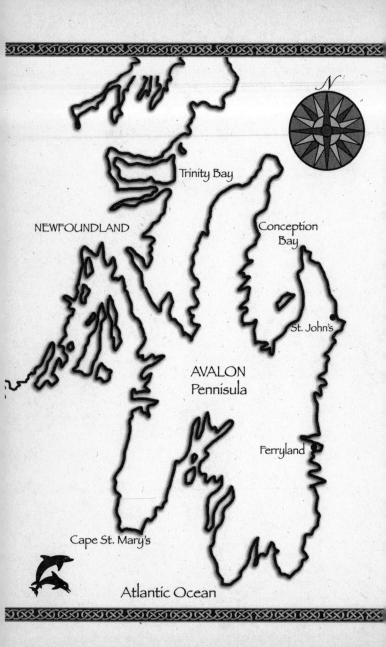

NEWFOUNDLAND

Trinity Bay

Conception
Bay

St. John's

AVALON
Pennisula

Ferryland

Cape St. Mary's

Atlantic Ocean

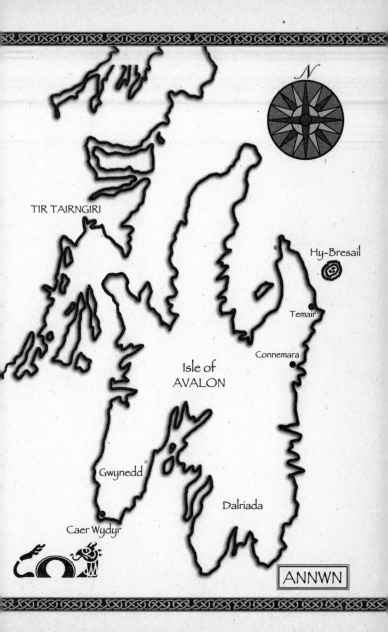

TIR TAIRNGIRI

Hy-Bresail

Temair

Connemara

Isle of
AVALON

Gwynedd

Dalriada

Caer Wydyr

ANNWN

On ne voit bien qu'avec le coeur. L'essentiel est invisible pour les yeux.

(It is only with the heart that one sees clearly. What is essential is invisible to the eye.)

Antoine de Saint-Exupéry
Le Petit Prince

Pronunciation Guide

IRISH WORDS

Author's note: the language I call "Gaelic" in this book is really known as Old Irish. There are some differences between Old and Modern Irish pronunciations, as shown below.

Put the stress on the syllable written in capital letters. Letters in brackets should be pronounced very softly.

* *ch* at the end of a syllable is a guttural sound (made in the back of your throat) such as the "ch" in the name "Bach"; "gh" at the end of a syllable is a softer guttural sound as in "lough" (i.e., Lough Ness).

** *ch* at the start of a word is a guttural sound such as the "ch" in "chutzpah"

Aengus	AYN-gus
airbacc Giunnae	AR-vack G(y)IN-a
ard-righ	ard-REE
Badb	BAWD(th)-iv (Old Irish)
	BOW (rhymes with "cow") (Modern Irish)
Brandubh	BRAN-duv
Cailleach Bheur	KY-yuck VAIR (rhymes with "fair")
Cathbad	KATH-vad(th) (Old Irish)
	KAFF-a (Modern Irish)
Cromm Cruach	KROM KROO-ach*
curragh	KUR-agh
Dana	DON-a
Daoine Sidhe	DIN-a shee
Dairmait	D(y)EER-mud
Domnu	DOV-new
dún	DOON

Éire	AYR-a ("ay" as in "hay")
Emain Ablach	EV-in OV-lach*
Ériu	AYR-you ("ay" as in "hay")
Finnabair	FIN-a-veer
Fragarach	FRA-gar-ach*
Grainne	GRON-ya
immram	IM-rov (rhymes with "improv")
Lia Fail	LEE-a FAW-il ("faw" rhymes with "paw")
Lochlannach	LOCH*-lon-ach*
Lugh	LOO(gh*) (Old Irish)
	LOO (rhymes with "blue") (Modern Irish)
Macha	MACH*-a
Magh Tuireadh	MAW(gh*)T(y)UR-ad(th) (Old Irish)
	MOY T(y)UR-a (Modern Irish)
Mannanan mac Lir	MON-on-non mock LYR ("lyr" as in "lyric")
Medb	MAYV
Morrigan, the	MO-ree(gh*)-an
Nemain	NEV-in
Niamh	NEEV
Nuada	NEW-ed(th)-a
Ogham	O(gh*)-em (long "O" as in "stone") (Old Irish)
	O-em (Modern Irish)
Padraig	PAWD(th)-rig (Old Irish)
	PAW-rig (Modern Irish)
rath	ROTH
Seanchan	SHAN-(c)hawn**
tarbhfheis	TOW-riv-ESH ("tow" rhymes withy "cow")
tine éigin	TIN-a AY-gin
Tir fo Thuinn	T(y)EER fo THIN (Old Irish)
	T(y)EER fo HIN (Modern Irish)

Tir Tairngiri	T(y)EER T(y)AR-in-gri ("gri" as in grizzle)
tuath	TOO-ath (Old Irish)
	TOO-a (Modern Irish)
Tuatha de Danaan	TOO-ath-a DAY DON-in

WELSH WORDS

In the Welsh language the consonants C and G are always hard (as in *car*, *goose*). The "dd" sounds like the "th" in "the" (not "thorn"). The "ch" is pronounced as in the name "Bach". The "ll" sound is made by placing the tip of the tongue against the roof of the mouth, just behind the front teeth, and breathing out: a "hissing" sound.

In modern Welsh the stress is normally placed on the penultimate (second to last) syllable.

Annwn	an-oon
Arawn	are-own (as in "ounce")
arglwydd	ar-gloith ("th" as in "the")
Arianrhod	air-ee-an-hrod
Caer Wydyr	k-eye-r we-dr
Cantref Gwaelod	kant-rev goo-eye-load
Craig yr Aderyn	kr-eye-g uhr add-air-in
Creiddylad	crayth-lad
Cymru	kum-ree
Gwern Abwy	goo-urn ah-boy
Gwion	gwee on
Gwydion	goo-uh-dee-on
Gwynedd	gwen-ith ("th" as in "the")
Llys Don	lees don
Mabon	mah-bon
Tylwyth Teg	tui-oith tayg
Ynys Afallon	uhn-is avallon

ACKNOWLEDGEMENTS

I would like to express my appreciation to the Canada Council, without whose assistance this book would never have been written. I would also like to thank my editor Meg Masters, and everyone at Penguin who contributed to the making of this book; Judith Diehl, for her advice and encouragement and most of all her friendship; and my Morgan relatives in St. John's, Newfoundland, especially Trudy Morgan-Cole, for all of their help with the research.

Two non-fiction works were particularly helpful in the writing of this story, and I would like to acknowledge them and their authors: *Strange Terrain: The Fairy World in Newfoundland* by Barbara Rieti, and *A History and Ethnography of the Beothuk* by Ingeborg Marshall. Thanks also are due to Anne Connon of the Centre for Celtic Studies at St. Michael's College, University of Toronto, for providing me with the Irish word pronunciations; and a heartfelt *diolch* to John Otley and Rod Branch, for assisting me with the Welsh.

I would also like to thank my family, especially my mother, Violet (Morgan) Baird, whose recollections of life in Newfoundland were the seed from which this novel grew.

THE HIDDEN
WORLD

Chapter One

IT WAS LISA WHO BEGAN IT. Things usually began with Lisa, then the others followed her lead—*like a chorus*, Maeve thought.

"So what makes you think you can act?"

"I *know* I can." Maeve was defiant, her voice a little tremulous, but she was still determined not to back down, not in front of Lisa Smith and her gang.

The girls were pretending to be amused, but she sensed their resentment of what seemed to them a completely misplaced confidence. They felt a need—almost, one might say, a duty—to set her straight, put her in her place.

"Quit dreaming, Maeve. Ashley will get the part, you know that as well as I do. She's gorgeous, and you—" Lisa hadn't bothered to finish the sentence, but had looked Maeve up and down contemptuously while her friends sniggered.

Maeve flushed. Her looks were one matter on which she could offer no argument. Though not stout, she was sturdily made—like a building designed to stand firm against onslaughts of wind and weather. In her limbs and in the moulding of her face there was an uncompromising solidity. But she had persisted. "What's that got to do with anything? I said I want to be an *actress*, not Miss Universe. Acting has nothing to do with what you look like. There're always character roles, and—"

"I give up! Catch *me* trying to help this kid again." Lisa had shouldered her backpack and turned away with an air of disgust. "Ashley's dad has offered to help pay for the stage sets." She threw this over her shoulder as she walked off.

And like a fool I didn't listen, Maeve thought now, wincing. *I must have been out of my mind.*

The street along which she was walking was lined with large, prosperous-looking houses, half of them designed in a Victorian style, with brick façades and pointed gables, the other half imitation Tudor. Like all the houses in the Balsam Heights development, they were of approximately the same height and breadth, with two-door garages, short driveways and one small strip of lawn at the front. There were few trees in the development, despite its name. Neat, close-clipped hedges were the dominant form of greenery.

It was early spring, damp and chilly, and a cold rain was falling. Maeve huddled into her coat and quickened her pace, her mind running over and over the events of the day. Lisa, of course, had been right. There had always been a sharp, knowing look in Lisa's grey eyes: she understood how the world worked. Maeve should have expected it; she should have guessed. But the possibility of real success for the first time ever had briefly intoxicated her, and she had been caught unawares.

Quit dreaming, said the remembered voice.

She pushed open the front door of her imitation Tudor home, then hesitated as she noticed an acrid smell on the air. Mom was smoking again: a bad sign. She'd quit last year—for good, supposedly. What had made her start again?

Mom was in the living room, reading a magazine—or at least turning its pages, quickly and angrily. Her eyes were fixed on a point in space that seemed to lie beyond the printed words. There were three butts in the ashtray in front of her. Somehow Maeve knew, without asking, that Mom and Brandon had been quarrelling again. The feel of it was in the air, bitter and lingering like the cigarette smoke. Brandon's stereo was blaring up in his bedroom—the kind of music he knew Mom hated.

Maeve stood in the doorway looking thoughtfully at her mother. She had been beautiful once—still was, really. Her hair was gold-blonde and luxuriant; it had been long in the old days, down to her shoulders, though she wore it now in a short, curly perm. Her eyes had lines about them, wrinkles of worry, but they were still the same bright china blue. They turned up to Maeve briefly, before returning to the magazine.

"Oh, Maeve." Her voice was flat, toneless, but the hands clutching the magazine shook perceptibly. "How was your day?"

It wasn't really a question, but some answer was required. To say nothing would seem rude, or be mistaken for sulking. Maeve thought of saying, "Fine," in the same dull voice, but she reflected that Mom would have to know eventually. "I didn't get the part, Mom."

"Part?" her mother murmured.

"The part I wanted, in the play." She could no longer keep a tremor out of her voice. "It went to—"

Her mother flung the magazine down irritably. "Oh, for heaven's sake, Maeve! I don't want to hear about it. I'm having enough problems of my own!"

But you asked, Maeve could have protested. Her mouth remained closed, however, her features schooled to an unresponsive mask as she turned to leave the room. *Not a good actress?* she thought drily, mounting the stairs with a slow, tired tread. Lisa had no idea. . . .

Maeve went straight to her room, pausing to glance in her mirror. Her short, straight hair was dark brown, lank and lustreless; beneath their straight black brows her eyes were hazel—not even a true green like Dad's, but an indecisive halfway hue, greenish-brown. Her features were of the sort that are described as "strong" by people who are trying to be kind. She sighed heavily. She was fifteen, an age when most girls began to blossom—like Ashley Robinson, she thought with a pang. Ashley could turn heads just by walking into a room. But Maeve Morgan O'Connor was plain—there was just no denying it. She'd got all her looks from Dad's side of the family.

Maeve quite liked mirrors, in spite of what they showed her. She had always enjoyed the strange reversal of things they presented. Mirrors gave you back the world, fresh and unexpected; presented new angles and perspectives; made you marvel again at shapes and colours. As a child she had often imagined entering a looking-glass like Alice, venturing into that backwards land. It had been her delight to wander

4

about the house holding a small hand mirror before her so that she might see everything anew. If she held it beneath her chin, it reflected the ceiling, and she could pretend that everything had been turned upside down and that she was walking along the stuccoed ceilings among the inverted light fixtures—peering out through inverted windows at blue deeps of bottomless sky.

"What on earth are you doing?" Mom had once demanded in bewilderment on seeing her little girl engaged in this activity.

"I'm walking on the ceiling, Mommy. It's fun." But Mom had just continued to look at her in blank puzzlement.

Poor Mom. She'd probably wanted a daughter who would be golden-haired and beautiful as she was. Instead, life had given her Maeve, who was not only plain but odd as well. "Thank God for Brandon," she had once overheard Mom saying to Dad. It was Maeve's brother who had inherited Mom's colouring, her fair skin and blue eyes and gold-blond hair. He was popular at school—unlike Maeve—and had always had plenty of friends. But now there was the raucous music coming from his room; there were the loud furious arguments in the small hours of the morning that roused Maeve from sleep. There was an atmosphere of stress in the house whenever he was in it, and Mom had not thanked God for Brandon lately.

Maeve hung up her damp coat and tossed her book-bag down in a corner. If only there was a way to escape all of this! There had been a "dress-up" drawer in her bureau long ago; Mom had given her some old dresses and costume jewellery so she could "play at being a grown-up." But Maeve had loved to put on different personalities with the dresses, to become other people, act out parts in stories of her own invention. She yearned for a dress-up drawer now. What a relief to put off your self just as easily as you'd take off your coat—put it off and set it aside, turn into somebody else, for a little while anyway. To *not* be Maeve O'Connor for an hour or two . . . But release would have to come from some other source now.

She looked at her bookcase, crowded still with her childhood favourites: the Chronicles of Narnia; E. Nesbit; L. M. Montgomery; *Alice in Wonderland*, of course; and *Peter Pan*. And there was the book of King Arthur and his knights, which Brandon had once been given by Grandma but hadn't wanted. It sat next to her book of Shakespeare's plays. Atop the bookcase lay a small paperback: *Adventure in the Otherworld* by Jean MacDougall O'Connor. On the cover were knights on horseback, with children riding behind them. She picked up the book and opened it. There on the flyleaf was the faded ink scrawl: "For my very favourite granddaughter, Maeve, with love, Jean O'Connor." This was a joke—Maeve was her only granddaughter—but there was real affection in the author's scrawled words. Maeve had read her late grandmother's book a hundred times at least— it was dog-eared now, and pages were falling out of it. But the story itself was eternally fresh and enthralling. It told of a young Newfoundland girl named Emma who one day wandered too far onto the barrens and walked right out of the world into another place. A land of fairies and giants and dragons, of knights and kings. The Otherworld.

As a child, Maeve had longed to pass through such a hidden portal herself; it became her favourite fantasy, replacing her looking-glass dream. She curled up now in her most comfortable chair with the book. The black-and-white photo on the back was of a younger woman than she remembered. For her, Grandma's face would always be as she had last seen it, all those years ago: her crinkled pink-white skin and silvery hair; her eyes, which could smile like sunlit water but were in repose a still and pensive shade of green, the colour of a pool in a quiet wood where no one ever goes. There had been something magical about her. Her home province of Newfoundland had seemed to Maeve a land of romance, with place names straight out of old stories: the Avalon Peninsula, for instance, which always made her think of the Isle of Avalon in the King Arthur stories.

"Grandma," a younger Maeve had ventured once when they were sitting reading a book together, "are . . . are there such things as fairies?" She had waited in fear for the answer, knowing that Grandma would certainly tell her the truth, but still half-hoping for a yes.

A curious expression had come over her grandmother's face, and at first Maeve thought she was not going to answer. Then Grandma had leaned close and said in a soft, low voice, "Do you know, I really think there *might* be." And for an instant, it had seemed to Maeve that she was going to say something else. But then she had just smiled and returned to her reading.

Maeve smiled herself at the memory, and plunged into the pages of her grandmother's book.

Maeve had just arrived with Emma at the great castle of Temair when voices from the room below jerked her back to the real world. Dad was home, his deep voice resonating throughout the house.

". . . I don't like that crowd he's in with. Coming home at two a.m., blind drunk! It'll be drugs next, you watch."

Her mother's voice rose plaintively. "What did I do? Where did I go wrong? Why couldn't I have had normal kids, like everyone else? I ran into June Robinson at the supermarket today, and she just talked and talked about her daughter. Her Ashley is attractive, a good student, always happy—"

Dad snapped, "Of course the kid's happy! Her father's a millionaire, so she'll never lack for friends. She gets whatever she wants: clothes, trips, racing bikes. Why *wouldn't* she be happy?"

At this point Brandon turned on his stereo again to drown them out, and Maeve tried to return to her book. But the bitter sarcasm in Dad's voice hurt her. She knew that at least some of that bitterness was directed at himself, and she longed to run down and console him, but there was nothing to say. The lines on the page before her seemed to blur, and she found that she was reading the same sentence over and over. After a few minutes Brandon switched to his earphones, and there were the voices again. Arguing still. Dad's voice now had an edge of desperation to it: "At least spare me the sight of the smug rich flaunting their expensive cars and clothes! If I must be poor, let it be in a poor province!"

"But Newfoundland!" Mom sounded appalled. "It's an absolute backwater! There aren't any jobs there at all!"

"Roy might find me something. And there we could buy a house outright—a real house, not one of these tacky jobs with their fancy fronts and plywood walls! No mortgage, no ruinous property taxes . . ."

Poor Dad. He was still upset about being laid off—"Just cast aside, after fifteen years!" he had said incredulously when it happened. "Not so much as a handshake. Just, 'Clean out your desk, please, you're not wanted any more.'" His work search was not going well, either. He had to be getting desperate if he was talking about going back to impoverished Newfoundland, where they didn't even have fish to catch any more. He must know Mom would never move *there.*

Maeve turned off the light and lay down on her bed. The streetlights were coming on, their sodium glow staining the overcast sky a dull, luminous copper. She closed her eyes, and in the darkness that lay behind their lids she sought the green and secret place in which she always found refuge. There were trees in that place; she formed them in her mind—not the bare budding trees of March but trees of late spring, enfolded in clouds of delicate, unfurling leaves. . . .

"I'm telling you there isn't any work! Not in this field. And a man my age can't just start over. Perhaps you should be looking for work—"

"And what kind of job do you think *I'd* be able to get now? *I've* been out of the workforce for seventeen years! I gave up a good, promising career to raise *your* kids, look after *your* house—that was the deal, remember? 'I don't want a working wife,' you said—"

They were both getting angrier by the minute. They'd be yelling soon. "That was then, this is now," Dad countered weakly. "The kids are grown. Can't you find something, even part-time?"

"As what? A waitress?"

. . . And lilacs, and magnolias, and apple trees all covered in white or wine-coloured blossoms . . .

Dad's angry misery rumbled through the room below. "For once I'd like to live in a place where I'm valued for *who* I am, not for how much money I make. I'm sick and tired of trying to keep up with the Joneses. And our kids, what are they learning here? Either to be greedy and acquisitive, or to envy kids who have more money and gadgets than they have. They could use some real values, Brandon especially, and they're not going to learn them here, that's obvious."

. . . There were trees and there was sunlight. It fell between the branches in long streams and lay in patches on the forest floor. Tall maples, birches with their silver bark and conifers too: resinous-smelling pines. Their needles crunched underfoot. But here where she lay there was moss, softer than the softest carpet. In the distance the tree trunks faded into a green dusk. Birds were singing all around her, large, dove-coloured birds that perched on boughs overhead or flew from tree to tree in a blur of white wings. Birds of the Otherworld . . .

"We can live within our means there. Don't you see? It's either go there and get by, or stay here and be poor."

"Then go there yourself. Who's stopping you?"

The voices faded, drowned by birdsong.

Chapter Two

MAEVE GAZED LISTLESSLY OUT THE WINDOW, lost in thought.

There was nothing outside but clouds, a dense, impenetrable, cottony layer of grey far below her through which nothing at all could be seen. It was like being a little girl again, looking out an upside-down mirror-window at a topsy-turvy sky. But these clouds really were beneath her. All around her the other passengers sat and read or dozed while the drone of the jetliner's engines reverberated through the cabin. She craned her neck, trying to see out the window ahead of hers, glimpse a gap somewhere in the cloud layer. There was none.

Maeve slumped against the window-pane. She had not wanted to take this trip, especially not alone. "I just want you to see my side of the family," Dad had said, almost pleading. She could see his face now: the greying hair all along his temples, the lines around his anxious green eyes. "We see a lot of your mom's people in Toronto, but never the Newfoundland relatives."

There had been a time, once, when the two of them spoke openly and easily about anything; when she ran to him with broken toys to be mended, problems to be solved. Now they both seemed to be struggling for words like strangers.

"Sure, Dad," she had replied, trying to make her voice sound normal to reassure him. She couldn't bear the haggard look on his face. Mom too looked worried and miserable, when she was not putting on the dreadful forced cheerfulness that fooled no one. Maeve knew enough about acting to be able to tell when other people were doing it.

They really must be serious about this Newfoundland move if they had spent all that money on airfare for her. They must be sending her there to give her a feel for the place, she thought, see how she would adjust to living there. She did not want to move; but neither could she summon any really strong regrets at the thought of leaving Ontario. *After all, it would be a fresh start. It isn't as though I'd be leaving any friends behind*, she thought ruefully.

The pilot announced that they were now over St. John's, Newfoundland, and would soon be arriving at the airport, but still she could see nothing below her. The plane banked, began to descend. They were among the clouds, and the dull greyness enveloped the plane. She could sense the steep descent, yet still the greyness persisted, opaque and seemingly bottomless. Was it cloud or fog through which they now flew? It was impossible to tell.

At last the clouds bgean to wisp away and she could see. Maeve stared incredulously at the view below. Her impression was one of utter barrenness—an endless expanse of igneous rock, scored and gashed by long-gone glaciers. Some of the scars had become long, narrow lakes reflecting the grey of the sky. A few stretches of dark green coniferous forest mottled the landscape. She saw no houses, no neat and orderly farmers' fields. It might have been the surface of an alien planet.

Her father used to refer to Newfoundland affectionately as "the Rock." It had never occurred to her to take the term literally.

Soon the stony land was falling away in cliffs, rugged and sheer. The plane was wheeling out over a sea like grey leather, dully gleaming and minutely wrinkled with waves. There were flecks of white in it—ships, perhaps? The sea drew nearer, the rolling waves had more depth to them: the surface now looked like a sheet of corrugated grey metal. And the white things . . . no, surely it couldn't be.

She gaped in disbelief at the cold, pale shapes adrift on the steel-grey waves. Icebergs. Real icebergs—in July.

The plane banked again, approached the cliffs, and there, suddenly, was the harbour, opening out of ramparts of rock. On the northern headland, she glimpsed a hill topped by a grey stone building with a square tower. And beyond, penned within the sheltering hills, were wharves with ships alongside, and above them, a sprawling city, countless rows of roofs and steeples rising in tiers from the harbour. St. John's, the capital of Newfoundland.

Her hand tightened on the strap of her carry-on bag.

The airport was small, to her relief, as was the crowd of people waiting for the passengers to disembark. Maeve, imagining a huge terminal like the one at Toronto, had wondered how she would ever find her aunt and uncle, whose faces she could not even recall distinctly from their last visit. As it happened, she saw them almost at once, standing near the front of the crowd. She remembered the small, bird-boned woman with the cap of neat dark hair: Aunt Ellen, the wife of Dad's brother. And there was Uncle Roy, with his thick, bushy beard (which she remembered as being sandy in colour, but was now mostly grey). He looked like a sailor or a fisherman in his heavy turtleneck sweater, though he was actually a professor of anthropology at Memorial University.

"Maeve!" Her aunt held out her arms and Maeve moved awkwardly into them. "Let me have a look at you. Goodness, you've grown. I think you were only nine or ten when we last visited Ontario."

"Sure we've got the right girl?" joked Uncle Roy. "I'd hate to take home the wrong one."

"It's really me," she said shyly. "Have I changed that much?"

"Oh, pay no attention to him!" snorted Aunt Ellen. "He's just codding, as usual. Now let's get your bags and we'll be on our way."

They spoke with an odd, almost Irish accent. So, Maeve soon realized, did everyone else here, and it added to the strangeness, the foreignness of it all. She followed her relatives out to the parking lot, wincing as an unexpectedly cold wind blew into her face. She had only a pair of shorts and a thin T-shirt on. In Ontario it had been hot and humid, with an air quality alert. The sort of smoggy, sweltering July weather that made you want to stay indoors. When her father had advised her to pack warm sweaters and a raincoat, she had found it hard to imagine actually wearing them.

Now she hastily removed the raincoat from her carry-on bag and flung it over her shoulders.

Her aunt and uncle chatted away in the front seat as they headed for the highway, asking Maeve about her parents and brother, her interests, school.

"How far away is the village?" Maeve asked, wanting to change the subject. "Is it a long way from St. John's?" Her father had described Mary's Bay as being rather isolated.

Her uncle shrugged. "It's about a forty-minute commute to the city. Not bad. And I've no summer courses this year, which helps." Her aunt explained that she was a teacher at one of the small local schools and didn't need to commute.

It seemed no time at all before the airport and nearly all signs of civilization were left behind. On both sides of the highway were vacant meadows, with the dark green expanse of coniferous forest far beyond.

"What sort of animals live here?" Maeve asked.

"We've got moose, some caribou, lynx, foxes, black bears," her uncle replied. "And the occasional polar bear."

Her eyes widened. "*Polar* bear? You're joking, aren't you, Uncle Roy?"

"Believe it or not, I'm not." Uncle Roy turned off the main highway onto a narrower, winding road with fewer cars on it. The coniferous forest slowly closed in around them, encroaching on the gravel shoulders of the road. All the trees were small, the size of Christmas trees. "In the wintertime, polar bears have been known to come down out of the Arctic. Sometimes they float here on pans of ice. There was one spotted roving the outskirts of the city a couple of years ago, and they had to go after it with tranquillizer guns."

They drove on, and presently the woods gave way to a vast open space. Trees grew only in isolated clumps, and interspersed among them were glacial boulders, some no larger than a man's head, some as high as houses. They had a strange, monolithic presence, and they reared up out of pools and streams and stood sentinel on the crests of hills— great rounded boulders perched improbably on granite outcroppings, as though placed there by giant hands. Glaciers had left them long ago, deposited them as they melted and retreated, bones of stone to lie bare beneath the sky.

"This whole area was cleared by a forest fire a while back," her aunt commented. "There used to be more forest in the old days, before the settlers came. They cut down a lot of timber, and the forests never really recovered."

"It's not all the settlers' fault, though," her uncle added. "Glaciers scoured off most of the good soil back in the Ice Age, so farming has never been a big business here. Some people are trying to raise sheep for wool now that the fishery's closed, but you certainly couldn't graze large numbers of cattle. Hard to believe this was once part of Africa, isn't it?"

"It was?"

He grinned. "Billions of years ago. You know about continental drift, of course? Well, my friends in the geology department tell me this eastern part of Newfoundland split off from the ancient continent of Gondwana when it drifted away from North America. So we lost our chance to be part of Africa and have nice tropical weather. Instead, we get all this fog and rain and cold."

"What kind of people settled Newfoundland?" Maeve asked.

"All kinds," her uncle answered. "English, Irish, Welsh, French. The Portuguese came here to fish. There are old French forts, Viking settlements up north at L'Anse aux Meadows—"

"Vikings!"

"Oh, yes. They were here long before Cabot, though they didn't stay. And of course there were aboriginal peoples here *thousands* of years ago."

Soon they were moving through more settled areas. There were small houses along the road, painted in bright surprising colours: lime green, cobalt blue, lavender. She saw lilacs in their gardens, and giant pink rhododendrons and golden chain trees: all were in full flower, as though time had moved backwards here and it was spring once more.

"Why do they call this the Avalon Peninsula?" she asked her uncle presently. "It sounds like something out of King Arthur."

"Ah, yes, the Isle of Avalon, where Arthur was taken by the three fairy women after his last battle and laid to rest. . . . Let's see, it was Sir George Calvert—later Lord Baltimore— who first used the name for his own tract of land, given him by Charles I. I don't know whether he was inspired by the Arthur legend or if he just named it after the place in Somerset. But some of the old myths said that Avalon wasn't in England after all—that it was a magical island far away across the Atlantic. If that was what he had in mind, it would certainly be a fitting name."

He broke off and hastily applied the brakes, to let a family of goats cross the road.

A few minutes later there was a turn in the road, and

suddenly the ocean was there again. A broad bay, embraced by hilly headlands dark with forests, spread before them and along its shore lay the village. There were many clapboard houses, most of them modest-sized and square—saltboxes, her uncle called them. The majority were painted white, though a few sported coats of brighter hues.

"Here we are," said Uncle Roy. "Scenic Mary's Bay—originally Murres Bay, after the seabirds called murres that lived on the nearby islands. Settled in 1597 by English Protestants as a fishing village. Later inundated with Irish, hence the name change. Site of numerous battles during the French-English wars."

Wooden docks extended into the bay. One was piled with lobster traps, while others had large boats moored to them. These were not pleasure craft, such as she had seen on Lake Ontario, but working fishing boats. All lay idle on the water.

"There isn't any fishing here now, is there?" asked Maeve.

"Not for cod, anyway," said her aunt sadly. "The biggest local industry is tourism now. They take people out in boats to show them the bird islands, and icebergs and whales in season."

Uncle Roy turned left, driving towards the northern side of the bay. Here the land rose in rounded slopes towards the hills; these were thickly forested on their slopes but bald above, grey with granite and scree.

"There was a small fort erected back in 1638 on the largest hill—Dutton's Hill, they call it. There's nothing left now, but a couple of cannon were dug up there. You see, St. John's was too well-fortified for an assault by sea: the

Narrows are a terrific natural defence to begin with, and then they added a fort and garrison. So attackers had to march overland to get to the city, and the place they usually chose to come ashore was Mary's Bay. An English warship was surrounded by French ships right here in our bay, back in 1696. The captain set fire to his own vessel to thwart the boarders, then he and his crew leaped overboard and swam to shore. The wreck's still there on the bottom."

"Yes, we had a TV crew filming it last summer," her aunt put in. "Divers and underwater cameras and everything."

Maeve was impressed. "A real shipwreck. Wow."

"There are lots of O'Connors here," her uncle added. "Have been from the first. One became something of a local hero, back in 1817. That was the year of one of the biggest fires in St. John's. All the winter supplies got burned up, and people here on the South Shore were literally starving. When a distressed brigantine, loaded with goods for the city, came to take shelter in the port, the villagers begged the crew for help. But they refused. Then a fisherman named John Patrick O'Connor organized a band to board the vessel and take supplies by force. The crew were told they'd be paid back, but they were furious and a bounty was put on O'Connor's head."

"Was he caught?"

"No, never. He'd become such a hero that no one in the village would turn him in. But he had to leave his family and go into hiding, and he was never seen again. A sort of Robin Hood figure, he was. You come of a famous lineage, Maeve. Here's Bayshore Road. We're almost there."

The road followed the north side of the bay, with the

densely forested northern hills on one side and the beach on the other. They passed a church, its wooden walls painted white, its roof and steeple tiled with dark green. There was a cemetery to one side, some of the headstones looking very old. The houses along this road were fewer, Maeve noticed, but larger; some looked quite new, with grand picture windows facing the bay and the opposite headland, which was very rocky and rugged and had an automated lighthouse at its tip. "There's our home!" announced her aunt at last. She pointed up ahead to a white saltbox house, which stood between the forest and the shore.

Grandma's house.

Maeve recognized it instantly from an old photograph Grandma had once shown her. It looked a little different: the shingles of the roof were not dark any more but had weathered to silver grey, and her aunt and uncle had added on a front deck. But the lines of it were poignantly familiar: the square box shape, the small windows on the second storey. "You'll come visit someday," Grandma had said, smiling as she showed Maeve the photograph. How she had yearned to visit that little house by the sea! Now here she was at last, but there was no Grandma waiting at the door for her. Maeve felt a lump form in her throat.

Uncle Roy pulled up in front of the house. Maeve got out, shivering as a raw gust of wind from the icy sea struck her bare legs.

The house was dark and still inside; she felt its emptiness as soon as she walked in the door. Her cousins, Sean and Keith, did not live here, she knew. They were older than Brandon, university age, and worked at summer jobs out west to pay for their tuition. Her aunt and uncle had only recently taken up permanent residence in the house (it had stood empty for a year or so after Grandma's death, and then been used mainly as a summer cottage).

As her aunt turned on the electric light, Maeve saw at last the interior Grandma had described: the wooden bannistered staircase that led up to the second floor; the door on the right opening on the parlour, with its large central fireplace and mantel of moulded plaster over a black grate; the tall grandfather clock in the hall. On the left a matching door led to the kitchen, which took up half the lower floor.

Even indoors she could smell the sea.

"This is the old part, the original house," her uncle said. "It's a fairly typical saltbox design. Your great-grandfather O'Connor built an addition at the back, a lean-to, and we've added a bit as well. The oldest part—the 1866 structure—has wider floorboards because trees were large and plentiful then. You'll notice the part at the back has smaller, narrower boards."

"We've still got the old iron woodstove in the kitchen," added Aunt Ellen. "It's in good condition, and it warms the room up so nicely."

The floorboards creaked. Maeve felt as though she would disturb ghosts, who would rise from them like dust. A large framed sampler hung on the kitchen wall—an ornamented text with the signature "Bridget Mary O'Connor" and a date, 1831. It wasn't like a modern house: people had been born here and had died here, whole generations of them. All belonging to the same family. Grandma had often visited here as a young girl, for her family and Granddad's had been good friends; later she had come here as his bride. Dad and Uncle Roy had slid down that bannister as boys, dried their wet feet before the iron stove. Long after them, Sean and Keith had come to visit Grandma, and to play all the same games in and around the house.

"Right this way, ladies and gentlemen, for the scenic tour." Her uncle ushered her through the kitchen, pointing out features of interest. "That's your great-grandfather's antique harpoon gun over there on the wall. It doesn't work any more, of course, but I find it very useful for beating off polar bears."

"We've put you in the left-hand front bedroom, Maeve," her aunt said. "I hope you'll like it. It used to be your grandma's study at one time."

She climbed the creaking stairs behind her aunt, up to the bedroom. It was a small, white-walled room with little in it besides a bed, bureau, desk, bookshelf and one cushioned chair. Aunt Ellen laid Maeve's suitcase down on the bed, which had an old-fashioned brass bedstead and was covered by a patchwork quilt that looked as though it was made of bits of old dresses. "There. I guess you'll want to change into something a bit warmer. Don't rush, dear. Lunch will be in about ten minutes."

As soon as her aunt had gone, Maeve pulled on some heavy corduroy pants, a sweatshirt and her favourite cardigan. It was forest green, which she always hoped would make her eyes look a bit greener, and had warm, deep pockets. Then she went and sat in the chair by the window, gazing out on the meadow that sloped towards the bay. A light rain had begun to fall, dripping from the eaves and thrumming on the window-pane. Had Grandma sat here once, gazing out on the sea? What had her thoughts been?

At last Maeve rose with a sigh and opened the bureau drawers to put her clothes away.

For the rest of her life, Maeve could never explain what she did next. It was as though some unseen hand guided her. She reached right in to the very back of the drawer, feeling about for—what? She could never say afterwards; yet when her groping fingers closed on something hard and cold, she felt no surprise, but drew the object out to look at it.

It was a brooch shaped like an interrupted circle, with a little gap at the bottom and a large pin at the top to fasten it. There were tiny, intricate designs worked into the metal, which was bronze in colour. Little snakes or dragons, they looked like. She turned it over and over in her hands, wondering how it had come to be stuck at the back of a drawer rather than tucked away in a jewel box. Perhaps it wasn't very valuable. Still, she should ask her aunt about it.

Maeve dropped the brooch in her cardigan pocket and finished her unpacking.

After lunch, Uncle Roy went up the road to talk to a neighbour while Aunt Ellen tidied the kitchen. Maeve, her offer of help declined, decided to go for a walk on the beach in front of the house.

It was a shingle beach, composed not of sand but of smooth, wave-worn stones about the size of her fist that clinked and rolled beneath her feet as she walked across them. ("We have a sandy beach here," her uncle had remarked. "The grains are just *very* large, that's all.") Beyond a wall of fog, she could hear the plaints of seagulls, the wail of the automated foghorn on the far side of the bay and the vast breathing of the sea.

The Atlantic. She remembered the year her family had gone to Prince Edward Island, back when there had been money for family vacations. Brandon was eleven and she was eight, she recalled. The red sandstone cliffs had reminded them of Mars, and they'd played awhile at being astronauts—for Brandon would play with her when there was no one else available—before heading to smooth Cavendish beach to build sand castles. Presently she had asked him (because Brandon was big and knew everything) why the sea was called the Atlantic.

"Because of Atlantis, stupid," he had said. "Atlantis was supposed to be a country that vanished beneath the sea."

"Was it *real*, Brandon?"

"Who cares?" Brandon had shrugged, bending his blond head over his castle. She had sat nearby, watching the wavelets lapping at the edges of the squat sand towers he raised, and had thought of ruined cities lying far beneath the blue, sunlit surface of the sea, of gloomy towers with fish circling them like birds. From that time on—even years later, when she found out that Atlantis had never existed—the word "Atlantic" would give her a little thrill of wonder.

There was nothing especially romantic about it at the moment, though: it was chilly and forbidding behind its veil of vapour, and presently she turned away from the grey stone beach and mounted the driftwood stairs that led to the house.

She did not go back indoors, however. The pine forest lay before her, the fog's first tendrils barely at its margin.

It beckoned, green and inviting with its floor of soft moss, its few deciduous trees rearing above the undersized conifers. It was a dwarf forest, somehow enchanting in its very smallness, friendly and welcoming. As she walked through it, she felt rather cheered. There were such appealing, tiny trees sprouting beneath the larger ones—each with its own personality. They seemed to her not only alive but also aware. There was an alienness, an *otherness*, about them that was not so much threatening as intriguing. They reminded her of an old Emily Carr painting she had once seen in the Group of Seven gallery at Kleinberg: *New Growth*, it was called. In it, the trees all seemed to be swaying and undulating with movement, and at the centre was a clump of little pine trees, paler and more luminously green than the rest, their blurred forms seeming to whirl in a circular dance. Did trees dance in the forest when no one was there to see? And those huge, strange, glacial stones—what if they came alive at night when nobody was watching?

You're weird, Maeve, she could hear Brandon's voice saying.

She reached out and touched a green bough almost shyly, then drew her hand back to smell the resin. But that was a mistake: the sharp green smell only brought back memories of Christmas trees and evergreen wreaths, of the old days when Mom had been Mommy and had smiled and laughed more, and Dad had looked proud and happy as he watched his children opening their gifts. . . .

Maeve pushed on, as if to escape the shadow of apprehension she had momentarily felt hovering above her.

The fog was now drifting like smoke through the woods. She noticed that she was in an area of larger trees—trees that were taller, with thicker trunks. There were birch trees here, slim and bone white; they shone palely through the mist. A little farther, and suddenly the trees thinned out and she found herself in a clearing.

It was not large, only about eight metres across and maybe ten metres long. A little brook wound through it, and it lay open to the sky. Flowers grew wild there, in unusual variety and abundance—perhaps they were sheltered by the trees. Amid the dandelions and purple-headed clover were drifts of daisies, forget-me-nots, buttercups and tall blue irises. There were many others she could not identify. Maeve ventured into the clearing, smelling and stroking the uplifted petals. Their blended fragrances filled the air. She turned at the stream's moss-grown edge and followed its meandering curves. It was quite clear, the stones at its bottom as distinct as if they stood in the open air, save that a little wavering pattern of ribboned light from the surface played about them. The water, she found, bubbled up out of the mossy earth at the clearing's western end: a natural spring.

Above the trees she could see the big stone-topped hill—Dutton's Hill, Uncle Roy had called it. The one that had had the fort on its summit. It was odd, though. He had said there was nothing left of the fortifications, but she could clearly see a rim of very old and worn stone near the top. Despite the weathering, the structure was obviously man-made.

Above the hilltop the sky was clear between banks of ragged cloud, and the sun suddenly burst through the fringed edge of one cloud and blazed down on her.

Maeve sat down on a large, flat rock to drink it all in: the sudden warmth, the scent of pine and flower, the drone of insects in the tall meadow-grass. Uncle Roy had told her that Newfoundland likely still had places in it where no human foot had trod. Surely no one had ever come to this clearing before: it was so pure, so unspoilt. No litter lay on the ground. She could not even hear the sounds of civilization here—not an airplane, or radio, or car engine disturbed the silence. The only sign of human life was that crumbling wall atop the hill.

She gave a deep sigh, suddenly feeling utterly relaxed. The trees, the flowers, the stream—none of these things was important in itself, yet somehow the sum of them was happiness. They reminded her of the make-believe forest into which she had so often withdrawn. There would be no need, here, for a green retreat of imagined trees.

If we do move here, I will come back to this place, she decided. *I'll come whenever I feel depressed, or angry, or unhappy. I will come here and sit and drink it all in. It will be my own special place, my refuge from the world.*

As she headed back towards the house, she heard her aunt's voice calling her name. "Maeve! Maeve, where are you? We've got visitors."

Two old women were sitting in the front parlour. One had neatly cut grey hair and was smartly dressed in a peach-coloured suit with matching floral blouse. The other was white-haired, plainly very much older—her shoulders were hunched and she clutched a cane in one liver-spotted hand. As Maeve came in, the older woman raised a face cobwebbed with wrinkles. Her eyes were faded with age, but Maeve could see from where she stood that they were green like Grandma's.

"Maeve, this is your great-grandmother," her aunt told her. "Your grandma's mother. And this is your great-aunt Fiona."

Maeve realized she was staring and hastily greeted the two older women. She had completely forgotten that she had a great-grandmother still living, and had been only dimly aware that Grandma had surviving siblings. Dad occasionally referred to his aunts and uncles in Newfoundland, but Maeve had never met any of them and never expected to. She could now see that Great-aunt Fiona bore a strong resemblance to Grandma, but the older woman was so shrunken and withered with age that it was impossible to tell if she looked like anyone else.

"I am sorry to drop in like this," her great-aunt quietly apologized. "But I was visiting with Mum, and when I told her Robbie's girl was arriving today, she took a sudden notion to see her. She hasn't been out of the nursing home in ages, and I thought I'd humour her."

"That's all right." Aunt Ellen smiled. "We're always happy to see family. Roy's gone up the road for a moment, but he'll be back soon. How about a cup of tea in the meantime? It's a raw sort of day. And we've got some scones left over from lunch."

Apparently both women lived in the city. Maeve was bemused at the thought of people travelling kilometres just to see *her*. Here in Newfoundland, though, she was someone quite different: here she was "Robbie's girl." The thought warmed her a little. But as Maeve and her great-aunt made polite conversation, Great-grandmother stared vaguely into space, seemingly having forgotten the reason for her visit.

Aunt Ellen returned from the kitchen with a tray on

which sat a teapot and a plate of scones and small, flat oatcakes. "Here we are. Milk and sugar for you, Fiona?"

The wizened old woman suddenly started, as if into wakefulness, and turned to gaze fixedly at Maeve. "Jeanie," she wheezed, holding out her hand.

"Steady now, Mum," said Great-aunt Fiona.

"It's Jeanie."

"No, Mum, that's Maeve," said her daughter. "Robbie's girl, remember? Your great-granddaughter."

"She looks like my Jeanie." The old woman moved closer, peered at Maeve. "Wrong colour eyes. Same face, though."

"Family resemblance, Mum."

"Jeanie were a sweet girl," mumbled the old woman, half to herself. "Loved ramblin' about. Always in the woods. She been *there*."

"Where, Mum?"

"There—where the fairies are. My grannie told me, back in the outport. She were from Ireland—the Old Country. 'Put a bit o' bread in your pocket to ward 'em off,' she said. 'An' never wear green.'" She gestured to Maeve's green cardigan. "They takes you away if you does. It's the fairies' colour. Jeanie knew that. You been there too, girl. I can tell." A mottled old claw reached out, seized Maeve's wrist. "You been there, like Jeanie!"

"Now, now," said Great-aunt Fiona, gently disengaging Great-grandmother's grip. "Let's have some tea, shall we? And scones and oatcakes—your very own recipes, Mum."

"Here, Mrs. MacDougall," said Aunt Ellen loudly. "I've got Jean's photo album. Would you like to take a look?"

The old woman nodded absently and ceased her unnerving

scrutiny of Maeve, who felt obscurely relieved. The album was large and plainly very old; the girl looked at it with interest as the three older women sat around it talking and pointing to pictures. There before her were whole generations of O'Connors and MacDougalls and others: her paternal great-grandmother as a young woman, with Granddad an infant in her arms; Uncle Roy looking very young without his beard; a sturdy little boy in a sailor suit who was still, somehow, recognizable as her father. She saw how, again and again, the same features cropped up, like variations on a theme: the high forehead here, the great long-lashed eyes there. She saw how like Dad her cousins Sean and Keith were. There was a picture of Grandma as a young girl, and right away she saw the resemblance to herself. Her own features leaped out at her from the other girl's face.

Her own life was in there too—photos of her as an infant in a bassinet, a toddler playing with her laughing father, a small stocky girl seated on a carousel horse. Brandon was there as well, and there were pictures of Mom from years ago, so beautiful with her long, sun-coloured hair and bright, vivid features. She was looking at Dad in one picture, a glow of happiness on both their faces that was almost too painful to see. Maeve averted her eyes until that page was turned.

The figures faded back in time, from colour to black-and-white and finally into the dimness of sepia. Faces taken out of time: Great-grandma as a bride, in a lacy waistless wedding gown that belonged to another era; Granddad O'Connor's parents with *their* parents . . . Aunt Ellen turned to the front inside cover of the book, pointing out a diagram. "There's the O'Connor family tree. The Mac-Dougall one is on the back, here."

A family tree—Maeve could see it. In her mind's eye it became a real tree, with myriad leafy branches and a great sturdy trunk, like a centuries-old oak. It would have roots too, that tree—deep and hidden, but strong. Her roots.

The old woman was speaking now, relating tales of these long-ago people in the present tense. Great-grandmother's mind must be like the photo album—past, present, past; to and fro and back and forth, without linearity. She pointed to a black-and-white photo of a man in naval uniform. "And there's my poor Andrew." The gnarled old hand moved across the photograph in a brief gesture almost like a caress. Maeve was disconcerted to see a tear well up in the aged woman's eye.

"What . . . happened to him?" she asked hesitantly.

It was her great-aunt who answered. "Oh, didn't you know? My brother was killed in the Second World War. He was in a convoy and his ship was torpedoed by a U-boat. Jean knew the precise minute when he died; it's a family legend. I was there at the time, and I remember. We were sitting in the parlour listening to the radio, and she suddenly went white as a sheet and cried, 'Andy, Andy!' Later we found out that was exactly when the torpedo hit. She always was a bit fey, Jeanie was. She used to see ghosts too—figures dressed like old-time settlers, walking through the village streets at dusk. Back in Scotland they'd say she had the second sight. It was supposed to be passed down in families."

"Aye, the sight." Great-grandmother seemed to have recovered from her passing sorrow, and she turned to Maeve with an almost impish look. "You've got it too, haven't you? I know. You see what others don't." She winked and nodded, grotesquely. "The hidden things."

Great-aunt Fiona stood. "I think perhaps we'd better be going now, Mum."

"Don't you mind your great-gran," said Aunt Ellen to Maeve after the two older women had left. "All that about fairies and so on is just rambling. She's extremely old, past ninety, and she's got confused and childish."

"The outport people really did believe in fairies until a couple of generations ago," said Uncle Roy. He had returned from his friend's house a few minutes earlier and was sitting at the kitchen table waiting for the kettle to boil. "The real old-fashioned fairies, that is, not those wee, twee people with insect wings you see in Victorian picture books. In the old Celtic tradition the fairies look like human beings, and they're usually human-sized—when they choose to be visible, that is. As a boy I once saw an old lady clutch her rosary at the sight of a whirlwind spinning across a farmer's field, tossing loose hay about. To her, you see, it wasn't just a random eddy of air: it was the fairies dancing."

"Why was she afraid?"

"Because around here the fairies were believed to be fallen angels, the rebels who were thrown out of heaven by St. Michael. They've sort of put two mythologies together. Fascinating, isn't it?"

Maeve gave a little shudder. "Kind of creepy, actually."

"Well, according to the old lore, the fairy world is a creepy sort of place. Not horrible or frightening so much as . . . alien to our experience, to our understanding of things."

"You make it sound almost real."

"It was real enough to the villagers. They were terrified of the fairies. There were stories of people who'd been carried off into fairyland; some just disappeared, it was said, while others came back mad. I can remember the old folks of Mary's Bay showing me the fairy paths—little trails that ran through the grass in the meadows. Goodness knows what really made them. If you crossed one it was bad luck, unless you turned your coat or some other article of clothing inside out. Then you'd be safe. I never did hear why. Those trails all seemed to lead up to the hilltops. Fairies danced there, it was said, that's why the summits were bare. They'd worn the grass away with their dancing feet." He sighed heavily. "It really seems a pity that Newfoundland should lose all her old folklore. Some of those traditions go right back to the Irish fairy-faith, and to practices of the ancient Celts. Very few places in the world have living oral traditions now."

"Just the ones with rampant illiteracy," observed his wife wryly, "which is what Newfoundland had a lot of in the old days. Your water's boiling, Roy."

"So now the villagers believe in alien abduction and government conspiracies instead, I suppose," grumbled Uncle Roy, attending to the kettle. "And they park the kids in front of the TV instead of telling them wonder-tales. Not much of a trade, if you ask me."

Maeve made herself smile, but there was something about the visit that had unsettled her. She almost imagined that she could still feel the grip of the old woman's hand on her wrist and hear the rasping voice: "*You been there, like Jeanie!*"

Gooseflesh was spreading along her arms. She felt a wave of cold, but it came from within her, not outside. It was as though her bones were marrowed with ice.

Someone walking over my grave . . .

Chapter Three

"THEY LOOK LIKE ENORMOUS SLUGS," declared Aunt Ellen.

Maeve and her aunt and uncle peered through the chicken-wire fence at the stone-coloured, flaccid forms lying next to the artificial pool. A sign attached to the fence nearby admonished: "Please Do Not Pester the Seals." As they watched, one of the animals lifted its head and began to undulate towards the pool.

"Slugs!" Uncle Roy said. He put on a phoney thick accent. "Slugs don't got big brown eyeballs what they rolls at you soulful-like."

"No, and a good thing too," said his wife briskly, "or you'd probably get sentimental about *them* as well." She turned from the holding pen and headed back towards the marine research facility's parking lot.

Maeve continued to gaze through the wire fence. "There were people in Grandma's book who could turn themselves into seals."

Uncle Roy nodded. "Selkies. They're part of Celtic folklore too."

The harbour seal turned to glance at them idly. Its eyes *were* very human: round, dark brown and expressive. For a moment it gazed at them solemnly. Then it yawned, a wide, tongue-lolling yawn like a dog's, and was suddenly an animal again.

Maeve followed her uncle back to the car, feeling vaguely guilty. Today the marine research facility at Logy Bay; yesterday it had been a trip to St. John's, to the museum and the shops on Water Street, and then to Cape Spear, where the old Second World War fortifications still stood, their huge guns facing out to sea. Her aunt and uncle were nice people, and kind, but she had been foisted upon them without an invitation and they didn't quite know what to do with her. And Uncle Roy was busy with his research projects too. She must find a way to amuse herself and not be such a burden to them both.

As she walked up the path, she noticed a splash of colour on the headland, unexpectedly vivid beneath the overcast sky. A number of people were milling about, attired in bright, colourful garments: gold, scarlet and green.

"A group of local players," her uncle said, seeing her look at them. "They're putting on a production of *A Midsummer Night's Dream* over there. Not the best climate for outdoor Shakespeare, but you have to admire their determination."

"Last year they did *The Tempest*," said her aunt, coming up to join them. "It was quite magnificent, with the real ocean right there and the surf pounding away on the rocks below."

Uncle Roy laughed. "As I recall, the actors got completely

upstaged in the final act by a bunch of humpback whales who had decided to come into the bay and feed and spout and play around. Stole the show, they did."

Maeve was thrilled. "Oh, I wish I'd seen that!"

"Come to think of it, Rob says you're quite the budding thespian yourself," her uncle said to her as they got into the car. "Have you been in a lot of plays?"

But Maeve didn't want to talk about that. "Not really," she mumbled, looking down at her hands.

She sat gazing at the grey sky and the spindly trees, but in her mind she was in the high-school gymnasium again, seeing the rows of chairs with kids sitting in them and, at the front, a handful of teachers. The auditions. *No, I don't want to be here again!* But she saw Mrs. Marshall, the drama teacher, sitting in the front row with a notebook on her knee, then heard her name called out: "Maeve O'Connor."

She was walking up to the stage, her heart pounding with nervous excitement. Ashley Robinson had just finished her audition—and she was terrible, Maeve realized with surprise. Beautiful, yes, golden and tall—she could easily play the part of a princess. But she'd just stood there stiffly, her hands at her sides, and her voice had been dull and toneless. Mrs. Marshall had had to keep urging her to "try a little more emotion, dear."

Then Maeve had found herself on the stage. She'd stood on it, looking down at the mocking faces of Lisa Smith and Cheryl Miller, the sneering grins of the boys. Up there on the suddenly enormous stage, alone and exposed, she'd known a frozen instant of fear. But she'd banished it, pushed it all away from her, and launched into the balcony speech from *Romeo and Juliet*.

She'd been thinking of Princess Gwenlian in Grandma's book, and of her feelings for Prince Diarmait (with whom Maeve herself had always secretly been in love). Longing, joy, fear—somehow the strange mix of emotions had come easily. Beyond it, she had been dimly aware of the spreading silence in the audience; the incredulous stares of Lisa and company; the exchange of glances between the teachers; the way Mrs. Marshall sat bolt upright, the eyes behind her spectacles following Maeve's every gesture. Triumph had swelled up inside Maeve. *I've done it, I've done it*, she had thought incredulously when she left the stage. *I've got the part!*

Now she stared listlessly out of the car window, watching the forests flow past and remembering Mrs. Marshall avoiding her eye; and the smug smiles of Ashley's friends; and the casting notice on the bulletin board, which she had stared at disbelievingly for an entire minute while the school bell jangled in the distance.

Another memory to bury. There were so many of them.

It was mid-afternoon when they returned to the house. The sky was heavy and looked as though it was considering a downpour. All the same, Maeve decided to go for a walk before dinner. Throwing on her cardigan, she thrust her hands absently in the pockets and gave a little yelp of pain and surprise as something sharp jabbed her right thumb. Of course—the brooch! She'd completely forgotten about it. Carefully she took it out, this time avoiding the end of the pin, and set it down on the bureau. Sucking her thumb, she grabbed her raincoat and ran downstairs.

She wanted to go to her special clearing again—*though of*

course it won't be the same, she admitted to herself. *It'll just seem ordinary this time, with the overcast sky and no feeling of surprise to make it magical.* Still, anticipation filled her as she hunted through the trees. She wished she'd paid more attention to her surroundings that first time she'd found it, but it had taken only about ten minutes to come across the place. It couldn't be that far away.

Yet fifteen minutes later, she still hadn't found it.

She looked about her, tired and frustrated. Only small evergreens stood around her, no tall birches like the ones that had surrounded the clearing. She altered her course slightly. There, that felt right. There were one or two things that looked familiar: a stump, a mossy glacial boulder surrounded by bushes.

Suddenly the trees thinned, but they did not give way to a clearing. Instead, she found herself looking at the white wooden church she had seen the day before, with a few clapboard houses beyond.

Funny. She must have got mixed up, taken a wrong turn somewhere. Her sense of direction had always been terrible, as Brandon had often pointed out to her. She turned around and made her way slowly back. There, that was the house's roof, rising out of the trees. She reoriented herself and set out again, taking a more westward course. She tried using the hill to get her bearings, but she could not see the low, crumbling wall of stone that she had noticed the other day. Perhaps it was over on the northward side of the hill? She set off through the woods.

But this time, when the trees came to an end, she found herself looking out on part of the paved main road that led to the village. Where on earth was her little clearing? How had she stumbled onto it so quickly the first time? As she stood there puzzling, there was a soft pattering sound in the forest all around her and a light rain began to fall.

She gave up and went back to the house, feeling unaccountably cheated and frustrated.

Back in her guest room, she glanced at the bookshelf that had been Grandma's: some old paperback novels, a dictionary, a few children's books. They looked as though they must have been here since Grandma's day. All had dust along their tops, so long had it been since anyone took them from the shelf. There must be *something* here for her to read to while away the rest of this rainy day.

One book, she saw, had no title on its spine. She pulled it out, curious, and discovered that the cover too was a plain navy with no words or pictures on it. She opened it, and found pages covered in neat handwriting. Of course, it was a blank book—a diary, perhaps. She was about to close it out of respect for that long-ago Jean O'Connor's privacy when a line caught her eye: "I entered the Otherworld again today."

Why, it wasn't a diary at all. It was Grandma's early notes for her book! A very old and different version too. How interesting that Grandma had initially written her story in the first person. She must have penned this early draft a very long time ago, for there on the cover page was her unmarried name: Jean MacDougall.

"Maeve!" Her aunt's voice came up the staircase. "Dinner's ready, dear."

Maeve hurried down the stairs, clutching the book and the brooch.

"That's a very old Celtic design, from Ireland," her uncle said, turning the brooch to and fro in his hands. "It's called a penannular brooch, because it's not quite a perfect circle—'annular' means ring-shaped. Notice the gap there at the bottom, and the ornaments at the broken ends of the circle—the terminals, they're called."

"Show-off," teased Aunt Ellen as Maeve bent close to examine the piece of jewellery.

Her uncle continued: "It can't be genuine, of course. If it was, it'd be incredibly old. It's a copy of an early form of the penannular brooch—the later ones, which date to the Christian era, are much more heavily ornamented than this. There's some debate over the origin of the penannular design. Some argue it's Roman, others that it's native to Britain and goes back to the Iron Age."

"You say it's Celtic? Who *were* the Celts, exactly?"

"Well, it's a bit complicated. The Celts weren't any one racial group, you know, but a whole lot of Indo-European peoples linked by common languages and traditions. It's a linguistic classification, really. There were different branches of Celtic culture—continental Celts, for instance, and another group who migrated to the British Isles, whom we also divide into separate branches. The Irish and Highland Scots are descended from what we call the Goidelic Celts—that's where the word 'Gaelic' comes from. It used to apply to the Irish and Scottish peoples, though nowadays it's used just for the Highland Scots language. The Welsh and Cornish and Bretons belong to a different sub-group, the Brythonic Celts, who—"

"Goodness, Roy, don't give her the whole lecture!" exclaimed Aunt Emma.

He grinned. "Sorry, Maeve: the Celts are an obsession of mine. Your grandma always had a thing about them, and she passed her enthusiasm on to me. They were our ancestors, after all—Scots, Welsh, Irish, they're all in our background." His attention returned to the brooch. "Found this in her room, did you?"

"Yes, at the back of a bureau drawer. As if she'd put it there and then forgotten about it."

"I never noticed it. So it's been lying there all this time," observed her aunt. She moved back to the stove. "I hope you like macaroni and cheese, Maeve."

"Yes, thanks." She held the book out. "This notebook . . . I think it might be an earlier version of Grandma's story—you know, about the Otherworld."

"Oh, yes," said her uncle. "Mum's book. Poor Mum. It wasn't exactly a bestseller, was it? It was quite popular here, but I don't think it was ever distributed outside of the province."

"I love it," said Maeve stubbornly. "I think it's wonderful. She sent me a copy years ago, and I've still got it. I've reread it about a thousand times."

"Oh, it's a rattling good yarn, all right," he replied. He sat back in his chair looking thoughtful. "Mum loved stories. She was always telling them to Rob and me, when we were little boys. I once told her it was *her* fault that I became a folklorist! But the tales she told us were always the old, traditional ones;

she never made up any stories of her own, aside from that one book."

"It's great! I like all those magical creatures, and those funny-looking words and names. It must have taken her forever to think them up."

"Well, she didn't really. All the foreign words and proper names in her book come from Celtic myths and legends."

Maeve stared at him. "You mean, they're *real* words? Even those weird, unpronounceable ones with all the *w*'s in them? Like Gwynedd?"

He corrected her pronunciation: "Gwen-ith. That's Welsh. Gwynedd, *arglwydd*—double *d* sounds like the *th* in 'that.' *W* followed by *y* is a diphthong, but for the most part it's pronounced like the double *o* in English. Annwn." He made the last syllable sound like "noon." "That was the Welsh name for the fairy world. If you translate it literally, it means the Notworld. But not all the words Mum used were Welsh. In fact, most of them were Irish—like the word for the fairy people."

Maeve nodded. "The Daoine Sidhe."

She pronounced it *Down Sid*; again, he gently corrected her. "*Din-a Shee*, that's how you say it. Mum took those words straight from Celtic mythology—and not just the words. The Fomori and the Daoine Sidhe and so on were all part of the old lore. The Otherworld, the fairy realm that lies just beyond our own world, that's a classic Celtic theme."

"But her magic country's in Newfoundland. At least, you get into it from a sort of gateway in Newfoundland."

"Yes, that's the clever part. You see, the Celts of ancient Britain believed in magical island paradises: the Isle of Youth, Tir nan Og; Tir Tairngiri, the Land of Promise; and

Hy-Bresail, the sunken island that could be seen by mortal eyes only once every seven years. These imaginary islands all had one thing in common: they always lay far away to the west, beyond the Atlantic Ocean."

"Like Newfoundland."

"Like Newfoundland." His face took on a dreamy expression. "There are ancient tales of ocean voyages, *immrama*, undertaken by bold adventurers who made landfall on a magic island. The *Navigatio Sancti Brendani*, for example, tells of a monk, St. Brendan, who sailed with his brother monks far across the sea in search of paradise—the Land Promised to the Saints, as he called it. They saw all sorts of wonders on the way: sea monsters; islands where devils worked fiery forges, and others full of white birds that were the souls of godly men. They landed on the back of a giant fish or whale, and saw a huge pillar of crystal rising out of the sea. And finally they came to a large island, one full of fruit trees and precious gemstones, and surrounded by a mysterious wall of mist."

"It doesn't sound much like Newfoundland—well, except for the mist."

He glanced out the window. The rain had ceased and a dense fog was now rolling in off the sea. "True enough." He laughed ruefully. "But back to Brendan. Every now and then, someone tries to prove that the Brendan *immram* was based on an actual voyage. It isn't all that far-fetched—Irish monks *did* travel by ship in search of new converts to the Christian faith. Scholars have pointed out that Brendan's crystal pillar could have been an iceberg, and his sea monsters could have been whales and walruses. There are plenty of islands where white seabirds nest, and the fiery forges sound a lot like volcanoes; he could well have passed Iceland, they say. Back in the seventies, a team of men sailed across the Atlantic in an old-fashioned Irish *curragh*, to prove that it could have been done. And then there's that rock near L'Anse aux Meadows, with the inscription that looks a bit like ogham."

"Like *what*?"

"Ogham is a very old linear script—just a series of lines and dots that people used to carve into stone. A sort of old Irish alphabet that goes back to the fourth century A.D. But if the ancient Celts did come here, what happened to them? There's no definite trace of their presence—even the Vikings left a few artifacts behind. So in her book your grandmother rather cleverly decided that Brendan and the others sailed right out of their own world and into another place, a world parallel to this one, then ended up on an island that exists in the same space as Newfoundland but on another plane. A land of the Otherworld." He thumbed through the notebook, looking pensive.

"Keep the brooch, Maeve," said Aunt Ellen gently. She took it and pinned it to her niece's cardigan. "I'm sure she would have wanted you to have it."

"Thanks." Maeve felt a little awkward. She glanced out the window. "It's still light. I think I'll go for another walk."

"Yes, why don't you? Fresh air will do you a power of good," said her aunt approvingly. "Help you sleep."

It was almost *too* fresh, Maeve thought as she stepped out into the backyard. The wind had picked up and was now blowing off the sea; there was more than a hint of iceberg in it. Her cardigan probably wouldn't be enough. She decided to go back for her raincoat. On the threshold of the back door, she paused. Her aunt and uncle were talking, and there was something in the altered tone of their voices that set off alarms inside her.

"Poor kid," Uncle Roy was saying. "Not much fun for her here, is it? Nothing for her to do."

"From what I've heard, she's better off here than at home."

"The sad fact is, Rob never felt half good enough for Maureen, and losing his job just makes it worse. They've been having problems, I know, but divorce? We've never had a divorce in the family before. Mum would have been very sad. . . ."

Maeve's heart gave a painful jolt, as though it had been squeezed in a vise. She turned and fled back outdoors.

Divorce. The dark shapeless thing that had hovered above her had taken form at last, in that one word. A word from books and TV dramas. *Divorce.* It was a word you often heard nowadays. Three kids in her class had divorced parents. It happened. It was only a word. Life continued in spite of it. She would not lose either parent: even if she and Brandon lived with Mom, of course Dad would visit sometimes, or they would go to see him. . . . There was a hard little knot in her stomach at the thought. No, it would not be only a word, a minor change. It would be the death of everything safe and familiar.

A kind of blind panic seized Maeve; she was suddenly running, as if she could leave her thoughts behind her. She ran sobbing through the thick, Christmas-smelling woods, blundering through the knee-high boughs of little trees, stumbling over roots.

So that was what this trip was really about. She had not been sent here to adjust to living in Newfoundland; she had been sent here so she would be out of the way, so she wouldn't know about any of this until it was settled and finalized and there was nothing at all that anyone could do about it.

And then, even in the midst of her tears and her terror, anger came. Wild, furious anger at her parents for doing this, for thinking only of themselves and not of her and Brandon, for putting their own problems first. "I hate you," she sobbed. "I hate you!" Yet even as she said it, she knew the hatred would not be so strong had there not been love at the back of it. But the love only worsened the hurt, the betrayal. She flung herself at a tree trunk, pounding it with her fists and weeping. Then she clung to it, her cheek against the smooth bark, her chest heaving and her eyes shut. After a few minutes, she opened them again—and only then did she realize that this was a birch tree.

She wiped her streaming eyes and looked around her. There were birch trees everywhere, and beyond them a clear space where the sunset shone down unimpeded. Her clearing! She had found it again, by sheer accident.

Maeve started forward eagerly. There it was—the sweep of meadow-grass and flowers, looking more beautiful than ever in the gold-tinted light of the setting sun. The spring bubbled quietly, the birds twittered in the dim inner recesses of the wood beyond. The wildflowers seemed almost to be glowing with their own internal radiance. The forget-me-nots were a mist of luminous blue, the chaliced petals of the buttercups brimmed with light.

Maeve flung herself down on the margin of the stream

and lay there, staring up at the sky. It was feathered with clouds—delicate, plumose shapes like the wings of birds, dyed to a fiery gold-orange that slowly changed, as she watched, to a deeper rose colour and finally a smouldering ember red.

A vast, primordial silence lay over the land; no drone of car or airplane disturbed it. Darkness crept from horizon to zenith by almost imperceptible degrees, and still she lay there, not moving, not thinking—just breathing and looking. She would let the darkness enfold her as it did the sky and forest, cover her up and blot her out. She watched as the moon—invisible from where she lay—tinted the winged clouds with silver at the edges. Stars slowly appeared in the night-blue spaces above, and she gazed at these in turn.

Suddenly she realized how late it must be, and she started up in alarm. Her relatives would be getting worried. This area seemed safer than her Ontario neighbourhood, but all the same . . . She leaped to her feet and hastened through the darkness under the trees, groping and stumbling. She must get back to the house, and quickly.

But ten minutes later, she was still wandering through the trees.

I don't understand this, Maeve thought, frightened.

Where was the house? Why couldn't she find it? She was lost—completely lost—and now it was growing dark, such a darkness as one never saw in the brightly lit suburbs. She blundered on through the dark woods. She was sure she had been walking for half an hour now, but still there was no sign of the house—of any house at all. No lights glowed through the trees, and there was a dead silence beyond the rustling sounds of the forest. Where on earth was she, and how could she have got so mixed up? Surely by now she should have come across civilization—there was a whole village out there, for goodness' sake!

She was beginning to feel quite frightened when at last a road appeared before her in the moonlight. It wasn't the familiar asphalt road that led from the highway to the village, however, but a narrow dirt road of the kind they had deep in the country. She must have gone the wrong way, ending up on the northern edge of the wood where it thinned and turned into farmers' fields. She stepped onto the rough earthen road and looked up and down it uncertainly. Which way would take her back to her relatives' home? She had a notion that left was south, but she'd got mixed up so many times before that she hesitated to trust her own judgement.

Finally, she decided that the road must eventually lead to *someone's* home, whichever way she went, and she could ask to use a phone and call her aunt and uncle. People were friendly here; it wasn't like the city. They would certainly help a lost young girl.

Fog was beginning to wisp through the trees as she set out, following the road to the left. The sky above the trees was still clear, however, moon and stars lighting her way. No cars passed along the road, which looked too narrow for vehicular traffic anyway: there were thin ruts in it from wagons or carts of some kind, along with the prints of horses' hoofs and some bootprints, but no broad tire tracks from trucks or cars. Presently she heard the sound of hoofs ahead of her. Thank goodness! Finally, here was someone to give her directions! She quickened her pace eagerly, moving towards the sound.

And suddenly the horse and rider appeared out of the mist, rounding the corner and emerging into the moonlight. The horse seemed to be swimming in the mist, breasting it like the water of a river. It was a white horse, moon-coloured in the moon's light, with a loose flowing mane and tail. It was all so beautiful, and so like something she might have imagined, that she stopped and gazed speechlessly. The rider didn't see her there in the shadows and the fog. He was about to ride right past her when she collected her wits and called out, "Excuse me! Hey!" The horse snorted and shied; the rider gave an inarticulate exclamation, pulling it to a halt.

And the moon's glow ran like lightning down the blade of the sword in his hand.

Chapter Four

MAEVE STOOD MOTIONLESS in shock.

The rider clutched at the reins of his plunging horse with one hand, holding his weapon aloft with the other. He was slender, with long dark hair that hung to his collar.

"Who are you? Who is there?" the rider demanded, stilling his mount at last. His voice sounded young, and he had a curious accent, not like the Newfoundland accents she had heard so far. Perhaps the villagers had their special dialect?

"It's just me," she said hesitantly. "I'm visiting, and I got lost. Is"—her eye went to the shining thing in his hand—"is that a real sword?"

The young man looked at the blade and then back at her, lowering his arm. "No," he said in a quieter voice, nudging his horse towards Maeve. It approached, with widened eyes and nostrils, as though it was still uncertain of her. "It is only a stage sword that I use in plays. I was trying to understand a character I am going to be playing—a soldier in olden times. I am sorry if I frightened you." He sheathed the sword a trifle clumsily, holding the reins in one hand.

"Plays!" She looked up at the figure on the horse. He was, she now saw, wearing an archaic-looking costume: a doublet, or was it a jerkin? She couldn't recall the correct word. He looked no more than fifteen or sixteen years old. "You mean, people in this village do drama too? Like Shakespearian plays?"

He smiled, teeth flashing in the moonlight. "Shakespeare— yes, we do his plays. You know them too? That is good, very good." He swung himself down out of his saddle. "I am Thomas Ryan. And you, what is your name?"

"Maeve O'Connor."

"You say you are visiting here?" he inquired.

"With my aunt and uncle. At the big house on Bayshore Road."

"Is that far from here?"

She stared. "Far? No, it's just a stone's throw, really . . . down by the shore. Don't you live here?"

"I have lived here all my life." He looked at her closely.

She ventured a smile. "Look, could I drop by your home, if you can't give me directions? Maybe your parents could give me a lift, or—" She'd been about to say, "Or I could phone," and then remembered she didn't even know Uncle Roy's number.

"Of course, of course." Thomas glanced at the horse. "Would you like to ride? Gwyn will take two, if they are not heavy, and he is a good mount, very steady."

Maeve hesitated. She liked horses and thought them very beautiful, but she had never ridden or even come very close to one, having spent all her life in the suburbs. The horse lowered its head and snorted, absently stamping a hind hoof.

It wasn't as big as she had thought at first—a pony really, not a horse—but it was still a very large animal, and she didn't much want to clamber onto its back. "Umm, that's okay. I can walk," she said quickly. "If it's not too far."

"No, no, not far at all. I will walk too." Thomas pulled the pony's reins over its head and tugged on them, making it follow him. The mist was lifting. In the moonlight she could now see every detail of the road's rough surface, almost as though it were daylight. Trees crowded thickly to either side, but she could still hear and smell the sea.

Thomas said little; he seemed shy, not much of a conversationalist. For the most part she did the talking, babbling on to fill the huge silence of the night—for beyond the sea sounds, the countryside seemed almost unnaturally still. After a time she stopped talking about acting and Shakespeare and fell silent too.

The night surrounded them, vast and overwhelming, and she marvelled at the stars. Of course they were always brighter in the country, away from city lights, but she had never seen them like this. They clustered in the sky like drifts of flowers in a meadow. It was almost difficult to find the familiar constellations—Cassiopeia, the Big Dipper—with those white multitudes thronging between them, scores of stars that the sodium glare of the suburbs had always concealed. And how they shone! Their light had a clear, cold, gem-like brilliance—she felt that she could reach up a hand and touch them—and they did not so much twinkle as throb, flaring and fading in rhythm, as though linked by a common pulse. Surely that was the Milky Way above them, that long, pale lane of light spanning the sky? She had never seen it before. The night sky had always looked to her like a flat ceiling hung with a few bright stars. Now its lights were layered, bright and near, dim and far; it had depth and dimension. She was looking out, as if through a window, at endless reaches of space.

"They're *wonderful!*" she exclaimed, and when her companion looked at her in a startled way, explained, "The stars . . . I've never seen them like this."

"Like what?" He seemed puzzled. "How else should they look?"

"Where I live, you can see only the brightest stars," she said regretfully. "Too much light pollution."

"What place is this?" he asked, still sounding bewildered.

"Oh, nowhere special. Just my little corner of soulless suburbia," she said with a deprecating laugh.

"I have never heard of it," he said. "Where is it, Suburbia?"

She turned to stare. "You've never—" she began, and then caught herself, fearing she sounded like a rude, stuck-up mainlander. After all, Newfoundland villagers might not be up on urban slang. "Never mind," she said quickly.

"We are almost there," he announced, a trace of relief in his voice.

She looked ahead and saw the welcome glow of warm-lit windows through the trees. The pony raised its head and picked up its pace, as though it knew it was nearing its stall. Soon the trees thinned and gave way to a wide, cleared area with numerous dwellings and outbuildings. Maeve slowed in surprise at the sight of them. She hadn't expected anything so rustic; not only the stables and sheds but also the houses themselves were plain wooden structures, shabby and ramshackle in design.

The boy tethered his pony to a tree and gestured to her to follow him in. "This is my home," he said shyly. Maeve was trying hard not to let her thoughts show. His home? Could anyone really live in such a place? It was cruder than a summer cottage in Ontario. Its walls, she could see even by moonlight, were of plain, unpainted wood. A small square shed at one end apparently housed several chickens; she could hear them clucking drowsily. The chimney was built not of brick but of fieldstones roughly pieced together and mortared.

Thomas opened the front door and she followed him inside. The large room within was apparently a kitchen, dining room and sitting room combined. At one end was a wooden partition, also unpainted and full of knot-holes. In the centre of the room stood a large wooden table, its surface stained and pitted from years of use. There were no chairs, just plain wooden stools. There was no fireplace. Instead, a fire burned openly on a raised stone hearth, right in the middle of the room. A funnel-shaped hood in the ceiling led the smoke up a primitive flue, but the air still smelled smoky. A large iron pot with legs, and some kind of soup bubbling in it, straddled the hearth. From the rafters above hung hams and strings of onions. The floor was scattered with . . . could it really be straw?

There were three people in the room. A woman in a drab brown dress, with a sort of bonnet on her head, was bending over the fire, and a little blonde girl sat at the table eating bread and milk out of a wooden bowl. Next to her sat a large, thick-set man. They all wore crude, homespun-looking clothes.

What were these people? Mennonites? She looked around for a telephone and was not surprised to see there wasn't one. In fact, there wasn't any kind of modern device to be seen: no stove or microwave, refrigerator or dishwasher, not even a sink.

The woman was ladling soup into another earthenware bowl, talking to Thomas. "Just in time, you are. I have made a nice frumenty; sit you down now and eat. Why, Thomas, who is this? I have never seen him before." She had turned and noticed Maeve. Her eyes were a light, warm brown, tea-coloured, with kindly lines about them, though she looked to be only in her late thirties. Her expression was one of utter astonishment as she looked towards her son.

"She, Mam. She is a girl. This is Maeve O'Connor," said Thomas.

"A girl?" The woman looked startled, and peered more intently at Maeve. "I do beg your pardon. My mistake." But her eyes looked a question at Thomas, who lifted his shoulders and shook his head.

"I found her out wandering on the road, Mam. She was lost, and I could not help her find her way, so I brought her here."

The little girl at the table spoke up. "Why is she wearing such odd-looking clothes?" she asked.

Thomas looked embarrassed. "That is enough, Cordelia. Do not be rude."

"But why is she dressed like a boy?" the girl persisted, pointing at Maeve with her spoon.

The large man now rose from his seat. When he stood, he seemed to fill all the room. Though not fat, he was very broad-shouldered, and a thick beard and shock of tawny hair surrounded his face like a lion's mane, making his head seem even larger than it was. He roared with laughter as he came forward. "Ah, you mustn't mind my family," he boomed cheerfully. "We are always like this. Barely civilized, we are, but we mean well. Welcome to our home. I am Padraig Ryan, and this is my wife, Branwen, and my daughter, Cordelia." He turned to his small daughter. "Our friend here likely wears men's clothing for her protection, being out on the roads by herself after dark. And no, I am not going to explain that." He patted her blonde head fondly, then turned back to Maeve. "Will you have a bite to eat? There is plenty."

"No, thank you," Maeve replied, feeling rather overwhelmed by their hospitality as they thrust a chair at her and tried to herd her towards the table. "I mean, it's really kind of you, and all that, but I have to get back to my uncle's house."

"And where does your uncle live?" the big man asked.

"Bayshore Road." They all looked blank. "My aunt and uncle have an old white house by the shore. The O'Connors. They said everyone in the village knew them."

Padraig plucked thoughtfully at his beard. "There are families of that name hereabouts—one of my own ancestors was an O'Connor—but I know of no Bayshore Road. How long were you out wandering?"

"Not long—just ten minutes or so. I went to a clearing in the woods, with flowers and a brook, and stayed there for, oh, about an hour." She hesitated, not wanting to mention why she had gone there. "I . . . I was there until it got dark, and then when I went back into the woods I lost my way."

"Did you say a clearing with a brook?" the woman Branwen asked, shooting an anxious look at her husband. "A spring, was it?"

"Yes, not far from here. Do you know it?"

"I know of such a place," Branwen said slowly. "And yes, it is not far, but . . . You say you went there and stayed for some time?"

Maeve was puzzled. "Yes. Why?"

"The Nemeton," said Branwen in an odd, hushed voice. "You have been in the Nemeton."

There was a sudden stillness in the room, and Maeve felt a trickle of unease. "What's wrong? What are you saying? Was I trespassing or something? It was just an empty place in the middle of the wood."

"Of course, of course," soothed the woman, laying a hand on Maeve's shoulder. "I did not mean to frighten you, only . . . that place is not one we ever go to, if we can help it. There are stories—"

"Hush, Branwen," said her husband softly. "Let us say no more. The child has taken no harm, that is plain. We will leave it at that."

Were they all crazy? The strangeness of it all was beginning to get to her: the puzzled, firelit faces; the anachronistic interior of their cottage; their peculiar accent and even more peculiar conversation.

"Look," she burst out, "is there anyone around here who knows the area well? I've got to get back to my uncle's. He'll be sending the police out if I don't get back. Do you know anyone else in Mary's Bay who has a car?"

"Mary's Bay?" they murmured.

"The village!" she almost shouted. "These houses are part of it, aren't they? The village of Mary's Bay?"

Branwen spoke. "Our village is called Connemara. There is no other, not for many leagues."

"What?" she cried.

Little Cordelia spoke up suddenly. "Papa, she's from the other side!"

Something in the way she spoke the last two words made everyone in the room go rigid, Maeve included. *Other side of what?* she wondered. *The tracks? Why are they all looking at me that way?*

Padraig laughed, but it sounded forced, not at all like the booming mirth he had shown earlier. "Now, now, Cordelia— we have been telling you too many tales, I think." But they had all backed away from her, and she saw the uncertainty in their eyes.

It was too much: the oddness of everything, her concern over her relatives' worry, the pending disintegration of her family and now this wariness in the faces before her. She burst into tears like a child.

But it was the right thing to do. At once, Branwen's face softened. Leaving the others to stand and stare, she came forward and put an arm around Maeve's shaking shoulders.

"There, now. There, my dear! You mustn't weep. Lost you may be, and all alone, but you are safe beneath our roof this night and no harm can come to you." Clucking and soothing, she led the sobbing girl out of the main room and into another that lay behind the wooden partition, a little cramped space with nothing in it but a pallet on the floor.

"I . . . I'm sorry," Maeve gasped, struggling to master herself. She rubbed at her streaming eyes. "I'm okay now, really."

"You are tired," Branwen said. "All that wandering about in the dark, and no food in you, like as not—no blame to you if you cry a little. Lie down here on the bed, and I will go get you something to eat. The men will go out riding and see if they can find your kin. Rest easy now—I will be back."

Maeve crumpled onto the pallet. Its mattress felt as though it was stuffed with dried grass or leaves, and it smelled faintly fragrant, as did the pillow. The walls were of plain, rough wood. When Branwen closed the door and the room was plunged in darkness, the light of the main room leaked through dozens of little knot-holes. It looked like a sky full of round yellow stars.

Maeve closed her eyes and tried to calm herself. Her heart was beating at twice its normal rate. Soon Branwen returned, bearing bread and some pale yellow cheese on a wooden plate. Cordelia was with her; she gazed wide-eyed at Maeve, clutching a rag doll in her arms. Then, solemnly, she proferred the doll.

"Thanks, Cordelia," Maeve said, managing a little smile. "But I'm fine now." She found she was hungry, and the food was unexpectedly good: the bread was homemade, as crusty and dark as varnished wood on the outside and as light as cloud within, and she had never tasted such tangy cheese.

"Sleep now," said Branwen when Maeve has finished, "and do not worry any more. We will get you home, if we must search all of Avalon Isle."

The flimsy door closed on her and Cordelia. Maeve was left to sit and stare after them, the chaotic whirl of her thoughts worse than before.

Avalon *Isle*?

Chapter Five

MAEVE SLEPT FITFULLY AND AWOKE WITH THE DAWN.

In the still, quiet moment before she thought to open her eyes, she was aware of a vague unease, like the memory of an unsettling dream. Then the unaccustomed feel of the straw pallet beneath her, the coolness of the air and the faintly floral scent emanating from the pillow brought her back to full wakefulness. Her eyes sprang open, wide and alarmed; saw the rustic interior of the room, dim and half-defined in the dawn light; and closed their lids against it.

No.

She lay still for a time, feeling her heart beat, listening to the few faint sounds that punctuated the deeper silence. There were birdcalls, some coming from quite close by and others more remote, their echoing quality describing a large cleared space. There were myriad rustlings of trees, the larger rumours of the air beyond and the distant respiration of the sea. No human sounds as yet invaded the dawn: no voice, real or electronic; no mechanical dronings of cars, planes, lawnmowers or chainsaws. The world breathed and sang and murmured and softly stirred, not as a pleasing background to human activity, but as though it was a thing entirely sufficient in itself.

Soon, however, human noises entered the soundscape. There were voices and the sound of feet in other parts of the cottage. No one disturbed her, but at last she found she could no longer lie still; sunlight was beating on her lids. Unwillingly, she rose.

Branwen was in the main room, kneading bread dough on the wooden table, but no one else was to be seen.

"Ah, good morning, Maeve." She smiled. "Can I get you something to eat now?"

"No, thanks," Maeve murmured.

She stood in the open doorway, gazing out. She saw rows of wooden buildings, sheds and houses, with the rounded stone tower of a church-like structure exulting above them. A bell rang in the tower, the sound carrying clearly over the roofs of the village. Connemara, Branwen had called it.

She knew of no such place.

People were working in fields that lay to the west of the village; she could see their heads and backs bobbing rhythmically as they weeded, or gleaned, or whatever it was one did in fields. Their clothes were strange, a mixture of different time periods. Some of the men wore rough trousers and shirts of linen, others tunic-like garments that would not have looked out of place in a Shakespearian play. The older women wore white caps that had an eighteenth-century look about them, but their long flowing gowns were almost medieval in design. Small shaggy ponies grazed freely in the open meadow beyond. Her uncle had spoken to her of the small and hardy Newfoundland ponies that had been able to live off the poorest pasturage. Settlers had used them for hauling fish and firewood, he said, but today they were a dwindling breed.

She walked out through the door, looked to the east. She saw a grey-headed hill—very like Dutton's Hill—but there was that ring of broken, weathered wall around its summit. The opposite headland, with its bare, rugged rocks, looked much like Sunker's Point at Mary's Bay, but there was no lighthouse perched on its tip.

She turned to look at the people again. A fantastic thought occurred to her, and she rushed back into the cottage. "What year is this?" she blurted.

"What *year*?" asked Branwen in amazement, her hands arrested in the middle of kneading the dough.

"Just tell me. Please!" Maeve begged.

"Why, 'tis the year of Our Lord, nineteen hundred and ninety-nine."

Maeve released her pent-up breath. The woman said it oddly, but it was the correct year. For a wild instant, she had almost believed she'd travelled back in time, like the heroes in the science-fiction stories Brandon used to read—back to some previous, primitive time when Mary's Bay was still just a settlement. Branwen had to think she was crazy. She laughed weakly at herself, but also felt a flood of relief. *This isn't Mary's Bay; it just looks similar, that's all. I wandered into another village last night.*

She walked back out through the front door and stood

gazing across the small meadow behind the house. It was covered in wildflowers: bright buttercups and daisies and the tall spikes of lupins, pink and blue-purple and white. Suddenly, she noticed the little girl, Cordelia, standing nearby, watching her just as intently as Maeve was watching the scenery. Cordelia's blue eyes were very wide—not in fear, Maeve sensed, but in a young child's unabashed, open stare of curiosity. She was clutching her rag doll.

"Who is that, Cordelia?" asked Maeve, trying to smile reassuringly as she gestured to the doll.

"Gwendolen," said Cordelia succinctly.

"Is Gwendolen your friend?"

Cordelia's eyes widened further. "Gwendolen is my *doll*," she said.

Maeve blushed, then turned at a laugh from behind her. Padraig came striding up, grinning broadly. "There, now! Good morning to you both! Are you being a good hostess, Cordelia?" He picked the little girl up, swinging her through the air. She giggled and hit him with the doll.

Maeve smiled at the sight, and sighed. Their mutual affection was as natural as the sunlight on the meadow. *Dad played with me like that once,* she thought.

Padraig set Cordelia down and beamed at Maeve. "Now, how are you this day? Better for a night's sleep?"

Maeve nodded. "You didn't get hold of my aunt and uncle?"

"I fear not, but we will ride out again later. Have no doubt, we'll find your family."

The kind assurances were beginning to sound repetitive.

"But Papa, she's not from here," objected Cordelia. "She's from the other place."

"What other place do you mean?" Maeve asked urgently, before the child's father could interrupt.

"*You* know," said Cordelia unhelpfully. "You're *from* there." Maeve looked in bewilderment at Padraig.

The big man looked apologetic. "I have told her all the old stories, and now she thinks the Shadow-world lies behind every rock and tree. You mustn't mind her. Cordelia is a romantic, like her old papa." He smiled ruefully.

"Shadow-world?" Maeve repeated. "You mean, the land of the fairies? The Otherworld?"

Both Padraig and Cordelia were wide-eyed now. "The Otherworld?" he repeated at last. "The Otherworld . . . But that is not the name of the Shadow, it is what the Shadow-people call *our* world—"

"You see, Papa? You see?" the little girl shrilled. "I was right, you see now I was right!"

"Well, I'll be blessed!" the man murmured, almost prayer-fully. "Come, sit down a moment and talk to me."

"What about?" asked Maeve, puzzled by his reaction.

"Oh, everything about yourself. Where you came from. Who you are."

He seemed curiously excited, seemed also to be holding that excitement back with an effort. Cordelia was almost dancing on her toes, her small, pointed face flushed and eager.

Padraig led Maeve to a rough wooden bench behind the house and sat down beside her. She proceeded to tell him, in detail, about her relatives, her family, her vacation, her home. As she spoke, a curious sequence of emotions crossed Padraig's face. There was confusion, and blank incomprehension, and curiosity. Once or twice he seemed about to interrupt, and then to think better of it; his already ruddy face became flushed, and his blue eyes grew very bright, as if with excitement. Cordelia, on the other hand, grew uncharacteristically still. Her eyes never left Maeve's face, and seemed to grow ever larger as she listened.

At last Maeve's voice trailed away. A little silence fell before Padraig spoke again. He shook his great shaggy head, like a dog coming out of the water, and smiled a little unsteadily at Maeve. Cordelia got up and moved closer to him, and he took her small hand in his great, rough, hairy one.

"Well," he said, "this could all be a tall tale that you are telling, trying to get a bit of attention for yourself—and heaven knows you tell it well enough that a priest would be convinced—but—"

"What are you saying?" Maeve demanded. "Why would I lie to you? I *am* from Ontario; I flew here just a day ago. I've never been in Newfoundland before."

"You . . . flew," he repeated, with an odd pause between the two words, and slowly shook his head again.

Maeve sprang up. "Look," she said desperately, "could you just explain something to me? What is this place and why are you all acting so funny?"

"Well," he said, looking at the ground and hesitating as if he did not know how to begin. "Well, we told you this village is called Connemara. You are on the eastern coast of Avalon, about a day's journey south of Temair—"

"*Temair?*" Maeve had a curious sensation, like vertigo, as if the ground had suddenly lurched up beneath her feet.

"Aye." He was looking full into her eyes now, his blue gaze

open and direct. "Temair, the seat of the kings in ancient times. Avalon's other royal city, far to the south of here, is—"

"Gwynedd." She finished the sentence for him, almost whispering.

"You do know of our land, then?" he asked.

"I read . . . in a book . . ." The dizzy sensation had gone, but she sat down suddenly on the wooden bench.

"No one has come into Avalon from . . . the other side . . . for many a year." His rumbling voice softened. He was gazing off into the distance now. "There were never many. . . berry-pickers who wandered too far on the barrens, and hunters who got lost in the woods. The forest folk and the people of the ice . . ." His words drifted into silence and he turned back to her. "But not for some time now. We had thought that perhaps all the doors were closed, that there would be no more. No travellers from the Shadow to enter our world."

"The Shadow . . ." She faltered. "You mentioned that before. What *is* the Shadow?"

"Our name for your world. Beyond our own world of Annwn, it is said, lies another—and it is to Annwn as a shadow is to the object that casts it. Like, and not like; similar, yet strange."

Annwn. This could not be happening; it couldn't be real. A feeling akin to panic seized her. She leaped up again, then staggered as the earth once more seemed to shift beneath her; she slowly fell forward as the sunlight was replaced by a seething greyness.

She never felt the ground come up to hit her.

When she came back to herself, she was once more lying on

the straw pallet in the crude, unfurnished bedroom. Branwen knelt at her side, holding a cold, damp cloth to Maeve's forehead. The sun shone in the doorway, but whether hours or minutes had passed she could not tell.

Branwen smiled down at her. "Eh, then, you're back with us! That is what comes of not breaking your fast—and naught but bread and cheese for supper, either! Little wonder it is that you fainted, child. No"—as Maeve tried to speak—"first you must eat, and then you may talk. Here, I have prepared a bite for you."

It was more of that wonderful bread, this time spread with honey, thick and sweet and the colour of sunlight, oozing through the bubbles in the bread as if through the cells of a honeycomb. With it there was milk, thick and creamy, in an earthenware mug. Maeve sat up and ate, her head clearing as the honey restored her blood sugar and eased the shock. When she had finished, she sat quietly. Now that she was free to talk, she felt disinclined to. It was Branwen who spoke.

"Ah, my dear, Padraig has told me your tale. I am so sorry if we alarmed you, but you see it has been so long since one of . . . your kind came through to us. And you with friends and family on your own side, poor lamb! But there is naught we can do about it. Here you are, and here you will have to remain, unless the magic sends you home."

"The magic," Maeve whispered.

"I mean the power that governs both our worlds, and permits the comings and goings between them. No one can say how it happens or why, but the Good Lord watches over all and His ways are often mysterious to us. For now, you are our guest, and there we must leave it."

"This is . . . weird!"

Branwen nodded. "You are right. Fate often has a hand in such things."

"Fate?"

"That is what 'weirde' means: destiny. Has it a different meaning in your world?"

My world . . .

The door opened on its creaky hinges and Padraig's big, bearded face peered in. "I thought I heard voices. I am glad you are awake again, Maeve."

"Annwn," said Maeve, looking up at him. "This is . . . Annwn."

"So it has been called since the dawn of time. It is not our own world, the world of men, at all. But over the years mortals have found their way into it, and we are their descendants. Some, like Brendan and his monks, journeyed here of their own free will. Others were lured in by the Good People—"

"You mean, the fairies?"

"Hush!" Branwen looked alarmed. "Do not call them that! To my people, to the Cymri, they are the Tylwyth Teg, and to Padraig's folk they were known always as the Daoine Sidhe, but we never call them by any name save the Good People. This land is theirs, and all of Annwn. We have never seen them, though—not in many long years have they been seen by any mortal. There are some, it's said, who have the gift of the sight, and they may see the Good People without their leave. But there has been no one with the sight here for many generations. Without such a one, we cannot know if the Good People are still here, or have gone out of Avalon to some other isle."

"Those without the sight can see them," put in Padraig, "at certain times."

"That is so. The Good People may be seen by anyone at dawn or noon, at twilight and midnight. But that is only by their leave, and ill luck comes to those who see them." She turned back to Maeve. "The Good People, you see, were once angels in heaven. But when Lucifer and his rebels rose up to challenge heaven, St. Michael and his hosts defeated them and cast them out. Those angels who did not intervene were also expelled from heaven, but Michael interceded for them, asking that they not be banished forever. And so they were not cast into the Shadow, but were sent here to Annwn; and they became the Good People. They were first to enter this world. It belongs to them and not to us mortals, who came much later."

Maeve tried to speak, but could not make a sound.

"My father's father's grandfather," said Padraig, "entered Annwn from the Shadow-world in a long-ago time when need was great and no living was to be had. He was an O'Connor too—so you see, we are distant kin. He lived in that Newfoundland you speak of." He pronounced it as though it were three separate words—New Found Land. "There had been a great fire in the city and no food was left, and many were near to death with hunger. So my ancestor, John O'Connor, rose up and raided a ship to feed the people of his village. For that, a price was laid upon his head, and he fled his home to seek refuge elsewhere.

"One night he wandered alone in a wooded place, where he fell asleep beneath a tree, and he awoke to find that he had left his world behind. All he had were the clothes on his back, a little food and a precious book that had been his father's, and that he had hoped to sell."

"A book?"

"A volume," said Padraig, "of Shakespeare's plays. It has become a family treasure, passed down from oldest child to oldest child. I have it now. We perform some of the plays, young Thomas and I and the guildsmen of the village—"

"This is crazy!" Maeve sprang up and paced the room. "Fairies . . . Annwn! It *can't* be real!"

"'There are more things in heaven and earth, Horatio / Than are dreamt of in your philosophy,'" quoted Padraig. "You know Shakespeare too, Thomas says. There is far more to the world than you realize, young Maeve. You saw those icebergs out there on the bay? They are larger than they look, for only one small part of them shows above the water. It is even so with the world—much of it is hidden to mortal eyes."

Fear made her stubborn. "But if this place was real, we'd *know* about it. Someone would have told us."

"Those who return to your world from ours are never believed. And in time, Annwn's memory fades from their minds and they cease to believe in it themselves. In like manner, your world of the Shadow soon became like a dream to those who found their way here. We cannot re-enter it now, even though our grandsires came from there. Annwn's power is too great; it will not let us go."

Maeve stood still. "I can't believe it," she insisted.

"And why is that?"

"You don't understand." She groaned. "None of this is true. Temair, Gwynedd, Annwn. It's all from a book my

grandmother wrote, which she gave to me. Don't you see?"
She implored the two blank, puzzled faces. "It's not real.
You're not real. This is all just inside my head, it has to be.
I'm dreaming—or out of my mind." *Maybe I'm still lying in
that clearing, under the stars. In a coma or something. They'll
find me there, sprawled out unconscious, my face turned up to
the sky....* She shivered.

"A book," said Padraig, "written by your grandmother?
Could it be?" His question was directed not to her but to his
wife, who raised her hands in a gesture of helplessness.

"Why should not one of her family have come here before
her? And have written what she knew before she began to
forget? Your grandmother, Maeve, does she remember nothing of our world?"

"She . . . she's dead," Maeve answered. Desolation filled
her. "I want to be alone now. Please!"

She ran out of the room, through the house and on out the
door. Sunlit fields, farm buildings and a backdrop of forest
greeted her eyes. She glared at them, her chest heaving.

Not real!

She plunged into the waist-high grasses of the meadow,
feeling their feathery tips lashing against her skin, hearing
the hissing rustle as she ploughed through them. She caught
at one slender reed and tore it from the earth, clenching her
hand around the green stem. It *felt* real. She was outraged, as
if at a lie. She bent and twisted the pliant stem in her fingers,
brought it up to her mouth. A bitter woody taste met her
tongue and she spat it out again.

She flung her face up to the sun, felt its burning heat on

her skin, saw the unbearable white blaze within the corona and dropped her eyes, dazzled. A round purple shadow blotched her vision for a moment, just the way it should.

"No," she said aloud, panting with fear.

If this was a dream or a delusion, it did not feel like one. Perhaps it was something else, something more serious: a deep coma, total insanity. It was easier to believe this than to believe that the universe had inexplicably changed, altered itself and left her the lone, isolated remnant of its former pattern....

"Maeve!" It was Thomas's voice, calling her. "Where are you going?" the boy asked, running up to her.

She stood still. "I don't know," she admitted.

His dark brown eyes were filled with concern. "You are going to look for your people all by yourself, aren't you?"

"No," she said. "I know I won't find my aunt and uncle *here*." This much she had had to accept. "I just need to walk for a while," she said. "To think."

"I will come with you."

Maeve didn't really want company, but there was no refusing that anxious face. That a stranger should seem so worried for her sake brought a lump to her throat. She looked away. "If you like," she rasped.

They walked on through the meadows. Here and there Maeve noticed curious little ruts, too narrow for wheels, worn into the earth. They seemed to form circles. Some were only a few metres wide, others the greater part of an acre across.

"Fairy rings," said Thomas, seeing her stare at them.

"What are they?"

"No one knows, but it's said that the Good People made them. The ponies and goats will not graze within those rings, and though crops may be grown on the ground where they lie, bad luck always seems to come to the harvester. Some say that the rings were worn into the ground by the dancing feet of the Good People, and that if you wander into the midst of one, you will be in their power." Maeve, who had been on the point of stepping into one circle, drew back hastily. "I do not know if that is true, or only a tale," Thomas added. "But no one here will go near them."

They passed an apple orchard, trees frothy with white blossoms; the trunks were pale grey, like pewter. Here she halted, overcome by the blossom scent blown towards her on the breeze; it was at once fresh and heavy, sweet and piercing.

"The apple trees bloom late this year, because of the sea ice. There are no such trees in any other land," said Thomas, a note of pride in his voice. "With branches the colour of silver, and in summer fruit like—"

"Like gold," finished Maeve.

"How do you know that?" he asked in surprise. "If you have never been here before?"

"It was in a book I read," she told him. "The Isle of Avalon is the island of the apple trees—"

"Ynys Afallon, in the old Cymri tongue," he told her. "To my father's people, the Gaels, it is Emain Ablach. The meaning is the same.

"When the hero Bran of Éire sailed the sea long ago, it was this land he sought. A spirit in the form of a maiden brought him a silver branch with golden apples upon it, a branch that rang with sweet music like a harp. She told him to seek the Island of the Apple Trees, the land of the sea god Mannanan mac Lir, which lay far to the west."

"I know," she said softly. Peace came upon her, as sudden and unexpected as the breeze-blown scent of the blossoms. "They say . . . they say that all the apple trees sing, and that their branches make a music you can hear if you only listen hard enough. . . ." She closed her eyes and let sound flood into her ears, as she had when lying in bed. Ocean, birds, leaves . . . and was there something else? She opened her eyes and looked at the trees again. The wind rocked their boughs, loosened a few petals that spun, glittering, as they fell. In this place everything had purpose, everything flowed and fitted as if it was meant to be. The woven music of the birds and the trees, the spiral dance of the falling petals, came together and were part of the same thing. "So beautiful," she said dreamily as he took her gently by the arm and led her away.

"Come, let us take the forest road. I think you should go to the Nemeton."

"I thought your family never went there," Maeve remarked.

"Not usually, but you mustn't mind Mam's stories. I never heard of any harm coming to anyone in the Nemeton. It is only a place." He led her across the field towards the road. "And it is where you entered."

"Entered?" she queried, trying to match her pace to his long-legged stride.

"Entered our world."

She blinked. The clearing, the Nemeton, it was the node, the still centre of the shifting patterns. Perhaps an answer *did* lie there. "So Padraig—your father—told you about all that? My being from somewhere else?"

"Some. The rest I overheard. I had just come in from riding about the area, looking for your Bayshore Road."

She pictured him galloping about on his white pony, his untidy dark hair blown back in the wind, searching tirelessly while she slept in and took her ease. Once again his kindness made her throat tighten. A world, real or imagined, where such things existed could not be so very terrible.

Dense forest hemmed in the road on either side, the trees much larger than those of the Newfoundland forest. Wildflowers grew thickly at the sides of the road: the ubiquitous lupins, doily heads of Queen Anne's lace and daisies, which Thomas referred to as "day's-eyes." The origin of the name had never occurred to Maeve before. Now, looking into the white raying petals, she saw the yellow sun. Occasionally they passed someone—a man driving a cart with a shaggy pony between the shafts, an old stoop-shouldered woman carrying a basket of eggs—but for the most part, they had the road all to themselves. She noticed many things as they walked; there was a clarity to the colours, to the air and especially to the sky, which seemed more intensely blue than the sky she knew. Her part of Ontario was near the international airport, and there were nearly always vapour trails of aircraft in the sky—thin white lines on blue, like scratches in paint. But this sky above her was empty, untouched; it domed the land with silence.

"That monk, St. Brendan," she said presently, "he came here too, didn't he?"

"Not to Avalon, but to another island—the one we call Tir Tairngiri. And he did not sail from Éire, like Bran. St. Brendan was of your world, the Shadow; he sailed from his own eastern island, your Ireland. He sailed in search of Paradise, and

77

because his soul was pure and his quest true, they say, he passed right out of your world and into Annwn. He made landfall to the north of here, in Tir Tairngiri, where there are many gems and fruit-bearing trees, and so he believed that he had found his Paradise. He and his monks did not stay there, though. They returned across the ocean so that they might tell of the wonders they had seen. And so they came again into the Shadow and vanished from our world. They did not return, and since that time no others of your world have made the sea journey into Annwn." Thomas stopped and pointed. "We must go through the wood here. There is no road or path to the Nemeton any more."

"You mean there was once?"

"Long ago, when the Druids met there for sacred rituals. They have been gone for more than two hundred years."

"But Druids have been gone for much longer than that, haven't they? Hundreds and hundreds of years."

"In your world, perhaps," he said, "but not in this. In the land of Éire they still exist, or so it is said—few ships now cross the great ocean that divides their land from ours. There are even a few Druids in Avalon still. In Annwn there are lands to the east, those we call Éire and Cymru and Logres. They are like the eastern lands that lie in your world, across your own ocean, yet also not like them. Once the two worlds were closer, and there were more comings and goings between them. In those days, your Shadow-Druids fled to the lands of Annwn, for they had seen that their traditions were dying in your world. With them fled many common folk too; they claimed those eastern lands and named them, and their descendants flourished. And some learned the art of sailing, and they journeyed across Annwn's sea to establish their ways here in Avalon as well.

"But then *we* came—Shadow-children of your New Found Land—just a few of us at a time, but bringing with us new words and new ways. And though our ancestors married with these people of Éire and Cymru, and learned their tongues and their customs, even calling themselves Gaels or Cymri, they did not follow the faith of the Druids but remained children of the church. English became the language of the common people, replacing the older tongues. As in the lands of the Shadow, new customs grew while the older ones diminished over time. Then the Druids retreated deep into the forests, where a few still live to this day. There are none here now. Only the Nemeton remains; the forest has never taken it over. The spring in it was sacred to them: a goddess dwelt in its waters, or so they said. People came, pilgrims, to bathe in it or to drink the water. It had a healing power, the Druids said. There was also the Dream of the Goddess."

"Dream?"

"Pilgrims would go into a sort of trance and have visions of the goddess, who would speak with them."

The forest was floored with moss, springy and soft. There were pines and firs and, farther on, white birch trunks.

The clearing! It was the one familiar thing in all this unsettling strangeness, and she ran towards it as though she was coming home. There was the quietly bubbling spring, and all around it the wildflowers. She stood for a moment at the stream's edge, gazing at the dance of light along its surface. "Where did the pilgrims stay when they came here?" she asked.

"There was a guest house not far from here. It is only a ruin now, all overgrown, but there is still a statue of the goddess standing in it."

"Will you show it to me?"

"If you wish."

He led her deeper into the forest, to a place where only a few rays of sunlight filtered through the heavy boughs, and there in the dappled gloom were walls, old and broken. In some places only the rectangular outline of the ancient building's foundation remained. Many strange forms had been carved into the stone: intricate braided patterns; mesmeric swirls and whorls; and beasts, ramping boars and stags. Some of the figures were fanciful: there were three-horned bulls, ram-horned snakes and a dancing man with deer's antlers growing from his head. The figures and designs seemed to move before Maeve's tired eyes.

Thomas led her into the midst of the ruin and showed her where the crudely carved image still stood in its niche of stone: a female figure with an overlarge head, one arm upraised while the other cradled the crumbling shape of an infant.

"This was their goddess?" Maeve asked. "What was she called?"

"Her name was Modron—Matrona, some called her. Her child is Mabon. He was a hero in olden times."

"Why didn't they put her statue in the clearing?"

"The Druids did not use images in their sacred places. And Modron was goddess not just of that little stream, but also of a great river that lies farther on, with all its streams and pools. The Nemeton was only one of many places sacred to her."

Maeve was silent. If there was indeed a presence in this place, she thought, then perhaps it could be appealed to, petitioned in some way. "Let me go back to my own world," she could say, and perhaps someone, somewhere, would hear. . . .

And yet, how much more pleasant it was here in the forest, listening to the breeze and the birds. On the other side, in that other world, lay anger and fear, and the betrayal of trust. She sat down by the sun-mottled, mossy wall and closed her eyes, ignoring Thomas's pleading and cajoling. "Leave me alone," she murmured, curling herself up. "I just want to stay here for a while."

"Here! But why?" he asked.

She had no answer for him, and did not try to come up with one. After a few minutes, she heard his footsteps reluctantly retreating, but she paid no heed. She felt curiously drowsy, but that too was all right.

Perhaps I will dream of the goddess, she thought.

She lay there, wrapped in a warm inner darkness while the scents and sounds of the wood receded, withdrawing into the still dark place that is the antechamber of sleep. It was an escape, and after the bombardment of her bewildered senses, she welcomed it. She could not say afterwards how long she spent in this in-between place. What brought her back was a sensation of cold. The warmth of the sun had gone, and she opened her eyes to darkness. Shocked, she remained where she was for a moment. Then she scrambled to her feet.

"Thomas?" she called out uncertainly. There was no reply.

Had she fallen into a deep sleep after all, and slumbered for hours? The sun had gone from the sky. There were trees nearby, but not the dense forest she remembered. She spun around, trying to make sense of the constantly shifting realities.

Evening now, and she was in a park-like place with a scattering of small trees. As she stood there, a cold white light touched the trunks around her, steadily building in intensity as she watched. The source of the light was approaching. . . .

She staggered out of the park and toward the paved surface of a road as a car drove swiftly past, its headlights sending shadows flying through the branches of the trees.

Chapter Six

FARTHER DOWN THE ROAD THERE WERE HOUSES. Maeve could see the light from their windows shedding a yellow glare on its asphalt surface. She was standing in a cemetery; to her left a church raised its dark spire against the sky. Slowly Maeve walked out into the road and headed towards the houses. Light was everywhere, blazing from the windows of homes and shops; in one picture window a couple sat watching TV, the whole room bathed in its cold blue, underwater light. A group of teenagers stood outside a corner store drinking pop from cans under a fluorescent sign: Dougherty's Variety & Video.

"Are you okay?" one of the teenagers called.

Maeve realized that she had been standing rooted in the middle of the street, looking dazedly about her. "I . . . I'm trying to find Bayshore Road," she managed to say.

There was a little pause, during which they must have been wondering how on earth anyone could possibly get lost in Mary's Bay. Then one of the girls spoke.

"You're standin' on it, girl. Just follow it back east," she said, pointing with her pop can. "It goes round the north side of the bay. So you're new here, are you?"

"I'm visiting," Maeve called over her shoulder as she fled back down the street.

She found her aunt and uncle's home without any difficulty—the white saltbox house was ablaze with lights—and as she ran around the lean-to at the back, she saw her aunt and uncle in the front hall. Talking together—about her, no doubt. Had they contacted her parents, called the police? Maeve put on a desperate spurt of speed, flinging open the back door and tearing into the house.

"Oh, there you are," said Uncle Roy as she ran into the passage. "We were just about to send out the bloodhounds." He smiled at her, then turned back to Aunt Ellen. "So I said, 'What about tomorrow for the meeting, since I'll be in town . . .'"

Maeve froze in place, her chest still heaving with exertion. His tone had been light, casual, his expression as affable as ever.

"How long have I been out?" she asked slowly.

Uncle Roy turned to her again. "Oh, not much more than an hour. It was getting dark, though, and we thought you might lose your way. Rob would never forgive me if I mislaid one of his kids—"

"Are you all right, Maeve?" asked her aunt, turning a keener glance in the girl's direction. "You look a little pale."

An hour, Maeve thought. *I've been gone* only *an hour. Then none of it happened.*

"Maeve?" her aunt persisted. "Are you feeling okay?"

Maeve took a deep breath. "I'm fine, it's just . . . I went to this place in the woods, and I lay down by a stream and kind of dozed off." She must have done, though the transition between awareness and sleep had been strangely seamless. "And I dreamed . . ." *Dreamed*. Was that really the right word? Her memories of sunlit fields, Thomas's family, the apple blossoms arose in her mind. *When did I ever dream about taste and smell before?* she wondered. And there was nothing vague or blurry about these memories, unlike the dim recollections of a dream. "I feel funny—as if I've been gone longer than I really was," she said.

"A nap will do that to you sometimes," Aunt Ellen said. "Leave you feeling a bit thrown off. And you may still be a bit jet-lagged. If you're that tired, perhaps you should make an early night of it."

Jet-lagged. She grasped the explanation eagerly, clutching at straws. That was it: she was overtired and a little disoriented still. Such things happened. She could put Connemara and Annwn and all that strangeness behind her now. It hadn't been real; of course it hadn't. For even in Grandma's novel, time had flowed at the same pace in Annwn as it had in our world. Emma Butler had come home to find she'd been given up for dead by her family. But Maeve's own "visit" to Annwn had seemingly taken only minutes (for an hour at least must have passed as she'd lain in the clearing looking up at the darkening sky). She breathed more easily as she mounted the stairs. *Delusion,* that was the word. None of it had actually happened.

As she thought this, she suddenly realized with amazement that she had almost believed—had seriously entertained the thought—that Annwn was real.

And then, to her further astonishment, she felt a pang of bitter disappointment.

When Maeve woke up the next morning, the fog had vanished and the sun had returned.

She ran over to the window and looked out. The view was utterly changed: its bleakness had gone, and the sunlight brought out the greenness of the fir trees and the sweep of wild grasses that served as a lawn. The sea was as blue as the sky, scattered with the dancing points of reflected light that Grandma used to call sun pennies. Even the stones of the shingle beach had changed. A uniform grey no longer, they showed a variety of softer shades—beige and purple and slate blue—and the sea-wet stones at the surf's edge gleamed as though coated in varnish. The great rolling breakers of yesterday had diminished to little rippling wavelets that made only the smallest of murmurs as they came ashore. So calm and clear was the water that Maeve could see every detail of the pebbled bottom; and farther out there were the great grey-purple shapes of submerged boulders furred with seaweed. Mysterious and forbidding no longer, the bay cheerfully revealed its secrets to the sun. Perhaps even the shipwreck would be visible today, if one went over it in a boat.

Maeve rummaged through the bureau drawers for some shorts and a T-shirt. As she did so, she remembered the curious dream, or delusion, of the previous evening. But it had no power to alarm her now; it had been explained away, and in the sunlight and warmth of the morning it seemed less real than it had before. Again, she felt rather sorry. Even if it had been only a sort of lucid dream, it had been an interesting, even a beautiful one. It really had felt as though she'd been plunged into an actual Annwn. Who could say what might have followed if she had remained unconscious? She might have seen the fairies themselves, as the fictional Emma had in *Adventure in the Otherworld*, or journeyed to Gwynedd and seen Gwenlian and Diarmait, now reigning as king and queen in their castle. It was odd that her subconscious had not simply repeated the plot of her grandmother's book, but instead had created a sort of sequel. Who could say where it might have taken her? It was like that computer thing people were always talking about, virtual reality: creating electronic images so convincing that you could imagine you were in some other reality. But this had been better; it had involved not only sight and sound, but also things like taste and smell. And because it had been a dream, she had actually *believed* it was happening—unlike virtual reality, where you knew it was all just a game.

She sighed as she went downstairs. *Why do I always wake from dreams just as they're getting interesting?* she moped. *I've always just won a big part in a play, or I've been accepted into the Stratford Festival or something—and the next thing I know, I'm awake. It's so disappointing.*

"Ah, Maeve." Her aunt looked up from the breakfast table. "How are you this morning? Feeling better?"

"Yes, thanks. The weather's much nicer today, isn't it?"

"It's still a bit cool, but it's not bad out." Aunt Ellen rose. "I'll put on an egg for you, shall I? Or would you rather have cereal?"

"Just a piece of toast would be fine, thanks."

Her aunt clucked a bit at that, but she slipped a slice of

whole-wheat bread into the toaster. "I've got some home-made strawberry jam, if you'd like it. Your uncle's going to be away for a few days, by the way. Some sort of conference in the city. He left earlier this morning."

"Did he? I never even heard him. I must've been sound asleep."

"Ah, that's the sea air—better than a sedative." Her aunt put out the butter and a pot of jam. "Well, I'm glad you're here with me, Maeve."

"Are you nervous when Uncle Roy's away?"

"Not really. Crime's pretty well non-existent around here. But it'll be nice for me to have some company."

Maeve understood that Aunt Ellen was kindly trying to make her uninvited guest feel needed and wanted. "It's such a beautiful day, I think I'll go for a walk," she announced as she took her toast to the table. At least Aunt Ellen shouldn't feel she had to come up with things for her to do.

"Actually," Aunt Ellen said, pouring herself a second cup of coffee, "I thought I'd show you around the village. You haven't really seen it yet."

"That's okay," replied Maeve carefully as she spooned jam onto her toast. "I can just walk around by myself. I'm sure you've got a lot of other stuff to do."

"No, I've no plans for today, beyond putting some flowers on your grandma's grave. I like to do that once in a while. We'll go for a walk together, shall we? There are people here who would like to meet you, people who knew your dad and your grandparents."

"Oh, well then, sure," said Maeve, surrendering.

They set out half an hour later, walking up Bayshore

Road towards the main street of the village. She marvelled anew at the colours of some of the small wooden houses— orange, butter yellow, dark green, even garish pink with turquoise trim. Perhaps their owners were trying consciously to combat the monochrome dreariness in which the landscape was generally plunged. In full sun, though, the bright colours did not seem imposed on the land. Rather, they appeared to belong to it, as natural as the colours of the wild lupins that grew in tall, festive spikes by the side of the road.

"Your dad and your uncle grew up here," her aunt was saying. "That's the very same store where they used to go to buy candy when they were little boys. It's been in the Dougherty family for almost sixty years now. But I suppose your dad's told you all about it."

"Not that I remember." Dad, in fact, had seldom mentioned Newfoundland when she was growing up. Only in the last year or so had he begun to speak of it.

"Your grandma's father was a good friend of your grandfather James O'Connor's dad, and when she and James grew up, they fell in love and married. Later on, they inherited the O'Connor family house. So you see, she knew and loved the O'Connor house long before she came to live there; it was like a second home to her."

She nodded towards the church. "That's St. Mary's, where the family went for generations. The present crop of O'Connor men," Aunt Ellen observed mildly, "has always been too lazy to get out of bed on Sunday mornings. Roy says everyone ought to believe in something, but he'll do his believing at home. Your grandma didn't attend here either—she was

Presbyterian, not Roman Catholic—but she's buried there beside your granddad."

How did I ever get there from the clearing? Maeve wondered as they approached the cemetery. *Was that clearing real, anyway, or just a part of my dream? Why can't I remember everything that happened? Did I black out?* Shock could do peculiar things to the mind, and she had suffered a terrible shock before fleeing into the woods. . . . But she wasn't going to think about that, not now.

They went to Grandma's gravesite together, and Aunt Ellen stooped to place her bouquet before the white headstone. "I visit her grave each week, and put fresh flowers here in spring and summer. And I planted that shrub rose"—she pointed to a bush growing next to the headstone—"for a memorial. The flowers are very pretty when they're in bloom, a sort of cream colour with pink at the centre. Your grandma loved roses, so I thought it would be appropriate."

"I'm glad," said Maeve a little hoarsely. "I'm glad someone else remembers her."

"She was a lovely person. I couldn't have asked for a better mother-in-law. I still miss her terribly. Her illness was so sudden." Aunt Ellen waved a hand at the rows of headstones. "All your O'Connor ancestors are here, going back to the early 1800s. Here's your great-grandfather Matthew, James O'Connor's father, and here's his wife, Sarah Morgan. She was Welsh, but converted to the Catholic faith."

"So that's why my middle name is Morgan," remarked Maeve. "I always wondered."

"There are lots of records in the church, too, of course; all the births, weddings and funerals in the family for decades. Shall we go in?"

The church's interior seemed dim after the sunlit street— its stained-glass windows turning the light to muted jewel hues—and there was a curious hush inside it, a silence unlike any Maeve had ever encountered. It was a silence that you *heard*, that you found yourself listening to, as you might listen to music or the sound of falling water. Just inside the entrance a plaster image of an angel stood, holding in its arms a shell-shaped basin. "Holy water," Aunt Ellen explained, dipping her fingers in the basin and crossing herself. The inside of the church was painted white like the outside, and an emerald green carpet ran up the central aisle into the sanctuary, where the curtained tabernacle stood over the altar. Banks of votive candles stood to either side of the sanctuary. They had been placed in red glass jars, so their flickering flames showed red, like rows of glowing embers. To the left of the sanctuary, a plaster statue of the Virgin and Child stood in a tall niche.

Maeve followed her aunt up a side aisle to the front of the church. As she did so, a middle-aged woman came through a side door with a tall vase full of summer flowers. Aunt Ellen did not call out, but approached the woman and spoke in a low voice, almost whispering. It still seemed loud against the silence, however. "Hello, Anne. I've brought my niece to see the church."

The grey-haired woman beamed over her flowers. "How nice to meet you, Maeve."

Maeve returned her smile. "Hello."

"This is Mrs. Murphy, Maeve," said her aunt. "A good friend of mine."

Mrs. Murphy beamed. "Go way back, we do. Now if you'll excuse me a moment, I'll just take these flowers to Our Lady." She nodded amiably at the statue of the Madonna.

Maeve looked up at the graceful female form in its flowing blue robe, the painted plaster face serene beneath its gilded crown, the rose-cheeked infant nestling in the crook of her arm. She had never seen the statue before, and yet it seemed oddly familiar. No doubt she'd seen pictures of similar statues in books.

Aunt Ellen smiled. "What pretty blue irises, Anne. Just the colour of her robe, aren't they?"

Maeve glanced towards the niche again—and froze.

In the dim light there was no statue now; it had been replaced by an alien image: a mother and child carved roughly in grey stone and weathered by time, cruder than, yet curiously evocative of, the figures whose place they had taken. They floated before her eyes, adrift in a seething gloom. *"Her name was Modron—Matrona, some called her. Her child is Mabon. He was a hero in olden times."* Where had that voice come from? Maeve's vision swam. There was a faint droning in her ears, then she blinked and the image was gone, the plaster statue had returned to its niche.

As Aunt Ellen and her friend talked on quietly, Maeve turned slowly around and stared about her. She saw, now, how the flowers in the vase echoed the shapes and hues of other flowers she remembered; how the white wooden pillars that supported the vaulted roof resembled the smooth boles of silver birches, and the green colouring of the carpet held in itself something of the living green of moss. At the doorway, the angel proferred his basin of holy water. . . .

Holy water, sacred water. *The spring was sacred . . . pilgrims came to bathe in it, or drink the water. The Madonna. Modron—Matrona.* The Virgin with her holy child. The goddess cradling her infant son.

The church and the Nemeton reflected each other, suggested one another in a hundred small and subtle ways. They were separate yet connected, like an object and its shadow. *The Shadow-world.* Where had she heard that? What had Grandma written in her book? "If you cover yourself with a blanket, you may note how the cloth fits itself in some places to your body, following the shape of a knee, hip or arm; but in other places, the blanket is stretched taut, and the shape of the body beneath is hidden. So it is with the two worlds: our own world comes very near to reflecting certain places in Annwn, but other places it masks and hides."

There *was* no clearing, not in this world. That was why she had not been able to find it the second time, why she had come upon the church instead. The church was its reflection in this world. . . .

Nonsense, thought Maeve desperately, and followed her aunt back down the aisle and into the sun.

That afternoon, Maeve slipped quietly into her uncle's study. It was a small room at the back of the house, pleasantly cluttered. Books lay scattered on every horizontal surface, including the seats of chairs and even the floor. They had titles like *Bronze Age Europe*, *Reign of the Celts*, *Irish Fables and Folklore* and *Creation Myths from around the World*. There was one called *St. Brendan's Voyage*; she leafed through this, gazing at the illustrations of the sailor-monk's adventures. Here was a little ship crammed full of tonsured monks, balancing on the back of a huge whale-like sea monster: "Brendan's ship lands upon the back of Jasconius, the great fish, and the abbot celebrates the Mass." Another picture showed the ship sailing past an island that belched out flames and flying devils, while yet another depicted a tiny islet where huge white birds perched, bigger than the trees they sat in.

She set the book down and picked up *A Dictionary of Folklore*, a massive tome with alphabetized entries for all the folkloric terms and themes. Opening it at random, she read: "Leprechaun: an Irish spirit, popularly described as the shoemaker for the fairies . . ."

She flipped on to the *N* section. Of course it wouldn't be there, she told herself. It wasn't in Grandma's book, so it must be only a nonsense word invented by her subconscious. Still, she scanned the entries; it sounded as though it was spelt with an N—E—M . . .

Her eye came up sharply against the word: Nemeton. There it was. "Among the Druids it was the practice to set aside groves in the forest as sanctuaries. Their name for these sacred places was Nemeton, from the Irish *neimed*. A possible origin of this word may be the Latin *nemus*, a clearing. . . ."

Maeve stared, her skin prickling. A clearing. Nemeton, a sanctuary of the Druids. The word was real; she'd used it correctly. *But how? It wasn't in the book. I never saw it before. It's not in* Adventure in the Otherworld. *I reread that book a thousand times. . . .*

She put the book down hastily and left the room, closing the door firmly behind her.

I must have read it somewhere else and remembered it. I must have.

That evening after dinner, Mrs. Murphy came to visit. Maeve sat quietly with the two older women at the table in the breakfast nook overlooking the bay, staring into her teacup and only half-listening to their conversation. Though Mrs. Murphy had more grey in her hair, she apparently had been a close friend of Aunt Ellen's back in their school days. Maeve found this difficult to imagine. Back home in Balsam Heights, no one stayed put for very long. The residents were mainly executives and business people, and they were constantly being transferred, moving their families out to Calgary or Vancouver before anyone had a chance to get to know them. The houses on either side of Maeve's present home had changed hands several times since the O'Connors had moved in five years ago—and now it looked as though the O'Connors themselves would not be able to stay. Maeve wondered what it would be like to live in the same neighbourhood all your life—to grow up with the same people always around you, see them change with time as you yourself changed.

"Are there any kids Maeve's age around this summer, Anne?" Aunt Ellen asked as she poured more tea into her friend's cup. "She's at a bit of a loose end, I'm afraid."

Maeve started to protest that it was all right, that she wasn't in the least bored, but the other woman replied, "Why, yes, there are a few teens about. My neighbour's daughter, Karen, is about Maeve's age, and she has some nice young friends. They rent videos and see them at each other's homes, have parties on the beach, that sort of thing."

Maeve looked down at her teacup to hide her dismay. *Kids my age! Just what I need.* Oh, things would be just fine at first; she'd go on an outing or two, see a movie or two at someone's house. She'd hate the movies, she always did—dumb screwball comedies, horror slasher flicks. The acting was always terrible. As hard as she tried to pretend she was enjoying herself, somehow they always seemed to guess that she wasn't. And she was always getting caught out. She'd wear the wrong brand of shoes or jeans, use slang that wasn't quite "in," give away the fact that she didn't watch their favourite TV shows or listen to the latest rock groups. Somehow she could just never get it right. Soon their voices would grow distant when they spoke to her; there would be swift exchanged glances every time she said anything. Later, there would be muffled sniggers and whispers that stopped abruptly when she turned around. Finally, to her relief, there would be no more invitations anywhere. It was always the same. Mom had often tried to get Maeve into her friends' daughters' cliques, to no avail. *No thanks! I'd rather be bored.* But she couldn't say that to Mrs. Murphy and her aunt.

She stared dully out the window as they talked, hoping they would change the subject. The sunlight was beginning to fade, to lose its daytime clarity: the beams were lower, more golden, the shadows they cast softer at the edges. The light on the bay no longer dazzled, and the sky beyond was a more muted blue. The kitchen door was open as always, and she could see the back garden, its trees showing through the window in the back door. They too were being slowly transformed by the approach of evening, the airy spaces framed by their boughs now a dimmer green, the colour of deep water. The boughs themselves lay half in that green shadow, half in the waning sunlight, which painted them in warm, red-edged hues. A bird perched on one of those boughs, dark and small in a leafy gloom; as she watched, it suddenly flew upward and the whirring wings were filled with light.

Then, just as suddenly, Maeve realized with a shock that this view from the back window was all wrong; that these trees were too large, had much thicker foliage, than the few spindly maples that really stood at the back of the house. With the little stab of fear came the same odd sensation she had experienced in the church—the feeling that her world was in some way becoming transparent, letting something beyond it show through. *No, that's crazy. It's just another hallucination.* If she sat very still, it would go away.

But she realized to her own surprise that she did not want it to go away, that something in her called to it even as it called to her. It offered itself, perhaps, as a release and an escape. She sat silently as Aunt Ellen and Mrs. Murphy chatted on about the old days, her eyes locked on the window and the impossible trees beyond.

At last the two women rose. "I must see your garden before I go, Ellie," said Mrs. Murphy. Aunt Ellen opened the back door and the two of them passed through it, still talking.

Maeve followed them as if in a trance. Would they see what she saw? When they opened the back door, would they walk through into Annwn? They seemed to notice nothing unusual. Aunt Ellen opened the door for Mrs. Murphy and they both went out, closing it behind them.

Maeve approached the back door hesitantly. She could still see the tall, evening-shadowed trees, but she found that she could no longer see the women. The garden was gone. Before her there were only the trees, and beyond them more trunks receding into the tinted twilight of a forest. She could still hear the voices of her aunt and Mrs. Murphy, but they were faint now and had a curious echoing quality, like sounds heard at a great distance or like the voices of disembodied ghosts. It was all right—it was not real. The women, invisible now to her eyes, continued to talk amiably, and she knew that the garden was still there. It had not gone away. The Otherworld forest was there for Maeve alone.

For me . . .

She felt an odd constriction of the throat.

Opening the door wide, she wavered for an instant on the threshold. Then she stepped through into Annwn.

Chapter Seven

"WHAT A PERFECT DAY," sighed Maeve.

"Yes," agreed Thomas. "I think summer has really begun at last."

They were strolling together along the well-trodden path that led to the shore, Cordelia capering along ahead of them. Maeve had been here for two weeks now—or rather, what felt like two weeks. *But I will go back, as I did before, and it will have been only a few minutes—if that.* She could put it all off indefinitely: the divorce and the move, everyone's pity and the "kids her age." *I could spend a year or more here, I'll bet, and still everything there would wait for me. Well, let it wait!*

Thomas had been waiting for her when she had returned to his world. She'd gone straight to the Nemeton and there she had found him, lingering by the stream. He had gone there on and off since her disappearance, he had said, hoping that she was all right, that she would return.

"I wondered if you might come here," he had told her,

and pointed between the tree trunks. "Look, these roses bloomed in the forest just today. I took it for a sign."

And Maeve had stared at the rose-bush growing up improbably through the mossy forest floor. It was covered in flowers, soft pink at the centre with creamy-white outer petals. "The villagers say that this rose-bush has been here for years. No one knows who planted it," Thomas continued, "or why they would put it in the middle of a wood. Some say it is magical. I never believed that myself. But when I came here this morning and saw that it had bloomed, I wondered if it had anything to do with the Shadow-world, and you."

"It looks like the rose-bush my aunt planted on Grandma's grave." The cemetery was right next to the church, as this part of the forest was next to the Nemeton. But why would the rose-bush be here in Annwn as well, in two places at once? What could it mean? *Don't be stupid*, she had scolded herself. *It doesn't mean a thing. This is a dream!* Dreams were made up of such things: little, inconsequential snippets of memory and experience that were thrown together without rhyme or reason.

She had said warmly, "I'm so glad to see you again, Thomas."

He had looked shy at that. "I am happy to see you too. I was afraid you would never return, and leave me always wondering what had become of you."

She stole a glance at him as they walked through the village, noting his sensitive face and dark, long-lashed eyes, his long brown hair moving restlessly in the breeze. *If Lisa and the other girls could see this guy, they'd go crazy over him*, she thought with a smile. It was a pity she couldn't really *believe* in Annwn's reality this time around, but on the other hand there wasn't any stress or worry about getting home.

Perhaps this hallucination could become like a drug, an addictive thing—but so what? Brandon was always having beer with his friends, and probably the occasional joint; Mom had her cigarettes, and Dad his daily drink. They indulged themselves in these comfortable addictions without apology. Why shouldn't she indulge herself too? And the Annwn dream was benign; there were no side effects, no headaches or dizziness or blurred vision or anything like that. It took nothing from her, not even time.

Once, when she had found herself alone in Branwen's kitchen, she had taken a knife and run the blade along her arm, feeling the cut and watching the blood well up from the broken skin. Pain, she realized, existed here as well as pleasure. She would have to be careful. But any hurt she received would be unlikely to harm her actual, physical body. This body, real as it felt, could only be a projection of her own mind.

And there was more pleasure here than pain. She fed upon Annwn, sating hungers she had not even known were there.

"Maeve," Cordelia said one day, "I feel as though you have always been here." Maeve had begun to feel the same. She slept now in Cordelia's tiny, narrow room, on a mattress placed on the floor. Cordelia did not mind, seemed in fact delighted to have someone to talk with at night. "I have never had a sister," she observed.

"Neither have I," Maeve told her.

Cordelia considered her a moment, then took her by the hand. "Now you have," she said simply.

The feel of the small warm hand in her own thrilled through Maeve like a strain of music, like the sun on a spring morning. *If only it could be real!* she thought yearningly. But as time passed, it became more real; there were moments, little lapses, when she forgot to disbelieve, and the joy and comfort enfolded her completely.

When Maeve had first arrived at Thomas's home, she had felt like a stray dog or cat the family took in out of compassion. But now she understood that it was more than that. They had taken her in as a pool takes in a droplet of rainwater, incorporating her wholly into the life of their home. She learned more about that home every day. The round stone hearth, for instance, was no mere fireplace: it was the centre of the house, a little sun about which the life of the family revolved. In addition to heating their food, it gave them warmth and light, and in the evenings the family would gather around it to tell stories or sing snatches of song. *Hearth—heart.* The words seemed to Maeve to mean the same thing. There were no fireplaces in the Balsam Heights houses, only fake mantelpieces with artificial fires beneath for decoration.

"I wish you could be here on May Day," Thomas told her. "Then you would see the ceremony of the need-fire."

"Need-fire?"

"Yes. On that day, all the fires in the villagers' hearths are put out, and in the evening a great bonfire is built atop the largest hill. This is the *tine éigin*, the need-fire. It is divided in two, and all we villagers and our animals pass one by one through the narrow path between the flames, to drive away bad luck for the year," he explained. "It is a very old custom that goes back to the time of the Druids. When all have passed through, one person from each household takes some of the need-fire back to rekindle the hearth. Very pretty it is, to see the torch flames going down the hillside in the dark, back to all the homes of the village."

Branwen was teaching her to bake bread, and Padraig showed her the tools and techniques of his carpenter's trade. He also loved to talk to her about Shakespeare. Sometimes he would speak some dialogue while he worked—Falstaff was his favourite character, and *The Merry Wives of Windsor* was apparently the most popular play in town. But they never performed *A Midsummer Night's Dream*.

"*They* would not like it," Padraig explained. "The Good People. They would find it disrespectful, I think. And who can say whether one of them might not be watching? We must show them the proper respect, all of us—even you, Queen Maeve." He had taken to calling her that. Apparently there had once been a great queen of that name in the faraway land called Éire—a warrior-queen, like the English Boadicea, who had led armies in her chariot.

This place was like, and not like, the Newfoundland she knew. That island's forests had been cut down by the desperate settlers, but this island was still heavily forested. The soil, too, seemed more fertile. Yet the people were the same; they possessed the same rugged cheerfulness, the same inexplicable contentment, that she had seen in the faces of Mary's Bay villagers. Here too, happiness and contentment grew like flowers between stones, springing up where they had no right to be.

Thomas once told her of one man in the village who had a curious heirloom hanging on his wall: "A great hollow tube of metal it is, with a wooden handle at one end. He says it once shot metal balls out of its mouth, with the aid of a fiery powder. But no one here knows how to make this powder, so the weapon can no longer work."

"A gun," said Maeve primly. "You don't want guns, Thomas. They're horrible things." But she was intrigued by the inventiveness of the dream, by the story that continued to unfold before her, seemingly of its own volition. It gave to her every detail of the villagers' lives, which appeared in every way realistic and convincing. For instance, the people here used a barter system, exchanging services rather than coins. She had heard that people in olden times did this. Eggs were traded for milk, fish for greens; various services were offered in exchange for food. Sometimes Maeve went with Branwen and Thomas to the communal fields to gather foodstuffs—root vegetables, for the most part. Maeve was accustomed to buying produce at the supermarket, where it lay neatly arranged in bins. It seemed to her very wonderful to see the familiar shapes of carrots and beets being pulled right out of the ground with bits of damp brown earth still clinging to them in places. The people, she learned, wasted nothing; even the leafy tops of the turnips were eaten as a green.

On her second day in the village the capelin came in, thousands upon thousands of little silver fish that washed ashore with the tide to spawn and die. The villagers all ran down to the beach to gather them in aprons and baskets; they were not only good to eat, but also useful for fertilizing the fields. Everything fascinated her: the net-mending and the hay-mowing, the boat-builders crafting keels from tree trunks, the potter with his wheel. Sometimes she and Thomas stopped to watch the blacksmith in his forge, pounding the glowing metal on his anvil before the roaring furnace; or they would peer in the windows as the village weaver worked her loom, her feet pedalling mechanically on the treadles, her head bobbing absently up and down as though she were herself a working part of the apparatus. Maeve had forgotten—indeed she could not even remember learning—where fabrics came from and how they were made. Now she watched in fascination as the warp and weft threads came together into cloth.

Life here was rough and often difficult. All the villagers slept on straw pallets on the floor, drawing these right up to the hearths for warmth on cold nights. Thomas's own pallet was in a sort of small loft at one end of the cottage, and was reached by a little flight of steps. There was no plumbing, and baths had to be taken in a barrel with bowlsful of water heated over the hearth. Even so, the people did not always smell clean. But they were unfailingly kind, and that was all that mattered to Maeve.

The houses and shops were all built close to the abbey, like chicks sheltering under a hen's wings. If the hearths of the village were like little suns, this huge stone church with its community of monks was the centre of their universe. The monks were learned as well as spiritual men; they had asked that Maeve come to visit them one evening and tell them all about the Shadow-world, and she had agreed. It would be fun, she thought, smiling—like being the Connecticut Yankee in King Arthur's court.

As it turned out, the meeting was not as much fun as she had expected.

The Ryans walked over to the monastery with her, and she met with the monks in the great stone hall where the abbot held audience. The monastery looked as she had always imagined such places would, all lofty stone arches and heavy pillars supporting vaulted ceilings. The church to which it was attached had the soaring grace of a small cathedral, and the same deep silence she recalled from the church in Mary's Bay. The monks wore hooded, homespun grey robes with rough cords for belts, just like monks in picture books about the Middle Ages. But their hair was peculiar. Instead of the usual tonsure, a bald patch shaved off the top of the head, they sported a shaven line that ran from ear to ear across the crown, dividing the front hair from the back.

There was something intimidating about these men, with their stern faces and long hooded robes, and Maeve's amusement quickly evaporated. The elderly abbot showed her an old map on a roll of yellowed parchment, pointing out to her the lands and seas of Annwn. Avalon, she saw, had almost the exact same shape as Newfoundland's Avalon Peninsula; but it was not joined to the main island, here called Tir Tairngiri. There were other small islands just to the north of Avalon. One of these was labelled Hy-Bresail. It was actually a group of tiny islets encircled by an outer ring of land.

"I thought that one sank beneath the sea," she said, remembering what Uncle Roy had told her. It was fascinating to see how this dream/illusion incorporated such small fragments of her real-life experience.

"A part of it remains above the surface, and there is more that mortal eyes may not look upon. We see as much of Hy-Bresail as the Good People allow us to see, no more."

The abbot crossed himself. "It is their island, and we do not go there."

Far across the parchment sea lay the British Isles, but they too looked subtly different, and their names were not the same: Ireland was Éire and England was Logres, while Wales was called Cymru. But what country was Kernow? It seemed to form part of what should be England. The names of Gwynedd and Temair, she learned, came from places in these old countries: the settlers, like those in the real North America, apparently had given familiar names to places in their own New World.

The monks questioned her at length on the land masses and seas of the Shadow-world, then on its history and customs. Maeve realized that her explanations did not sound convincing. When she told them of her own world, of radio and television and airplanes and space travel, they were not impressed, but instead demanded to know how such things could be. And to her embarrassment, she was unable to explain the technology beyond a few vague comments about electricity and engines, which only perplexed them further. She was woefully ignorant, she had to acknowledge, and in her humiliation had to keep reminding herself that none of this was *really* happening. The monks were soon shaking their heads and looking askance at her. It was plain that they thought her either a liar or mad. She was almost relieved when they were interrupted by a knock at the door.

"I beg that you will excuse me," the old man said courteously. But the rest of his sentence seemed plain to Maeve: ". . . while I deal with more important matters." The audience was clearly at an end.

Maeve and the others walked slowly back through the narrow dirt roads of the village.

"They didn't believe me, but it's all true," Maeve said disconsolately. "I've just never learned how those things work. Honestly!"

Padraig patted her shoulder comfortingly. "Never mind now. *We* believe you, Queen Maeve." He launched into yet another of his Shakespearian quotes:

> . . . now I will believe
> That there are unicorns; that, in Arabia
> There is one tree, the phoenix' throne; one phoenix
> At this hour reigning there.

Maeve smiled, but she could think of another quote that was far more appropriate: "*We are such stuff as dreams are made on.*" That was the real truth. *You're nothing but part of a dream, poor Padraig—you, your family, the abbot, everybody. I only wish you could be real.*

The following day was also fine, and she joined Thomas and his sister as they went to get some fish for supper. There was, of course, no fishmonger's shop here. Everyone went down to the shore, where the small fishing boats unloaded each day their rich catch of herring and halibut and mottled codfish, fresh from the ocean. In this dream-world there was no shortage of fish, and the cod were huge, some of them nearly as long as a man was tall.

Cordelia preceded them down to the shore, prancing

about and holding her doll on her shoulders; she was, she announced, a horse and Gwendolen was riding her.

"As you say, Brat," replied Thomas. He often called his little sister by such names, but they were said with tolerance, even affection. Cordelia skipped up to him and took his hand, and the sight gave the watching Maeve a sharp little twinge.

Thomas got the fish as usual from Old Ned, who bartered with Padraig for produce from their little farm. He was an aged, weather-beaten man with skin like wrinkled brown vellum, but his thin arms had a surprising strength as they hauled on the loaded nets. His big black dog was with him. All the dogs here were of the same breed, like a sturdy version of the black Labrador—water-dogs, the villagers called them. They were excellent swimmers and could even retrieve fish that had slipped off hooks.

"I get my living from the sea," Ned was telling Thomas and Cordelia, "but I respect it too. That's why I have lived so long. Terrible dangerous, the sea. It looks very pleasant just now, with the sun dancing on the waves, but there are strange things in it, marvels and dangers. Beasts big enough to swallow a boat. Seals that aren't seals, and that look at you with human eyes as they swim past." He stroked his dog's glossy black head absently, gazing out to sea. "Once, when I was a young lad, I went out fishing with my father, and we came to a place where the sea was clear as glass, or so it seemed to me. I gazed down, down through the deeps, and below me I saw a country. Down there at the bottom, where there should have been weeds and fishes, I saw the tops of trees, hills, whole meadows covered in wildflowers—all as they would look to a bird flying high above them. And—strange to see—there were lakes too, and winding rivers."

Thomas looked puzzled. "Lakes and rivers in the *sea*?"

"As I live and breathe, I saw them. And towns as well."

"Towns?" repeated Cordelia, her eyes wide.

"Aye." He raised his thin, strong arms. "Great cities that lifted up their towers to the sun, and roads winding among the hills and fields. In a moment it all vanished, though, and when I asked my father and the other men in the boat about it, they said they had seen nothing. I have never seen the country in the sea again. But I've heard the bells in the towers ringing down there under the sea, tolling in the tide. It is a country of the Good People perhaps, a magic place. Or it may be that I saw where the Fomori have their home."

"What *are* the Fomori?" asked Maeve. Grandma had mentioned them only briefly in her book.

The old man thoughtfully rubbed his forehead with his sleeve. "I don't really know what sort of devil or elf they may be, but it's said that they dwell down there in the deep. That's what their name means: 'the undersea dwellers.'"

"My grandmother mentioned them in a book she wrote," Maeve said. "But she didn't say a lot about them, except that they were allies of those evil sea-raiders, the Lochlannach, and were the enemies of the . . . the Good People."

"That they were. They were hideous-looking monsters, though some say they could alter their forms at will, being magic folk, and looked monstrous only when they wanted to frighten their foes. Balor was their king in olden times, Balor of the Evil Eye. He appeared as a great giant with one terrible staring eye in his forehead. Long ago, in the isle of Éire, he fought against the great race of the Tuatha de Danaan, the mortal offspring of the Good People. But the Fomori lost that battle—the Battle of Magh Tuireadh, the Plain of the Stone Towers. The children of the Sidhe drove them out, and they have not been heard of since. Perhaps they have gone back to their home beneath the sea."

"How could anyone live in the ocean?" asked Maeve.

He gave her a long look out of his dark, creased eyes, and for a moment she was afraid she had offended him. But there was no annoyance in his voice when he spoke. "There are ways, for magical creatures. The Fomori are not the only ones who can dwell beneath the waves. There are the merrows too."

"Merrows?" asked Maeve.

"Merrows they are to some, others call them *mari-morgans*. Many a fisherman's seen them, and they come ashore sometimes, when they think no one's about to see. They look like us, but the women are uncommonly beautiful. Their fingers and toes are webbed like a seabird's feet, and they wear magic caps that let them pass through the water. There was one came ashore here nigh on a hundred years ago. A man from the village saw her a-sitting on a rock, combing her lovely long hair and singing. She'd taken off her magic cap—it was lying to one side—and quick as a wink he up and snatched it away. And she started a-weeping and a-wailing, for you see, she couldn't return to the deeps without it. But he never would give it back, for he'd fallen in love with her and wanted her for his wife. Back with him she had to go, and they were wed and had a child. But always the sea called to her. One day she found out where her husband had hidden the magic cap, and away she went to the seashore and plunged straight into the waves—and was never seen again."

"What a wonderful story," said Maeve.

"It is no story, but the truth," said Old Ned, and he held up his hand for her to see. Between the splayed fingers were webs of pale, translucent skin, reaching almost to the knuckles. "The sea-maid was my grandmother," he said.

"The wonderful thing is that it's *true*," said Maeve delightedly.

She and Thomas had delivered the fresh cod to Branwen, and were now sitting on boulders by the shore, watching the fishing boats bobbing on the blue expanse of the bay. Here and there an iceberg reflected the sun dazzlingly, but the wind was warmer than it had been.

"What's that?" asked Thomas.

"What Old Ned said, about being a mermaid's grandson," she told him. "It's not just a story, it's true."

"Of course it is true. Ned would not lie."

"In—" she was about to say "*real life*," but quickly changed her sentence, "my world, things like that never happen. It's so dull and ordinary. But here there are sea-people and magic and the Good Folk. And castles with kings and queens, the real old-fashioned kind. Have you ever been to Gwynedd?"

"I? No. It is a great journey, of many days. No one here has ever been so far."

Of course. She was forgetting. "In the . . . the Shadow-world we travel much faster. In a car the trip would take only hours. You could be at the south end of the penin— I mean, the island, by nightfall."

"Ah, yes, your horseless carts! And the strange craft that

fly through the air . . . You find my world wonderful, and yet it seems to me that yours has all the greatest wonders in it."

"Oh, it's not that special, really," she said. But as she spoke she realized the wondrousness of her world, the things she had always taken for granted. It was as though Annwn mirrored them back to her, charged with a strange splendour.

"I would gladly see your world," Thomas continued. "But those who have dwelt all their lives in Annwn cannot leave it by any door. Even those who come here from the Shadow do not find it easy to return home."

His wistful tone saddened her. *It's only a dream*, Maeve reminded herself. *That's why Thomas and his people can never leave Annwn—because they and their world exist only inside my head!* She kept forgetting that these people weren't real—she would find herself thinking how Uncle Roy would like Padraig, for instance, bracketing the real people with the unreal ones. Indeed, sometimes the inhabitants of Annwn seemed more real than many real people she knew. This disturbed her slightly.

"I'd love to see Queen Gwenlian," she remarked, lying back on the sun-warmed stone, "and King Diarmait. But I guess they never come here."

"No, they travel very little now that they are old."

"Old?" She sat bolt upright again, staring at him.

"Yes, they are both well past their seventieth year. Did you not know? Prince Gwion, their eldest son, now is king in all but name, dealing with all the weighty matters of the realm. He is close to fifty himself, a good and sober man, or so the travellers tell us."

Maeve was silent. Gwenlian and Diarmait old—she could

not imagine it. They were a prince and princess of fairyland, eternal in their youth and strength and beauty. How could it be otherwise? Time should not be able to touch them. *If this is my dream,* she thought rebelliously, *then it should do whatever I want. I want to live the adventure Grandma wrote about, not some kind of depressing sequel.*

"Gwion too has a son, by his wife, the Princess Siobhan," Thomas continued. "Arawn, they named him, after Gwenlian's father. But the people call him *Gwalchmai,* Hawk of May, for he dearly loves hawking and hunting. Most say he will not see the kingship for many a year, as his father is in good health and like to live as long as his grandparents. The young prince spends all his time jousting and riding about the country with his hawks. The people love him; it is said by the old folk that he has a strong look of his grandsire, the king, when Diarmait was that same age."

Diarmait—what she would have given to *see* him, young and vital and in the "flesh," as it were, instead of a character conveyed only through printed words. It wasn't fair. She felt cheated, resentful of this new controlling influence on her precious dream-world, which now seemed so independent of her will.

"Let's go home," she said abruptly, and sprang up from her rock.

A *ceilidh* was held that evening on the village green. This was something like a large square dance accompanied by the music of bagpipes and fiddles. Maeve had come to enjoy these revels very much—the merry reels and jigs and the gracious slow strathspeys had seemed complicated at first, but once she got the hang of them she found them great fun and beautiful to watch. She recalled the school dance her mother had once made her go to, where she had stood miserably by the wall as the loudspeakers boomed and the strobe lights flashed, watching all the other girls being asked to dance while she was ignored. The humiliation of that evening had never left her, and she had refused to go to any dances after that. But here the couples danced together in big groups, and no one was ever left out; the women, if they could find no male partners, laughingly danced with other women. Even the children joined in, and all was merriment and light-heartedness under the stars.

But tonight she could not summon that carefree feeling, and she watched with dull eyes as the village fiddler struck up a merry jig. (Someone from the Shadow-world, it was said, had long ago brought a fiddle with him into Annwn, and the instrument had been carefully studied and copied.)

"Tom, who are those men over there?" Maeve asked, pointing. She couldn't recall ever having seen them in the village before, and visitors were rare. They looked to be in their late twenties or early thirties. One was in a kilt of muted greys and browns, with a coarse shirt and a draped stole-like garment that matched the kilt, and the other was plainly dressed in a black tunic and leggings.

"They are Duncan and Aengus, two huntsmen from the southeastern cape, the part of Avalon that we call Dalriada. They just arrived today."

Duncan was a broad-shouldered giant with curly red hair and a ruddy complexion. His companion Aengus was slenderer, though no less tall, with hair of so dark a brown that it was almost black, and a short trimmed beard. Both were very handsome, and many of the village girls were finding a reason to stand close by them. For their part, the men seemed amused and eager to be a part of the festivities.

"Bring out your pipes, Duncan," called the dark-haired Aengus. "See if you can drown out that fiddler!" Laughs arose, and the grinning Duncan strolled off into the night to return a few moments later with a set of bagpipes over one arm.

"Come," said Thomas, taking Maeve by the hand. "If you do not want to dance, then let us go up the hill and see the moon on the water. It is a fine night."

"Okay," agreed Maeve, summoning a smile for him. Perhaps something nice could still happen; it was the sort of evening that people in the real world liked to call magic or enchanting. *Let something magical happen,* she silently urged the dream. *Have a mermaid come up out of the water to comb her hair on the shore—or a Selkie, to change its seal body for a human one. Show me something beautiful and wonderful, something the real world never gives me.*

They climbed the hill and sat down on the old broken wall that ringed its bald summit. This had once been a hilltop fortress, Thomas explained, but it had been allowed to fall into ruin. Once, too, the village would have been surrounded by a wooden pallisade for protection, but there was no need for such protections now. The Lochlannach no longer came to trouble these shores.

"We are safe now from all enemies," he assured her.

Up here they could see everything: the great moonlit sweep of the bay, the glowing windows of the cottages far below, the torchlit green where the dancers swung and whirled to the music of fiddle and pipes. From this lofty vantage point, they could clearly see the precise geometric patterns of the dances: the sets advancing and retreating, the dancers weaving in and out of one another's paths to form figure eights, the round reels that spun back and forth like cartwheels.

"I don't understand why the monks wouldn't believe me," Maeve commented presently. "I mean, wasn't Princess Gwenlian helped out by a Shadow-person back when she was a princess? Don't they remember Emma?"

"Emma?" he repeated. "I know of no Emma. Princess Gwenlian was aided by the Lady Jehane. And it has been many, many years since Jehane left Annwn for her own place."

"Her name wasn't Jehane! It was Emma—Emma Butler! I know, I've read the book a hundred times." She felt peevish and irritable. Why must everything keep changing? Why couldn't it just follow the story?

But Thomas was not looking at her.

A light was moving through the dark forest, a yellow flicker of fire; it came and went from view as the trees concealed it, speeding like a will-o'-the-wisp beneath their boughs. A torch, held in the hand of a rider. As his horse burst from the forest margin, they saw the blur of his firelit face. He was heading at a full gallop towards the green.

Maeve felt a sharp pang of unease. "What is it?" she asked, turning to Thomas.

He shook his head. "I do not know, but something is wrong, I think." His face was openly curious, even a little excited. "Come, let us go down and find out what is happening!" He caught hold of her hand and they ran back down the hill together. Already the patterns of the dances had fallen apart, and people were crowding around the rider.

Branwen and Padraig met them on the dancing green, drawing them in with anxious arms. Branwen's face was white in the torchlight. "Oh, have you heard? Gwynedd is fallen! They were surprised, from the sea—" Her voice faltered and broke, and Padraig finished for her.

"Fomori, a great force of them. A Fomori army has landed, and . . . the royal family is slain." His huge voice was hushed, flattened nearly to a whisper. "King, queen, princes and all! All dead!"

Cordelia began to wail, and Branwen tried to hush her. "There, there, now, my *Creiddylad*." But her own voice trembled and Cordelia cried on.

No! Maeve protested silently. *This can't be happening! I don't want this sort of adventure. I don't like it. I want to go back . . .*

She fled, her departure unnoticed in the general confusion, and ran headlong through the deepening night propelled by her rage. *I want to go back!* Why had the dream taken such a horrible, sinister turn? It was more like a nightmare now, the sort of dream one desperately wants to wake up from. At the back of her mind was fear, fear that perhaps she could not return and was trapped in this dream state for the rest of her life, in this living nightmare where Gwenlian and Diarmait had unforgivably aged and were now dead, killed by enemies . . .

She tripped and fell her length on cool damp ground, then realized that she was weeping.

It can't end like this. This is all wrong! Let me go back! I want to go back now! I want . . .

"Come back, Maeve!" a voice said nearby.

"Wha—?" Maeve blinked as Aunt Ellen waved a hand before her face. The girl realized that she was standing in the kitchen doorway, staring out into the garden.

"That must have been some reverie." Her aunt laughed. "You were miles away."

Maeve stepped back from the door to let her aunt pass, feeling dazed and disoriented. What day was this? What time? Was it the same evening when she had sat with Aunt Ellen and Mrs. Murphy at the kitchen table, listening to their talk? She glanced at the table, saw the teacups sitting there and the steam still rising from her own unfinished drink. Confusion roiled in her mind. With an effort, she pulled herself together.

Serves me right, she thought shakily as she climbed the stairs to her bedroom. *I went into the dream deliberately that time, let it take me over. It's my own fault if it turned nasty on me. That's it—I've learned my lesson! No more running away from reality. I'm through with Annwn.*

The dogs appeared at noon the following day, in the yard behind the house. Maeve noticed them when she came down to lunch and glanced out the kitchen window. The dogs were large and gaunt, the size of Great Danes but leaner in build, something like enormous greyhounds. They were both a flawless white in colour, and in the strong noon-day sun their pricked ears had a reddish transparency. The dogs were pacing to and fro restlessly, their muzzles raised as if straining after a scent. She saw no collars on their necks, and no one was with them. It seemed odd to her that any-one would let such large dogs roam free; it certainly wouldn't have been allowed back home in Balsam Heights.

"Whose dogs are those, Aunt Ellen?" she inquired as she joined her aunt at the table by the front window.

"What dogs?" her aunt asked absently.

"Out there, in the backyard. Those huge white ones. It looks like they're running loose."

Aunt Ellen rose to get the sliced bread, glancing out the side window as she did so. "I don't see any dogs."

"They're right over—" Maeve walked to the window and then went rigid. A wave of fear washed coldly over her, and she spoke with an effort. "They .... they've gone now. Into the woods, maybe ..."

"Must be strays. I don't know anyone here with big white dogs." Aunt Ellen returned to the table with the bread.

Maeve remained by the window. The dogs were still there, had been there all along. Her aunt had been looking right at them. As Maeve watched, they were joined by a third dog of the same kind—tall and lean and pure white. It glanced towards the window, and for a moment seemed to look right into her face. Its eyes glinted red in the sunlight.

"Coming, Maeve?" Aunt Ellen asked.

Act normal, Maeve thought frantically as she joined her aunt. *Don't let her see there's anything wrong.* She'd almost betrayed herself. As it was, she could feel a film of cold sweat on her face and was afraid to meet her aunt's eyes. It was the dream, of course. It was taking over, breaking through. Until now, it had come in response to a yearning, to a desire for solace or escape. Now it was intruding on her daily life of its own accord. She might be through with Annwn, but Annwn plainly was not through with her.

Am I going crazy? Is this what it's like? Should I tell her? She envisioned waiting rooms and hospital corridors, tests, therapists, drugs, and her stomach cramped with terror. *Tell her, you coward. You've got to be treated for this. It's not a game any more. Tell her!* But she couldn't speak.

"Would you like some mustard with your sandwich, Maeve?" her aunt asked.

"I . . . no," said Maeve weakly. "No, thank you."

As the afternoon progressed, the dogs lost some of their solidity; they became like white shadows, like wisps of fog through which the sun shone. This encouraged her a little. But they did not go away or fade competely, and late in the afternoon she saw that they had been joined by more. Half a dozen dim white shapes now paced and prowled about the house, and whenever she went to a window at least one of them was there. There were human shapes now too: faceless, half-defined forms wrapped in what looked like hooded cloaks. They were at the very edge of her vision, almost invisible save when they moved. The white dogs became excited at their presence and ran to and fro in front of them, baying soundlessly. It was like a hunt, or rather the close of one—that moment when the hounds hold the helpless quarry at bay and the hunters move in to take control. And as for the quarry . . . she could not escape the conclusion that presented itself to her unwilling mind. She stared at the faint figures and tried repeatedly to *will* them away, but they were stubborn and persisted despite their transparency.

She avoided windows for the rest of the day. But she could feel the watchful presence throughout the house, as oppressive as thunder. And somehow she knew that they could sense *her* as well.

"Your uncle will be back this evening," said her aunt at dinnertime.

Maeve felt a great relief at that—to have another person in the house, especially kind, comforting Uncle Roy, was a reassuring thought.

He came back a little after nine in the evening. When she heard his car drive around to the back of the house, she almost ran downstairs. Her aunt was in the parlour, settled in a corner with a book and a cup of tea.

"That sounds like Roy," she called. "I knew he'd get in about now. I've got the teapot in here if he wants a cup."

"I'll tell him," Maeve replied as she ran through the kitchen.

But at the back door she froze, staring through the window.

The dogs and their masters were still there, and now they looked more real. As when a candle reflected in a window seems to burn in the midst of the garden, or when ghostly transparent reflections of people indoors seem to mingle with passersby on the street, so the Otherworld figures were imposed on this world. They had that same translucency; yet like reflections, they were also distinct and highly detailed. She shrank back as a pair of hounds stalked through the backyard trees, moving through the trunks like mist, moving within a metre of Uncle Roy so that she almost cried out a warning to him and just stopped herself in time. It was as though two worlds coexisted in a state of uneasy flux.

One of the black-clad figures was standing there in the yard and she *heard* him as the door opened: a low, chanting voice, rising and falling rhythmically. Was it some sort of incantation?

"So how are you, Maeve?" her uncle asked jovially as he strode in the door, briefcase in hand.

She managed to murmur something and give a sickly grin that passed for a smile. As he walked across the next room, she saw in terror that he was fading—his figure had a dim translucency at the outer edges, and she could see things through him. She closed her eyes, opened them again. He had set the case down on the table and was heading for the parlour, cup in hand, talking to her aunt. His form was even fainter now, the ghostly wraith of a man. And it was not just Uncle Roy. The whole house was fading, slipping away. She could see the trees through its walls, as though the wood had been replaced by pale, milky glass. The robed men and the hounds were waiting beyond. Now it was their forms that were solid, opaque.

"No," she choked, raising her hands in a feeble fending gesture. Soon the whole house was transparent, its rooms as empty as bubbles. She could barely see the outlines of doors, windows, walls, and her aunt and uncle were gone. The shapes of tree trunks materialized within the room, supplanting its furnishings. There was grass beneath her feet in place of the floorboards, and where the roof had been there were stars.

"No!" She was screaming now, but her aunt and uncle did not come running. They could neither hear nor see her, any more than she could hear or see them. Her second scream was wordless, a harsh shriek that tore her throat. She reached frantically for the pale outline of a kitchen chair, saw her hand pass right through the rungs of its back. The tree trunks, however, were hard and real to her touch—they were gaining solidity as the house lost it.

The white hounds with their shadowy masters were advancing, strong and confident. The hounds' eyes glowed red through the night, not reflecting light like a normal dog's but burning from within like heated metal. She knew, with a spasm of horror, that the hounds could see her now as well as sense her. Two of them approached to within metres of where she stood trembling, but at the house's glassy wall they halted abruptly, as if it was still a barrier to them. But Maeve sensed that it would not be so for long.

"Please!" she begged the vanishing walls. "Stay . . . oh, please, please don't go!" Silently she added, like a prayer, *Grandma, help me.*

As agonizing seconds passed, it seemed to her that the walls were, in fact, holding firm, ceasing to fade. In another instant, she was sure of it. The whiteness of the paint was coming back into them, a smooth pallor that spread like light. Bridget Mary O'Connor's sampler was there, its stitched letters hanging in the air. Slowly the frame reappeared, and then the panelling of the wall around it.

She sobbed aloud. The walls raised by her ancestors, walls that had sheltered her family for more than a hundred years, were reasserting themselves in answer to her plea. The men and the hounds were now half-hidden from her view. They drew back, the dogs with thwarted snarls and the men with oaths, as the house rematerialized around her. And then even the sounds were gone. The house had returned, and Annwn fell back before it like the surf retreating from shore.

Her relatives' voices came from the next room. "More tea, Roy?"

"I'll have another half-cup, thank you. The top half of the cup, mind. I said the *top*, woman. You done filled up the bottom!"

"Oh, you and your jokes!"

Maeve backed towards the rung-backed chair, which now received her crumpling form. Her legs would no longer support her.

Chapter Eight

MAEVE PACED NERVOUSLY ABOUT THE BEDROOM. She yearned for home, for security, even for the prosaic fears of yesterday. She would give a great deal to believe she was insane. Only insane! Insanity seemed a safe and comforting thing now: a mere ailment, to be diagnosed, treated, controlled. There was no escaping this new terror.

Outside, the dim, waiting shapes had returned, though fainter than before, as if discouraged by her show of resistance—or so at least she hoped. Sleep had been impossible. If she closed her eyes, she saw shrouded, faceless figures and the heads of dogs with burning eyes coming through the walls; several times in the night she had started up from her bed, her heart pounding wildly, convinced that they had returned. She had heard the grandfather clock downstairs chime every hour from bedtime to dawn.

It was no use trying to convince herself that the incident had all been in her head, or that her eyes and ears had deceived her. There was no escaping the truth: the attack had really happened. She had certainly screamed; all evening her throat had been raw and her voice was still hoarse from it. Yet her aunt and uncle, one room away, had not heard her. They had not really faded away, nor had the house: it was Maeve who had nearly disappeared, drawn out of her own world into Annwn by the hounds and their sorcerous masters.

She sat down on the bed, her hands clenched together, rocking to and fro. It was all there—in Grandma's book and in her diary—for, of course, it was a diary. Maeve had spent the remainder of the evening poring over the pages, the scribbled notes. *I entered the Otherworld again today . . . Princess Gwenlian calls me Jehane now; I told her I didn't care for my name . . . The fairies gave me a brooch, which they said would take me back to my own place—and back in time too, so that no one here would know how long I have been gone . . .*

Maeve reached out to the cardigan that lay on the quilt, ran her fingers over the bronze brooch that was pinned to it.

Yes, the notebook was plainly a diary, kept in an effort to hold on to Annwn's elusive memory. Maeve picked it up from the small bedside table and flipped through the pages, hoping to find something new, something that could help her. But except for a few name changes, it was the same account Jean had put in her book: the attacks of the Lochlannach sea-raiders, Diarmait and Gwenlian, the quest. By the time of the book's writing, Jean/Jehane had forgotten that her "adventure" was real, and she had used these notes for her story.

It was here in the notebook, and also in the textbooks Maeve had borrowed from Uncle Roy. She looked at them fearfully where they lay piled on the bureau. The translation of the word "Fomori" was there, and descriptions of nemetons and the need-fire ritual . . . all there. Yet none of these things was to be found in Grandma's notebook or in her story. Nor had Maeve read of them anywhere else. She could not have forgotten such interesting pieces of folklore had she encountered them before, so they had not come from her memory.

They came from outside her mind.

From Annwn.

She snatched up the textbooks and walked quickly down the narrow upstairs hall to her uncle's study. "Thanks for the books, Uncle Roy." She set them down on a chair, then stood hesitantly behind it.

He scarcely glanced up from his own studies. "You're welcome."

She rested both hands on the back of the chair. They were trembling and the palms were damp. "Uncle Roy, do people here *really* still believe in the"—she caught herself on the verge of saying "the Good People"—"the fairies?"

He looked up at that. "Well, I've talked to people here in the outports—old-timers, I admit, but healthy, normal people—who swear they've been fairy-led."

"Fairy-led?" repeated Maeve.

"Led astray by fairies, into some kind of otherworld or country unlike our own. One old fellow in Duck Cove told me about going out for a walk in the woods when he was a boy and getting lost. He ended up in a place he'd never seen before, a large, cultivated garden full of flowering shrubs and trees. But there was no house, he said, and no one there—just this beautiful garden. He left the place and wandered in the woods for hours, going in circles, before he finally found himself back on the road. And no matter how many times he went back to the forest afterwards, he could never find that garden again. When he told his folks what had happened, they said there wasn't any garden like the one he had described; there never had been anything there but pine forest. 'You bin in the fairies, boy,' they told him, and wouldn't let him wander any more on his own after that. Interesting, isn't it?"

Maeve felt faint. She gripped the back of the chair. "You don't really *believe* that story, Uncle Roy?"

He scratched his bearded chin thoughtfully. "The old man himself believed it. That doesn't mean it's literally true, of course. He could have been senile, I suppose. Still, there's something about hearing a tale of that sort from someone who's completely sincere . . . I don't know what to make of it, to be perfectly honest. Even some scientists say there may be more to our universe than we can ever know."

It was not what she had hoped to hear. Maeve's hands tightened on the chair-back. "Oh . . . I see."

"All right, enough of this beating about the bush," he said suddenly, closing his book and looking her straight in the eye. "You didn't really come in here to talk about folklore, did you? Something's bothering you. Is it what's happening at home?"

Home. Incredibly, she had forgotten. Her parents' quarrels, the threatened break-up—it all seemed so distant, so unreal, when set against this larger fear. Uncle Roy was looking at her in concern. He thought that she'd guessed somehow, that she was miserable about the pending divorce.

"I think perhaps it's time for a family conference," he said quietly. He rose and called out the door, "Ellen? Could you come up here for a moment, please?"

There were voices in the downstairs hall, then footsteps quickly ascending the staircase. Aunt Ellen came in, looking slightly harassed.

"What is it, Roy? We've got company." She turned to her niece. "Maeve, your great-grandmother has come for another visit. Would you mind seeing her again? I think she's confused, poor thing. She must have forgotten that she came by before."

Maeve looked at her blankly. She would have to sit through a visit now, struggling all the while to act normal? A kind of desperation filled her.

Her aunt read her expression. "Don't worry, dear, it'll be all right. I'll be there, and Uncle Roy too, if she has another odd spell."

She thinks I'm afraid of the old woman, thought Maeve. *If only it were just that.*

She followed her aunt and uncle downstairs and into the parlour, her feet as heavy as stones. There sat Great-aunt Fiona, and with her was Great-grandmother. The old woman was swaying from side to side on the sofa, her right hand clenched on her cane. She looked up, her pale green eyes unusually alert as Maeve entered the room, and the girl immediately saw the anxiety in them. Perhaps her own distressed state of mind helped her to see it. The two of them gazed at each other, linked by their shared agitation, while the other adults exchanged pleasantries.

"Come here," wheezed Great-gran. Her free hand came down on the sofa cushion beside her—once, twice. It was not an invitation, but an urgent command.

"Maeve?" queried Aunt Ellen, concerned.

Maeve drew a long breath, as if preparing for a dive into deep water. "It's all right," she said, and went to sit by the old woman.

"Got something for you," said Great-gran. She fumbled in an ancient battered handbag and drew out a silver chain and locket. "For you," she repeated, holding it out.

Maeve could see the relief in her aunt's eyes. So the old lady wasn't confused; she had merely wanted to bring a gift for her great-granddaughter.

"Thank you," said Maeve awkwardly, taking the necklace.

"It were Jeanie's," said Great-gran. "Long ago."

"It's Mum's locket," declared her uncle, stooping to study it with interest. "It's got her picture and Dad's inside." Maeve handed it to him, and he opened the locket to show her the tiny photographs: Jean, her straight hair touching her shoulders, Granddad as a handsome young man.

"Oh, let me see," said Aunt Ellen.

While Uncle Roy, Aunt Ellen and Great-aunt Fiona were admiring the locket and reminiscing about Grandma and Granddad, the old woman motioned to Maeve to sit closer. She reached into her handbag again and took out something else: a small object wrapped in what looked like a paper napkin. "Fairy bread," she whispered hoarsely into Maeve's ear. "It wards 'em off. I gave it to Jeanie, to keep her safe."

A fragment of dry crust lay inside the paper. Maeve's heart raced; it seemed to shake her entire body with each beat. "Safe from what?" she rasped.

"From them. She were crossing over, into *their* place. Same as you." The pale green eyes held her own. "My grannie told me, my grannie from Ireland, but I never believed in it—not till Jeanie. Then I wondered. So I gives her bread, same as Grannie used to give me. The Good People lets you alone then."

The Good People.

Maeve shivered violently, and the ancient woman reached out and laid a hand on hers. It was as cold as a bird's foot, but its grip was surprisingly strong. The girl looked down at the aged, rheumatic claw—the large, knobbed knuckles, the pallid skin, the raised veins that were like blue cords binding the bones—and then at her own smooth young hand beneath, its veins only blue shadows as yet under the smooth, firm skin. Yet she felt the kinship of the hands, the intimate, invisible bond of their flesh and bones and the blood in their branching veins. They were like one hand seen at different times: past and future commingled. Her trembling eased.

She knows . . . she understands. She can help. This was why Great-gran had come, Maeve realized. The locket had been only a pretext for the visit, and a diversion: it took the other adults' attention off her while she spoke with her great-granddaughter.

"She were gone a whole day once. Jeanie. We looked for her everywhere. Found her out on the barrens at dusk. But she couldn't have been there, not all that time. We'd looked." She leaned close again. "Fairies got her, took her to where they live. And she went back again. They gave her something after that, some magic thing what always brought her home on time so no one'd ever notice she'd been gone. But I always knew. I could tell when she'd been *there*. It were somethin' in her eyes, her voice. Once I overheard her singin' a song that

I'd never heard in me life. Words and tune were strange, not like anything she'd ever pick up in the village. It were a fairy song—she learned it there. And so I gave her the fairy bread, to keep 'em away from her, keep her safe."

"Just bread?" asked Maeve in a low voice, turning the little package over and over in her hands.

"Just bread, you say. Tell me, when the priest lifts the holy wafer at Mass, is that just bread?" The faded green eyes were steady. "There's a strength in plain and simple things, my grannie always said. Here it's just bread, but there—in *that* place—it's power."

Strength in simple things. The walls, reforming before her terrified eyes; old walls raised and mortared with strength, with suffering, with endurance. A barrier against the dark.

"Don't be afraid, me love." The old hand patted hers. "Don't walk on their ways. Don't eat of their food. Keep your distance and they'll do you no harm."

Maeve sat by the window in her room, facing the bay.

It was evening and very calm, the waves hardly more than ripples stretching away to the expanse of blue-black sea. She looked across the bay to the main village, the half moon of houses following the shape of the shore. Their lupin colours had faded in the dusk, but their windows glowed, squares of warm, butter-coloured light. People would be settling in for the night, reading in chairs, washing up after dinner, getting small children ready for bed. Farther out, on the rocky head of Sunker Point, the lighthouse swept its wheeling beam through the night, a steady pulse of light against the darkness. Here all was safety, stillness, comfort. But in that other, parallel place, what events were transpiring? The faces of Thomas and his family kept arising before her eyes.

She peered out the window. Nothing moved in the shadows below . . . the otherworldly figures had vanished. Whether that had anything to do with her great-grandmother's visit she could not tell. She reached into her cardigan pocket and touched the morsel of dry bread. If the Otherworld did, in fact, lie beyond the world of familiar things, then the lore surrounding it must be true as well. Which meant she was safe now.

But Thomas and his family were not.

Annwn held dominion over them; they could not escape it as she had done. The figures she had seen, the spectral hounds and men, were real in Thomas's world. And they were still there, waiting in the darkness of that other night.

She thought of her relatives here in Newfoundland and the ancestors who lay in the cemetery at St. Mary's church— people linked to her across distance and time, by no cause or connection other than the simple, homely bonds of the flesh. "Blood is thicker than water," it was said. That bloodbond ran like a river through the ages, a red river of life. It reminded her of the family tree that was like a real tree, green and growing. For a river, too, had the shape of a tree, its flowing course like a trunk joined to countless branching tributaries.

And did one branch/tributary of her family extend into Annwn? *Was* the John Patrick O'Connor who had vanished from her world the same one from whom Padraig had claimed descent?

She had never even repaid the Ryan family for their

kindness to her. Her own once-looming troubles now seemed small and petty next to theirs. She *must* know what had become of them all—Padraig and little Cordelia, kind Branwen and Thomas . . . Thomas. She could see his open, honest gaze, his shy, hesitant smile. Never to know what had happened to him?

There was still a little fluttering of fear within her, but it was overridden by a greater sense of urgency.

Once more—she must enter Annwn once more. . . .

The next day was cool and overcast, with a threat of rain in the heavy clouds hanging over the sea. There was a stillness in the house that was due only partly to the dull weather: Maeve, her mind preoccupied with her worries, could find little to say to her aunt and uncle. They, in turn, seemed uncomfortable in her presence, even the usually jovial Uncle Roy. They imagined, naturally, that she was depressed about the situation at home, and she said nothing to contradict this. It was easier than the truth.

After lunch she left the strained silence of the house and went for a walk through the woods and up the side of Dutton's Hill, almost to its stony summit.

She had to make her point of entry a place far from the house, in case the dogs and men were still lingering. She turned, looking back at the view—the village, bay and forest now lay spread out beneath her. She lay down on the coarse, gravelly ground, ignoring the discomfort. Then closing her eyes, she reached out for Annwn.

When she opened her eyes again, the sun was blazing high above her out of a blue sky lightly streaked with cloud.

She sat up. The land below was thickly forested, except for the cleared area where Connemara lay. The village was still and quiet, without a wisp of hearth smoke, and no figure stirred on its rough roads. Maeve swallowed. She got up and stepped over the wall, moving slowly and warily down the hillside, which was not the same one she had come up. The village seemed utterly deserted. She saw no dark-robed figures lurking there, no questing hounds.

But they had been here. Once she was down among its buildings, she saw that the village had been ransacked. The damage was not heavy; it was as if the attackers had been too contemptuous of the villagers and their humble possessions to waste much time before moving on. Window-panes were shattered, tables and chairs smashed or simply overturned, a fire set on the straw floor of one home. In the earth before its door was the footprint of a dog.

She entered Thomas's house trembling, fearing what she might find, but here too there was only spiteful vandalism. It was the emptiness that was the worst. She stood motionless amid the ruins of the great wooden table. The large chest in which clothing was kept was empty—but was that because the family had taken away their belongings, or because the clothes had been stolen?

The hearthstone was cracked, and the ashes of the fire had been scattered across the floor.

She walked outside again, looking about her. Suddenly she saw something lying in the grass and ran to snatch it up. It was Cordelia's doll, Gwendolen. It had been lying like a discarded rag on the ground. She held it in trembling hands.

What happened here?

From building to building she wandered, from houses to outbuildings to the little village shops. All were the same. The abbey with its protecting walls was quiet and empty too, and many of its stained-glass windows were smashed. The great stone church had a different silence now, vacant and cold.

At least she had not found what she feared: no bodies, so everyone must have survived. Perhaps they had all had a chance to flee before the enemy came. Or had they all been taken prisoner?

She returned to Thomas's house and lay down in Cordelia's room on the pallet that had once been hers. So this was how it ended. She would never learn what had happened to the villagers, what the Ryans' fate had been. The mystery must last forever, tormenting her to the end of her days. . . .

Suddenly she sat bolt upright, listening.

Voices. There were voices coming from outside.

Was it only her imagination, her hunger for other human presences? But the droning voices increased in volume and clarity as she sat there, straining to make out what they were saying. Were they villagers, or some of the enemy come back to loot and destroy again? She sprang up, hastened towards the nearest window, her heart thudding behind her ribs, and peered fearfully out.

Three figures were standing in the meadow behind the house—they were all men, and there were horses tethered nearby. She froze, every muscle taut, before she noticed that one of the horses was a white pony.

Gwyn!

With a low cry, she ran out the door, her caution turned

to wild joy. She saw the two adult men whirl around to face her, their bodies tense; there was a scraping and flash of steel in their hands, but her eyes were only for Thomas.

He had been standing somewhat behind the men, their bigger bodies half hiding his thin, awkward frame and long hair. He recognized her in the same instant, and came forward to meet her headlong rush. They did not so much meet as collide, staggering and holding one another fast to avoid falling. His play-sword was sheathed at his side, and the scabbard banged against her shin.

"Maeve, Maeve, thank God!" he was saying breathlessly.

The two other men relaxed. She now recognized them as the visitors, Aengus and Duncan.

"I presume this is your mysterious lady, boy?" observed Aengus in a dry voice.

"It's she—thank God she's safe," said Thomas. "When we saw what had happened to the village, Maeve, I was afraid you had come back and—" He could not finish.

"Oh, Tom, what happened? Where is everybody?"

"We all decided to leave the village, to move inland. The Fomori surround the island, and it is not safe to be so near the sea. The holy brothers took the sacrament from the abbey, and we all packed our belongings. And not a moment too soon, it seems."

She was still clutching Cordelia's doll; she held it out to him now. "I found this. I thought you had probably escaped, but . . . I wasn't sure." Her voice shook.

He took the doll from her and put it in his saddlebag. "Cordelia will be glad to see this again. She mislaid Gwendolen before we left. Maeve, don't look so distressed; we are all safe. They have gone on ahead, all of them. I planned to follow as soon as I knew about you. I refused to leave, in case you came back, and were caught by the Fomori. Aengus and Duncan stayed with me. We have been camping in the forest."

Duncan turned to his friend. "Aengus, I think we must make for Temair. It is well-fortified against attack by sea. We shall have to make our stand there."

The grim-faced Aengus nodded. "Our last stand, you mean. But first we must make our way there, avoiding any Fomori patrols *and* all the sorceries they may call up."

"Would . . . would this be of any use?" asked Maeve. Feeling slightly foolish, she held out the tiny package Great-grandma had given her.

Aengus's dark brows rose when he saw what lay within, but he shook his head. "Hearth bread, from a Shadow-home. It may well put you beyond their power, but for us Avalon-born I think it will prove of little use."

She told them then of the dark figures in the Otherworld forest that paralleled her uncle's house, and of the pale hounds.

"I have heard of such monster hounds," the red-headed man commented. "There are the *Cu Sith* of Dalriada—big as a bull calf with fur as green as grass—and the black dogs that haunt the old Sidhe ruins."

"But these dogs were white," Maeve told him. "White with red eyes." She was still afraid, but what a blessed relief to be able to discuss the apparitions like this, seriously and matter-of-factly, not hide them away like a guilty secret! She felt as though she had cast off a tremendous burden.

"And you say there were men with them? I think you saw the *Cwn Annwn*," said Aengus, "the Hounds of the Otherworld. They are fairy creatures, and pursue their prey without mercy. Some call them the Hounds of Hell, but the *Cwn* are not evil. They are a power, part of the land itself, and it is simply their nature to obey whomever summons them to the hunt. The Fomori must have discovered the spell that commands them."

"Is it true that the members of the royal family were all killed by the Fomori?" Maeve asked the two men.

"So they say," Duncan answered heavily. "We were not there ourselves. Would to God that we had been. Many of the Fomori would have paid dearly for their deeds then!"

"Some of the villagers say they heard rumours that the young prince survived," said Thomas.

"Rumours," said Duncan shortly.

"But some say they heard that he was not in the palace, that he was out stag hunting at the time of the attack, and so escaped."

"What if he did?" Aengus snapped. "Would you pin all your hopes on that careless young pleasure-seeker?"

Thomas went rather white, and she heard the slight tremor of emotion in his voice, though he strove to control it. "He is the king now."

"Aye, so he is . . . if he lives," replied Aengus. "But what of it? He is not one-half the man his sire and grandsire were, for all his airs and his hawks and horses. A man is but a man, whatever blood runs in his veins. You would do better to sharpen your sword, lad, and hone your own courage than to await salvation from such as he. *Gwalchmai!*" He almost spat the name.

To Maeve's alarm, Thomas stepped forward, his hand on the hilt of that ridiculous sword.

"I serve the king, wherever and whomever he may be. You talk like a traitor."

Maeve cried out, and Duncan stepped between the two other men. "Hold! No more! Have we not foes enough without going for one another's throats like dumb brutes?"

Aengus had not moved. "Well said, Duncan," he said, speaking more quietly. "And you, lad . . . your loyalty speaks well of you. May your king prove worthy of it."

"Enough," said Duncan. "Aengus, we must ride now and rejoin the villagers if you do not wish to go to Temair. They will have need of our swords."

Aengus considered a moment. "We will take them north with us, but by an inland route. The enemy is attacking settlements along the coast."

"Yes," said Duncan with a shudder, "by all means, let us leave the sea behind. But there are no safe places now, especially if the Fomori are calling on the old magic. Many of its creatures cannot even be seen, if they do not desire it."

"Not by us," put in Thomas, "but Maeve could see them."

Duncan looked at Maeve. "She has the *an da shealladh*, the second sight?"

"Yes," Maeve replied. "It . . . runs in my family."

"This is a wondrous thing!" remarked Aengus. "Even here in Annwn that gift is rare. But you will be returning to your own place, lady, now that you understand the danger here?"

"No," said Maeve. "Please, I want to help. If there's anything I can do." She was thinking of John Patrick O'Connor, hero of Mary's Bay; of the great-uncle whom she would never know outside of a photograph. She remembered how Andrew's eyes had gazed steadily at her out of the past. "I want to help," she repeated, forcing a firmness into her voice.

"As you will," said Aengus after a pause. "You could be our eyes on this journey. There was once a woman of your world who performed a like service for the Princess Gwenlian."

"I know. Jehane—Jean—was my grandmother," Maeve told him.

"I did not know that!" exclaimed Thomas in surprise.

"I found it out myself only just recently," she explained, turning to him. "She must have come here long ago, and then remembered enough of what happened to turn it into a book." She touched the bronze brooch on her sweater. "My grandmother brought this brooch back with her from Annwn. The fairies gave it to her. There's a sort of magic in it: any visitor from my world who wears it is returned to the exact place and time when they left."

The two older men were staring at Maeve. "Jehane's own blood-kin," murmured Duncan, shaking his head.

Aengus held a hand out courteously to Maeve. "Lady, if you will mount my horse, I will ride with you and see that you do not fall. Young Thomas tells me that you do not ride."

"Maeve can come with me," said Thomas a little sharply.

"My steed is larger and can take more weight. Also I have a true sword, and can defend the lady if need be." Aengus swung himself up into the saddle and looked down at Maeve.

His gaze had the same quiet confidence and assurance as his voice. Maeve found herself following his directions obediently, letting Duncan give her a leg up into the saddle. Also, being called "lady" gave her a curious little flutter beneath her ribs. The word resonated with a meaning it never carried in her world. There was a gentle reverence in Aengus's voice as he spoke it, and though his grey eyes remained keen, there was the slightest softening in them.

The bay stallion was tall, and it was strange to perch on its glossy back with the warm living roundness of the flanks between her legs. She put her arms shyly about Aengus's waist. Then his arms were gathering up the reins in front, and she felt the firming of his muscles as he took control of the horse, urging it forward.

"There now, you cannot fall. Try to grip with your knees, my lady. That is right."

The other two mounted, and they moved in haste into the western woods, leaving the village to its silence.

The ride took what felt like endless hours on the hard, jolting back of the great horse, over the roughest terrain—forest and meadow and muddy bog—for they dared not take the roads. There was no sign of the fleeing villagers. Occasionally there were distant howls behind them that made the horses roll their eyes and prick their ears. "Wolves," said Duncan. "Or so let us hope."

At last they came to a place where the trees thinned out altogether and a rolling plain covered in glacial boulders stretched before them, like the fire-cleared barrens Maeve had seen from her uncle's car.

Like, yet not like, for as they rode through it she began to see ordered patterns in the stones. They marched in long, motionless lines, straight as roads, or stood in great rings that made her think of Stonehenge. *Menhirs*, these were called, weren't they? Standing stones. It was as if her odd fancy of the glacial boulders coming to life was true: they had been moving in strange processions, huddling together in secret councils here on the barrens, where there was no one to see.

"Those stone circles are the Druids' old temples," said Thomas, seeing her looking at them.

Aengus shook his dark head. "Nay, not the Druids'. They may have used the circles for some of their rites, but it was not they who made the stones dance. Older hands than theirs accomplished that feat."

Fog was rolling over the barrens now, thick as white smoke. Through it, they saw more standing stones, great rings within rings. There were dolmens too, like crude tables of stone.

"We are nearing the Rath of Morgana," said Aengus. "This is no natural mist, I think."

Morgana. Maeve gasped. "You don't mean . . . not the *same* Morgana? The sorceress that Gwenlian and Diarmait fought?"

"The very same." Duncan pulled his horse to a halt and sat staring at the menhirs with a blend of horror and wonder.

"But she *can't* be still alive. Queen Morgana was a grown woman when my grandmother was just a young girl!"

"You forget she is of the fairy blood," Aengus told her.

"You mean she's immortal?"

"Not immortal perhaps, but the children of the fairies do not age in the same manner as we. Time has not such a hold on them. They may live in its flow as do we, or tarry almost forever. They are like a man walking in a stream and resisting the pull of the current, while we are like the leaves and sticks that are carried helplessly along. That is the difference between her kind and ours."

Maeve glanced down at her brooch. It could alter time too, seemingly. Was it of fairy make, then? "Are there any others like Morgana here?" she asked.

"Nay, that race is gone from Avalon. They went to Tir Tairngiri, to dwell with the Daoine Sidhe, and have never taken mates from among common mortals again. There is very little human blood left in them now; they are one with the Sidhe. Only Morgana has lingered, in the place that was her father's before her."

"We must not go near her Rath, Aengus!" Duncan adjured his companion.

"But there the *Cwn* would not follow us," Aengus replied. "Her power is as great as theirs—greater. It would be as though we rode through a stream, throwing the hounds off the scent."

"You cannot be thinking of riding through that evil place! Each stone in it, they say, is connected to the next by a strand of fell magic, and she who sits at the centre feels in her mind the trespasser's footfall as the spider feels a fly upon the web."

"Aye, and some say that the stones are merely aligned with celestial bodies, marking out the seasons and all the revolutions of the heavens," responded Aengus mildly.

"I do not believe that and neither do you! 'The work of old hands,' you say? You know as well as I that it was the Sidhe themselves who wove this web of stone. It is filled with their sorcery. In olden days, its centre was not her tower, but the *sid* mound on which that tower now stands."

Thomas's voice was hushed. "She built her keep upon a fairy mound? How could she dare?"

Duncan's expression was bleak. "There are few things

Morgana will not dare. She is, after all, of one blood with the Sidhe, and counts them as her kin."

More howls arose behind them—nearer now. The horses stirred and snorted. "Those are no wolves! It is no use, Duncan. We must enter the Rath or be overtaken by the *Cwn*," declared Aengus.

"A choice between flood and fire!" muttered Duncan beneath his breath.

Aengus made no reply to that, but led them on into the stone circles.

Chapter Nine

THE MIST SEEMED TO COME OUT OF NOWHERE. It did not roll in on them as they rode, like the heavy, gauzy sea fogs, a thick and palpable wall, but began, rather, as the finest of vapours, trailing low on the ground as though the earth was breathing it forth in pale wisps. But as the minutes passed, it rose and thickened until hills and sky and forest were blotted out, and they moved through a grey void in which only the looming menhirs could be seen. All landmarks were gone; there was nothing to help the travellers orient themselves.

"You were right. This is no natural mist," said Duncan darkly.

Aengus remained grimly silent, but Maeve felt the tension in his back muscles increasing as they rode.

She tried to recall all she could of Morgana from her grandmother's account. The fairy queen claimed direct descent from King Arthur's sister, Morgan le Fay. She was a shadowy figure, a half-mortal sorceress who had ultimately used her magic to aid the powers of evil in the war. Maeve had never thought of the dangerous and terrifying things in the book coming to life as the pleasant ones had done. But then, she had thought Annwn existed only for her pleasure. How childish that seemed to her now! If dreams could be real, so too could nightmares. Maeve turned her thoughts hurriedly away from her grandmother's description of the dark queen.

Then she noticed the humming.

It was a low sound, barely audible at first, that seemed to come from all around them—out of the air itself, or out of the earth. It was steady, neither rising nor falling in pitch, but growing ever louder as they wound their way through the stones.

"You hear it, Aengus?" said Duncan hoarsely.

"Aye."

"What is it?" asked Thomas. But Aengus made no answer.

Maeve suddenly caught her breath. One of the stones had moved.

She had seen it distinctly: a small, squat, grey shape that had stirred and scuttled away to one side, vanishing in the mist. For a moment she could only stare dumbly, wondering if she had just imagined it. Then, as they rode on, there was another blur of motion off to the right. She just caught it with the corner of her eye, and by the time her head moved, whatever it was had gone.

"Aengus," she whispered. "There's . . . something . . . alive out there."

He halted the horse and looked about him. Duncan and Thomas also reined in their mounts. A few metres away, another circle of grey upright shapes was visible through the mists. There were eight of them, each less than the height of a man, and the droning sound seemed to come from them.

"Who is there?" called Duncan.

One of the shapes moved, turning to face them. Maeve saw that it was not a stone after all, but was a human figure swathed in a shapeless grey cloak. A gnarled witch-face peered out at them from beneath the coarse cloth, and where the cloak divided at the front was the hem of a black gown. The humming sound rose to a wailing chorus—an eerie sound, like a lamentation.

And now the sound of running feet came through the mist on every side. They were surrounded. Human forms burst through the greyness, huge men with naked swords in their hands. The men wore tunics and trousers of coarse cloth, their hair was long and wild, their faces and arms painted or tattooed with blue swirls and jagged patterns that gave them a savage air.

One tall man stood apart from the rest. Like the eight women, he wore a black robe under a cloak of grey, and his hair was cut like the monks', with a band shaved across the top of his head so that the hair above his brow was separated from the long locks straggling down his back. The hair was iron grey, matching in hue the thin beard that streamed down his chest, and his face was hollow-cheeked and deeply seamed with age.

He shouted something in one of the old tongues—Gaelic or Cymri, Maeve could not yet distinguish between the two—and Aengus answered him in the same tongue. The strange men advanced, swords at the ready, but did not attack.

"We are to go with them," Aengus told Maeve and the others in a heavy tone of resignation. "They will do us no violence so long as we do not attempt to escape."

Duncan swore an oath in his own tongue, adding, "These are Morgana's creatures, her Druid and priestesses. And the men are Fianna warriors, sworn to protect her with their lives. They bear us no love; we might as well fight now as die later, in her lair."

"No, Duncan," said Aengus. "Now is not the time. There is the lady's safety to think of. Give up your sword now or they will surely attack." He was already removing his own sword belt. His tone was stern, authoritative, and to Maeve's surprise the other man obeyed him without further protest.

They dismounted and let themselves be led through the hanging mists and past the lowering stones. The fierce shaggy-haired warriors did not speak, not to their prisoners or to one another, but kept a grim silence. The cloaked women spoke among themselves, but in the language Maeve could not understand. Ahead of them, the dark-robed Druid strode; his bearing was erect and proud, and not once did he glance back at the captives.

Soon they noticed that the mist had wisped away as suddenly as it had come. And there before them, under the grey sky, was a high grassy bank: a ring of earthworks raised as a protective wall. The Rath of Morgana. In the centre was a gap, which was sealed by a high gate built of strong timbers. Sentries wielding spears stood upon the earthen ramparts to either side. Maeve felt a wave of sick fear wash over her. Atop the gate was a row of yellowed human skulls, teeth bared to the winds, bleakly staring.

"Those who follow the old ways like to place such trophies on their gates," said Aengus, seeing her stare. "To them, the head of an enemy is a cherished prize. It is the throne hall of the soul, a sacred thing."

"Who . . . who were they?" she whispered.

"Who can say? Wanderers, perhaps, who strayed into the Rath. Morgana would have no pity on those who trespassed on her domain. It is the only part of Avalon still under her sway."

One of their sword-wielding guards called up to the sentries, and received an answer that made him smile in satisfaction. With a great creaking, like the long, slow fall of a mighty tree, the wooden gate was opened from inside.

"Are our families in there?" asked Thomas. "The people of Connemara?" No answer was made, but as they rode in at the gates they saw huddled groups penned within a vast central enclosure like frightened sheep. There were monks as well as villagers there, and many familiar faces. Maeve, anxiously scanning the figures, recognized Padraig, and Branwen standing with Cordelia, but she did not dare call out to them.

There was a small cluster of houses within the enclosure, odd circular structures about fifteen metres across, with wooden sides and thatched, conical roofs. They had a primitive look about them; she was reminded of the round, grass-roofed huts built by African villagers in the days before the white settlers arrived. Their inhabitants stood at the low doorways, staring out at the prisoners. The men wore trousers, the women dresses shaped like long, loose tunics. All wore large rectangular cloaks draped about their shoulders. They seemed to be very fond of jewellery: not only the women but also the men sported bronze brooches, armlets and torques about their necks. Their hair was thick and luxuriant, and both sexes wore it long, either falling freely down their shoulders and backs or tightly braided. All, including the women, were tall and muscular looking, as though they had plenty of exercise; there was not an overweight person anywhere to be seen.

Beyond the houses, at the centre of the vast cleared space, the earth rose in a massive mound, too smooth-sided and flat-topped to be a natural hill, and on this there stood a round tower built of stone so weathered and ancient that it appeared almost black.

Thomas had now seen his family and had started to move towards them, but the guards held out their swords. "No, you four must go to the queen," said one in thickly accented English, and they had no choice but to obey.

They were led up the smooth slope of the mound, and on through a high door in the base of the tower, which was also guarded by sentries. Within was a huge, dim, circular chamber. Animal-skin rugs were thrown down on the clammy stone floor, and torches burned in metal sconces on the walls, blackening them further. At the northern end of the chamber, a throne-like chair of heavy dark wood was set on a stone platform, and seated on it was a woman.

So, at least, one had to call her. She who sat on the throne had the outward form and semblance of a woman, but the word was too human for her, too warm, too *alive*. Nor was she at all like Maeve's idea of Titania, or any other of the fairy queens from storybooks. When she tried later to describe Morgana, Maeve could never quite find the words. The queen was beautiful, but not with the sort of beauty one thinks of in connection with women—not prettiness, or delicacy, or elegance. Morgana was beautiful as stone or sea-sculpted ice is beautiful: hard, strong, wild, magnificent. Her black hair was incredibly long and flowed about her, cloaking her shoulders and spilling over the arms of her throne, almost to the floor. Her eyes were true green, emerald green, though like the gemstones they resembled, they were hard and cold. Her pale skin was flawless, her features finely formed, but she did not seem young or old. She was as ageless as a statue, which keeps its grace and beauty because it is not flesh and cannot change with time. But with the beauty there was also something strange and terrible. The mere sight of her chilled, as if one touched cold stone.

The queen's slender, long-limbed figure was draped in garments of sombre hue: a sleeveless black gown like those worn by the priestesses and a square, bronze-coloured cloak fastened at the shoulder with a huge brooch in which a green jewel was set. She wore a torque of twisted gold about her neck, but no crown was on her head. She had no need of one. Her cool, level gaze, her proud, erect bearing, both proclaimed her royalty as no coronet could.

"Your Majesty, these are more of the fugitives from the village," the Druid intoned as the black-clad women moved to flank the throne, four of them to each side. "The last stragglers, or so I believe."

The queen said nothing. It was the witch-like woman, the oldest of the priestesses, who spoke. "Are all these people mad? They know what befalls all outsiders who come within our Rath."

"We none of us meant to come here," snapped Duncan. "We have been driven hither by the Fomori, with the aid of the *Cwn Annwn*."

"Oh, indeed?" the crone retorted. "And what is that to us? By Macha, you shall pay for your trespass all the same!"

Throughout this exchange the queen had said nothing, but sat silent and statue-still upon her throne, her hair like a mantle of shadow about her. Now at last she stirred. Her eyes turned to Maeve.

"This one is not of our world," she said.

Her voice was a contralto, deep for a woman's and powerful. Maeve trembled at the sound of it. All in the room were looking at her now; Thomas moved to stand by her side.

"How came you here, Shadow-child?" demanded Morgana. She stood, and Maeve saw that she was very tall, as tall as any of the men in the room. She approached the trembling girl, but Aengus spoke just before she reached her.

"You cannot harm her, Queen. She bears with her a token, bread of grain grown in the Iron Earth." He did not speak challengingly, but in a dry, matter-of-fact tone.

"Indeed. We shall see about that." The queen turned her piercing eyes on Maeve. "So you come from the world of iron and shadow. There are still portals that lead from that world to this?"

The Druid spoke. "The cave of Cruachan, which lies in the isle of Éire, was said to be such a portal. Many came into this world by its gate. And there are other portals here in Avalon, though none now knows where they lie."

Maeve could not meet the queen's emerald eyes, but fixed her gaze instead on the brooch at her shoulder with its staring stone. Morgana, in turn, seemed interested in Maeve's own adornment. A long white hand reached out and tore the penannular brooch from her cardigan. "How came you by this?"

The old woman at Morgana's side caught her breath when she saw it and turned accusingly to Maeve. "This is Sidhe jewellery, from the Old Kingdom! It was not made for such as you to wear."

"It was my grandmother's," Maeve gasped.

"A likely tale!" retorted the old woman. "You have stolen that brooch, a thing you had no right so much as to touch!"

But Morgana had turned now to Aengus. "And you, Prince? Why are *you* here?"

"*Prince?*" blurted Thomas.

Maeve started, stared.

The queen ignored them both, intent upon Aengus. "You forget, Arawn ap Gwion, I knew your grandsire when he was but a boy. Your face is cast in the same mould as his. I know those eyes, that brow. My old enemy." Her voice grew harsh. "Where is he now, the mighty Diarmait? Withered by time, like all the sons of earth. A sword blade cut him down at last, but he was scarcely worth the reaping. And all his house gone too—all but one."

The man who had called himself Aengus stood very still, but Maeve could see his hand clenching and unclenching at his side. *Prince Arawn?* Could it be? It would explain his suppressed anger, his dour and bitter mien. He must be mourning for his slain family. But why then had he spoken of the prince with such disdain?

"Queen and sorceress though you may be," the young

man said very quietly, "if the royal family fell by your command, you shall answer for it one day. They were . . . dearly loved." And again his hand tightened into a fist at his side.

"That may be," said Morgana calmly, "but it was no deed of mine. Tethra, king of the Fomori, has put forth his hand to take this isle. For many a year, as you children of the earth have flourished and made merry and lived your brief little lives, I have felt the steady growth of the power that is in the sea. And now that it comes, I welcome it, aye, receive it with open arms. Fools!" Her voice was cold. "Did you not know that it was fear of *me* that kept him from these shores? For I am of the fairy blood, and the Sidhe and the Fomori have been foes since time out of mind. But no longer."

"Then you *are* in league with him!" accused Duncan.

"Say rather that I did not defy him when I felt him approach this isle, and that knowing I would not rise against him made him bold. I shall meet with him soon, and what follows upon that meeting will decide the future of Avalon."

"If you ally yourself with the Fomori," said the prince, "you may regret it bitterly. They are the enemies of your race—"

"Silence!" cried the crone, scandalized. "Will you speak so to one who is both queen and high priestess of Dana?"

Morgana looked with narrowed eyes on the prince. "You speak to me of enemies, you who are the heir of Diarmait and Artos the accursed."

"Artos? Do you mean Arthur Pendragon?" said Arawn. "You know well that Arthur had no heir of his blood save the traitor Mordred, whom he slew."

"You of Gwynedd continue his reign. You honour his

name and your standard is the Pendragon's. There can be no peace between your people and mine."

"But was not your ancestress Morgan le Fay reconciled with Arthur at the end?" Arawn asked. "Did she not, with her fairy companions, bear him across the sea to Avalon? Did she not place him in a deep cavern here, to heal and sleep an enchanted sleep until the time came for him to arise again?"

The queen made no answer, but looked at him with eyes of ice. Then she turned and motioned to the Fianna. "Remove the men, but leave the maiden. Keep the prisoners in the village for now." The guards bowed low and forced Maeve's companions from the tower at spear-point. Thomas looked as though he might try to resist, but Arawn laid a hand on the boy's shoulder and shook his head.

When they were gone, Maeve felt horribly alone and helpless, standing there in the middle of the vast torchlit chamber with the dark-clad women all around her. Panic dried her throat, and she wondered if she could leave Annwn by her will. But however hard she wished herself back in her own world, the tower room did not fade. She could enter Annwn at will, but could not leave it whenever she chose.

The dark queen approached, appraising Maeve with her icy eyes. "You—child of the Shadow-world. What do you here in Annwn? Answer!"

"I . . ." Maeve's voice cracked and died in her dry throat.

"You say the brooch was your grandmother's? She has been here also, then? But hold . . . her name was not Jehane Mac Dhughaill?" Morgana demanded.

Maeve dared not lie. "Jean MacDougall . . . yes."

"Ah." The queen nodded, as though it was all beginning

to make sense to her. She fingered the brooch thoughtfully. "Does Jehane live still?"

"N-no. She's dead. I . . . I found the brooch in her house."

"And you . . . what is your name?"

"Maeve O'Connor."

"What!" exclaimed the Druid, as though Maeve had said something unbelievably shocking. The old man turned to the queen. "Maeve—*Medb*. The name of the queen of Connacht, in ancient Éire, *and* an O'Connor, a child of the royal line of Connacht . . . What can this mean?"

The queen's face was cold, still. "How come you to bear the name of O'Connor, girl?"

"It's . . . my father's name," said Maeve faintly.

"A son of Connacht, descendant of the high kings of Éire. And he named you for Connacht's warrior-queen?"

"I . . . no, it was Grandma who came up with the name. Jehane."

"This is a portentous name," the Druid declared. The priestesses were silent, staring at Maeve. "Jehane had the second sight. What did she see, to name the child thus? What did she know?"

"More than she has told the child, that much is plain," said Morgana. "Maeve—Medb—is a name of power. It was old when the queen of Connacht bore it. Medb is the goddess of the earth. It was to her that the kings of ancient Éire swore their allegiance, and to her they were wed in the ceremony of the Lia Fáil. She was the power of the land, a goddess without whose sanction they could not rule. A child of kings, come to summon a king to the throne. Is this what Jehane foresaw?"

They were discussing Maeve as though she was not there, or as though she was a mere inanimate object.

"Then she must die," said the crone.

At that, the round chamber seemed to reel about Maeve, but the queen shook her dark head. "Nay, Grainne. You cannot cheat fate so. I knew a warrior once who was told by a Druid that his newborn son would one day cause his death. He decided to kill the babe so that it could never grow to manhood and wield any weapon against him. But as he hastened from his house with the child, he stumbled and struck his head upon a stone. The babe lived, but the man died: so was the doom fulfilled for all his efforts. This girl is woven into the world's cloth now, even as we are. Removing that thread could be our destruction, not our salvation. In any case, we do not know what role she will play, what king she will bring to the Lia Fail or what the fortunes of that king may be. It might even be Tethra whom she makes king. But you do not approve of that either."

"I say nothing, Majesty."

"You speak your thought with your eyes. I know you well, Grainne. I remember the day you were born. I know what it is you would say now: the Fomori have never been friends to my race or to yours."

"Something of that sort, perhaps," muttered the old woman.

Morgana seemed at last to remember that Maeve was standing there listening. "Remove her," ordered the queen with a peremptory gesture to the seven younger priestesses. "I will decide later what is to be done with her."

Chapter Ten

SHE WAS AWAKENED BY A SCREAM.

The echo of it lingered in her ears as she sat up, cold and stiff and disoriented. It was not so much a sound as the sleep-distorted memory of a sound. She was not quite sure that she had not dreamt it. All around her people lay on the ground, wrapped in their cloaks or in coarse blankets like the one Branwen had given her, huddled together for warmth. She saw many familiar faces: Old Ned, with his big black dog lying beside him, and the baker and the blacksmith and the weaver-woman. Not all the monks and villagers were here, however; it seemed that one group had gone on ahead of this one. Nearby, Cordelia was snuggled between her parents, and Thomas lay not far off, his long brown hair covering half his face. Guilt filled her. Had the Ryans delayed their departure because of her? Would they have got safely away with the first group had they not waited for Maeve to return?

Aengus—*no, not Aengus*, she remembered—was also

awake, standing apart from the slumbering villagers, an erect dark figure gazing pensively at the sky. Had he slept at all? She rose, wrapping the blanket about her like a cloak, and approached him shyly.

"Prince Arawn—I mean, Your Majesty . . ." she stumbled when she realized he must now be king.

He turned to her, and she saw the noble lines of his face, firm and well-defined, the steady gaze of the grey eyes. It was not hard, now, to imagine a circlet of gold on his dark hair. From now on, whenever she read *Hamlet*, she would always see this man's face and his brooding dark-clad figure. Melancholy hung about him like smoke over a banked fire, but she felt that anger might yet flash through it, quick as flame.

He had not always been thus, she knew. This man had been young Gwalchmai, the merry huntsman beloved of his people, the man he himself now bitterly derided. She had glimpsed that man briefly at the village *ceilidh*—so long ago now, it seemed. All that gentleness and mirth had been stripped from him. It was like erosion, she thought. Suffering cut away the soft parts and left only what was hard and durable. Arawn looked as though he had been carved down to a solid core of strength and endurance. Did he feel guilty for being alive when all his loved ones were dead? Guilty that he had not been there to defend them?

"There are no titles any more, young Maeve," he said in his quiet voice. "Can there be a king without a kingdom?"

How could he be so calm when he was so close to death? Even she knew the fate of heirs to a throne when the land is invaded.

"I'm sorry," she burst out miserably, and then fell silent, feeling the pitiful inadequacy of the words.

He spoke softly, as if to himself. "My grandsire and grandmother loved each other deeply, so much so that I was filled with dread at the thought of one dying before the other. The grief of the one left behind would have been hard to see. That they should perish together, then, and know no separation, is perhaps not such a dreadful thing as you might think. And they had led long, happy lives. But my father and mother are another matter. Many long years they had ahead of them still, and their blood demands justice." Again, as in the tower room, his hands clenched tightly at his sides.

He's so brave, she thought with a pang. *So noble. It's not fair.* "Isn't there anything we can do? Aren't there any allies who can help?" she asked desperately. "That big island, Tir Tairngiri . . ."

"Tir Tairngiri has but few people in it," he told her. "A people called the Skraelings once dwelt there, but they suffered greatly from the assaults of the Lochlannach in your grandmother's day and I doubt there are many of them left. The only other inhabitants of that land are the Daoine Sidhe, and they will care little what becomes of us common mortals."

"But not all the fairies hate humans, do they? In my grandmother's book there were some who were good to people."

"Those Sidhe departed Avalon and Tir Tairngiri many years ago. They no longer hold their courts here."

"Oh. Then is there any way we could make peace with *these* people?" she asked hopelessly.

She jumped when a man's voice answered from behind

her, speaking rough English. "There will never be peace between our peoples," it said sternly.

She turned, saw that a small group of the pagan Celts had emerged from their low, round houses to stare at the captives. The latter were now stirring, sitting upright in blinking confusion as she herself had done, looking about them.

"It is your own fault. When your Christian faith came to our lands," declared the man who had spoken, "the powers of the earth faded. The people turned from the old gods and no longer made the sacrifices that fed the earth. The bonds of the great magic were weakened and broken."

"You wear the *airbacc Giunnae*, the fence cut through the hair, like our Druids," said another man to one of the monks, pointing to his odd tonsure. "Why is that, if you are holy men of the Christian faith?"

The abbot stepped forward. "We are Druids of a sort," he replied. "We preserve old knowledge and pass it on. We lead the community in the rituals of our faith. Priests and Druids were not always at enmity. In elder days, we learnt much from one another."

"Your rulers in the Shadow-Rome would not have had it so," said the man who had first spoken. "Was not your church governed by the men of that otherworldly city?"

"Once that was so, before the two worlds were so deeply divided. But we live beyond the Shadow now. We are far removed from that Rome of which you speak, and follow our own traditions. It is our own abbots, not bishops sent by a pope, who are the leaders of the church in Avalon."

A woman now stepped forward, looking at them curiously. "Your ways are very strange to us. Why do you never marry? Our Druids do, and the priestesses may take what men they please. And is it true that even a man who is not ordained must have only one wife, and a woman only one husband? But what if you should come to love another?"

The abbot replied, "I think what you are calling love is what we call lust. It is not love but only a kind of hunger, which is quickly sated and fades from the mind."

"Yes," put in Branwen in her soft voice. "To us, you see, love is a thing that grows slowly between two people. Only after many years—" She broke off with a little shriek as Padraig pounced on her from behind and lifted her bodily, whirling her around.

"This is my lady!" he roared. "My queen, my heart's desire! And I'll have no other, though I live a hundred years! Let any man take her from me who dares!" He put on an expression of pretended ferocity and some of the watching men actually stepped back. Branwen's face was flushed with laughter. She looked, with her hair wisping down around her face, almost like a girl. "Oh, Padraig, put me down!" she exclaimed breathlessly.

Thomas turned away, as he always did when his parents became embarrassing. "Come, Maeve," he said, walking over to her. "Let us go apart for a while. Such talk is hard for you to hear, I know."

"Why?" she asked.

"Well, because of your own father and mother. What you say is happening between them."

Maeve looked at him blankly. "My father and mother . . . It's funny, Tom, but I haven't thought of them much. They seem so distant somehow."

He stared at her. "They were a great trouble to you once."

"Not any longer. It doesn't seem to matter any more."

He gave a little exclamation, pointing to her sweater. "Maeve! Your grandmother's brooch—it's gone."

"Oh, yes. Morgana took it," she said vaguely.

He looked at her more closely. "Maeve, is all well with you?" he asked worriedly.

She shrugged. "As well as can be expected, I guess."

The two of them walked apart, away from the buildings.

Beyond the houses, goats, cattle and horses grazed the green sweep of turf. All Celts, Duncan had told her, loved horses and valued them highly. Cattle too were important. Here a man's worth, his "honour price," was reckoned in kine. The more beasts one owned, the greater one's prestige.

"I asked Prince—*King*—Arawn what he thought we should do," Maeve said presently, "but he doesn't seem to have any ideas. Tom, I'm scared. I don't see any way out of this."

"Can you not return to your own world?"

Again Maeve strove to visualize her own world, but it all seemed blurred and faint and far away. "I don't know, and anyway, what about the rest of you? How could I just go off and leave you?"

"There is nothing at all you can do. Arawn is a king and Dugall a great lord, and even they can do little against Morgana."

"Dugall? Who's he?"

"The man we called Duncan. He is really Dugall, thane of Dalriada in the south. Arawn fostered with him as a boy, as is the royal custom. They are close friends, as dear as brothers. The prince was staying with Dugall at his castle when the

Fomori attacked. The two of them had decided that it would be amusing to rove about the countryside in the garb of simple huntsmen and dwell among us village folk for a time."

Maeve suddenly gave a little gasp and stood still. A horse lay sprawled on the earth a few metres away, its dull dark eye turned up sightlessly towards the sky. Blood pooled beneath its neck, which was scored with gaping wounds.

"I *thought* I heard a scream," said Maeve, her voice shaking.

"A sacrifice," came Arawn's voice behind them, "to their gods."

Maeve was appalled. "I thought all the Celts loved horses!"

"They do, so this must be a very important sacrifice to them. Morgana seeks the aid of her gods."

More of the captive villagers were wandering in the same direction, including Thomas's family. When Cordelia caught sight of the horse's carcass, she stopped in her tracks. Her lower lip trembled, then she burst into a loud wail.

"Stop it, Brat!" hissed Thomas. He looked anxiously towards the tower. Morgana and the Druid had emerged from its dark entrance and were also walking towards them. "This is no time for bellowing!"

The Druid threw a sharp glance at the little girl, but where another child might have quailed, Cordelia cried determinedly on. The pagan villagers stirred uneasily; something in the child's laments seemed to unsettle them. A woman with a small child clinging to her own skirts seemed particularly upset. She went to one of the houses and returned with something in her hand—a sweetmeat, perhaps—

which she held out awkwardly to the girl, but Cordelia took no notice.

Then Morgana approached, her pale face stern. Cordelia fell silent at once and ran to Branwen's arms. Her mother seemed small and drab and frail next to the towering queen, but she looked up with the eyes of a lioness. For the space of a heartbeat, Morgana and Branwen stood silently confronting one another; then the dark queen walked on, to join the Druid in contemplating the sacrifice.

Maeve expelled a long breath. So might some huge and fearsome predator pause before a small animal standing desperate guard over its young—pause, briefly consider and turn aside, not in fear, but from a kind of instinctive respect. Morgana might be contemptuous of weakness, but courage apparently did not anger her. That might be useful to know, should she demand that Maeve be brought before her again.

As the day progressed, the captives and the pagan people drew apart, the latter retreating into their houses or caring for their livestock in the field. These people, Maeve learned, were apparently the descendants—the children and grandchildren—of the Fianna guards and priestesses who had dwelt with Morgana in Grandma's day. In Jean's book, Maeve now recalled, the queen's warriors and the original eight priestesses had chosen to join their evil ruler in the Rath. Their offspring now carried on their traditions, awaiting the time when the queen would be freed from confinement.

For all the ferocity of their appearance, the Fianna were not savages; they had their own code of honour, Arawn told her, rather like the knights of the Round Table. In olden days, such men had been held in awe by the common people—minstrels and cup-bearers had waited on them as if on great lords. The founder of the Fianna, he said, was none other than the great Irish hero Fionn Mac Cumhail. Like him, the Fianna feared no threat, natural or supernatural, and many a Fianna warrior of old had even dared to wed a fairy bride.

The Druid puzzled her a little. Among the characters in Grandma's book there had been a great Druid, but he had had exceptional powers: he was able to alter his shape at will and control the elements. Arawn explained to her that only a few Druids could command such magical powers. All Druids had great knowledge, for they began their training by studying under a master for twenty years; but they learned for the most part about astronomy and herbal lore, religious rituals and the Gaelic laws. They might invoke the gods before a battle, or read the future in the entrails of a beast, but they were regarded as learned men, teachers and magistrates, rather than sorcerers.

"Morgana would have no need of a Druid with magical powers," Arawn said. "Her own are great enough to defeat any foe."

"She couldn't leave the Rath, though," Maeve pointed out:

"That is true. A wall of fairy power surrounds it on all sides. But years have passed and the ones who cast that spell have left the land. Its power is weakening, and she will soon be able to break free."

At midday the prisoners were given a meal of plain bread and water. When they were finished eating, a company of Fianna warriors herded them like cattle into long double lines. None of them dared ask where they were being led—

their captors' grim faces, as much as their spears and swords, discouraged questions.

Out of the inner ring of the Rath they were led, on through the plain of dancing stones. The sky had cleared and was now full of scudding clouds. Presently they heard the sound of hoofs behind them, and turned to see many riders leaving the enclosure at a gallop. At their head rode Morgana.

Her mount was a large stallion, midnight black save for a white star upon its forehead, and she rode astride it rather than sidesaddle; her cloak and her cloud of black hair streamed out behind her. Her gown today was green, the fairy colour; it matched her eyes, which shone intensely bright. No longer did she seem like a cold and lifeless statue. The wind had stung a wild rose colour into her cheeks, and her features were fiercely alive.

"Macha herself!" murmured Dugall.

"Who *is* Macha?" asked Maeve.

"The goddess of war in the old legends of the Gaels. There are three goddesses: Macha and Badb and Nemain. Sometimes they are spoken of as a single goddess, the Morrigan. Macha-Morrigan is a great horsewoman, so they say."

"It's a magnificent horse," said Thomas enviously.

Arawn nodded. "That is one of the fairy steeds whose ancestors were bred in the land of Éire long ago by the Tuatha de Danaan, the half-fairy race whom we now call the Daoine Sidhe. Their horses are like no others: they can run faster than the wind, and there is magic in their blood. They were bred to bear the Sidhe in their fairy rides."

Morgana had spied Arawn and pulled the stallion out of

his gallop with superb control, directing the snorting and prancing beast close to the line of villagers. "So, Prince, who is the victor now?" she called. "Your grandsire robbed me of my rule and penned me within the Rath, but see, I ride free again! The walls of air that hemmed me in have now fallen before a greater power. I shall call up all the spirits of the land: *boggart* and *banshee*, *urisk* and *glaistig* shall again walk its earth. You grew careless over the years, you and all your house. Did you think I slept in my tower all that time?"

Arawn made no answer, but continued to march with his eyes fixed ahead of him.

"I told Diarmait and Gwenlian that the Sacred Isle would be mine again to rule," said Morgana. She tossed her head, black hair flying, and her eyes were as wild as the stallion's. "You see now I spoke true! Avalon is given to those you called enemy—the children of the gods and the lords from the deep!"

She urged the horse forward, the mounted Fianna and priestesses following after her.

"So," muttered Dugall, "it is the Fomori we ride to meet."

"Do they really live in the sea?" Maeve asked.

"So it is said. Their magic arts allow them, like the Merrows, to dwell in the deep like sea creatures, needing neither light nor air. They have a city that lies beneath the waves— Lochlan, it is called. It sits upon a crag above a great abyss, in whose depths their goddess is said to dwell. The sea-raiders whom our grandsires fought also gave their allegiance to that city and its deity, and so they were called the Lochlannach. But they worshipped many gods. The Fomori bow only to one: Domnu of the Deep is their ruler."

"And she is a cruel one," said Arawn grimly.

"Will Tethra seek Temair, and be crowned at the Stone?" asked Dugall.

"I think he does not care for any sign of approval, from the Lia Fail or from any living being," said Arawn. "Temair is nothing to him but a fortress to be stormed, and the land a thing to be conquered."

Thomas looked puzzled. "If the Fomori come from the sea, why do they ride overland to Temair? Why would they not attack the coast?"

Maeve remembered her trip to St. John's with her aunt and uncle, remembered how they had gone up to the top of Signal Hill and seen the water of the harbour far below. Ancient cannons had stood upon the stone fortifications there, and on the far side of the harbour was Fort Amherst, built in the Second World War. She remembered her uncle telling her that the steep-sided Narrows made a natural barrier against forces attacking from the sea. "My uncle told me that the French forces used to come ashore at Mary's Bay and try to march overland to St. John's because they could never get at the city from the harbour. It had too many defences."

"Aye, and the harbour of Temair is also well-guarded, with a fortress and many men-at-arms," confirmed Arawn.

Presently they glimpsed another great host approaching them across the boulder-strewn barrens: many men, both mounted and on foot, with shields and mail. There were also figures in black hooded robes, like those Maeve had seen surrounding the house—the memory seemed curiously faint now, but it still sent a shiver through her. At the head of the army, on a large grey horse, rode one who could only be their king: a huge man, broad of chest and shoulder, with long black hair and a flowing beard. His eyes were dark, almost black, and his face whiter than Morgana's, as white as a drowned man's.

The sight of him filled Maeve with foreboding; even Morgana seemed taken aback for an instant. She pulled her horse to a halt, and her eyes were suddenly wary. Maeve thought of two cats sizing one another up, the fur on their backs bristling.

The Fomori king now spoke to Morgana. His voice was deep, as might be suspected of so large a man, but was curiously flat and expressionless. He spoke in the Gaelic tongue first, then in English for all to hear.

"We are come to take this land at last, to rule it as it ought to be ruled. No more will we linger at the edge of the Black Abyss, in the dark places of the sea. We will live in the light and the air again, as we did long ago. It is the mortals who will be driven into the deep."

Morgana nodded. "The powers of Avalon will be reawakened now. Already I hear that the *Cwn Annwn* have arisen to hunt their prey again, and that the spirits of the wood stir in their leafy halls. The true gods shall be revered again, and shall receive the sacrifices to which they are entitled."

"Aye, and to Domnu her sacrifices also. It is to her power that this victory is owed. Henceforth she must be honoured above all other gods in Avalon."

Morgana eyed the cowled figures. "The Black Druids of the Fomori perform human sacrifices, is that not so?"

"It is. And that is why you will be permitted to retain some of the mortals who serve you—so that Domnu may be honoured upon her holy festivals as is fitting. It has been long since she received the proper offerings."

The flame was kindled again in Morgana's eyes. "They are *my* people!" she flashed. "My *tuath*. I will not have them sacrificed. Sate your goddess with the blood of others!"

"I shall," said Tethra. "Beginning with some of those you hold here. And there is one mortal in particular whom I seek."

At that, Maeve felt her blood run cold, and she could not look at Arawn.

"I hunt a hawk," said Tethra. "One of a brood that escaped me. If it remains free, it shall raise up another brood to be a trouble to me in days to come. I seek the Prince Arawn, called Gwalchmai. Is he among those whom you hold?"

There was a small eternity of silence, then Morgana answered in a neutral tone. "That may well be," she said.

So Morgana had no intention of giving away her revenge to another. Maeve shot a glance at the queen, then hurriedly looked down at her feet again. She must *not* look at Arawn . . .

"Then see that he is delivered to me. I shall make an end of that royal line, once and for all. And I shall not suffer any of his subjects to remain on this isle. In future, it must be peopled by those of the old faith only."

The horse of the Fomori king suddenly stretched out its dull lead-coloured neck, snapping at Morgana's mount as she rode past. The Sidhe stallion bared his teeth in turn, and the queen pulled his head around, letting the horse wheel and dance out his anger on the turf.

"*You* . . . will not *suffer* . . ." she said. "Is it you, then, who shall rule this isle alone? You forget, Tethra, Avalon has a queen." Her eyes blazed now, and the Fianna moved, quietly and unobtrusively, to flank her.

"And you forget, daughter of Morfessa, to whom you owe this triumph. Your gods have not delivered you, for all your prayers. Had you offered them human lives instead of pigs and chickens, they might have heard you. Domnu has made me *ard-righ*, high king over all this land. You shall keep your Rath, but look not to reign over this isle again."

A stillness seemed to have come over Morgana. The fierce wild animation had gone from her, the colour in her cheeks had ebbed. The flame in her eyes was extinguished; they were stone-cold once more. "Very well," she said, and her words fell into the silence like chips broken off a block of ice. "I shall return now to my tower and consider all you have said to me this day."

"Consider then, well and wisely—and not for too long."

He made a gesture of dismissal, but Morgana had already turned her back on him and spurred her horse away.

"Ahh, she didn't care for that!" said Arawn softly.

"Will she dare to defy him?" murmured Dugall.

"I would not be surprised."

"Then Morgana has made a bad enemy this day."

"So, I think, has he," said Arawn, looking thoughtfully after the departing queen.

Chapter Eleven

"YOU CANNOT BE SERIOUS," objected Thomas, incredulous.

His father looked up from the book on his lap. "Indeed I am."

"A play? Here? *Now?*"

"It will be something of a challenge, I admit, without a proper stage or costumes—"

"That isn't what I meant!"

They were back in the great enclosure, huddling together on the ground in little groups. The pagan folk still watched them curiously, though not with the wariness they had shown before. It was as if Cordelia's tearful outburst had somehow broken the barrier between them.

They had seen nothing of Morgana for a day and a half. After the encounter with Tethra, the Druid Cathbad had offered to perform a *tarbhfeis*, a ceremony in which he would consume some of the flesh and blood of a newly slaughtered bull. This sacred rite would then cause him to have visions of the land's next ruler. That afternoon, the air had resounded with the tortured bellowings of the selected animal; this was followed by a long silence that seemed to Maeve to have an ominous quality to it. That silence persisted into the night and all through the following day. Whatever the Druid had learned in his trance, Morgana seemed not to have liked it. She did not leave the tower or give any directions as to the fate of her prisoners.

The pagan villagers murmured among themselves. "They say she has gone into the mound, to the fairy court that lies within it. She has gone there alone, to sit in its dark hall and draw upon the power that lingers there."

Then, yesterday evening, a man whom they had not seen before had come out of the tower and approached them. He was young, with wavy cinnamon-coloured hair and a short spade-shaped beard, and was clad in a yellow tunic and brown trousers, with a many-coloured cloak about his shoulders. He had stood watching the prisoners with great interest, until at last an irritated Thomas had boldly asked him what he wanted.

"Oh, I am just wondering," he'd replied, "what sort of stories you folk tell among yourselves. I am Finian," he gave a little bow, "bard to the queen."

"A bard!" exclaimed Padraig, turning an affable smile upon him. "An heir to the mantle of Taliesin the bright-browed! You will know many legends, then."

The young man grinned at him. "Indeed, yes. I know more than two hundred sagas and romances by heart. I can tell you of the battle of the Sidhe and the Fomori at Magh Tuireadh, or of Fionn Mac Cumhail and his Fianna and all their adventures. Or recite the tale of Gwydion and Arianrhod. But Christian folk, they say, have no bards. Their monks write down our old tales and embellish them with curious Christian themes, and they have in their courts many minstrels who sing songs of love to the ladies. But they have no one who can tell a grand and moving tale."

"Now there I must correct you," said Padraig, raising an admonishing finger. "There is at least one with whom I am acquainted, a Christian gentleman called Shakespeare."

Finian raised a cinnamon-coloured brow. "Shake-spear? With such a name he should have been a warrior."

"'What's in a name? That which we call a rose / By any other name would smell as sweet.' So said the poet himself in one of his works. But such is his fame that many call him simply the Bard, as though there were no other in all the world."

"Say you so? And is this celebrated poet among your company, then?"

"He is, in a manner of speaking." Padraig held up the battered book of plays. "Here lie his words, preserved by generations of scribes—for my friend Shakespeare has been dead many a century, alas. But in his plays, he lives on."

"Plays? You mean those pastorals your villagers perform at Whitsuntide?"

"Similar, yes, though rather longer. I would gladly have one performed here for you. All of our player-troupe are here, and Shakespeare must always be performed to be properly appreciated."

The bard laughed, and Maeve found herself liking him. "Now that would be a sight worth seeing. But I hardly think he can be a rival to Taliesin. Tomorrow, then?" And wrapping his cloak about him, he had returned to the tower.

Now Padraig was leafing through his precious volume of Shakespeare. "What play, I wonder?"

"*The Tempest*," suggested Maeve at once.

He nodded, looking thoughtful. "Hmm, yes. Not too long, and with lots of magic and wonder—the sort of thing these pagan folk delight in. We have done it several times in the village; the last performance was only a year ago. I played Prospero."

Maeve smiled. "Of course."

"And most of the actors should remember their lines. But Branwen can hold the book and prompt us. Maeve, you must be Miranda. We used a boy last year, but he was no good."

"He kept looking at his feet," recalled Cordelia, "and giggling."

"Women do not play-act," said Thomas frowning.

"Ah, but these are exceptional circumstances. We must have the best players for the parts. Thomas, you will be Ferdinand again?"

The youth raised his arms in a gesture of surrender. "Oh, very well!"

"The mind of one who hears a tale," declared Padraig, "is a canvas on which the tale-teller paints. And these minds will be most receptive, I think. There is nothing the Celtic soul loves so well as a grand tale of magic and marvels."

The play was acted out that afternoon in abridged form, there on the turf. The spectators were mesmerized, and Finian too seemed fascinated. Even the Druid Cathbad came out of the tower and watched from a distance, though with a frown on his face. They used one of the small wagons for the shipboard scene, with a sail hastily made of a cloak hung on two sticks lashed together. Maeve was given a shawl to wind coif-fashion about her face, and one of Branwen's dresses. Padraig used a blanket for his sorcerer's mantle, but he scarcely needed a costume or a prop. He *was* Prospero, sorcerer and deposed duke. The power of his big resonant voice was all that was necessary to work the transformation.

Before he began, Padraig made a little explanatory speech to the curious crowd that had gathered about their makeshift stage. "I pray you, good folk, help me in the telling of this tale. Furnish forth what we lack with your own imaginations, as though you listened to a hearth-tale on a winter's night. See with your minds the heaving billows of our stormy sea and the strange wonders of our southern isle. Let your mind's eye clothe us according to our stations, in the garb of lord or slave. Imagine me one Prospero, a mighty thane and Druid cast out of his throne; and this my beloved daughter, Miranda; and these my servants, one a monster foul of aspect, the other an airy spirit. . . ."

There was hardly any need to act. From the moment Maeve felt the warm weight of his hand on her shoulder, and heard the affection in his rumbling voice, she *was* his daughter. Caliban and Ariel—played by the blacksmith and the baker's boy—*were* his inhuman servants. They were all able to give strong performances because of him, and seldom needed help from the prompters. Maeve found herself looking at Thomas as though he truly *was* Ferdinand, the very first love of her sheltered life. He was a good actor, she noticed with slight surprise, getting right into the part; his thin cheeks actually coloured a little at her fervent declarations of love. Or perhaps he was only embarrassed?

The onlookers murmured at first, but soon fell utterly silent, as if entranced by the strange drama unfolding before them. The schemes of Caliban and the usurping duke's men, the merry caperings of Ariel, the reconciling love of Ferdinand and the sorcerer's daughter—all seemed to enrapture them.

At last, Padraig stepped forward for the final speech of the play, in which the actor must drop out of character and plead for the audience's applause. "As you from crimes would pardon'd be, / Let your indulgence set me free."

Maeve suddenly saw the double meaning he had put into that last line, and looked anxiously at Cathbad. The Druid was approaching, a heavy scowl on his face. But before he could speak, Finian came forward, smiling.

"A most magnificent tale," he declared, "and to see it performed thus, as though all were truly happening before my eyes—ah, you would put a poor bard out of his living! I am glad that the queen was not here to see!"

"A foolish tale," grumbled Cathbad. "What manner of Druid was this Prospero, to get his incantations out of books? No true magic was ever created thus. Druids never commit their knowledge to paper, but memorize it all. The power is in the breath of the spoken word, not its written form."

"All the same," said Padraig, "there is a sort of magic, called poetry, made with written words and that must be preserved if it is to survive."

The Druid merely grunted and turned away. Finian smiled.

"You must not be troubled by his moods. Cathbad is a dour man, but he is wise for all that. He could be no wiser had he supped of the salmon that ate the nut of wisdom, or drunk from Cerridwen's cauldron, or lived as long as the Eagle of Gwern Abwy."

"The eagle of where?" demanded Cordelia.

"Ah, that is a tale even longer than your romance of Prospero! I shall not tell it now, but one evening, perhaps." He smiled again, then headed back towards the tower. As for the pagan folk, they had scarcely moved from where they sat or stood, and seemed almost bemused.

"Well," commented Padraig, "I think we may have made a friend of this Finian. It does not hurt to have an ally in the enemy's court. Not that many could sway Morgana. But all the same, it eases my heart a little."

Maeve hoped he was right.

"Now what?" asked Thomas nervously.

The Fianna and the eight priestesses, headed by Morgana, had emerged in a solemn procession from the tower. The prisoners were told curtly by one of the Fianna that they must make a journey. But they were not told what their destination was to be.

Once more they were herded out of the enclosure while Morgana and the others rode by. But this time the pagan folk came too, bringing with them all their own horses and cattle as well as the prisoners', and large bundles of possessions. As they marched, a mist like that which Maeve and her companions had first encountered began to seethe up from the ground and enfold them in its cold whiteness.

Morgana waved a hand at the mist. "Earth and sea may be under Tethra's sway, but the air is yet mine to command. There is a magic in this mist. Within it we shall be not only invisible, but impossible to hear as well. Moreover, any foe who enters it shall be stricken with confusion and terror. Follow me, and stray beyond the mist at your peril."

On and on they trudged, through grey vapour and standing stones, through the barrens beyond and then into a dense forest of fir and pine. They startled a small group of caribou, which made off in alarm, fawn-coloured coats blending into the barrens. But no other living thing showed itself. The mist accompanied them all the way, a moving shield. Only at the margin of the trees did it begin at last to wisp away.

Finally Morgana called a halt. "We will camp here amid the trees," she announced, "and this evening we must sacrifice to the gods. Now, Finian, why these faces?"

"It seems a waste of a good beast," muttered the bard, dismounting from his horse.

"I agree," said Morgana coolly. "Let us sacrifice a man, then."

"Ah, well, perhaps after all a beast is best," said Finian hastily.

They set up a primitive sort of camp in the forest, with jury-rigged tents made of carts and draped cloth. The people of Connemara, the abbot and his monks included, were once more forced to sit on the ground while the Fianna stood guard. Morgana, Cathbad and the priestesses vanished into the wood.

"Now what fate awaits us?" one of the monks asked. "I would not put it past Morgana and her Druid to make a human sacrifice. All Druids are accursed magicians. They cast spells and try to read fate in the stars instead of trusting to divine Providence."

"The Magi of the East," observed the abbot mildly, "read of Our Lord's birth in the night sky and followed his star to Bethlehem. So let us not condemn."

"But they worship trees, and animals, and unholy spirits!"

Maeve was looking thoughtfully at the silent ranks of trees. She had suddenly remembered paintings on a wall, a green world where trees danced like flames. "I think I know why the Druids worship trees," she said slowly. "Trees have a sort of *presence* about them, haven't they? Almost like a soul."

The monk looked shocked.

At sunset, the prisoners were made to walk into the forest to the place of the sacrifice. The trees all had immensely thick trunks, eyed with staring knot-holes. Presently they came to a place where the trees opened out into a clearing that measured about fifteen metres across. Here the ground was strewn with more glacial boulders, some as high as a man's head. The space was ringed about with massive trees—oaks, judging by their notched leaves. So huge were they that their branches almost met overhead, and much of the clearing was cast in shadow.

"The Drunemeton," said Finian, seeing her stare. "The most sacred nemeton of all. Here the Druids came to reap the mistletoe from the boughs of the holy oak and slay the sacred bulls."

Padraig murmured softly:

There is an old tale goes that Herne the Hunter,
Sometime a keeper here in Windsor forest,
Doth all the winter-time, at still midnight,
Walk round about an oak, with great ragg'd horns . . .

"Don't, Papa!" squealed Cordelia, and he said no more.

Maeve looked about her in awe. The oaks were incredibly old, their thick trunks gnarled and pitted and caverned with age. They must be hundreds of years old. A sense of great antiquity hung about them, and an atmosphere of sanctity also. As the Nemeton had been to a church, so this place was to a cathedral: a living holy place to whose confines only the highest priests could come. What had they been brought here to witness?

The eight priestesses, with Morgana at their head, stood in a tight group at the very centre of the grove. Some carried torches in their hands. Once all the people had been brought in and made to sit on the grass, the priestesses began to chant.

"He comes who is hunter and hunted, master of beasts, the king crowned with horns."

Maeve heard people gasp all around her. A figure had appeared out of the dim green dusk within the forest. It walked erect, like a man, but its tall form was swathed in rough grey fur and from its head there rose the palmated antlers of the caribou. It stood on the edge of the clearing, shadowed and unreal, watching and waiting.

"Cernunnos," whispered Finian. "The man-beast, the Lord of the Wood."

"Herne," squeaked Cordelia, and huddled against her father.

The figure stepped forward into the clearing, and Maeve

suddenly saw that it was Cathbad the Druid, costumed in skins and a horned headdress. But his eyes were strangely glazed and his expression that of a man in a trance.

"What is happening? What is he doing?" she asked Finian in a low voice.

He bent to answer in her ear. "He is becoming the god."

"Becoming?"

"That is and yet is not Cathbad before us. He has taken a part of the Divine into himself, and has become what he worships."

The Druid was dancing now, a fierce, wild dance without order or pattern. The eight black-gowned priestesses joined in, yelling and waving their torches so that the wild, winding paths of their dance were traced in fire. Only Morgana stood apart, her face watchful.

"Shall he dance alone?" called Grainne. "Who shall be his partner? Shall it be Ériu, fair island goddess?" The words seemed to be part of a ritual.

In her deep voice, Morgana answered. "Nay, not Ériu— far away her throne is. Hers is the Green Isle, Éire across the ocean."

"Shall it be Medb?" called another priestess.

"Nay, not Mother Medb—deep is her dwelling. Hers the soil and all its yield, earth is her body. Rich are the Mother's gifts, yet we seek another."

"Then call her by name."

Morgana held her head high. "We would call the Morrigan, in her threefold aspect: Macha, Badb and Nemain, goddesses of battle."

Grainne spread her arms wide, the flame of her torch

smoking and fluttering. "Hear our summons, goddess of the gore-crows!"

"She comes," cried another priestess. "The goddess is come! She is in this place! Sacrifice to her and she will hear your pleas!"

"Give to her one of the prisoners!" someone yelled.

Morgana did not even look at the cringing villagers. "Nay, their lives are naught to me. For such a sacrifice, only the life of one dear to me can suffice."

"Oh, mistress," cried Grainne running to her, "take *me* then! Have I not served you for many years? And few more are left to me. When I was young, I prayed to the Morrigan that I should win glory for you and die in battle. That wish was denied me. Can I not give my life now, my queen? If I must die an old woman, let it not be in my bed!"

Morgana laid a hand on the bowed grey head. "Nay, Grainne. The Morrigan is not Domnu; she requires no such sacrifice of you. And my choice is made already." She gestured. "Bring Brandubh." *Brandubh?* Maeve wondered.

A Fianna guard now came out of the wood, leading Morgana's black horse behind him. He passed the reins into the hand of one of the priestesses and withdrew.

"Her horse?" exclaimed Maeve in surprise and relief. "Is that all?"

"Ah, child, you do not understand," Finian told her. His face was stricken. "No mere human creature could mean to her what this Sidhe horse does. Brandubh is the last of his kind in Avalon, as she is the last of hers, and he is dearer to her than anything that breathes."

The Druid reached below his robe of hide and drew out a long, curved knife. Morgana took it from him and moved to the horse's side. "Brandubh, Brandubh," she murmured as she stroked his nose. He turned and nickered gently, nuzzling at her face as if to say that he understood.

Maeve moaned softly. Cordelia began to whimper and Padraig held her close.

The queen laid her head against the horse's neck, her black hair mingling with his mane. The dance had ceased, the torches were still. Maeve could see the queen's bare shoulders heaving, the trembling of the hand that gripped the knife. Suddenly, she could bear it no longer.

"No, you can't!" she shouted without thinking.

A shocked silence filled the holy place. The Druid came abruptly out of his trance-like state. His horned head turned to Maeve, glaring. Morgana, too, started and swung around. "Let her speak!" the queen cried. "Words have more weight here than in other places, and she has the second sight."

"Madness! The goddess is summoned. You cannot deny her the sacrifice you owe!" exclaimed the Druid in horror.

"And why not?" demanded Morgana in anger. "What has she or any of the gods given me thus far, in exchange for all my prayers and sacrifices? An ocean of blood have I spilled for them, and all for naught. In all the years I called on them, the mortals of the new faith never ceased to thrive, while I remained bound within my Rath. I have been so long without hope that I even looked to the Fomori sea demons for aid. And now this Shadow-daughter comes to me with counsel born of the sight, and you wonder that I turn to her?" She gestured at the cowering Maeve. "Did she not enter our world through the gate of a goddess, the Nemeton of Modron? It may be that the powers we honour have sent her to us."

"A child of Jehane's line!" gasped Grainne.

"A child in whose veins the old magic flows with the blood." She turned again to Maeve. "Speak, child, if you are moved. I will hear you." She pointed, unnervingly, with the knife.

All eyes were on her, Maeve realized in panic. "I . . . I don't know about your goddess," she stumbled, "but I can't believe she would take Brandubh from you. If . . . if she's like a mother to your people, then she must care for her children." A vision came to her of a smiling face, blue eyes and golden hair and a voice that was always soft and tender. *Mom . . . Mommy.* A vision from the past, which brought a lump to her throat and made her voice hoarse when she spoke again. "A mother would help you no matter what you did—just because you were her child. Because she loved you."

Morgana stood silent. "So have I often thought in my heart of hearts. Must there always be payment? Can there be no love?" And as they watched, she sprang nimbly onto Brandubh's back. The horse lifted his head and neighed, and her black hair flowed about his black neck, as though they were one creature.

"Now there stands one who could challenge the gods themselves!" said Finian softly.

"Aye, and win!" said a warrior behind him.

Morgana and her mount turned and thundered from the grove.

They did not see the queen again until late the following morning, when they had broken camp and begun to march once more. The wooded land gave way to a glacial landscape of stony fields and lakes and hills, and here they saw Morgana on her black horse galloping towards them. Queen and steed looked exactly as they had when they had left the Drunemeton: full of life and fierce energy.

"Was she out riding all night?" Maeve wondered aloud.

"I would not be surprised if that was the case," commented Arawn, "given that particular woman, and that horse. Both are creatures of the Sidhe, and do not grow weary as quickly as we mortals do."

Morgana did not speak to them, but rode on ahead at a great pace, leading the way. Soon she was little more than a black dot on the landscape.

"She leads us inland," observed Dugall. "What can that mean? Does she fear the sea, or is there some other place she seeks—a seat of power like the Drunemeton?"

"The latter, I suspect," the young king replied. "She seems much excited, as though she still expects to find help."

"What made you speak out like that in the grove, Maeve?" Thomas asked. "Were you really moved by the sight?"

"No. At least, I don't think so," she replied confusedly. "I just felt terribly sorry for her and spoke without thinking."

"If things go ill, she may blame you for preventing the sacrifice," remarked Thomas worriedly.

The same thought had occurred to Maeve, though she had tried to suppress it until now. She huddled into the cloak Branwen had given her, staring at the ground as she walked. *How could I have been so stupid?* she asked herself miserably. *I should never have interfered.* But it was too late to take back her words.

She looked unhappily at their surroundings. It was a dreary landscape. Only grasses grew here, and rocks lay everywhere: scattered in the fields like rubble, rising from the surface of pond and lake.

"This was once the *Cailleach Bheur*'s domain," commented Dugall. "I can feel her presence yet, something that has no love for life and growth."

"The Blue Hag." Again Maeve remembered her grandmother's book. "She's a sort of goddess too, isn't she? The old woman who rules the winter."

"Aye, she is a powerful spirit, and a cruel one. Ice and snow are in her power, and she relinquishes her grip in the spring with deep reluctance. Once, long before our people came here, before even the reign of the Sidhe, these lands were ruled by the *Cailleach Bheur*. Ice covered all of Avalon and Tir Tairngiri, deeper than the hills are high. But the Blue Hag was driven out by the greater powers, and her cold kingdom destroyed. The ice that enfolded the isles melted and withdrew like a vanquished army, though the land still bears the scars of her ancient reign. But far away to the north there lies a realm of never-ending cold, and there the Blue Hag reigns perpetually."

They were walking now along the edge of one of the deep glacial lakes, and some people had stopped at the shore to fill waterskins and bottles or to let their animals drink. Mist rolled down from the hills beyond to trail on the still, cold surface, which reflected the leaden hues of the sky. Far out on that misty surface, Maeve thought she saw a dark, upright shape, like a pole or a tree from which the branches had been stripped. As she watched, it seemed to move, swaying sinuously from side to side. Her blood froze in her veins. It was alive, that thing in the lake. She saw now that the long, slender neck, supple as a swan's, terminated in a dark, oblong head. She was too thunderstruck to speak; she merely stood gaping, trying to grasp with her brain what her eyes were telling her. She blinked and the dark thing was gone, as though it had never been there at all. There was no ripple on the water, no sign that anything had broken the surface.

"Maeve! What is wrong, dear?" Branwen asked, seeing her expression.

"I saw . . . I saw . . ." Maeve stammered. What had she seen? A mirage, or some quite ordinary thing that her fatigued brain had distorted? "I *thought* I saw something out there in the lake. Like some kind of creature, but it can't have been real." Had she imagined it? She must have. And yet she still felt the stirrings of unease.

She stared at the lake again, then went rigid. Along the mist-shrouded surface, a long stretch of bubbling, disturbed water had appeared. It was moving, heading towards this side of the lake, to the shore where the people had gathered.

"Look out!" she screamed.

Chapter Twelve

EVERYONE TURNED TO STARE AT HER, and a Fianna warrior stooping at the water's edge for a drink whirled around, drawing his sword reflexively. At the same instant, the surface of the lake behind him erupted into a fountain of foam, and something long and dark that glistened like a wet log thrust through it, seizing hold of his leg. He fell, howling in pain.

His comrades immediately rushed to his aid, swords drawn. The creature let go its prey and reared up, hissing.

It was greenish-black with dark mottlings, its head larger than a horse's. The long, swaying neck was as thick around as a man's body, and was covered in fish-like scales. The head bore a finny crest of webbed spines. There was a frothing of the water behind the neck, and a great green arch rose from it, scaly and dripping: a coil of the creature's long, serpentine body.

People streamed back from the water, added their cries to the terrified bleating and lowing of their animals. Belatedly,

Maeve too began to run, but her legs were uncertain beneath her and she stumbled. The Fianna charged as one man, but the monster did not retreat. The dark head seemed to split open, like a cloven melon, and there was a huge salmon pink mouth lined with serrated teeth. It lunged with lightning speed, snapping at the men.

And then Morgana was suddenly there, riding her horse at the monster, her face grim. Holding out her arm, she spoke in Gaelic, her voice high and commanding. The beast paid no heed, but snaked its long, glistening neck towards her horse, making him rear and scream. As Morgana fought to control him, Arawn bent to seize the sword of the fallen man, who now lay clutching his bloodied leg and groaning. Swinging the blade in a long arc, Arawn hacked at the scaly neck.

The other Fianna joined him, their blades rising and falling almost in unison. Dark wounds gaped from the green-black hide. With a hiss like water thrown on fire, the injured beast recoiled, diving back into the lake. There was another flurry of foam, and then a long slick, like oil or black blood, tinted the churning bubbles of its retreat. The waters smoothed, were still again beneath the grey sky.

Arawn was left standing at the water's edge, sword in hand. The Fianna now turned their weapons towards him. He faced them with a savage light in his grey eyes, and for an instant Maeve feared he would take them all on at once. But then he gave a little shrug, as though it was of no importance, and flung the sword away. Maeve breathed again.

"What *was* that beast?" asked Thomas, shaken. "I never saw the like of it."

Dugall gazed at the water in wonderment. "A *péist*—they are ancient creatures, older than the oldest magic, and many of us had thought that their kind was long gone from the world. The old things truly are stirring again. No one knows where these water dragons come from. Perhaps they are spawned from the great sea serpents and find their way up rivers and into lochs. Are there any such creatures in your world?" he asked of Maeve.

"No," she answered, "at least . . . there are stories of a monster that lives in a loch in Scotland. But not many people believe in it. Or in sea monsters, either."

"It is said in Dalriada that there is only one serpent now left in the sea—Cìrein Cròin, he is called. He is the largest beast that lives, and he roves about the ocean hunting whales for his food."

The *péist* did not resurface, but fearing that it was merely lurking in the lake and might try another attack, they hastened from the place. The Fianna warrior it had nearly taken was in a bad way. His injured leg had been bound up and his comrades had helped him onto his horse, but despite his stoicism, all knew that he must be in terrible pain.

When the lake was finally at a safe distance behind them, Morgana signalled again for a halt.

"We are come now to the parting of our ways," she said, turning to face Arawn. "I must go westward and seek the others of the old faith; they may provide me with fighting men and chariots."

"I did not know of these others," said Arawn sharply.

"You were not meant to know, King. Not all of my followers were confined within the Rath; those that escaped lived on in hiding, and have borne many sons and daughters. They hoped to fight you one day; now they will fight the Fomori. But you must go now to your *dún* at Temair and prepare for your own battle."

The Connemara villagers gasped audibly, and Arawn raised an eyebrow. "Your Majesty is most . . . generous."

She looked away. "I could not control the *péist*, and that for me should have been no hard task. The land is Tethra's now, and he is turning it against me. You see how he has not even troubled to pursue me: he knows that the land itself is his ally and my enemy. I have no use for prisoners, and I will give to Tethra nothing that he desires. Your death would please him greatly. So fly away to your eyrie, Hawk, and defend your nestlings as best you can."

He stepped forward, the Fianna now clearing a way for him. "I shall do so, and to any of your people, Queen, who are willing to come with me to Temair I will give shelter as though they were my own."

There was a slight softening in Morgana's pale face, but she said only, "So be it. Let those who would accompany you do so. These are simple people, most of them, who know not how to fight, and I will not lead them into greater danger. Seanchan, the man who was wounded, should go with you too. And the children and their mothers and the aged. Cathbad, you go with them. They will have need of your knowledge and powers to protect them."

"Such powers as I possess," said the Druid gloomily.

"Finian, you are not a warrior, and I shall have little need of a bard where I am going. You also, Grainne, must go with the king."

The old woman rushed forward, her face desperate. "No, my queen, I beg you. Take me with you! I would not leave your service while I have breath. Give me one last boon: to ride with you, even to the end."

Morgana looked long at her, considering, then nodded. "So be it," she said simply. "And let us all make as valiant an end as we may, when the foe comes upon us."

"You do not believe we will win?" asked Arawn.

The queen's face was shadowed. "I do not look for victory, King. I have cut myself off from the gods, and the Fomori king's power grows. He gives the land much blood, and it rewards him." Her eyes flashed. "But I shall not fall under his sword, at least not before I have taken many of his demon-folk with me." She dismounted in a graceful swirl of gown and cloak and long-flowing hair. "One last thing: I give you Brandubh to be your steed."

Arawn looked nonplussed. "Queen Morgana—"

"You must have him. If the goddess is displeased at my failure to sacrifice, I must make amends. I cannot slay my Brandubh, but neither can I keep him." She put the reins in Arawn's hand. "Bear him, Brandubh; carry him into war against the foe. And you, Prince, if you would return good for good, then do this one thing for me: fight Tethra's minions, harry them like hounds, and leave not one living if you can."

"That," he said quietly, "I shall do with pleasure."

"I go to raise my own army. Fare you well, King Hawk."

She mounted another horse, and with her Fianna and her priestesses and several of the younger men and women she rode off through the barrens at a thundering gallop. Arawn stood gazing after her, and would not speak or move until she had passed from his sight.

They journeyed to the northeast, making better speed now that more of them had mounts, for the pagan folk had returned the villagers' ponies and other beasts to them. Thomas and Maeve rode together on Gwyn behind Dugall and Arawn. They were moving back through the hill country to the great forest, heading in the direction of Temair and the coast. The pagan folk of Morgana's Rath seemed almost bewildered at the sudden turn of events: their queen was gone, her prisoners now their protectors, and all at her command. They would not think of disobeying her, though, however great their amazement.

"Who would have thought it?" marvelled Thomas.

"She's a wonderful woman," said Maeve.

"You admire her?"

"She's strong and powerful and ambitious," declared Maeve with passion, "all the things women aren't supposed to be. I think she must be lonely, too, being the only one of fairy blood in the land. I just wish my grandmother had had a chance to know her better," said Maeve softly.

Late afternoon found them surrounded by forest as deep and dense as that surrounding the Drunemeton. The path had dwindled to the merest track, heavily grown over in places. Yet there were some signs of human habitation: footprints in the soil and here and there an arrowhead—usually of iron, though some were made of stone. Towards evening they came upon a curious sight: a tree from which all the bark had been stripped, its trunk painted in alternating rings of white and rust red. Attached to the denuded branches were many caribou antlers, as though the tree grew boughs of bone.

They all dismounted.

"What can this mean?" asked Dugall. He looked at the Druid and the queen's bard.

Finian shook his head. "It has naught to do with the old faith, that much I can swear to."

"It is not a creation of Druids," agreed Cathbad, examining the tree. "What it may mean, I cannot say."

"A warning, perhaps?" mused Dugall. "Or the sign of a holy place? There is a people who dwell deep in the woods, known to us as the Forest Folk, though the Lochlannach called them Skraelings. Little is known of them: they follow neither the old way nor the new, but have rituals and customs of their own."

"Are they friendly or not?" asked Arawn.

"I have never encountered them myself, but I have heard they are not so friendly as they once were, preferring to keep to themselves. Certainly we must proceed with care, if this is indeed their territory."

"What are these people called?" asked Maeve suddenly. "I mean, what do they call themselves?"

Dugall looked at her. "I am told they use the word 'Beothuk' for their race, but I do not know what it means."

Maeve breathed in sharply. "I know about these people! They lived in my world too, a long time ago. . . ." She remembered pendants of bone, a model canoe, arrowheads . . . and her uncle's voice, explaining. She had been taken to the Newfoundland Museum by her uncle, and he had shown her the exhibit of native artifacts. *Beothuks.*

"And these, if I mistake not," added Dugall suddenly, "are the folk themselves."

While they had stood talking, figures had materialized, slowly and silently, out of the gloom under the tree boughs. They were simply clad in loose-fitting clothing of caribou hide: tunic-like garments, trousers and heavy cloaks. Pendants of carved bone hung on thongs about their necks, their feet were shod in moccasins of caribou hide. Both their clothing and the skin of their faces and hands were daubed with the same rust-red pigment that had been used on the tree. Their teeth and the whites of their eyes seemed startlingly bright by contrast.

The men carried metre-long wooden bows, with fletched arrows at the ready and more in quivers of birch-bark on their backs. The points of the arrows were aimed directly at the villagers.

Another memory came to Maeve. "We must carry green branches—that's their peace sign!" She reached up and snapped a twig off a fir tree, holding it out with shaking hands. Arawn and the others quickly followed suit. The arrows wavered slightly.

One tall man came forward, his face stern under its strange red mask. "Why are you here?"

He spoke English!

Arawn stepped forward, green branch in hand. "Are you the chieftain of this tribe?"

"I am Longnon," the man said impassively. "You?"

"I am a chieftain also, the leader of my people. We did not mean to intrude upon your lands. I wish only to take my people to a safe place beyond the forest. Is that acceptable to you?"

The man's expression was difficult to read under its layer of red pigment. "Your kind bring trouble always. Death follows after you—killing, treachery, sickness. Go back to where you came from."

"Chief Longnon, there is no going back. This island is under invasion by the Fomori, the people of the sea. You will have heard of them. We must flee, and you also, or they will destroy us all."

The Beothuk chief considered them in silence for a long time. Then he spoke a single word: "Come." Turning away, he and his men returned to the depths of the forest.

After a moment's hesitation, the travellers followed them.

They were led to a small settlement beside a lake that was smaller than the lake of the *péist* and completely surrounded by trees. Along the shore was a cluster of tall, conical, wigwam-like dwellings made of birch-bark. Smoke wisped from openings in their tops. There were also a few square structures made of branches woven together. Canoes were drawn up on shore in neat rows. Like the wigwams, they were made of birch-bark and had a curious shape, the gunwales rising in curved peaks halfway along the hull. There were tall wooden poles surrounding the settlement like signposts; these were tipped with an array of curious symbols or totems—one had the shape of a half-moon, another that of a whale's fluked tail. Everything—wigwams, canoes, sheds, poles—was covered in more of the strange red stain.

There were many more Beothuks here, women and children as well as men. They watched with wide dark eyes, half curious and half afraid, as the large crowd of pale people approached their settlement. Some of the smaller children ran and hid behind their mothers' legs.

Presently a woman stepped forward and addressed Longnon in her native tongue. He answered her with many gestures towards the travellers. Finally, the woman—she seemed about Branwen's age—came closer to them, a look of friendly interest in her large brown-black eyes. Like all her people, she had the red clay-like substance smeared all over her face, but her fine features showed plainly through it, the high cheekbones and broad brow. Her hair was very black, and streamed freely about her shoulders.

"I am Zosweet," she said in a gentle, melodic voice, "wife of Longnon. If you are friends, you are welcome here."

Arawn returned her greeting courteously. "Lady," he said, bowing, "we would be glad of your friendship. We are two peoples, travelling together; some are the followers of the old ways and of Queen Morgana, the rest are under Gwynedd's rule. I am Arawn, newly king of Gwynedd, and it is my charge to lead them safely to Temair."

Her teeth flashed in her red face. "Ah, Gwynedd! We have heard much of your people: stories of your great stone houses and of your mighty chieftain, Arthur, who was brought here from across the sea. Guashawit, we call him; that is 'bear' in our language. For he was placed in a cave, was he not, to wake one day like the bear that wakes in spring?"

"That is so," replied Arawn, smiling.

The chief's wife returned the smile, then gestured to a tall youth standing behind her. "This is my son, Nonosabasut," said Zosweet. "It is a name of high honour among my people."

"Because of Demasduit," said Maeve.

Her eyes widened. "You know that tale? But it comes from the Shadow-world."

"I know. I'm from there too."

Longnon looked at her with astonishment, and many of the native people backed away from her. But Zosweet was smiling in delight. "From the Shadow! Now that is a wonderful thing! Few come to our world from that place. I would gladly hear more of this."

"What is this tale you spoke of?" Finian asked Maeve curiously.

"A long time ago," Maeve told them all, "some settlers of my world took Beothuk men and women captive, to teach them our language and to learn theirs. But they were taken by force and were terribly frightened. Nonosabasut was the chief of a Beothuk tribe; his wife, Demasduit, was taken, and when he heard her cries he fought the settlers, trying to free her. And he was killed."

"Yes." Longnon's voice and eyes were cold for an instant. "We tell that tale every year, with other tales of the wrongs done us by our enemies on both sides of the Shadow."

There was an awkward pause. "Why do you paint yourselves in this fashion?" Finian asked, to change the subject. "What dye is it that you use? Our warriors do something similar, but with a blue dye called woad."

Zosweet touched her red-smeared cheek. "This is red ochre. It is holy to us, for red is the colour of blood, the colour of life. Earth blood, we call it, and we gather it from cliffs and riverbanks. Our first layer of ochre is put on us when we are but newly born. Every year it is renewed, in the ochring ceremony that comes in the spring. For ten days, we have games and feasts and dancing."

"On what do your people live, if you do not farm and have no cattle?" asked a woman of the pagan folk.

"In winter we hunt the caribou, herding them into fenced-in areas that we build with wood. In spring there are seals to harpoon at sea, and later seabirds and their eggs. Now, in early summer, we depend greatly upon the salmon. But it is the caribou who sustains us through the leanest times. We dry the meat and live off it for months, and always we give thanks to the caribou."

"Why are you not camping by the coast, if you seek the salmon?" Dugall asked.

Longnon answered. "We fear the powers that are in the sea: the Fomori, as you call them. They rise from the deeps and attack our canoes, even though we do them no harm. We have been sending hunters in small groups to the coast since spring, to catch fish and seals for our people to eat, but many of those we sent never returned. The last was a band of six young warriors, one of them my brother's son. We cannot spare any more; my tribe, our whole people, is much diminished." He turned and regarded Maeve. "You say this girl, here, comes from the Shadow-world? What more can she tell us of our kindred on the other side, those whom we left behind long ago?"

Maeve swallowed. She had no wish to discuss the fate of the Beothuks in Newfoundland, but she had to answer and she could not lie. "Chief Longnon, I'm sorry, but they're all dead."

"All?" said Longnon after a breathless silence. "All dead? But how can that be?"

"They were killed, many of them, by the settlers. My father's ancestors." She could not look him in the face. "And there was disease and . . . and hunger, because they couldn't get to their hunting grounds any more. My uncle says there weren't many of them to begin with—only about a thousand—and they couldn't survive all the new threats. . . . They died out more than a hundred years ago. A woman named Shanawdithit was the last of the Beothuks. She died alone, among the white people."

"All gone," said Longnon in a flat voice. The Beothuks murmured. "We, on this side of the Shadow, are all that remain. And we are not many, either. Nor are there any doors into other worlds for *us* to escape through—only the door to the spirit world, the door of death."

"But there lies the Happy Island," said Zosweet.

"Happy Island?" repeated Maeve.

"Far from this island," said Zosweet, "there lies another: the Happy Island, we call it. We go there when we die, in the form of spirits. There is no trouble or sorrow there, only feasting and fishing and hunting. It lies where the sun sets."

"We know this western isle," said a pagan man. "We call it Tir nan Og. It is of this world, yet not of it. When one of our people dies, we bury with him tools and other things he will need there in his next life."

"We do the same," Zosweet told him.

The abbot spoke up. "We also are taught that there is another, higher realm. And that place is the highest of all, and is ruled by God and His angels. Those who obey God's laws may go there when their lives are over."

Zosweet nodded. "We believe the Happy Island is ruled by

the Good Spirit, and we must all be very good, and not be cruel or hurtful to others, if we are to go there when we die."

"Enough. Ask the wise woman what she thinks of these visitors," said Longnon abruptly.

"Wise woman?" repeated Dugall.

"That is Mammadroust," said Zosweet, pointing to an aged, leathery faced woman sitting before a wigwam. She was humming tunelessly to herself as she made a container of some kind out of a piece of birch-bark. "She is our wise woman and sees what others cannot."

"You mean she is a sorceress?" asked Cathbad. "I am a Druid of the old faith. I too commune with the spirit world."

"She is a little like you, then. She can bring healing, ward off evil with charms, consult the spirits of the ancestors. I will tell her who you are."

She spoke to the old woman in the Beothuk tongue, gesturing to Cathbad. Mammadroust looked at the Druid, then nodded her white head and smiled in gracious condescension before turning back to her work. Finian gave a little half-stifled snort of laughter, and Cathbad looked annoyed.

"I will ask Mammadroust about the Shadow-girl, and all the rest of you," Zosweet told them, and she spoke again to the wise woman.

Mammadroust glanced up at her, then put the birch-bark aside. The wizened face under its mop of whitened hair considered the strangers solemnly for a few moments. Then the old woman spoke in a thick guttural voice.

"She does not speak your tongue," explained Zosweet. "She says . . . she says that evil is coming."

"Not us?" said Maeve anxiously. "Tell her we mean no harm, Zosweet!"

"She knows," the woman replied. "She says that there is evil behind you and evil before you, but that you yourselves are good. She wishes to warn you of the danger that comes from the sea."

"The Fomori?" asked Thomas.

"Perhaps, though we have legends of another, more terrible being who dwells in the sea depths. A being who has no name, who is never seen. But this being has power over all things that dwell in the sea."

"Can she mean Domnu?" a woman asked.

"I know not that name. But not all spirits are good. Many of the ancestor spirits are cruel and vengeful, and there are others, older beings that have never known a human form and have no love for our kind. Near a lake not far off lives Aich-mud-yim, the Black Man; he appears as a short, bearded man in a robe of black beaver skin. To all those who see him he brings evil. And just as there is a Good Spirit, there is also a Bad Spirit. The Good Spirit sends us friends and allies, the bad one enemies."

"*We* come from the Good Spirit," said Thomas quickly.

"So Mammadroust seems to believe."

"Well," said Chief Longnon, "the wise woman has spoken. She has always been quick to find out any evil. But she sees none in you. So be it: you may pass on through our land."

"But Husband," said Zosweet, "it grows dark now, and they are weary. It has always been our custom to share our food with those with whom we have made peace. Shall we not do so now?"

Longnon was silent a moment, his face still stony. Then he grunted assent. "Let them remain for this one night, then. But tomorrow they must go, and take with them the evil that follows them."

That night they feasted around the fires of the settlement on fresh-caught trout from the lake and wild fowls. Stones heated in the fire were dropped into birch-bark containers filled with water, bringing it to a boil, and then the meat was added. It came out steaming hot and juicy and tender. Nothing had ever tasted so good to Maeve. Famished, she took each boiled morsel offered her as though it were her first food. The injured warrior, Seanchan, had been helped to the fire and was able to take a little food. Mammadroust was examining his leg wound with the serious look of an experienced physician.

As they sat around the fire, Maeve asked the chief's wife about the poles with their curious symbols. Zosweet explained their meanings: the semicircular one was called the *kuus*, she said, and it represented the moon. The whale's tail was the *ow-as-posh-no-un*; it was a hunting totem. Maeve then asked her about the painted tree with its antler-hung boughs.

"That is the tree of life," answered Zosweet. "It is always a birch tree, and we hang it with bones and antlers of the caribou. From the birch comes the bark with which we make our homes, our canoes, the pouches in which we carry food and the vessels in which it is boiled. The chosen tree is always near water, which is life's source. We paint it with red for the blood of the earth, white for the clouds that give rain. In its branches are caribou antlers, which are cast off and renewed each year as the leaves of the trees are renewed and as the caribou himself is renewed. For though we kill him in wintertime, each year he returns to feed and clothe us. Do you think because we kill him that we hate the caribou? We love him above all things that live. For without him, we would surely starve and die."

Near at hand, Maeve could hear Cordelia's chattering voice. She was learning Beothuk words from a native girl about her age.

"What is your word for girl?"

"*Emamooset.*"

"Salmon?"

"*Wasemook.*"

Maeve turned to Thomas, who was sitting beside her eating as eagerly as she. "I hope these people won't get in trouble for helping us," she said in a low voice.

"The Fomori make friends with no one," he replied. "I think they would be in danger no matter what they did."

"That's not very comforting."

He shrugged. "Perhaps they will come with us to Temair."

"How do you say seal?" Cordelia's voice asked behind them.

"*Bidesook.*"

"Bake-apple?"

"I do not know bake-apple."

"It's a wild berry—like a raspberry, only orangey coloured."

"Ah, *abidenashuck.*"

As night fell, the sparks of the fire spiralled up into the dark, seemed to dance among the stars. Watching them, Maeve was aware of a happiness that seemed to grow with the flames, in defiance of the danger they all faced.

"*Tine éigin*," Maeve murmured, looking at the ring of fire-lit faces. By the ruddy glow, it was hard to tell the ochred faces from the pale ones. *The need-fire.* This, then, was the origin of the hearth: it all went back to the beginning, when ancient tribespeople had gathered about their open fires, revelling in the safety of the flames that banished wild beasts and darkness. *Is that why people in my world sing and tell stories around campfires?* she wondered. *Is there a part of us that remembers?*

It was a ritual feast, this, a sharing of more than meat. They were one people tonight, pagan and Christian and Beothuk. She was only sorry that it had taken not a genuine reaching out in friendship, but the fear of a common enemy to drive them together and forge this firelit peace.

Chapter Thirteen

THE WIGWAM-LIKE STRUCTURES, or *mamateeks*, as the Beothuks called them, were surprisingly comfortable. Unlike a true wigwam, a *mamateek* was a permanent building, its birch-bark walls supported by a foundation wall made of stones. The occupants slept in hollowed-out, fur-lined depressions in the earth, while the embers of the central firepit warmed them. So many members of this community had left or died or gone missing that there was plenty of room. To the children from Morgana's realm, the circular shape of the foundations was soothingly similar to their own round houses, and the Connemara children were delighted by what to them was an unusual design. They had now forgotten their fears, and seemed to feel that they had embarked on a sort of adventure.

Maeve was offered a place in one of the *mamateeks*, but, finding the atmosphere stuffy and the children's excited whispers distracting, she chose to sleep outside with the adults. She was growing accustomed to lying on hard ground, and the banked fires gave off a comforting warmth, but sleep still eluded her for some time. Whenever she closed her eyes, she saw the swaying neck and lunging jaws of the péist.

Presently, there arose in the night a long, mournful cry. She was not alarmed at first, thinking that it was only the call of a loon out on the lake. But the wailing voice was joined by others, an eerie chorus, and she started up, her heart beating hard. The howls were coming from the direction of the barrens.

"It is not the Cwn," Dugall reassured her as he walked by, doing sentry duty. "Only wolves."

Only wolves! She sank back, listening with trepidation to the distant howls. Wolves. *Canis lupus beothucus.* Now where had those words come from? She lay still, trying to remember. The Shadow-world . . . Newfoundland. Yes. There had been a mounted wolf skin in the museum, she now recalled, with the skull displayed beneath. And a sign explaining that this was the last known specimen of the Newfoundland wolf, hunted to extinction decades earlier.

But here the wolf lived on, as the Beothuk did.

She lay gazing up at the sky. It was clear tonight, and filled with those wondrous stars. Looking straight up, with trees and tents removed from her field of vision, she could almost imagine that she was suspended in the midst of the heavens and the stars were all around her. Presently, the stars themselves were dimmed by a greater wonder. A pale light flickered above her, so quick and faint that she thought for a moment she was imagining it. It came again, brightened—and the sky burst into flame. Great tongues of fire sprang up to hide the stars. Unlike earthly flames, they were a pale fairy hue—green with edgings of blue and violet—though here and there, as they wavered and rippled, Maeve saw flowerings of gold and rose. They flared, dimmed and died, then blazed forth again to fill all the sky. She sat up, staring at them in wonder.

"You seem amazed, young Maeve," said Dugall. He and Zosweet were standing by the fire, looking at her with amusement. "Are the Fir Chlis, the Merry Dancers, not known in your world, then?"

"Yes, we call them the Northern Lights. But I've never seen them like this. They're almost . . . alive."

"So they are," he answered. "The Fir Chlis are spirits of light and air, angels who left high heaven to dance beneath the stars."

"To us they are the messengers of the Good Spirit, who sends them to watch over us," said Zosweet. "But it is the same thing. Your angel spirits are messengers, are they not?"

"True enough. It is as you have said: we believe in the same things, though we call them by different words."

Myths, Maeve thought as she lay down again. The auroras were just natural phenomena, weren't they? Solar rays colliding with the atmosphere. But perhaps that was only what they were in *her* world, that place of shells and shadows where the outward part was all. In Annwn, the inner selves of things showed more clearly—everything here was more real, more alive and aware. Who could say what the auroras were in this world?

It took Maeve some time to sink into sleep, and even when she did she got little rest. Her dreams were dark and full of the sea, of its sound and smell and the broken moonlight playing on its waves. For some reason, the images seemed filled with menace, and yet she still felt drawn towards the heaving surf. She tossed and turned, moaning softly.

When she awoke the fires were burning high again and people were gathering around them for a breakfast of fish cooked over the open flames. She rose, stretched her stiffened muscles and went down to the lakeside to splash cold water on her face.

"Did you sleep well, child?" Zosweet's voice asked behind her.

Maeve turned. The chief's wife was standing about a metre away, with the old wise woman at her side. "Quite well, thanks. I dreamed a lot, though."

"Mammadroust thought you might." Zosweet turned and spoke in the native tongue to the old woman, who nodded sagely.

"She did?"

"She had many dreams herself last night. Visions sent by the ancestors."

"Mine were just jumbled-up images. My dreams never make any sense."

Again Zosweet translated, and the old woman murmured a response. "Mammadroust says that in your world dreams may be meaningless, but here in Annwn they are sendings, messages. Here we are closer to the spirits, and they speak to us often."

Maeve could not imagine what message might be hidden in the dark, confused images her subconscious had presented. Her fear of the Fomori and their sea realm must have something to do with it. But why, then, had she felt so *drawn* to the sea?

She headed back to the settlement with the two women. Music now arose on the cool morning air: Finian was sitting on a fallen trunk, strumming on his bard's harp and singing.

Under the greenwood tree,
Who loves to lie with me,
And tune his merry note
Unto the sweet bird's throat,
Come hither, come hither, come hither;
Here shall he see
No enemy
But winter and rough weather.

"Where did you learn that song?" Cathbad demanded. "I have never heard it before."

"The tune is of my own devising; as to the words, my friend Padraig there taught me them," replied Finian. "It is a work of our old friend Shake-spear the Bard."

"*Your* friend, perhaps, but none of mine." Cathbad sniffed. "He is a fool, and knows nothing of Druids. As for you, your mood is most light for one who flees in fear of his life."

"And yours is most gloomy, for one who has escaped the battle and seeks now the safe citadel." Finian smiled.

"A citadel full of Christians."

"Would you prefer Fomori? Come, Cathbad, matters could be worse." The Druid looked unconvinced, and Finian began to sing again.

Who doth ambition shun,

And loves to lie i' the sun,

Seeking the food he eats,

And pleas'd with what he gets,

Come hither, come hither, come hither;

Here shall he see

No enemy

But winter and rough weather.

Cathbad walked away, grumbling.

"You must forgive his manner," said Finian to the others. "He loves not the mornings, for he spends all his nights in contemplation of the stars while we are getting our rest. And it seems he has read in the skies nothing that is to our favour."

Arawn turned to Chief Longnon. "I thank you for your hospitality, and now we will take our leave as we promised. I hope to make Temair by sunset."

"Nonosabasut will go with you," replied the chief unexpectedly. "He can guide you through the forest. He has asked for some time to be allowed to go and search for our missing brethren. I have now given him leave. We may need them here to help defend us from the sea demons when they come." He gestured to the youth, who was already shouldering his bow and a birch-bark quiver as though he was impatient to be gone.

Zosweet held out to Maeve the little packet of birch-bark on which the wise woman had been working. "Mammadroust wishes you to have this. It is filled with red ochre, for you. Perhaps its power will keep your safe."

Maeve thanked both women, stammering a little.

"Will you not change your minds and come to the fortress with us?" Dugall asked the chief.

"No," answered Longnon. "We will not die between walls of stone. We will fight and fall in our own land, die where we were born."

"Perhaps after all you are safer here," said Arawn, "at least for the moment. The Fomori armies are concentrating on the large cities now. But there will come a time when no one will be safe anywhere in Avalon, if Tethra has his way."

"Then perhaps we will all meet again one day, in the country of the Good Spirit," said Zosweet softly.

They set off once more, with their beasts and their baggage and their chattering children, the long-limbed Nonosabasut striding before them as a guide. A low droning sound arose from the Beothuk camp behind them. Longnon and his people had begun the rite of mourning for their lost Shadow-kin.

The forest seemed endless to the villagers, its dim spaces threatening. But they saw no Fomori and met with no dangers. Once, a pair of lean grey wolves crossed the track right in front of them, staring at the procession of people and animals with curious golden eyes. But to everyone's relief, the wolves quickly turned aside and slipped back into the trees.

Nonosabasut showed no fear of them. "I know those wolves: they are the chief of the pack and his wife."

"Wolves have chiefs?" said Dugall disbelievingly.

"And wives?" asked Branwen.

"Yes, they stay true to their mates all their lives. And each pack has a pair that lead and rule the others. Those were the

Longnon and Zosweet of the wolves." The boy smiled for the first time.

"Where is the rest of the pack?" asked Dugall nervously.

Nonosabasut merely shrugged, appearing unconcerned. But the travellers clumped closer together after that, and kept wary eyes on their goats and cattle.

Maeve walked at the front of the procession with the Beothuk boy, looking warily about her. After the incident with the *péist*, many were convinced that Maeve's second sight had saved them, and she had noticed some of the pagan villagers looking at her with awe. She had explained, in vain, that she might merely have caught sight of the creature when no one else was looking, but they insisted that she go ahead to warn the others of any dangers. She was not really unhappy about the arrangement, though it forced her to walk at a more gruelling pace than those behind. For one thing, Arawn also walked at the front, leading by its leather reins the great Sidhe horse, which he had never yet attempted to ride. He talked with her and Thomas to while away the hours, speaking always with courtesy to Maeve, as though she were royalty herself. It made her feel pleased and honoured and shy all at once, so that she hardly knew what to say to him in return.

"What is Gwynedd like?" she asked him at last. "I know it only from my grandmother's writings."

A rare smile broke over his bleak face. "Ah, Gwynedd! I would that you might see it, indeed. Perhaps someday you shall. It is a lovely land, not so wild as this, except where the sea meets the shore: there are great cliffs along the southern coast, and deep caves, and beaches with tumbled boulders. I played on those shores as a lad. At the tip of the southwestern cape, a great rock pinnacle rises from the sea: Craig yr Aderyn, it is called—the Bird Rock—for on it, the gannets make their nests. In the summer months, all the air is filled with their white flying forms and their never-ceasing cries. And on the high crag facing the rock of the birds sits Caer Wydyr, the royal palace of Gwynedd. Some say it is like Arthur's Camelot reborn, but I cannot think even Camelot was so fair. The walls and towers of its keep are as white as the birds that circle them, and the curtain-walls that surround the keep are the great wonder of this world. They were raised by the Sidhe in days long gone, and they are made not of stone but of clear crystal that glitters in the sun like glass. Four towers there are, facing the four winds; at the top of each tower there is a chamber like a cave of ice, and windows paned with finest crystal." Longing filled his voice, the first really strong emotion she had seen him show. She wondered sadly if he would live to see his home ever again.

The land slowly lost its wildness as they walked, trees giving way to barrens crossed by many rutted roads. Before long, they were passing cultivated fields and silver-trunked orchards still laden with blossoms that tossed and sang like the sea. But there was no sign of habitation in any of the farms they saw: the buildings stood empty, and they passed no other travellers on the roads. Many of the homes and outbuildings were damaged and pillaged, as the houses of Connemara had been.

"Do you see anything, Maeve?" Arawn asked her as they passed one small settlement. "Any creatures of the Sidhe?"

She gazed long and hard at the sad little collection of abandoned buildings, then shook her head. "There's nothing there." She was rather flattered that he should turn to her thus, even though it was perfectly logical for him to do so. Perhaps it was the respect, even deference, that always tinged his voice when he spoke to her. *Respect . . . from a king!* she thought, marvelling.

They feared every minute that they would encounter Fomori, or some terrible creature in their service, but no enemy was spied. Save for the occasional wildfowl flying far overhead, the land seemed utterly empty of life.

Day's end found them at Temair, ancient seat of the Gaelic kings.

Those who had never seen the city of Temair before exclaimed in wonder at its size, at the austere majesty of its buildings and at the grandeur of its natural setting. But Maeve stood silent as she contemplated it. She knew this place, though she had never been here before. She had visited it in the pages of her grandmother's book, and she also knew the land on which it lay.

Temair was a twin of the city of St. John's. She knew it at once. Though the buildings were different—the houses built of grey stone rather than brightly painted clapboard, the streets paved with granite blocks instead of asphalt—it was still, somehow, the same place her aunt and uncle had shown her. There was the harbour, and the steep-sided, hilly headlands of the Narrows, and the sheltering South Side Hills. To the left of the harbour mouth, Signal Hill reared up—only it was not Signal Hill; it was higher than its earthly counterpart, its rocks more rugged and its sloping skirts of barren lands broader. The hill she had seen in her own world was to this like the fading echo following a trumpet's blast. Atop its summit, where only the small grey shape of Cabot Tower stood in her world, there sprawled in this a mighty high-walled *dún*.

A *dún*, Arawn had told her, was the Gaelic word for any castle or fortified place. This great fortress of Temair was the largest *dún* on the island. Many acres of the hill's broad summit were enclosed within its weathered walls, and its four square towers gave a commanding view of land and sea.

The steep streets of the grey stone city were empty as they passed through—no face looked out of the dark windows as they went by, no child played on the granite flagstones. All Temair's inhabitants, it seemed, had fled to the keep. Now the travellers, too, ascended the winding road to the *dún*.

On the rolling barrens that sloped towards the hill there was a large mound surrounded by rings of earthworks, like a smaller version of Morgana's Rath. In its centre, on the mound, stood a single upright stone. "The Lia Fail," said Arawn, seeing her and Thomas look at it as they rode by, "the Stone of Destiny, brought here long ago by the Tuatha de Danaan. For the Gaels of old, that place was the centre of things, the world's pivot. There the Gaelic kings once stood at their crowning, and if the land approved its ruler, a sound of roaring went up from the stone."

She gazed at the grey stone column. The Lia Fail: here was yet another thing of which Jehane had written. This throne of the earth had raised its enchanted voice at one point in the book, and she had often wondered what that sound would be like. Thunder, perhaps? But no, she thought now. Thunder was too light and airy a sound for the Lia Fail. Its voice would be deeper, darker: a roar, like lava boiling up from a volcano's throat or an avalanche crashing through a mountain valley. Whoever stood upon that pillar of rock would feel the vibration of its voice in every bone, be bound by it to the land forevermore.

Onward and upward they rode, past stony hollows and large wind-wrinkled pools. The silence and the absence of life on the barrens were beginning to fray at everyone's nerves, when Arawn raised a great shout.

"See where the dragon flies!"

Maeve looked up sharply, fearful of seeing some winged monster swooping overhead. Instead she saw, high above the topmost tower of the keep, a long banner with a red dragon on it waving on the wind. "The sign of my house," declared Arawn in a ringing voice. "The dragon flies still!"

That glad cry put hope back into them; they hastened towards the *dún* talking eagerly among themselves. The great drawbridge was lowered for them, and they went in under the mighty gate; and here at last they found the thronging crowds and noise that the city had lost. Within the outer ward of the *dún* were many men-at-arms, all wearing coats of mail and tabards emblazoned with the red dragon. They greeted Arawn with cries of joy, for though they had heard the rumours of his survival, few had dared to hope that these were true. Soon he and Dugall were surrounded by shouting men.

There were real storybook knights among them, men clad in shining armour of polished steel.

And the women! They came flocking out of the keep, a living torrent of youth and beauty. Their gowns were of bright summer colours, lavender and yellow and rose, and they followed the fashion of the Gwynedd court. Long trains flowed from their skirts and their pointed sleeves hung nearly to the ground. As the women hastened across the pavements, their sleeves billowed out behind them like wings, giving them the look of great exotic birds or butterflies. Their lovely heads seemed poised on their graceful long necks like flowers on stems, their eyes were liquescent jewels, and their features delicate. Their long hair hung loose down their backs or was braided with silken cords. Every shade of raven and mahogany, copper and gold was flaunted before Maeve, and she was suddenly conscious of her own drab, short locks.

Nonosabasut had seen several Beothuks among the men and he now ran to them, calling out their names. The rest of the weary travellers proceeded to the central keep, where the families of the city now sheltered. Branwen and Padraig began to set up their own little corner in one of the great halls, putting down blankets and folded cloaks on the flagstone floor. But Thomas quickly slipped away to watch the knights. Maeve, too, wandered off on her own.

She knew what she was seeking, though not where it lay. Many great stone rooms she passed through, some hung with colossal tapestries depicting adventures in olden times. One was designed for banquets, with huge oaken tables and a minstrels' gallery at one end. Another, with great racks of spears and swords and maces hanging on the walls, was plainly the armoury.

At last she found the long hall with the cavernous fireplaces and the bright banners hanging from lofty beams—the hall that she had never seen, never been to except in the pages of a book. She knew it at once, and stood in silence before the dais on which the two carved oaken thrones still sat.

Above her in the dim space beneath the vaulted roof hung the banners of a dozen noble houses: there the stars, moon and sun blazed, surrounded by heraldic rays; there lions, stags, unicorns and griffins motionlessly ramped. But she barely noticed them, because the tapestry on the wall behind the thrones held her attention. It was not the hunting scene that the book had described, but a new one, woven since her grandmother's time. It showed Gwenlian and Diarmait holding court in this very throne room while rays of light descended on them from above. The figures were very stylized, like those in a medieval painting, but she knew Gwenlian at once by her long golden hair. And that could only be Diarmait, so tall and dark and princely. Maeve's eyes searched to and fro among the other stiff figures around the throne, looking for the one that represented Jehane. That must be she, the woman in the blue gown with shoulder-length hair. She stood to the left of the throne with her arms crossed and her face uplifted.

Grandma, she thought in sudden longing. She had been here, Grandma-Jean-Jehane, stood perhaps in the very spot where Maeve was standing. Not until now had Maeve felt the tugging at her heart that was the yearning for home, for family. There was a bittersweet comfort in knowing Grandma, too, had been here, long ago.

There was a large oaken chest below the tapestry and between the two thrones. It was exquisitely carved, with braided knotwork and stylized serpents whose mazy coils made their own intricate patterns. Maeve approached it with reverence, knowing what must lie within. Still, she caught her breath as she raised the lid, contemplating the object inside.

It was a sword—a sword of extraordinary beauty, its hilt and crosspiece patterned with interlacing ribbons of silver and studded with precious gems. She did not touch it, but merely gazed on it reverently. The decorations had been added to it later, she knew: the original weapon had been a simple thing of bare and gleaming steel when its first owner wielded it. *The* sword, wielded by Diarmait himself and by many a king before him going back to the dawn of the worlds. It was *Fragarach*, the Answerer, called also the Sword of Nuada. No mortal hand had made this blade; it had come from the forges of the Sidhe. The sword had been left here, no doubt, to be near the crowning-stone of the kings: a ritual object only, its great work done in the battle of Avalon nearly sixty years ago. But a new danger had arisen to threaten the isle, and the sword was now Arawn's to wield.

She closed the lid on it, and quietly left the hall.

Chapter Fourteen

IN THE CORRIDOR, MAEVE MET WITH A BEVY of court ladies in flower-coloured gowns who said that they had been sent to find her. Laughing and chattering, they swept her up with them and took her to a chamber high in the keep where a bath and new garments awaited her. The gown they chose for her was amber-coloured with trimmings of bright gold, and when she was dressed, they held a little mirror before her so that she might see herself.

She caught her breath. Never before had she been taken unawares by her own face, regarding it in the instant of surprise as though it were a stranger's. How often had she gazed in a mirror and wondered, *Is this really me, this face? Is this what I am?* Now she asked the same question, but for another reason. The girl in the glass was not the Maeve she knew. There was something subtly different about her, something new. She turned her head from side to side in puzzlement. The face was thinner, but that was only to be expected after living on frugal traveller's fare. The cheekbones looked sharper, and the cheeks beneath now had a flush of colour in them. The newly washed hair framed the face with softness, and the light glancing through the layer of outer hairs gave her head an aureole. The green in her eyes showed more in that light, and their expression was brighter, keener. But she saw many other things that she had never noticed before: the warmth and sensitivity in those eyes, the hints of humour and generosity in the folds of flesh that framed her mouth, the stubborn strength in the bones that supported the face.

When the ladies were through with their preparations, they led Maeve downstairs again and took her to the throne room. It was filled with people now, and Arawn and Dugall were there, seated in the two thrones. They too had been transformed: they were king and thane, clad in the rich and splendid garments of their offices. She could not take her eyes off Arawn. A mantle of royal blue hung about his shoulders and the red royal dragon of his house ramped across the front of his golden tabard. On his dark hair was a heavy circlet of gold, and on his hand gleamed the royal signet ring. Yet these trappings seemed to her but the outward expression of Arawn, of the all things that she had come to see in him: courage and courtesy, and steadfastness in the face of despair.

He smiled when he saw her, and beckoned to her to approach.

She was led up to the dais. Arawn took her hand and held it high, and proclaimed to all the gathered court who and what she was. And the people bowed—to her, to Maeve. Her cheeks burned with self-consciousness. *Because of Grandma,* she thought, and she seemed to feel behind her the woven image in the tapestry, as though it were a watching and living presence.

Then Arawn motioned to the other throne. Dugall, grinning, had vacated it. They could not mean her to sit *there*! But they did; their strong and gentle hands guided her to it, and she took her seat on the velvet cushion and clutched at the carved armrests. She could not meet all those eyes before her, so she looked instead at Arawn, and listened as he spoke to them of the fears and trials they had all experienced and the danger that was yet to come.

When at last Arawn was done speaking, and the people had begun to file silently out the great doors, Finian remarked flippantly, "We have here monk and Druid, old way and new. It seems to me that the Fomori have little hope, for we have many gods to their one."

"Do not blaspheme," growled Cathbad. "And do not underestimate the power of hate. It is like a raging fire, consuming all it touches; the more it feeds, the greater is its hunger."

One of the court ladies offered Maeve a chamber of her own, but she chose to stay with the Ryans in the great hall. The people of the keep offered what comforts they could to the refugees, and as the fortress had been designed and stocked to accommodate all the townsfolk in times of war, they did not suffer greatly. The worst part, Maeve decided, was the waiting. A week passed by under leaden skies, and still there was no news, no end to the gnawing anxiety. Time weighed on them, as heavy as the stifling air of the keep. Yet they did not give in to despair. Their king's strength and resolve had inspired them, the walls of the *dún* were a constant protection and there is always comfort in company. Maeve started once at the sound of a woman's laugh echoing through the stone hall: it was as though a bird sang in the dead of winter.

The fortress had become their world—a world of stone corridors and stairs, of high-roofed halls and paved courtyards, all bounded by the great grey curtain-walls. Cordelia joined a group of wild-haired, ragged children and ran about with them, shrieking and laughing as her mother looked askance.

"Let her play," said Padraig softly to Branwen, "while she can. We do not know what the future holds, for her or any of us."

Terrible stories were being told among the refugees, accounts of Fomori attacks and other horrors. There were invisible monsters that stalked the land, and one had no warning of their coming unless one saw their tracks appearing in the soil, or cattle suddenly sprouting deadly wounds and falling to the ground. The Fomori themselves had been glimpsed only in the distance.

"Horrible creatures they are," said one man, shuddering visibly as he spoke. "They are not human, but a sort of devil, vile and monstrous."

"Those we saw had the appearance of common men," Padraig told him.

"They can have any appearance they choose," replied the other. "The old tales say that they can alter their forms, wear the heads of horses or goats. Nay, do not laugh! That may sound amusing to you, but imagine such a creature approaching you in the light of day: a man from the shoulders down, but with a beast's inhuman visage staring at you. The sight would frighten a man mad."

This time they all shuddered.

"But what have we done to the Fomori to have them hate us so?" one woman asked despairingly.

Hate is like a raging fire, Maeve thought, remembering Cathbad's words. Memories came back to her from the Shadow-world: Lisa Smith and her friends, their taunts and sneers and the glinting malice in their eyes. Who could explain that? And had she herself been immune to that rage? Another memory rose before her, one from which she recoiled in shame.

Ashley Robinson . . . she was as lovely as any lady of Temair. Her eyes were a deep, clear blue and her skin fair with a peach-pink blush on the cheeks; her hair was as smooth as silk and the colour of ripe wheat, and always it fell neatly about her shoulders without so much as a straying strand. Whenever one saw her, she was laughing and smiling in the carefree way of one to whom everything in life comes easily. She was smiling now as she walked towards Maeve.

"Oh, Maeve! No, wait, I have something to tell you."

Ashley's voice . . . Ashley's blonde head coming towards her through the crowds around the lockers. Maeve closed her eyes against the memory, but against the darkness of her eyelids it only showed more vividly.

"Look, Maeve," the girl's voice was gentle, soothing. There was no mockery or unkindness in it. "I know *just* how you feel. You must be disappointed about the play. Don't feel bad about it, okay?" Ashley hesitated, then laid a hand on

Maeve's shoulder. "You know what? I bet someday you'll find something you really *are* good at. You just wait and see."

Maeve recalled that speech with a new clarity: the kindly tone of it, the encouragement. *She didn't mean to be patronizing. She really thought she was helping me.* So said Maeve now, to herself. But the Maeve in that time had shaken the other girl's hand off, turned on her in fury. Had spat out words of rage, contempt and . . . venom, she thought, recalling them with a wince. Had told Ashley what she thought of her and her rich, set-buying father. Had watched in savage exultation as a red flush crept over the girl's face and the beautiful blue eyes dropped in confusion.

Lisa and her gang were the mean ones, the cruel ones. But I saved the worst of my hate for the one person who'd never meant me any harm, she thought miserably. Oh, yes, she too had felt that consuming fire. Its power could not be denied.

Thomas too was deeply unhappy, though for a different reason, and he cared little who knew it.

"Why can't I take part in the battle, Father?" he was arguing now. "You always make me stay with the women and children! Arawn asked for every able-bodied man to take up arms. Nonosabasut is my age, and he will be fighting! *His* people consider him a man!"

"His people are different," Padraig replied. "And he will not be fighting in the field, but will be up on the battlements with the archers." Since they could not leave the *dún*, several of the Beothuk hunters had offered their archery skills in its defence.

"You have no skill in fighting, Thomas," Branwen told her son.

"Neither has Father! He's fought only on the stage."

"I've fought with my fists on occasion," his father remarked. "In my younger days, to be sure, but now I have even more weight to use against an adversary."

Thomas flushed. "And I am a weakling, is that what you mean?"

"Son, Son!" Padraig put his big hands on the boy's shoulders. "You look for insults where there are none. If I go out on the field, who will care for your mother and Cordelia and young Maeve? You must be the man of the family while I am gone."

Thomas looked sullenly at the floor and made no reply.

The Fomori advanced on the *dún* the following day.

For those sheltering in the inner keep, there was a sense of unreality. Cut off from the outside world by castle and curtain-walls, they had to rely on what reports they could get from the pages who ran to and fro in the corridors, carrying news to the king and his councillors. After a sleepless night, they learned that Arawn and his troops were riding out to defend the castle that day. Rather than await a lengthy siege, they would seek to reduce the enemy's numbers as much as possible.

Many of the men from the surrounding farms and villages offered their services as foot soldiers. Padraig was one of these. Branwen wept quietly and embraced him, but made no effort to stop him from going. Maeve could not bear to look at her face as he left with the rest of the men for the outer ward.

She and Tom followed, and stood in the outer ward watching as the men were given pikes and shirts of mail.

Padraig raised his weapon and gave it a hearty swing. "*O Dhia!*" he shouted. "*Gach an cathair!*"

"What does that mean?" Maeve asked Thomas. "Is it Gaelic?"

"Aye." The boy's eyes held a fierce light she had not seen before. "It is the old battle-cry of the O'Connors."

Not far away, Dugall was arguing with Arawn, who had chosen Brandubh for his warhorse. "You're never going to ride that black beast of hers! It looks like a kelpie. Most likely it will carry you away across the country and drown you in a loch!"

Arawn just smiled as he gathered the reins and pressed his spurs lightly against the glossy black flanks. Brandubh snorted and rolled his eyes a little, but he obeyed the king's command and trotted to the front of the assembling army.

Thomas sidled up to Maeve, whispering in her ear. "Now is our chance! Let us go to the curtain-walls quickly, before they see us and send us back inside. If we cannot fight, we can at least watch."

Maeve was not at all sure that she wanted to see a battle, but the suspense of waiting in the keep seemed worse. At least they would know how their side was faring. As the knights and soldiers moved into formation, Maeve and Thomas headed for the arched entrance of one of the towers. Climbing the tight coils of the spiral stair within, they found an unoccupied arrow-slit and stationed themselves by it, taking turns looking through the narrow rectangular opening. They heard the rumble of the drawbridge, then the clatter of hoofs and booted feet as the army moved out onto the hillside.

"Can you see my father?" Thomas asked Maeve as she stood peering anxiously out the slit. She looked around for Padraig's big blond head, but there were so many figures out on the field now, all riding or running to and fro, all dressed in the same heavy mail shirts. Where was the king? She scanned the ranks of men and finally spotted the dragon standard streaming high above the helmeted heads. Arawn himself was indistinguishable at this distance from his men, but she saw the arched black neck and proud head of Brandubh. The stallion was prancing and pulling at the bit— upset at having to carry someone other than Morgana, or just overeager to go into battle?

The ranks of the Fomori, by contrast, were nearly motionless. They might have been rows of statues, and even their horses were oddly still. She could see Tethra sitting on his horse beneath the Fomori banner of a green *péist*—his black beard and bone-white face were unmistakeable. Many guards surrounded him, though there was something wrong with the shapes of their heads: their helmets seemed to have large horns and snout-like projections. Or *were* they wearing helmets? A chill went rippling down Maeve's spine.

"Nothing's happening," she told Thomas as she relinquished the arrow-slit to him. "They're just waiting."

"I should be out there," he complained under his breath as he stared out the slit.

She looked at his lean young body, crouched tensely at the slit. *What was it about men and fighting?* she wondered. *How could they be so unafraid of violence?* Great-uncle Andrew had been the same, no doubt—going off on the convoy because it was the thing to do. Had he ever felt any fear? Or was that only at the end, when the enemy came up out of the dark sea beneath and the ship shattered all around him? She couldn't even bear to think of it, or of those spears and swords out there on the battlefield.

"The king and Tethra are exchanging challenges, I think. All the weapons on both sides are out now. King Arawn has unsheathed Fragarach and is pointing it towards Tethra. They're lining up . . . they're charging!"

"Let me see," said Maeve in agony.

He hesitated. "Perhaps, after all, it is not a good thing for a girl to—"

"Let me *see*." She practically shoved him aside in her anxiety. The fragmentary view offered by the arrow-slit was frustrating, but she glimpsed, above the roiling mass of bodies, the dust clouds and the blades that flashed sporadically like lightning, the royal standard still aloft. The shouts and the clashing of steel sounded faint and far away. Still the Fomori came on. Their rising was relentless, like the rising of the sea.

Then she gasped. Leaping through the mêlée were pale, lithe forms, swift and deadly. White hounds. As she watched, men and horses stumbled, torn by the savage teeth. Why didn't they fight back? They just stood there, letting the *Cwn* leap on them. . . .

She reeled away from the slit, sickened and in shock. Thomas immediately took her place.

"What is the matter with our men?" he asked, frustrated. "They are all just running to and fro, and falling off their mounts—"

"It's the hounds," Maeve told him.

"What hounds?"

She stared at him. "Oh, no," she gasped.

And then she was sprinting frantically up the stone staircase, up to the battlements.

Of course! The invisible monsters the country folk had spoken of! They were the *Cwn Annwn*! Why hadn't she thought of that? They were fairy creatures and therefore invisible to the men. Only she, with her second-sighted eyes, could detect them. Arawn's men hadn't a chance.

Up on the crenellated rampart, the archers were all at the ready, waiting tensely for a foe to come within arrow range. They did not notice Maeve as she dashed up behind them, staring at the scene below.

The battle was spread out before her now in all its savage fury. Total chaos reigned: prone men and horses were scattered on the barrens; other men and horses stumbled over them and fell. The Fomori king had barely moved from his position. He was just watching, calmly and coolly, as his enemies were thrown into confusion and slain one by one. She looked for Arawn in terror and saw that he was as helpless as the rest, unable to see the five hounds that were now moving in to surround him.

But Brandubh could see the *Cwn*. The big stallion reared up and then leaped sideways, kicking out with his hind legs. A hound springing at Arawn's back was knocked to one side and fell to earth. A real dog would have been killed; as it was, the stallion was well away before the hound had regained its feet.

Maeve wanted to cheer, but she knew the king was not out of danger yet. The four other hounds were in hot pursuit.

"Listen to me," she cried, tugging at an archer's mailed sleeve. He turned to stare at her in astonishment. "The *Cwn Annwn* are down there . . . the fairy hounds. I'm the only one who can see them!"

All the archers were staring. "Please!" she begged them. Out on the barrens a horse screamed, a hound hanging from its throat. The knight was still looking around in bewilderment when his mount staggered and fell, pinning him under its body.

She saw Nonosabasut standing at the far end of the battlements and ran towards him. "The hounds! There are creatures down there, spirit creatures only I can see, and they're attacking our side. What can I do? I can't use a bow myself."

The Beothuk boy eyed her calmly. "I can," he replied. "Show me where these creatures are and I will shoot."

"*Could* an arrow hurt them, though? They're fairy hounds, not real animals."

He reached out, tapped his arrowhead. "My shafts are tipped with *monazeemit*, what you call iron. Your people say that the fairy spirits love not that metal. Show me, and I will shoot."

She looked at him desperately, then turned back to the battle. "There!" she cried, pointing. "There's one just below us. It's crouching over that man, worrying him." The pikeman had one arm up, trying to fend off the unseen fangs. "Go on, shoot! You won't hit him—the hound's between him and us. Aim as though you were going to hit his chest."

Nonosabasut hesitated only a fraction of a second. The bowstring twanged, the arrow hissed down and struck the white hound between its shoulder blades. The unearthly creature sprang up off its victim, howling with rage. For an instant, the red eyes seemed to stare straight up at Maeve. Then its body faded, began to dissolve into vapour. The arrow dropped to the ground as the hound shape turned to wisps of formless white that poured away into the ground like water.

"You did it! Oh, you destroyed it!" Maeve shrieked.

Nonosabasut remained coolly focused. "Show me another," he said, fitting a second arrow to his string.

"There, I see one standing by the . . . oh no, too late, it's running now. There's another, snapping at the heels of that brown horse, just there." Maeve pointed, then dropped her arm and groaned. "It's no use. There are so many of them, and they move so fast—"

Suddenly, one of the archers gave an exclamation and pointed. Everyone looked across the barrens. A huge fog bank was descending on the field in a moving white wall, but at more than twice the normal speed—and it came not from the sea but from inland. Maeve's heart sank. What new Fomori sorcery was this? The mist billowed up the hillside and then broke against it like a tremendous wave. There was a din like the baying and bellowing of thousands of huge beasts, and out of the cloudy depths shapes came hurtling: chariots of wickerwork, each with a spear-wielding warrior beside the charioteer. Some of the warriors were men, some women. On their heads were helms of beaten copper or bronze, but they wore no other armour, only sleeveless deerskin tunics that left their arms free. Their faces and their bared arms were patterned with jagged lines and whorls of woad. The bellowing noise that accompanied the charge came from the gaping mouths of curious, trumpet-like instruments with tall vertical necks of bronze that ended in stylized animal heads. Men ran to and fro, blowing mightily through these horns. There were tongue-like clappers in the bronze mouths that made a clanging sound. No doubt the noise was intended to startle and confuse the foe.

"Morgana! It's Morgana!" cried Maeve.

"The sorceress-queen!" shouted an archer. "She has thrown in her lot with Tethra after all."

Maeve shook her head vehemently. "No, no! She's come to help us!"

The queen rode in a chariot at the head of her mist-shrouded army. She stood tall beside her driver, her hair bound back for war in a long black braid, a helm of beaten copper with spikes like jutting horns upon her head. In her hand was a spear whose tip gleamed like gold. The two fierce, rough-coated ponies drawing her chariot were galloping with all their might, foaming at their mouths and rolling their eyes, but the charioteer controlled them expertly. They were heading directly for Arawn.

"The king!" the archer yelled. "She is going to slay the king!"

Arawn was once more surrounded by *Cwn*, the spectral hounds snapping at Brandubh's flanks as the horse spun and reared. The spear leaped from Morgana's hand, its tip flashing like flame: through the air it soared, swifter than thought, then arcing down it passed right through the body of a hound. The beast instantly wisped away to nothingness, and the other *Cwn* recoiled snarling. Brandubh seemed to recognize his mistress: his head jerked up and down on its long glossy neck, the white star upon his forehead blazing beneath the sun. Morgana sprang down from her chariot and drew a sword, running fearlessly into the fray. Some Fomori warriors who had been stooping over the fallen spear gave way before her fury. Other chariots were also halting to let their warriors leap out onto the field. Maeve could hear the wild war howls from here, rising amid the rattling blasts of the animal-headed trumpets. The charioteers, meanwhile, swiftly drove their teams this way and that, watching the progress of their warriors, swooping down to carry them off if they were outnumbered, depositing them again in another part of the field.

So sudden and savage was the onslaught that both Tethra's and Arawn's armies seemed disoriented by it. Maeve saw the king of Avalon trying to gather his troops together, riding Brandubh to and fro before them and shouting. As Morgana swept by in her chariot, her spear once more at the ready, the black stallion turned to run at her side. Arawn seemed to be shouting something to the queen, then he turned and waved his arm to his men. Armed knights and charioteers merged behind them like two rivers flowing into one. With a mighty roar, they charged the Fomori ranks.

Many of the foe did not wait to meet them; others were cut down. Tethra had vanished. The *Cwn* were still on the field, but they now ran willy-nilly, as dogs will do when separated from the master who commands them. The Fomori were defeated.

Once the drawbridge had closed safely behind them, the two armies gathered in the *dún*'s outer ward. Maeve and Thomas ran out of the tower to watch as the weary fighters streamed past. Padraig was there, to their relief. Arawn's councillors, who had emerged from the keep to greet their ruler, stood transfixed at the sight of the Sidhe queen.

Morgana still held the great spear, which she'd retrieved from the battlefield. Its shaft stood upright in her hand, as tall as a sapling, and she had wiped the gore from its golden head. "Aye," said Morgana, seeing them look at it, "it is *the* spear, the same that once was Lugh's. My people found and kept it and watched over it these long years, hoping that I might yet take it up against you. But all that is past. Now it will fight the Fomori."

"Your Majesty, this sorceress—" began the oldest councillor, but Arawn cut him short.

"The queen is our friend and ally. I have told you how she released us, out in the wild. Now, in our need, she has come to give us aid. We must repay her with our hospitality." He swung himself off the black horse's back as Morgana set down the spear and approached him.

"We meet again, Hawk," she greeted him.

He bent low over her outstretched hand. "And well met, indeed. How went the battle in the wilderness?"

"Not well." Her face clouded, and she turned to stroke the horse's neck. "Ah, Brandubh, my war raven. I would that you had been there! King Arawn, you see before you the only survivors of my secret army. Tethra sent a great force against us. A third at least of our company was lost." She shook her head sadly, the great cable of hair swaying to and fro. "And Grainne is dead."

"My sorrow to hear it."

"She *would* be my charioteer—it was ever our custom that

driver and warrior be close companions, and she deserved the honour. But it was too much for her. Her strength soon failed her, and she was slain by a Fomori arrow in the first of our frays."

"Then she had her wish: to fight and die in battle," said the king gently. "You shall have shelter within my walls," he added, "and I will see that you are provided with chambers and anything else you may need. And if we are attacked again, I would gladly join forces with you once more."

She nodded, met his gaze. "Tethra did not send his full force against you, so sure was he of victory. He will return ere long with a greater army, and leave naught to chance. Our only hope now is in each other's strength."

He removed his helmet and put a gauntleted hand to his sweat-sheened brow. "Forgive me, Queen, but I am very weary and would rest now."

Thomas was looking all around him. "Your Majesty! I don't see the thane of Dalriada. Where is Dugall?"

Arawn made no reply.

Chapter Fifteen

DUGALL WAS DEAD. That strong, robust, vital young man—gone forever. Maeve could not believe it, still half-expected to see his red-curled head somewhere amid the crowds in the castle corridors, hear his deep powerful voice cut through the clamour. If a man like Dugall could die, what hope could there be for any of them?

"Poor, poor Arawn!" she mourned as she sat with Thomas that evening in the large hall. "I'm almost more sorry for him than for Dugall. He's lost *everyone* he cares about: his family, his best friend. How can he stand it? I guess he feels he has to be strong for the rest of us."

Thomas looked at her with an odd expression in his eyes. "You love him, don't you?"

"Prince Arawn?" Maeve was taken aback by the question. She sat for minute thinking of Arawn's strength and determination, his bravery on the field of battle, the odd little flutter she felt whenever he called her "lady." And he was certainly handsome. But Maeve never let herself think too much of handsomeness. At school, she remembered, good-looking boys had been the unquestioned property of girls like Ashley Robinson, who accepted their attentions with laughing grace. As for Maeve, the boys only liked to torment her. Back in grade school, they used to come up to her and say, "Hey Maeve, I think you're pretty . . ."—a pause—". . .*ugly*!" And they'd run off with squeals of laughter. They said even worse things now, when no teachers were around to hear. Maeve sometimes had stolen glances at attractive boys in class, but she never dared be open with her admiration, knowing the taunts that would follow. She had learned to dismiss handsomeness from her mind. And the young king was even further outside her sphere than these—beyond even the thought of love or yearning.

"Well, I admire him," she began. "But of course I'd never presume—"

"No, you shouldn't." Thomas looked disapproving. "He is the *king*, Maeve."

Why was he being so testy with her? He must know she could never dream of marrying royalty! *King Arawn and Queen Maeve?* He could see for himself how ridiculous that was. Could he really think her foolish enough to believe she had any sort of chance with a titled, older man? And what did any of this matter, anyway? Thomas was probably still just annoyed about not being allowed to fight, and was taking it out on her because she happened to be near.

She got up and left the boy to his brooding. What she needed, she thought, was a little fresh air—it was so stifling in here with all these people crowded together. She could not leave the keep, of course, but perhaps she could go to the top of one of the towers, feel the cold, bracing wind off the sea. She had put on her jeans and shirt again, wanting to feel reconnected to her other life—that safe and sheltered existence in the Shadow-world—but the cardigan would not be warm enough, so she took up the short cloak Branwen had given her.

She met no one on the winding stair of the seaward tower. When she pushed the wooden trapdoor open and stepped up onto the roof, the wind nearly drove her back down again, so cold and powerful was it. A crescent moon shone above, and the sea was jewelled with light. Here and there a white floe drifted on the waves, and one huge iceberg, jagged and many-towered, had come to rest near the harbour mouth. It lay there like some white-walled fortress, vast and menacing. She could feel the chill of it from here.

She saw the dark forms of sentries patrolling the walls below, and a lone figure standing in the inner ward of the keep. In his arms was something that he cradled gently, as one holds an infant. The light of the moon and stars shone on his elegant clothing, the tabard and matching hose. Arawn. He shifted the bundle in his hands, put it to his shoulder: a set of bagpipes. The ones that had belonged to Dugall, perhaps? A wail arose from the pipes that fanned beside his head; it was high and piercing and strong, yet despairing too.

She stood there alone, listening sadly to the dirge as it echoed from the high stone walls. The sorrow in it was almost more than she could bear, yet she could not tear herself away. The music filled the ward, echoed off the high stone walls, filled the star-strewn sky. Then, with the same abruptness with which it had begun, it ceased. Yet it still seemed to fill her ears. In the sounding silence, she stood as motionless as the man in the court below her, as though bound fast by his grief.

Presently there were soft steps behind her, breaking the spell. She turned, expecting to see a sentry who would tell her to get below. But it was Morgana who stood there.

The queen had changed from her deerskin charioteer's tunic to a long, loose gown, and had a square cloak wrapped about her shoulders. Her hair, unbound now, streamed over it, waving in the wind like a long, black banner. The torque of twisted gold gleamed at her throat.

"What do you here, Shadow-child?" Morgana asked. "No, do not go! We will watch the night sky together a while."

Auroras spun and ribboned across the northern sky, but even their green dance was ghostly and subdued. Maeve remembered Dugall telling her about the Merry Dancers, and tears came to her eyes.

"You spoke to me, child, of love between gods and mortals," the queen said. "Of a bond that goes beyond ritual and sacrifice, that is more like the tenderness a mother feels for her child. Such a love had the goddess Dana for my ancestors, and they for her. They named themselves after her: the *Tuatha de Danaan*, Dana's People. But we cannot seek her aid now. When my people began to dwindle from the earth she forsook it, returning to the heavens: see where she sits amid the stars." Morgana pointed to a constellation. "That is the celestial court of the goddess Dana. The Cymri call it *Llys Don*."

Maeve gazed skyward. A fleeting recollection came to

her—of looking up at the night skies on warm summer nights with her brother. She had not been able to recall Brandon's face for many days, but now, looking up at the sky, she remembered the summer stars.

"In my world," she told the queen, "we call that constellation Cassiopeia."

"I know not that name, but perhaps in your world the gods are different."

"I think Cassiopeia was a queen, actually." Maeve tried to remember what Brandon had told her. "I . . . I'm not sure. It all seems so long ago."

Morgana pointed upward. "You see that circle of stars, child? Does it too shine in the skies of your world?"

"Yes. . . . Yes, I remember. We call it the Northern Crown."

"Here it is Caer Arianrhod, the dwelling place of the great goddess Arianrhod. She, too, has gone back to her bright home in the heavens. And there, above the stars, that great span of light across the sky—"

"The Milky Way."

"To us, it is Caer Gwydion. . . ." Morgana's voice trailed away into silence, then she sighed and spoke as if to herself. "Ah, it is no use! I cannot read the stars tonight: the Shining Ones keep their counsels." A gust of wind blew her cloak and hair out behind her. "How bitter is this wind! It is like the breath of the *Cailleach Bheur* herself." She looked at the massive iceberg, her expression bleak. "It does not bode well that the sea ice should linger so, or that the winds of summer be cold. I think that in this strife, she serves Domnu. It is said, after all, that the *Cailleach Bheur* takes the form of a sea monster at times, and lives in the deeps like Domnu the Dark."

"Everything's gone wrong," said Maeve, frightened. "In your world and mine. Back home, all the fish are gone and there's no work and people don't know what to do."

"Your world is Annwn's mirror. What happens here will be reflected in some way in your own place."

"And the Fomori will be back." Maeve looked back over the barrens, beyond the keep and curtain-walls. She could not look at the dark, motionless shapes still strewn upon it.

Morgana saw her expression. "Fear not, child," the queen said softly. "The dead do no harm. The soul, the essence and the pith of them, is not here but in Tir nan Og."

"The Happy Island," Maeve whispered, remembering the Beothuks. "But where is it, Majesty?"

"Tir nan Og lies where the sun sleeps at day's end, far in the west of the world. But even could we travel there, we would see but an island like other islands. Its beauty and its wonders are only for those who have known death." Morgana looked westward, the long tendrils of her hair playing about her face. "You have been told that your world is a shadow of ours, and it is so. But there is yet another world, to which Annwn herself is but a shade. Three worlds there are, and the one that lies above this is too subtle for our eyes to see. Even you and I, gifted as we are with the second sight, may not look upon that place."

Maeve was silent.

"It is said that there was a cauldron once that raised the dead to life," the queen continued, "but raised them mute. This, the bards say, was because the reborn dead were not permitted to speak of what they had seen in that other world. But I think it more likely that they *could* not speak of it, that words are weak vessels and there are things that speech cannot express. It is so with those of your world who return from Annwn, is it not? Speech fails them utterly when they seek to describe it and ere long they forget, save for a few great poets who can find the words. But as for that other world, we shall all know it one day. . . . Yes, even I. Long-lived I may be, but I shall not live forever. That which is mortal in me ties me to time and chance."

Farther down the hillside, the Lia Fail showed as a dim grey shape atop its mound; from this height, Maeve could clearly see the concentric ring pattern formed by the earthworks around it. The pole star gleamed high above, the centre of the circling sky. It was as if star and stone shared a common axis, as if this was the heart and the hub of things.

"You feel it," said Morgana, watching Maeve's face.

"What is it?"

"It is the great magic, the power that binds all things to itself. Perhaps that is what those Christians mean when they speak of one god. I do not know. But I feel a power in this place that is sovereign to all others in Avalon."

"The Lia Fail—it was one of only four ancient treasures, wasn't it?"

"Aye. Four treasures were brought to this isle by the Tuatha de Danaan in days of old: the Sword of Nuada, which came from a city called Findias; my spear, which was made for the god Lugh in the city of Gorias; the Stone of Destiny, which stood first in the city of Falias; and the Graal, which was kept in the city of Murias. Of all the treasures, this last was the greatest. "*Graal*" means serving dish, but some say it was a cauldron, and others a cup. The Christian monks call it the Vessel of the Sacred Blood and say that it belonged to their Christian god. It may be that, being magical, the Graal took different forms in different times. For in it was the power of creation and rebirth, the very essence of life." In the moonlight, the shifting hue of her eyes had become a fathomless grey-green, like the surface of the sea. "So great a power! Tethra could never stand against it. But it lies beyond our grasp: the Sidhe hid it well. Some say it rests now on an island, guarded by fairy maidens; others that it sits in a temple atop a hill surrounded by water. But no one can say for certain which tale is true."

They were both silent for a time. Presently, Maeve summoned her courage to ask, "How did you come here to Avalon, Your Majesty?"

"I was born in this place. My mother was of the Sidhe, my father the Druid Morfessa, who was descended from Morgan le Fay. On his side too were many merrow women, or so it was said. And so my name has two meanings: I am the descendant of Morgan and of the sea folk. For the merrows are called *morgans* by some."

"*Morgans*," said Maeve slowly. "There were people in my family called Morgan too. It all comes back to the sea," she murmured, turning to stare at the moon-jewelled waves. Her sea dream came back to her, as vivid as though she had just awakened from it. She told Morgana of it.

"I think you were meant to come here, Shadow-child," said the queen.

"But why?" she asked. "What is it that I'm supposed to do?"

"That you must learn for yourself, I think. It was your sending."

Maeve thought of Old Ned, and of what he had said of the sea. There were terrors in it, and wonders: beasts large enough to swallow boats, undersea lands with cities and towers and bells that hung tolling in the tide . . .

"Majesty, do you know about the country in the sea?" asked Maeve.

Morgana too gazed on the heaving surf. "You speak of Tir fo Thuinn, the Land Beneath the Wave. It is a fairy realm that lies under many fathoms of sea. No mortal can go there and live. Even I cannot."

"Is it the Fomori's country, or the merrows'?"

"That I do not know. Why so many questions, young one?"

Maeve struggled to explain. "It's a . . . puzzle. Something I must solve. The dream was a clue, I think. This undersea fairy country . . . what did you call it?"

"Tir fo Thuinn."

"It's connected to everything happening here. The Fomori, you . . . and me too. Somehow." She stared at the shifting patterns in the foam far below. "Why would anyone live beneath the sea? It's dark, cold. Not a place for people."

"Not for mortals, perhaps. The fairy folk are different."

"But some of the Daoine Sidhe are descended from the Tuatha de Danaan, aren't they? So they have some human blood. My grandmother wrote that they went into the sea, into bays and coves, to live after ordinary mortals started taking over the land. It was a refuge, not a place they chose for themselves. Maybe the Fomori did the same—maybe they started out on the dry land. And the merrows look human, from what I've heard. Their feet and hands are webbed, but they need magic caps to move through the water without drowning. Fish and whales don't need magic to live in the sea. So the merrows must once have lived on land."

"There is a tale of a princess in the old city of Ys who became a *morgan*. The Princess Dahut. Her city was smitten by a curse and sank beneath the sea, but for many years afterwards she could be seen swimming in the surf with the ease of a fish. Ys and Lyonesse and fair Cantref Gwaelodd, off the coast of Cymru—all are gone now, lost beneath the sea."

Lost beneath the sea. Maeve saw castles of sand, squat sandy towers slipping into the waves.

Why is it called the Atlantic?

Because of Atlantis . . .

"Atlantis," Maeve said aloud.

"What is that you say?"

"A story I once heard. In the Shadow-world. Not a true story, I think, but so many things that aren't true in my world *are* in this one. You were telling me about sunken lands. Well, in my world there was supposed to be a whole continent that sank into the sea. Atlantis, it was called."

"I know of no such place."

"Here it might have another name. You told me about Tir fo Thuinn. Perhaps it wasn't always beneath the sea; perhaps it was drowned like those other countries you mentioned. And that's where the Fomori come from, and the merrows. They lost their land, but their magic let them go on living there, like your Princess Dahut." Maeve was becoming excited. "Yes, that must be it! The Land Beneath the Wave is a drowned country. Just like Atlantis."

"Child, even if what you say is true, I do not see how it can help us."

Maeve felt her mind straining towards the sea. In one of Uncle Roy's books there had been a map of Newfoundland that showed the seabed all around as if the water had been taken away: the Grand Banks, an immense plateau of the continental shelf on which the island rested. A hidden landscape, shrouded by the sea. Perhaps unknown lands might be beneath these moonlit waves? If there were submerged kingdoms off the coasts of Annwn's old country, there might lie other lowlands lost to these shores as well. And those islands might be a part of them. She recalled her uncle's voice telling her about the prehistoric continent of Gondwana, about the drifting and shifting of tectonic plates. Perhaps Annwn's geological history was slightly different from her own world's. There were those islands, for instance, that were not part of the Newfoundland she knew. What other lands here had risen, fallen, vanished from sight?

"Hy-Bresail," she said aloud. "That's the fairy island, isn't it? Where the Good People are still supposed to live? Where is Hy-Bresail from here, Majesty?"

Morgana's sea-deep eyes turned back to her. "It lies not far off this coast. You can see it from here. That small isle out there, in the path of the moon: do you see it? It is called Bird Island, and if you look to the left of it you see another, farther out. That is Hy-Bresail, or all of it that mortal eye can see. To those without the sight, it appears as a group of barren islets surrounded by a ring of rock. To the sighted, though, it is a paradise of the Sidhe. It is said that a mighty monarch, Bresail the Great and Wonderful, king of kings, once dwelt there. But our lore says little of him, and there are no tales of journeys to his land."

"If it's a Sidhe place, then do the fairies still live there? Could they help us fight the Fomori?"

Morgana turned to face her again, and for an instant a fierce hope was kindled in her eyes. But it was quickly quenched. "Child, those are the true and ancient Sidhe, immortal and unchanging. No human blood runs in their veins."

"But they're your kin—"

"I call them so, for my mother was of their race. Whether they would call *me* kin is another matter." Her mouth twisted with bitterness. "In any case, we cannot take a ship and cross the sea. It is filled now with Fomori and the minions of the Hag."

A keening sound rose into the night from the neighbouring tower: the prince was playing on Dugall's pipes again. It was as though Arawn mourned through music, as though he passed into the wail of the pipes the grief he could not speak. The sound seemed to pierce Morgana as the wind had not.

"A *coronach*," she muttered. "A song of mourning. But for whom, Hawk? For your friend, or for all within these walls?" The pipes keened on. "Enough!" cried Morgana suddenly. "My sorrows I can bear, King, but not yours as well!"

She turned swiftly and left the tower. Maeve continued to stand alone, gazing out to sea.

"Tom, I've got to talk to you." Maeve's voice was low, urgent.

"In a moment," Thomas replied.

They were standing before the doors of the throne room,

one of which stood slightly ajar. A little crowd had gathered to peer at the war council now taking place within. Maeve could see Arawn and Morgana seated on the two thrones. The king was speaking earnestly with his councillors, but the queen did not appear to be taking part in the discussion. She was gazing at Arawn, her chin in her hand and her face had somehow changed. To Maeve it looked as though the shield of pride and hardness had dropped from Morgana's face, and it was now curiously open, vulnerable—*more human*, the girl thought. The queen's dark brows frowned very slightly, as though she confronted a puzzle she could not quite solve, a mystery that just eluded her.

Finian was coming out through the hall doors. As he squeezed past them, Thomas plucked at his sleeve. "What news, Finian?"

The bard snorted. "The queen has a perfectly good bard, but what music does she ask to hear upon the eve of battle? She asks that Arawn play the pipes for her. The pipes! Anyone who can be soothed by that hellish din must have nerves of the finest. 'Twould frighten a banshee. Well, if my harp is not wanted, I shall take up a sword, instead."

"Finian! You're not fighting?"

"I must. Many we lost in the battle, good fighting men." Finian looked ruefully down at his hands. "They were not made for war, these hands, but for holding a harp while I sing of others' valorous deeds. Aye, well, we must all do our part. It is a pity that no one will sing of *my* deeds."

"We shall see," grunted the Druid, passing by. "If you live, you will sing loudly enough of them, I am sure."

"Ah, Cathbad! Will you not give me a spell of protection?"

"My powers, such as they were, are spent," the other replied shortly, "since my link to the land was severed in the Drunemeton. But I'll not let it be said that I stood idly by and watched others fight. I too will join in the battle."

"Druids need not fight, Cathbad. It is not expected."

"It is my fight too. If I cannot raise up wind or storm to foil the enemy, as the Druids of old did, then I can at least fight like any other man."

"Good luck to you, then, my friend. If we come not alive out of the fray, perhaps we shall meet again in Tir nan Og."

They walked on down the corridor, still talking. Maeve grabbed Thomas's arm and dragged him away.

"But what can *we* do?" asked Thomas.

They were sitting in a stairwell in one of the castle towers, perched on the stone steps. There was no one in this part of the castle: Arawn's council continued in the great hall and the villagers were sharing their noonday meal.

"We'll run out of food," said Maeve. "That's what happens in sieges. The people starve and can't defend the walls, and the enemy breaks in. I suppose we could all try to get out the emergency tunnel, but sooner or later the enemy would round us up. So we're all caught here. Trapped."

"We must defend the castle as long as we can, then. We shall fight them, man to man, when they break in."

"You'll be too weak by then. That's what Tethra's doing: waiting, biding his time." Her own words turned her veins to a net of ice. She thought of the terrible inhuman patience of those dark figures—like vultures waiting for a wounded animal to grow feeble. "Time is on their side, not ours. No one is coming to rescue us. Gwynedd's fallen, and this part of the island is all in chaos. The Beothuks are too few in number to help. The pagans likewise. So who's left?"

"No one. You have named all the peoples of Avalon."

"What about outside Avalon?"

"You mean Tir Tairngiri? Most likely no one lives there now but the Sidhe."

"Maybe they would help us. They fought the Fomori once, in Éire, and some of them *were* friendly to Diarmait and Gwenlian and my grandmother."

"That was years ago. The Good People have little to do with mortals now."

"Morgana's their descendant. They might help *her*, if only we could find them."

Thomas shook his head. "No one can get to Brendan's isle. The Fomori would stop him."

"There may be some help nearer than that. Thomas, I let the queen believe that I was some kind of prophetess back at the Drunemeton, that I was speaking for her goddess." She winced, remembering the brief yearning flash of hope in Morgana's eyes. "This is all my fault."

"You speak as though you have a plan of some sort."

"I have," said Maeve, and she told him of Hy-Bresail.

His face brightened a little as she spoke, but when she had finished he shook his head. "But how to get there? Even if we had a ship, even if the king and his men were to sail there, the Fomori are in the sea. They would know right away what our rulers were about, and would go after them and sink them."

"A big ship," said Maeve, "sailing straight to Hy-Bresail

would be stopped. But what about a Beothuk sea canoe? A little canoe going out to Bird Island for some egg gathering? Would they care about that, with a war on?"

"Perhaps not. Would the Beothuks undertake such a mission, though? They have sworn binding oaths to return to their people if they can."

"*We* will be the Beothuks," said Maeve. "You and I."

He stared at her, blank bafflement giving way to understanding, and understanding to excitement.

"The adults would never let us," he said as soon as he could speak.

"They don't have to know," said Maeve.

"But how could we do it without their aid?"

"There's a group of Beothuks leaving at dawn by the secret messengers' tunnel," said Maeve. She was amazed at how calm her own voice sounded. "Nonosabasut told me. They're going to try to get back to their village and defend their people when their turn comes. Not that they really think they can do much good, but it seems it's a matter of honour for them. Arawn told them they could leave whenever they wished, and they've decided to move before sunrise. We could go with them, in disguise. Then we'd separate and go down to the harbour. There are some abandoned Beothuk canoes down there, Nonosabasut said."

"I have been in boats before, but never a canoe."

"I have." She did not tell him that it was years ago, at a day camp, crossing a small lake with an instructor. "And Bird Island isn't all that far. If the sea were dry land, you could *walk* there in about twenty minutes." *But it isn't dry land.* "From there to Hy-Bresail isn't too far, either," she continued desperately. "We'd be breaking up the journey by stopping at Bird Island. That's what Brendan did: he crossed the whole ocean just by going from island to island. *We* have to cross only a tiny piece of it."

"An *immram*," said Thomas. His eyes glowed, afire with the longing for adventure. "A sea voyage of our own."

"And at the end of it, perhaps, the Grail," said Maeve.

She fell silent. Talking about her own plan had made her realize how hopeless it really was, how insanely dangerous. But Thomas had taken to the idea, as she had known he would. His boyish enthusiasm was her only hope: it must carry them both through the perilous journey to follow.

Chapter Sixteen

NONOSABASUT SEEMED BEWILDERED by their request.

"You wish to look like our people? But why?"

"Just a couple of cloaks will do, if you can spare them," said Maeve. "To fool people at a distance. We know we couldn't fool anyone up close. If they got that close to us," she added grimly, "it would all be over, anyway."

"You are trying to escape?" the young Beothuk asked.

"No, no," said Thomas. "Maeve has a plan. We are trying to get to the isle that lies beyond Bird Island. There is something there that may help us all. A magical object."

"But not a word to anyone," said Maeve hastily. "It must all be done as quickly and quietly as possible. Will you help us, Nonosabasut?"

"I think this plan is not a good one," said Nonosabasut, looking disturbed. "But," he added, "I will help you. For I think that I would do the same thing in your place."

Maeve suddenly noticed the short sword hanging in a

scabbard at Thomas's side. She did not ask him where it had come from.

The poncho-like caribou cloaks were very heavy—Maeve had not realized how much real animal hide weighed—and the one she was given hung nearly to her ankles, hampering her movements. Thomas's fit him better, neatly draping his tall, lean frame; it might have been made for him. At least their clothes were well-covered, Maeve noted. She had chosen the jeans and cardigan again, for their warmth.

"Where are you going?" demanded a small voice. Thomas jumped and swore. His little sister was standing behind them in the corridor.

"What are *you* doing here, Brat?"

"I've a right to go anywhere, same as you," retorted Cordelia. "Why are you wearing Beothuk clothes? Is it a game? Will you let me play too?"

"Yes," said Maeve before Thomas could speak. She bent and whispered in Cordelia's ear. "It's a game. We're going to see if we can fool some people into thinking we're Beothuks."

"But why?"

"Shhh, Cordelia, not so loud! Listen, I can't tell you everything—it's a secret. You mustn't tell anyone what we're doing—not your mother, not your father, not anyone. Do you understand? That way, you'll be part of our plan. Just say we're in another part of the castle, if anyone asks. That will help us, because no one will look for us."

"That's lying." The blue eyes were serious.

"No, no, Cordelia. It's acting. We want you to be an actress, do you see? To pretend for us, so no one will try to find us or guess where we've gone."

"All right," said Cordelia at last. "But I'd rather play Beothuks too."

"We haven't any clothes that fit you." Maeve was relieved to have a practical argument to offer. "Now run along, Cordelia, please! And remember, don't tell anyone—at least for today."

After today, nothing may matter, she thought as she watched the little girl walk away reluctantly.

Mammadroust's red ochre, applied in thick layers, easily masked the fairness of their skin. "Do you suppose she knew?" Maeve asked suddenly.

"Cordelia?"

"Mammadroust. Did she know about this in advance? Is that why she gave me the ochre?"

Thomas shrugged. "Perhaps. She has the sight too, hasn't she?"

His rather long dark hair looked just like a Beothuk's, she thought; her own brown locks were a bit too light in colour, but perhaps that would not be so noticeable from a distance. She still felt as though they were putting on costumes for a play, and she knew with a stirring of unease that she was not yet frightened enough. Thomas, by contrast, seemed to have come to life with the promise of action. He kept gazing at Nonosabasut as the Beothuks quietly discussed their plans in their native tongue, and she knew that he was envying the other boy's calm assurance, his easy assumption of the mantle of adulthood.

At last the muttered conference was over. "Now we go," said Nonosabasut simply, and he led the way to the tunnel.

The secret messengers' tunnel was down in the castle cellars, a chill, dark network of low-roofed passages gouged into the living rock of the hill. The word "tunnel" had led Maeve to expect a passageway through which one could walk upright. But the dark opening before her was so low that even she would have to stoop to enter it. It was plain that they would have to progress on hands and knees. *And how far?* she wondered. It would be exhausting, claustrophobic . . . but there was no use thinking about it.

The sentry by the entrance did not notice Maeve and Thomas. The light here was dim, cast by the one guttering torch, and apparently he saw only red-smeared faces above loose-hanging garments. The Beothuk men stooped and crawled, one by one, into the opening. In a moment it would be her turn. Would the sentry notice now that there was a girl among them? Would he try to stop her? She almost hoped he would, but he gave her undersized figure not so much as a glance. He had been given his orders—to let a number of forest folk out through the tunnel—and his duty went no further. Her stomach cramping with worry, Maeve resigned herself to the quest. She stooped and crawled in, Thomas following her.

The journey through the tunnel was a long, nightmarish progress, creeping on hands and knees over hard, damp rock. She could feel walls of rock to either side, narrow and confining; the darkness was absolute, and the presence of others was not a comfort but only made her feel more claustrophobic. The rock was cold, the air musty. She felt that she was stifling, that there would be no end to this blind crawling and fumbling.

Horrific scenarios kept occurring to her unwilling mind.

What if the roof caved in on them? What if something happened to one of the men in front, and they could not crawl forward over his body? What if the Fomori were waiting for them at the other end of the tunnel, ready to pick them off as they climbed out? She clamped her teeth to keep herself from whimpering out loud. And crawled on, and on, and on.

After what seemed an eternity, she felt a cool current of air on her forehead and looked up. At last, at last, fresh air was blowing into the tunnel, into her face! A trapdoor of some sort was being opened up ahead. Light flooded in, cold and grey. She saw the profile of a Beothuk hunter outlined against that pallid square. He paused there, as a rabbit will hesitate at the mouth of its burrow. What if a company of Fomori attacked now, seizing the man at the entrance, and then came swarming down the tunnel? It would be impossible to retreat fast enough; they would be caught like rats in a trap. . . .

Thomas tapped her heel gently, and she looked up to see that the men ahead of her were climbing out.

Now it was her turn. She emerged, gasping with relief, into a chill grey dawn. They were standing in the barrens, in a field that slanted towards the sea. Heaving skeins of foam surrounded a rocky shore. Far below lay the harbour with its silent ships.

"We must part now," said Nonosabasut, turning to her and Thomas. "May the spirits you honour give you protection."

Much as she had hated the tunnel, Maeve now yearned to go back into it. The sea was vast and dark, the wind off it, bitterly cold. There would be currents, rip tides, all manner of dangers they could not imagine. Bird Island was only a dark-grey blur, and Hy-Bresail could not even be seen in this dim light. For the hundredth time, she doubted the wisdom of this venture. But Thomas was eager and excited, and she knew nothing would change his mind now. She must go with him, or he would make the terrible journey alone.

As the natives melted away into the grey landscape, their caribou cloaks blending perfectly with the tall meadow-grass, Thomas and Maeve descended the long, steep slope to the harbour.

Below Newfoundland's Signal Hill there had been a place called the Battery, where clumps and clusters of small wooden houses were set among the bare, rugged rocks. In this place also there were many houses, crowded together like the craggy nests of seabirds. Or, rather, like the nests of birds in autumn when they have flown away across the sea—for here too was the emptiness and desolation they had seen in the city. On a wooden wharf, many boats were moored or drawn up on the planks: leather-hulled *curraghs* with furled sails and dories made of wood. Here were the abandoned birch-bark canoes of which Nonosabasut had spoken, lying together in a row. They were of varying sizes, some large enough for half a dozen occupants, some designed for two paddlers. She and Thomas chose one of the smaller ones and eased it into the water. Two paddles were already inside it, and from one of the bigger canoes Thomas added an *a-a-duth*, the toggle-headed sealing harpoon of the Beothuks. "For we never know what we might meet, out there on the sea," he said. Maeve wished he had not brought that subject up. Old Ned's yarns were coming back to her with an unpleasant vividness, and she was wondering how many of them might be true.

"Why is it full of stones?" asked Thomas, looking at the canoe's bottom.

"Ballast, I think," said Maeve. "And the turned-up part on each side, that's called a hogged sheer. It helps keep waves from splashing over the sides and swamping the boat."

"It will still leak in the bottom, I think."

"There are some birch-bark pouches over there, do you see? We can use them to bail out."

They climbed in carefully, trying not to upset the craft. Once safely in, they squirmed about in an effort to make themselves comfortable amid the ballast stones. The paddles were of an unusual shape, with large, sharp-pointed blades, but they were not too heavy for either of them to handle. "Right, let's give it a try," said Maeve, trying hard to sound confident, and dug at the water with her paddle. At the bow, Thomas, looking back over his shoulder, copied her movement on the opposite side. This might not, she reflected, be so hard after all—not as bad as the blind journey through the tunnel. Here at least their goal would always be in plain sight.

Canoeing was much more complicated than Maeve remembered, however. The water in the harbour was as calm as a pond, almost flat but for a few gentle ripples, yet still they ran into difficulties. Maeve had spent most of the night rehearsing in her head the paddling instructions she had been given, and most had soon come back to her: forward stroke, back stroke, draw and pry. She remembered that the upper hand went on top of the knobbed end of the paddle, and that the lower hand went just above the blade. She remembered that the paddle should be raised from the water with its blade held flat, parallel to the surface, to reduce wind resistance. She remembered all these things, but once they were on the water everything seemed more difficult.

"No, this is no good," said Maeve presently. "We're working against each other. We have to get a kind of rhythm going here." There had been a school song about canoeing that had the beat of a paddle in it, but she couldn't recall it. She felt a flash of panic. Surely some unfriendly watcher would see how inept was their handling of the canoe and realize that they were not true Beothuks? It didn't help that she kept wanting to glance nervously around.

You call yourself an actress, she scolded herself. *Now's your chance to prove it. Act! Get into the role! You are a Beothuk boy, going out to Bird Island for food. You are a Beothuk boy . . .*

Aloud, she said, "I'll say, 'Stroke,' and we'll do it together. Ready? Stroke!"

As they paddled towards the mouth of the Narrows, a new difficulty arose. The canoe wouldn't travel in a straight line, but always wanted to veer to one side, away from the stern paddler. She had a vague notion that this always happened, that there was some way to correct it, but she couldn't recall how. In the end, she and Thomas solved the problem by regularly changing sides, simultaneously raising their paddles and crossing them over to the opposite gunwale every half-dozen strokes.

The sea was not as mild as it had seemed from the top of the hill. The waves were larger than Maeve expected, and when she and Thomas were out of the harbour, they felt the full strength of the swell. Maeve began to panic. They were managing to meet the waves head-on, but too much water was coming in; they'd soon swamp and capsize. And when a canoe turned over, there was nothing you could do but cling to it and hope for rescue—something which, in their case, would never come.

Suddenly, she realized that Thomas was moving back from the bow.

"Tom!" she screamed. "What are you doing?"

"Too heavy," he gasped. "It's my weight making the bow go down. You must move too. Forward, closer to me."

In a moment she saw what he meant. The bow, lighter now that he had shifted his weight from it, sprang higher up into the air and its tall, upturned prow easily repelled the waves. She hastily scrambled forward to balance the boat, taking up a new position just behind Thomas. The canoe moved now with a rocking-horse motion, its ends bobbing lightly up and down, and no more spray came over the bows.

"Tom, you're brilliant!" she shrieked as she paddled. He did not take his eyes off the sea, but she sensed in the proud, renewed vigour of his strokes and the set of his shoulders the pleasure he felt at her compliment.

As they paddled on, they were grateful for the superb design of the craft: the raised bow and sides, which met the waves and deflected them. But as Thomas had suspected, water still got in through the bottom seam, and it was ice-cold. Maeve longed for a pair of gloves. Her hands were numb, and she suddenly recalled Uncle Roy telling her that you would die of hypothermia in ten minutes or less if you fell into the Atlantic. If their boat tipped over, they would not live long even if they managed to hold onto its hull.

The giant iceberg now loomed out of the water ahead of them. From this perspective it looked even more like a castle, with a ring of sheer white walls from which shapes like sharp-horned towers rose high into the air. As they drew nearer, they saw that the ice was like fine porcelain in texture, smoothed by its passage through the sea, but the walls were veined here and there with gaping seams and crevasses. The ice inside these showed sapphire blue where the rising sun glanced upon it. Blue? What did that make her think of? *The Blue Hag, the Cailleach Bheur . . .*

"Down!" cried Thomas suddenly.

They ducked. With a whistling sound, an arrow struck the hull, its flint tip piercing the birch-bark just under the gunwale.

"Where did that come from?" she gasped.

More arrows came hissing through the air. But again the high bow and hogged sheer shielded them: perhaps they had been designed with this danger in mind too. Lying huddled in the bottom of the canoe, her face pressed against hard beach stones and lapped by frigid sea water, Maeve heard a chorus of bird-like shrieks rise into the air from somewhere near at hand. But these were not the voices of birds. That was laughter she was hearing, harsh, mocking laughter without a vestige of human warmth or mirth.

"They are on the iceberg," Thomas whispered.

"Fomori," she choked. The sea demons could easily survive on the ice. Or were these some other sort of creature? Polar bears, her uncle had said, sometimes drifted down from the north with the pack ice. What armies of unknown beings might have come down from the Cailleach Bheur's frozen realm, riding on spring bergs and floes?

Long moments passed, but there were no more arrows. The enemy suspected nothing, then. Those shafts had been loosed only in idle malice, perhaps as a way of passing the time while they waited for larger prey. After a few minutes, Maeve dared to raise her head. "Tom, the canoe's filling with water. We've got to start bailing or we'll sink."

"I know." He was already scrabbling around for the birch-bark pouches. These had been designed for carrying dead birds and eggs, and were not fully watertight, but by working quickly, the two of them managed to keep their craft afloat. In the meantime, they had drifted off course: the island now lay behind them. But at least the iceberg was out of range; its unseen inhabitants could not shoot them from here. Maeve looked warily at the other, smaller icebergs and drifting floes, but saw no menacing figures on any of them.

Paddling furiously, they managed to turn the canoe. After a few minutes, it seemed they were making progress. But the island, like a taunting mirage, never seemed to grow any nearer.

Thomas gave another warning yell.

"What is it now?" gasped Maeve, almost dropping her paddle.

Then she too saw the great grey backs arching out of the waves only metres away, heard the loud, hollow inhalations that followed the vaporous spouts. Long white flippers gleamed like ice below the water.

Thomas groped in terror for the harpoon, but Maeve caught his sleeve.

"No, Tom, it's all right. They're just whales."

"I have seen them before," he replied, "from Old Ned's boat, when he took me out fishing. But I never saw them so close. The size of them! What if they attack?"

"They don't attack people. They're humpback whales, I can tell by those big white flippers. They eat only fish and little shrimps. And they sing."

"Sing?" He looked at her as though she were mad.

"Yes—like birds, beneath the water."

"What if Domnu has sent them to find us? They may be in her power."

"I don't believe they have anything to do with her. They're *good*, Thomas. I'm sure of it somehow. They're not on her side."

Maeve looked at the great grey backs, the tall spouts, and suddenly recalled the picture in St. Brendan's book of the monks in their *curragh* resting safely on the giant fish's back.

"Jasconius," she murmured softly. The warm, moist respirations of the whales were somehow reassuring; they sounded more human than the cold laughter of the creatures on the berg.

And now Bird Island, after seeming not to draw any nearer for so long, finally appeared to increase rapidly in size. It lost the misty vagueness of distance, exchanging its flat grey hue for the darker grey-browns of granite and the green of grass along its upper slopes. It revealed great cracks and striations along its stony sides, cave-like crevices into whose mouths the sea ran foaming. And with the new wealth of detail, the birds for whom the island was named came into view.

They literally filled the island. The craggy ledges and shelf-like strata of the cliffs were lined with their bodies. They crowded the upright pinnacles and the flat boulders surrounding the stony shore, nested amid the tough grasses that topped it like a thatch and filled the air as bees swarm about their hive. Dark shapes circled, hovered, darted and whirred against the sky, flew low over the waves in search of fish. Some seemed to run on the water as though it were solid ground, raising trails of little splashes as they skimmed along the surface. The noise, a blending of thousands of guttural or piercing voices, croaks and cries, was overwhelming. So too was the smell, a musty barnyard stench that made Maeve gasp and breathe through her mouth.

There had been trees once on the upper part of the island where the grass grew, but they were white skeletal shapes now, killed by the birds' droppings. She could see, as they drew closer, little round openings like rabbit burrows amid the green. In them squatted little black birds with white breasts and bright-billed harlequin faces.

"Puffins," she said aloud. The relief of having made it so far made her voice cheery. "I've seen pictures of those. What are those bigger black-and-white ones, perching on the cliffs?"

"Murres," he told her. "There are many of them here. And gannets, and gairfowls, and herring gulls, and great black-backed gulls."

"It's like Brendan's *immram*," she panted as she strained at her paddle. "The Paradise of Birds."

"Hardly a paradise," said Thomas. "Old Ned has often been

to the bird islands beyond Connemara Bay. He says he has seen them kill each others' nestlings—has seen a black-backed gull catch a puffin in his bill and swallow it, whole and alive."

"Ugh!" She shuddered, and turned her attention back to more practical matters. "Where should we put in?"

"I don't know. It is so rocky, and we don't want to damage the bottom of the canoe. Let's keep circling the island and see if there is anything like a beach."

The water around Bird Island was turbulent. Rising mountain-steep from the ocean's floor to jut above the surface, the island disturbed the natural motions of the sea and transformed them into a churning mass of deflected and colliding waves. *Getting the birch-bark craft ashore in one piece is going to be difficult,* Maeve thought, as she examined the spray leaping up the granite cliffs. Rocks reared out of the surf, ranging in size from modest boulders to towering sea stacks that were themselves like little islands and carried their own colonies of birds.

On the north side of the main island, a huge cave gaped like a vast open mouth, its dank grey-black interior large enough to shelter several boats.

"Could we take the canoe in there?" Thomas suggested. "There is a bit of gravel to one side, look—almost like a beach. And it would be safely out of sight."

As they considered this possibility, a tremendous wave rushed into the cave mouth. There was a hollow, booming roar and a flurry of white foam filled the cavern right up to its rocky roof. They stared, shocked by the swiftness and brutal force of the surf. *We would have been smashed to pieces if we'd gone in,* thought Maeve in horror.

"All right," said Thomas, "forget about the cave."

They finally found a place where a semicircle of rocks formed a sheltered spot, almost a little harbour, and here there was a slanting shelf of granite that ran into the sea like a slipway, only not as smooth. They paddled right up to it and Thomas clambered out, wincing as he stepped into the chill seawater. Maeve followed, and they dragged the canoe awkwardly up the stone slope, stumbling frequently on its slick, slimed, underwater portion. They decided not to try to hide it, since a Beothuk canoe would not look suspicious on this island. At least that was how they explained it to themselves, but the truth was that they were too tired to search for a hiding place. Once safely on the grassy part of the island they lay down, completely exhausted. All around them rose the ceaseless clamour of the birds, and the guano stench filled their nostrils, but they were too weary to care. For nearly an hour they lay there, silent and still, with the sun beating on their closed lids.

At last they rose and looked about them. The island was not large, Maeve saw—about the size of a city block. The grassy slope on which they lay levelled out farther up, becoming as flat as a table. Beneath them lay the colonies of seabirds, crowding on the cliffs. The murres, Thomas told Maeve, built no nests: they laid their eggs directly on the stone ledges. Gulls nested among the boulders beneath, and the puffins claimed the grassy upper reaches of the island. Down by the shoreline, she saw a great crowd of white-aproned and black-backed birds, similar to the murres only much larger. They were plainly flightless, like penguins.

Their flipper-like wings were much too small to carry their body weight. One cocked its black head sideways as she looked, and Maeve saw that it sported a round, white patch between its beak and eye. She made a choking sound.

"What is it?" Thomas asked, seeing her expression.

"Those birds . . ."

"The big ones you mean? We call them gairfowls, though Cordelia says the Beothuk word for them is *apponath*. Ned brings dozens of them back to the village for food in the spring. But why are you so upset?" Thomas asked in bewilderment, seeing her expression.

Yet another fragment of memory had come to Maeve from the Shadow-world, a picture of a bird in a school textbook. "I'm not upset, it's just . . . oh, you can't imagine what it's like to see something you never, ever believed you'd get a chance to see. Something you thought was lost forever." How could she make him understand—he who lived in the world where wolves and Beothuks still dwelt in the forests of Avalon? He saw only the gawky, awkward birds: there was no wonder in them for him. "We call those birds great auks in my world, but they don't exist any longer. They're all killed off, extinct. Your world is so . . . so unspoiled."

"But we have the Fomori, and Domnu."

"We have other things that are just as bad in their way: terrible rulers, terrible weapons. You don't know about any of them because I never wanted to tell you." She added with vehemence, "I hope your world is *never* like mine, Tom."

They climbed higher, then stood for a while looking out to sea. Hy-Bresail lay to the northeast, and they could clearly see its rocky ring enclosing the central islands. But its shores were uniformly grey in colour, like Bird Island seen from the mainland: discouragingly distant.

"We can do it," said Maeve, and then she wished she hadn't spoken, for she had only acknowledged the difficulty aloud.

"Of course we can," said Thomas, making it worse.

They wisely dropped the subject then, by unspoken consensus, and turned to look at the coast of Avalon, instead. "How far off it looks!" observed Maeve. "Just think, we came all that way." But they fell silent again, considering the sheer cliffs, the hill with the fortress now looking small and lonely and vulnerable on its summit. They were all in there—Arawn, Morgana, Padraig and Branwen, little Cordelia, Finian the bard. All wondering by now where she and Thomas had gone. She felt a twinge of conscience. "If only we could tell them that we're safe," she said. And she wondered if it might not have been better to stay in the *dún*—to die surrounded by others.

But they both knew there was no point in having regrets now. Maeve swept her glance across the sea: it appeared relatively calm. But would the weather hold for the second leg of their journey?

As she gazed seaward, she saw white water burst upward and a grey shape rise through it and fall again. A breaching whale. She caught her breath at the sight. She had seen them leaping like this in documentaries, but never before in real life. The whale breached again, higher this time, and she saw following it a whole pod, dark backs one behind the other breaking the surface in rhythmic unison. It was curious how they all seemed to be moving in a straight line . . .

Suddenly Maeve's blood froze. What she had taken for a

group of whales swimming in single file was, she now clearly saw, the half-hidden body of a huge, single creature moving just below the surface. The fleeing whale spouted, desperately, and flung itself out of the water once more. White water roiled in front of the undulating coils, swirled, became a spinning maelstrom. At the bottom of the watery funnel was a glistening pink maw—like the *péist*'s, only many times larger. The whale tried to dive. They saw the fluked tail come up, flailing. In the same instant, the pink-lined jaws came together in a glinting clash of teeth. Water spurted skyward, hiding hunter and hunted in a white wall of spray. When it fell back into the sea, there was nothing at all to be seen but a troubled patch on the surface.

Maeve reeled. "Tom—"

"I know."

"We were out there. Bumbling around, in a little canoe—"

"I *know*," he said. She wondered if her face was as pale as his. "There is no use thinking of it, Maeve. We are safe now."

"But we have to leave this island!" She was close to tears with frustration.

"We will, we will." He put his hands gently on her shoulders. "It has gone now. By tomorrow, perhaps, we can safely leave."

"What if there's more than one?"

"Dugall said there was but the one. You remember? Cìrein Cròin is the last of his kind. The great sea monster."

Maeve's knees sagged. Was it true? A legend? What was truth here and what was tale? And what did it matter anyway? She knew perfectly well that she would never be able to get into that canoe again, not with the memory of those gaping jaws within the whirlpool. How could she ever find the courage?

"I guess I should be like Andrew," she said, laughing humourlessly at herself. "But look what happened to him."

"Who is Andrew?"

"My great-uncle. He was killed long ago by a submarine. Another kind of sea monster," she explained grimly.

"Well, we can do nothing now," he said, as if in answer to her unspoken question. "We must rest, and we must eat."

How like a man. She surprised herself by smiling.

They quickly ate all the meagre supply of bread that they had brought with them. To replace these provisions, Thomas went off and killed a couple of murres, returning with their limp bodies dangling from his hands. He would have preferred great auks—they were bigger and fatter—but Maeve would not let him kill any.

"Oh, Tom," she sighed. "What *are* we going to do? I don't think I'll be able to go on with this."

"Yes, you will," said Thomas. "You're the bravest lass in the world, Maeve."

"I don't feel all that brave right now," she replied, looking at the sea.

"It is not what you feel that makes you brave, but what you do. You were very brave when those whales came up to the boat."

"That's different. I knew *they* were harmless. No, I'm a coward, Tom, and that's the truth. My great-uncle Andrew, now *he* was really brave. I'm just an actress. I try to make people think I'm all kinds of things that I'm not, and brave is one of them."

"Ah, Maeve, why are you always so hard on yourself?" His dark-eyed gaze was very intense. Suddenly, he reached out a hand and very lightly stroked her hair.

Maeve was taken completely aback. She sat with her mouth open foolishly, staring at him. He moved his hand to her cheek, gently running his fingers down to her chin. "Maeve, my Maeve, how I love you!" he whispered.

This could not be happening. On top of all the other shocks she had experienced today, this was more than she could cope with. Incredulity filled her.

"What eyes you have, Maeve—like great pools they are, so deep. . . . Ah, but I was jealous when I thought you loved Arawn! I know he is a great man, and royal too, but. . . . Could you ever care for me, Maeve, as I do for you?" Again his hand brushed shyly across her cheek, gentle and tentative with inexperience.

Maeve fought the urge to draw away from him. What to do? To reject him now was to give him the deepest of hurts, yet to let him continue would wrong him too. . . . How absurd, to think of plain, odd Maeve in such a position, in such a place and time as this! She almost laughed, which would have been devastating to him. Finally, she leapt to her feet and turned away. Let him think she was overcome with emotion, as in a sense she was; that would be easier for him.

"I . . . I don't know what to say, Tom," she stammered.

"Very well," he said after a pause. "But I'll not stop hoping, Maeve—not while we're both still alive. I've loved you from the first, you see, ever since you came into our world."

She could find no reply to give him. After a moment, he too rose, and walked away.

Maeve spent the next hour or so resting her aching back and arms, lying on her caribou cloak in the long grass. She took care to keep apart from Thomas, her thoughts still a whirl of confusion, overlaid with many other fears and her mind-clouding fatigue.

She was not the sort of girl boys fell in love with. Ashley Robinson now, she'd had plenty of admirers: boys who hung about her locker and walked with her to school. Even the male teachers had flirted with her a little during classes. But boys brushed past Maeve in the crowded hallways, their eyes flicking over her, dismissing her, moving on.

How could Tom love her? His eyes had looked on the exquisite delicacy of the ladies in the *dún*, the wild magnificence of Morgana. He had all of this beauty to compare her with. To look at her sitting there beside him—tired and windblown, her face grotesquely masked with ochre—and love her? No, the thing was impossible.

But then, in her own world only her outer form had been visible, the image that mirrors showed, the shadow and shell of what she was. Everything in Annwn was more real, clearer, showed more of its inward self. The same, it seemed, was true of Maeve while she was here. For had she not seen it at the *dún*, in the lady's looking-glass? Could *he* see what she had seen there?

The sun had come out of the clouds, and here, out of the

wind, she could feel its warmth. In the end, she dozed off and slept—too deeply, and too long. She had, after all, not slept the night before, and she was overtired.

Maeve was awakened by the feel of hands on her face. She stirred and feebly tried to push them away, muttering, "No, Tom, *no*." Then there were more hands clutching at her, not gently. She started up with a scream, staring into the absolute dark of night on the island and thinking for a moment that it was only a nightmare. But the hands were still there, and as she tried frantically to beat them off she realized that they were cold, far colder than any human hands should be. She could see no faces, only vague silhouettes against the dark and clouded sky.

"Tom! Tom, *help*!" she cried.

The sea-cold hands were dragging her down the slope towards the water.

Chapter Seventeen

ALL WAS DARKNESS AND CONFUSION. Maeve tried to yell, but got a mouthful of seawater. She was being dragged down into the surf. She could not see the faces of her attackers, but felt the grip of their heatless hands on her limbs. She still did not know who was trying to drown her, but in the back of her mind, behind the immediate terror and desperation, she feared the Fomori.

She felt something being forced over her head as she raised her face above the water, gasping for breath. Some kind of cloth cap or hood. Again her head was forced beneath the water, and again she flailed wildly at her attackers. It took her a moment to realize that, though once more underwater, she was not drowning.

She could breathe.

The water was all around her, but it no longer flowed into her mouth and nostrils. She was breathing normally, as though she were in air. And the deathly chill had gone from the water too—it now felt merely cool.

In her surprise, she stopped struggling. At once, cords were slipped around her wrists and ankles, drawing them together: soft, slimy cords that made her think of seaweed. Her eyes, no longer stinging with salt, peered into watery darkness. Her captors were dragging her along by the cords, pulling her down into the deeps with them.

Exhaustion overcame her, and she lost consciousness.

When she came to again, she was no longer underwater. The cap, or whatever it was her assailants had forced onto her head, had been removed. She lay on a floor of cold stone. Thomas was lying beside her, his eyes closed and his wet hair slicked across his face. He was very pale, but she saw his sides heaving and knew that he lived.

Her own clothes were wet, and she shivered. They were, she saw now, in a vast stone chamber. Pillars of white marble supported the vaults of the roof, which was intricately carved with floral medallions and garlands interspersed with the figures of people and animals. It was badly damaged, though: large, ragged patches of rough stone sprawled where carvings had crumbled and fallen. A globe-shaped lamp suspended from the ceiling gave a cold, pearly light.

Maeve sat up—and saw that she and Thomas were not alone. At the far end of the room was a throne, also of white marble, and on it sat a woman, while several other figures stood to either side. Like the Fomori, these people were deathly pale, but they had another peculiarity: their hair was a dull, metallic green in colour. Next to a normal human face it would have looked startling, but somehow it suited their unnatural pallor. The hair of the throned woman was long, and was crowned by a silver circlet. Her gown was a simple sheath of silver white, glittering like the belly scales of a fish; a belt of scallop shells clasped her slender waist, and her feet were bare. Beside her throne there lay a large animal that Maeve took at first for a massive broad-faced dog, a New-foundland dog, perhaps. Then she saw that it was a huge seal, longer than a man is tall and slate-coloured with pale-grey blotches on its neck and flanks. It fixed its great dark eyes on her, but remained motionless and made no sound.

The crowned woman spoke in a toneless voice. "You wear the garb of the killers of seals, whom we hate," she said, "and for such we took you. But then we found that beneath the red clay your faces were fair. Who are you?"

"Please," said Maeve, struggling to her feet. Beside her, Thomas coughed and stirred into wakefulness. "We've come from Temair. We have to get to Hy-Bresail. Please let us go."

The pale people were silent. In the cold glow of the lamp, the scene was dreamlike and unreal, the figures scarcely human.

"Where are we?" asked Thomas huskily, sitting up.

"You are in the land of Tir fo Thuinn," said the queen.

"I've heard of it," said Maeve. "The Land Beneath the Wave."

"We are under the sea?" Thomas exclaimed, looking wildly about him.

The queen waved a hand at the window, and Maeve saw the webbing between her long white fingers. *These people are merrows!* She did not know whether to be relieved or not. "It is not the dark of night alone that you see there, but the dark of the deeps. Though this house is filled with air, it is surrounded on all sides by water. You cannot leave it, except by our will."

Thomas slumped back to the floor, his face drawn. Maeve continued to look steadily at the woman on the throne. "Why do you live here in the deeps?"

It was plainly not the sort of question the merrow queen expected. She paused for a long moment before replying. "It is our own country. We care not for the dry lands."

"But this was dry land once, wasn't it?" She gestured towards the ceiling, to the beasts and birds carved there.

Again the merrow paused before speaking, and when she did, it was not to answer but to question. "What do you know of our history?"

"Nothing," Maeve replied. "I just put it all together—bits of stories from my world and yours."

"Your world." Pale eyes stared.

"I'm from the Shadow."

The merrows about her throne murmured, but the queen showed little reaction. "Indeed."

She doesn't believe me. Maeve reached into her jeans pocket and drew out the little package Great-gran had given her. After all she had been through, the fairy bread was, strangely, still dry and firm and untouched by mould—as though it was completely unaffected by the laws of this world. The throned lady leaned forward to look at the crust, then she drew in a sharp breath and sat back. "So you tell the truth. And have you any token of this world with you— a weapon, or perhaps a jewel?"

284

"I had . . . a brooch," said Maeve slowly. "Round, with a pin. It was my grandmother's once, but it came from Annwn. It was magical. It could alter time so that she would never be missed when she went to Annwn, and it did the same for me."

"You say you *had* this brooch. Is it no longer in your keeping?"

"No. It was taken from me. It's in a fairy mound now, beneath Queen Morgana's tower. She said it belonged to the Sidhe."

"Ah." The green tresses shimmered as the woman nodded. "So it did, indeed. Such brooches come from the dawn-time; they were crafted by the ancients in Hy-Bresail. Like the beings who made them, they could change time's flow—and that was not the limit of their powers. Your brooch enabled you to recall this world when you were in the Shadow, and also to remember your own world clearly when you were in this. Many such jewels and talismans were made by the ancestors of the Tuatha de Danaan, long ago when the two worlds were one. There is a great and ancient magic in them that is not subject to the division of Annwn and the Shadow. So long as that brooch was upon your person, therefore, you could perceive both worlds as though they were still one. When you removed it in your world and set it aside, your memory of Annwn grew dim—is that not so?"

Maeve nodded. "I think my grandmother forgot about it too. She put it away and for years she never thought about Annwn, except to turn it into a children's story."

"And now that you have it no longer, Annwn will be the only world that you know. Your memory of the Shadow is fading and will one day be lost to you altogether."

Maeve knew she should be distressed at this, but she could not seem to summon any emotion for that other, shadowy realm. All she could think of now was Annwn and its plight.

"I was right, wasn't I?" she asked, stepping forward. "This country sank beneath the sea long ago, and your ancestors wouldn't leave it. They lived on, in their drowned cities, by magic. Like Princess Dahut."

The green-tressed head nodded. "It is as you say. They loved their land that much. We know, for we live in both: the drowned land and the land that was."

"I don't understand."

"There are two countries here," said the merrow lady. "Tir fo Thuinn, the land that is, and Hy-Bresail, the land that was."

"Hy-Bresail?" repeated Thomas. "But is that not the name of the island?"

"It is the name that was given by the Tuatha de Danaan to their homeland. The little island you call Hy-Bresail was once a part of a greater country. Tir Tairngiri and Avalon also belonged to it. This is the history your people do not know, the tale of which no bard sings, for you have all forgotten it. But the sea folk do not forget.

"Long ago, Mannanan mac Lir, the Son of the Sea, took a mortal maiden for his bride. He built a palace for her in the fairest of all lands, atop a holy mount whose summit was in the shape of a bowl; and there were their half-mortal children born. The oldest of these was Bresail the Great and Wonderful, mightiest of kings. He reigned over his nine royal brothers as *ard-righ* and gave his name to the land. It was a lovely country in those days, a very paradise full of trees and flowers and beautiful dwellings. Atop Mannanan's hill was a grove of sacred trees, and beside it a great temple in which stood an image of the sea god. All who came to pay homage in the temple were welcomed, and those who supped at the table of Mannanan mac Lir had their fill by enchantment of all that they desired, be it wine or flesh or fowl.

"But Hy-Bresail and its people had a dire enemy. She who dwells within the abyss has no love for living things, and in those days she caused the sea to rise that it might whelm all the world. Across the sea, Cantref Gwaelodd and Lyonesse were lost, and Hy-Bresail was all but destroyed. Then the goddess Dana took the part of the earth's children, fighting Domnu and beating the waves back. So it was that Avalon and Tir Tairngiri, which were once the highlands of Hy-Bresail, were saved. But the side of the holy hill was cloven asunder in the flood, and flames spewed forth; and all the lower land perished in fire and water.

"Those of the people who yet survived fled to the isle of Éire. There they fought the evil Firbolg race and came to rule all that land. They named themselves the Tuatha de Danaan, the people of Dana, for she had preserved their race from destruction. Many centuries they reigned there before other mortals from the Shadow came with weapons of cold iron and drove the Tuatha de Danaan out of Éire forever. Some of Dana's people fled to the depths of the sea and the country that they had lost. With their magic arts, they learned to live beneath the water, dwelling once more in their ancestors' houses: some became merrows, some chose to swim the deeps in seal form. And so we, the children of that mighty race, reclaimed the realm that was ours from of old.

"But the kingdom of Hy-Bresail is gone forever. Many

wonders are vanished from the world—only in our memory are they cherished still. The palace that the sea god built for his bride and the temple where the sacred bulls were sacrificed, the great cities and other mighty works of old, the fresh-flowing springs and the forests with their beasts and birds—all these are gone beyond recall."

"And now Domnu's trying to take Avalon and Tir Tairngiri too," Maeve told the merrows. "But with the Fomori instead of a flood."

The queen's cold eyes narrowed. "The Fomori! They were ever an evil people. Domnu protected them from the rising waters with her magic; *we* had to devise magical caps and cloaks in order to live here. So they desire the dry land? Well, it is nothing to us. Our homeland is gone. We live now in a land that is half a dream, a dream of the past.

"There is a *glamourie,* an illusion cast by our people, the work of many minds. It preserves the memory of our land as it looked before the flood. The crafting of this image was passed down from our land-dwelling ancestors to all the generations that came after. *Glamourie* is an old art of the fairy folk. Had you our eyes, you too could see Tir fo Thuinn as it once was, when it was Hy-Bresail—the divine land of a divine people. But it is only an image, alas."

As the merrow woman spoke, Maeve noticed that the view outside the windows was changing. To her amazement, she saw not dark ocean depths, but a view of blue sky and green grass, tall fruit trees laden with flowers, the white walls of a large building—a palace, perhaps? This, then, was the illusion of a past country that the merrows spoke of—and that Old Ned had glimpsed once as a boy. She opened her mouth, then decided not to tell them that she could see it too. The queen fell silent, and slowly the vision faded away again.

"Please, won't you help us?" pleaded Maeve. "We just need to get to that island."

"Your concerns are not ours."

"But you don't like Domnu any more than we do. And you said the Fomori are evil."

"If the Fomori go to the dry land, so much the better— then we need not share Tir fo Thuinn with them."

Maeve struggled to make her voice persuasive, but she was tired and her hope was dying. "One of our leaders is Queen Morgana. Her ancestors were Tuatha de Danaan too. She . . . she's your own kin."

"Then let her come down into the sea. We would welcome her."

"She wants to live in Avalon. She loves it the way you love your own land, and won't ever leave it."

"That is as she will have it."

"Then perhaps the fairies themselves—"

The queen laughed without warmth or humour. "You know not what you say, child. Do you know what the fairies, the true Sidhe, are? They are life without breath, form without flesh. What are your little mortal affairs to them? They will not help you." She rose, her sea-green hair waving and rippling to her knees. "I would know more of this Shadow-realm of yours, however. I will keep you here a while longer, and you shall tell me of it."

The great grey bull seal had been watching them silently all this time. His eyes, Maeve had noticed, did not drift like an animal's, but had an alert, focused intelligence. Now he suddenly heaved himself with paddling motions of his fore-limbs towards a corner of the room, where an open archway led to a spiral staircase. The lower half of the staircase was flooded, Maeve now saw, forming a pool of dark water. The seal plunged into it with a great splash and was gone.

The merrows followed him. From hooks in the stone wall, they took down round red caps and donned them. *Why red?* she wondered idly. Perhaps to make them more clearly visible in the deeps, like those red hats hunters wear in the bush? The queen fitted hers over her coronet, then walked over to the dark well of water and slipped into it easily, as though she too were a seal. Her green hair floated up around her as she decended the submerged steps, until at last it alone drifted like seaweed on the surface. Then it sank down out of sight. One by one, her courtiers followed her. When the dark water had closed over the last red-capped head, it smoothed and lay still.

Maeve ran to the window. She saw nothing now but the flat darkness of the depths. Not far away, cold pearly globes like the one that lit their chamber were mounted on tall columns: they cast a pale, diffused glow through the brine, like lampposts shining through fog, illuminating little. Maeve thought she could just make out the shape of a building far-ther on, a dim oblong rising from the seabed. She glanced down. Square patches of light from their windows revealed slimed rocks, a few waving weeds and the darting forms of small fish.

Maeve turned away from the window in despair. They were trapped here as no prisoner could ever be confined on land, beyond any hope of rescue or escape.

As day approached, the blank darkness outside the windows began to change—though as Thomas said, it did not so much brighten as grow less dark. They were given food, which they stared at in dismay after the server had gone. Served in large scallop shells, it consisted of damp strands of seaweed and small fish, whole and raw.

"I guess this is the merrow idea of sushi," said Maeve, trying to sound cheery.

"What?" said Thomas. He was pacing about the room restlessly. "We must leave this place, Maeve."

"We *can't*," she said, for the fifth time. "There's nothing outside but water."

"Do not speak of it." He shuddered, and she saw a sheen of perspiration on his brow despite the coolness of the chamber. Perhaps the thought of all that water outside weighed on him as the thought of the metres of solid rock above the messengers' tunnel had weighed on her.

"Here," she said, pushing a plate to him. "Try it. It won't kill you, and we need to keep up our strength." She could not bring herself to touch the limp slimy fish herself, but tried chewing on a weed. It tasted bitter and salty.

Maeve looked about her at the wall carvings. There were people dancing and playing flute-like instruments; loose draperies and loincloths seemed to be their only clothing. There were many birds and animals too.

"Atlantis," she said aloud.

"What is this 'Atlantis' you speak of?"

"Just an old story. In my world, a man named Plato, a philosopher, wrote about this country of Atlantis thousands of years ago. He lived in a far-away country called Greece.

Atlantis was supposed to lie somewhere to the west; it was a country surrounded by the sea. It was ruled first by a god named Poseidon, who took a mortal woman as his wife. They had children who were half-human, half-divine, and their descendants went on to populate the whole country. Atlantis was named after the very first king, Plato said. King Atlas. Ten kings reigned under him in ten kingdoms, but he was the chief ruler. The kings were all brothers, the children of Poseidon and this young woman, Cleito. Only that wasn't her real name."

She knew the story well. It was one of her favourites, along with the tales of King Arthur and Shakespeare's plays. "Plato said in his book that another man, Solon, got the Atlantis story from a priest in another country called Egypt. Solon is supposed to have translated all the names of these people and places into Greek names—they were originally in some unknown foreign language." She was becoming more excited with every word she spoke. "It's incredible! This is just a made-up story in my world. There *is* no sunken land in our ocean, and Plato was probably just using his imagination. But Tom, what if Shadow-people's imaginations reflect *real* things in your world? King Arthur . . . fairies . . . monsters." She was silent a moment. Then she murmured softly, "King Atlas— *King Bresail*. Atlantis—*Hy-Bresail*. Poseidon—*Mannanan mac Lir*. Are these the original names, then? Is our Atlantis your Hy-Bresail? Tom, I can't believe this is just coincidence!"

"But what has this to do with the Grail?"

"The drowned land in your world was the homeland of the Tuatha de Danaan. They're the ones who had the four magic treasures, including the Grail. The other three are in

Avalon—the spear, the sword and the stone. The cup was returned to its holy place, Morgana said."

"Somewhere in this undersea land?"

"No, I think it's on the island. We were going to the right place all along!"

"How can you know that? Is it a part of the Atlantis tale?"

"It might be. According to Plato's story, there was a sacred bowl in the temple, which was used to hold the blood of the sacrificial bulls. And the Grail is sometimes described as a serving dish or a cauldron—the monks call it the Vessel of the Sacred Blood. Blood . . . holy . . . sacrifice. Do you see, Tom? The island of Hy-Bresail, the little bit of land that's left, is a sacred hill half-drowned in the sea! That's where the Grail was taken—back to its temple on the hill. Only the hill's now an island! It all fits beautifully. Queen Morgana told me that the Grail was kept in a temple on a hilltop in one story and on an island in another. But maybe both stories are true!"

Thomas still looked dubious.

Maeve was about to speak again when there was a sudden splash and the wet, gleaming head of a seal broke the surface of the stairwell-pool in the corner. It held in its mouth something red, which they took at first for the bloody remains of some prey or other. Then they saw that it was a mass of fabric. The seal let go of the fabric, which as it fell to the floor resolved itself into two cloth caps. Then the animal looked very intelligently at Maeve and Thomas with its large, liquescent eyes and hauled itself onto the stone floor.

It was not the same seal that had lain beside the merrow queen's throne. This one was smaller and lighter in colour, silver-grey dappled with dark spots. For a moment, it lay quietly regarding them. Then it raised its whiskered muzzle, tilted its head back at an unnatural angle—and disappeared.

Grey seal hide flowed to the floor in loose folds, to lie there like a snake's discarded skin. Kneeling on it was a young girl clad only in a tight-fitting grey tunic; masses of soft brown hair surrounded her delicate, dark-eyed face.

"Do not be afraid," she said softly. "I have heard the story of your troubles and am come to give you aid."

Maeve's heart leapt. "You'll help us get away?"

"I will, for when my father and Queen Niamh told the court your tale of war on the dry land, and your errand to the fairies, I was deeply moved. We have grown cold, we sea folk, from dwelling in the deep, and will end like the Fomori, with neither hearts nor souls. You should not have come so far, through such great perils, only to be hindered in your quest by us."

"Who is your father?" demanded Thomas.

"He is the king of the Selkies. You saw him, here in this hall, though he disdained to take his human form in front of you. But we must make haste! The revels in the palace will soon be ended, and you must be away from this place. I have brought you merrow-caps to help you to breathe in the water."

"Can you show us how to get back to Bird Island?" Thomas asked.

"I could lead you there, but I fear it is of little use: the merrows destroyed your boat. And I must return, ere I am missed. I am sorry, but you must find your own way to the island that you seek. I wish you well."

"But how could we ever—" Thomas began.

Maeve interrupted. "I can see the illusion of the dry land, Tom, so I will know where to go. I just have to spot that volcano that became the island—the sacred hill. We'll head in that direction."

"You have the second sight?" asked the seal-girl. "I am glad, for you will have need of its protection on this journey, I think. Come."

"We don't even know your name," said Maeve, touched.

The great brown eyes turned to her. "I am the Princess Finnabair. Now come!"

The princess knelt and drew her sealskin cloak about her. At once, the strange transformation took place again. In an eyeblink her human form was gone, replaced by the long, heavy body of the seal. It slithered awkwardly into the pool. Maeve and Thomas quickly pulled on the cloth caps and followed it.

It was strange to descend into that cool, dark pool—to feel the seawater lapping about her ankles, then her knees, waist and shoulders. When it came up to her chin, Maeve could not help hesitating. The instinctive fear of drowning dominated her mind. But a cap like this had saved her when she was dragged beneath the sea by her merrow captors. She leaned forward, dipping her face into the water, and took a tentative breath. It was all right: no water came into her nostrils, only air. She took another step, and the water closed over her head.

She descended the spiral stair, relieved to find a dim light coming from below. Here, in the flooded lower chamber, more cold lamps glowed through a subaqueous gloom. She saw walls carved in bas-relief, in a style that reminded her of ancient Greece. The figures were beautifully proportioned and lifelike, filled with grace and the suggestion of movement. She would have liked to examine them, knowing now that they were vestiges of a lost civilization. But all was fear and haste.

There were no doors at the main entrance of the under-sea house. It gaped, an open archway, onto twilight deeps.

The seal came gliding out of the gloom towards her. Here in the water her clumsiness was gone, and she was as grace-ful as a swallow in air. She was holding something in her jaws. As she swooped down upon them, she dropped it at Thomas's feet, and Maeve saw that it was his sword-belt, the weapon still in its scabbard.

She waved and smiled her gratitude. The Selkie rolled above their heads, waving a webbed forepaw in a farewell gesture. Then she swam swiftly for the door.

Maeve turned to see Thomas behind her; he too was floun-dering along, neither walking nor swimming but awkwardly combining the two. Would the caps enable them to speak too?

"This way, Tom." Her breath rose in a swirl of bubbles, but he seemed to understand. Together they followed the Selkie outside, to where the pearly lamps shed their light on the deeps. Not far away was a great rectangular structure with light glowing in its windows. The Selkie palace? Finnabair was heading in its direction. Maeve looked about her, trying to orient herself. In what direction would the island of Hy-Bresail lie?

Suddenly, without warning, the green dusk gave way to daylight. A cloud-streaked sky spread high above her, with the sun blazing down from its zenith. She was standing on a hill with a flattened top, which rose from a plain surrounded by other hills. The image dimmed and flickered. *Concentrate,* she thought. She must *will* herself to see it. The image blurred, swam, cleared again, held steady.

The Selkie palace was overlaid now by the illusion of its more ancient self: its stark stone was faced with whitest marble, its roofs bright with gold leaf. Another ruin, the mere outline of a foundation, supported shadowy walls and the suggestion of windows. Atop a broken plinth, a ghostly figure stood: the marble statue of a young man. She concentrated and the images took on sharper definition, seeming to solidify before her eyes. The gloom of the deeps was gone, and she could no longer see Thomas.

Maeve spun, seeking the lost landscape. Where was north? She turned in a circle, seeing a great plateau or escarpment in the distance, stony slopes reaching up into the sky like a bank of low-lying cloud. These must be the vast tablelands that would become Avalon and Tir Tairngiri. Which way led to what was now the island of Hy-Bresail? They must find it. But there were so many hills rising from the broad valley below ...

Then she saw it: the majestic peak rising high above the others, more mountain than hill, its summit a smooth, almost perfectly cylindrical cone. A volcano.

"Thomas?" she called softly.

"Here." An invisible hand was slipped into hers.

"I can't see you while the *glamourie* is visible. Hold onto me."

The warm hand closed more tightly around hers. "I won't leave you. Now lead the way."

There was a dreamlike quality to the journey that followed, in part because of the wonder and strangeness of the sights she saw, in part because she did not walk through the illusory landscape but rather drifted through it, as one drifts in dreams. Her body was nearly weightless in the water, but she could not see the green depths through which she moved. And so she had the odd experience of floating through what seemed to be air, over land that her eyes told her was dry. Of course, the landscape had changed over its thousands of years of submergence. Often she bumped into a rock she had not realized was there, or absentmindedly put out a hand to steady herself against a tree trunk and ended up overbalancing and tumbling helplessly, head over heels. At such times, she relied on the invisible Thomas to catch hold of her and help her find the seabed again. They helped one another along, each aiding the blindness of the other.

She regretted the haste and fear with which they had to move, for she saw marvels on that journey beyond anything she had yet seen in Annwn: fair houses roofed with gold leaf or with silver that dazzled like water in the sun; elegant statues of men and women with a beauty unlike any mortal's. Some of the houses were built of white marble, some of a tawny-coloured stone; still others were of a stone so dark that it was nearly black—volcanic, perhaps. A few of the buildings used all three types of stone in their walls, and the variegated colouring and elaborate patterns gave them a cheery, festive look. There were lovely pleasure gardens where brightly coloured birds, such as one sees only in the tropics, flew from tree to tree. And all about her were the ancestors of the Tuatha de Danaan: tall, regal women who reminded her of Morgana; equally handsome men; beautiful children. The latter played and frolicked about the streets like children anywhere, but the adults carried themselves with pride and grace, as befitted the offspring of a god. They strode by talking silently to one another, graceful phantoms; or gathered wildflowers at the roadside; or waded in the pure, clear streams.

All this was preserved in some communal memory, like a film or a photograph; she was looking at a projection of countless living minds. But how real it seemed! Maeve continued to hold Thomas's hand, relating to him all she saw. It must, she thought, be terrifying for him to have to trust her so blindly.

As they descended into the plain, she saw that the land around the volcano was quite flat. The Tuatha de Danaan had surrounded the mountain with a system of circular canals arranged in concentric rings and crossed by bridges—just like descriptions she had read of Atlantis. This, then, was the sea god's country as Plato had described it in her world thousands of years ago. He had given her a map to follow. Somehow the tale of Mannanan mac Lir's western paradise, long lost to the bards of Annwn, had been transmitted to her own world in fictional form. All the Shadow's poets and storytellers might well be conduits for Annwn, their tales dim reflections of its realities.

The silver apple trees grew here, she saw, in summer-green orchards, with golden fruit gleaming between their leaves. She almost imagined that she could hear the elusive song of their wind-tossed boughs. And there were white, moon-horned cattle in the fields, mild-eyed cows and majestic bulls. Sacred bulls, perhaps, destined for sacrifice in the temple by the priests who were the forerunners of the Druids?

They passed over the first canal, crossing the bridge to the outermost ring of land. In the water below were vessels like Viking long ships, their banks of oars moving rhythmically. The bridges were so high that the ships could pass beneath them with ease, and there were also passages bored through the land-rings for the ships to sail through. The scale of the work was staggering; it must have taken centuries to complete.

The second ring of land had fortifications coated in what looked like shining silver, but which Maeve knew was really tin. On this smaller ring-island were many temples, also roofed with tin or copper. And there were park-like spaces, with sheltering trees and beds of bright flowers, and dusty yards where young men, bare-torsoed in the sun, were exercising horses.

"There's a sort of procession ahead of us, Tom," Maeve announced. "A man in fine robes on a white stallion, leading a great company of riders. Of course, he's a king. It's a royal procession. The rulers of the ten kingdoms must all be travelling to the palace of the high king, the *ard-righ*. They met once a year, Plato said, to make sacrifices in the temple. So if we go up to the hill, we'll get to see it all: the sacred grove, and the bulls, and the blood bowl that was used for the sacrifice."

"And that bowl is the Grail?"

"Perhaps. I can't say for sure, but maybe we'll know when

we see it." One more circular canal separated them from the hill; it coiled about its base. Morgana had said something about the Grail lying in a temple on a hill surrounded by water, hadn't she?

The last of the fortifications rose beyond the canal. They were plated, not with bronze or tin, but with a metal of a strange fiery hue, too red for gold and too bright for copper. "Orichalc!" said Maeve aloud, forgetting that Thomas could not see.

"What?" he asked. "What did you say?"

She hastened to explain. "There was supposed to be a metal used by the Atlanteans—the Hy-Bresaileans, I should say—a metal like no other in the world. It was found only on their island. *Orichalc*," she repeated, and her eyes feasted on the flame-coloured wall. On past it she went, clutching Thomas's hand, through the lofty gates and into the city beyond. Stone houses, larger and grander than those of the plain, nestled in the foliage of the hillside. A path, paved and well-tended, led up to the summit.

"The ground is beginning to slope," observed Thomas. "And it is not so dark."

"We're going up the side of the hill—the island, I mean," she told him. After a while, she said, "I can see some little children bathing in a spring. A hot spring, I think. It's steaming just like a bath."

"I feel a warmth upon my face," said Thomas's voice beside her. "Like a wind that blows from the south."

"I feel it too. The hot springs are probably still pouring out their water, even though they're under the sea now. Tom, we're almost at the top! Can you see?"

Instead of replying, he gave a sudden yell and shoved her to the ground, hard.

He had indeed seen something—something that she could not, enfolded as she was by illusions. She looked up. The dream-sky above her trembled as the sky reflected in a pool's surface trembles when the water is disturbed. It wavered and was gone, and in its place there was a green darkness and a huge, shadowy shape lunging down at them.

Chapter Eighteen

THOMAS SEIZED HER BY THE ARM and dragged her along with him through the green murk. Her beautiful dream had now become that most hideous kind of nightmare, in which one is pursued by some half-seen horror but can move only in slow motion. She flailed helplessly against the water, hampered by her body's own buoyancy. High above them the colossal shape loomed, black against the dimly luminous surface. She saw a gigantic head swinging from side to side, searching. The sea monster. Was the creature only hunting, or looking for them in particular?

"Faster," Thomas urged, the word escaping his lips in a silver stream of bubbles. He yanked again at her hand. Maeve risked a glance back over her shoulder, saw the long sinuous shape now winding towards them. It was still vague and indistinct through the cloudy brine, but she clearly saw the dull glint of teeth.

"There," Thomas was shouting. "In there!"

A deep shadow had appeared in the weed-hung slope: the

gaping entrance of some narrow cave or crevice. There was no time to check how large the inner cavity was, to decide whether it could provide enough shelter. Thomas pushed her in so hastily that she struck her arm on a projecting granite outcrop with bruising force. She squirmed farther in, disregarding the pain, leaving room for him to join her. Uneven rock faces met her groping hands. The cave seemed to go quite far back.

Thomas was now clawing his way through the fissure beside her. Behind him, the weak, watery light coming through the opening was eclipsed by a sudden darkness: the head of Cìrein Cròin. Looking back, they had a glimpse of grey-green scaly hide, serrated teeth, flat silver eyes as soulless as a fish's. The jagged jaws opened, revealing the huge pale mouth and the throat like a tunnel leading down into darkness. *It's too big*, thought Maeve in relief. *It can't get in . . .* Then the water around them stirred. They felt the dragging force of suction, like the pull of the tide, saw weeds and small fish spiral out of the crevice and vanish into the gaping maw. Thomas threw himself in front of Maeve and braced himself with all his might against the rocky walls. She clutched at him in turn, terrified that he too would be sucked out. For a small eternity, they clung there, silent in their shared fear, muscles screaming with stress.

At last the jaws closed again, and the head turned sideways. The staring, lidless eye, with its great black pit of a pupil—an eye made for piercing the darkest deeps—was thrust up against the crevice.

Thomas spoke in her ear. "Quick, while its mouth is closed. Go farther in!" He squirmed past her. "The cave narrows and goes upward, see?" He eased back again. "Go on!" he urged, pushing her ahead of him.

She scrambled forward, feeling her way with shaking hands. The crevice did indeed go farther back. She moved as quickly as she could in the darkness, hearing Thomas scrabbling along behind her. Then she felt the sudden movement of the water again, the deadly current that caught at her body and strove to drag her back; she braced herself once more against the slimy stone.

"Tom!" she cried, panicking. "Tom, are you there? *Tom!*"

A tiny heart-stopping pause, then: "Go on, Maeve. I'm right behind you."

She squirmed ahead. Still the narrow space went on and on; it twisted and turned, but no dead end met her fumbling hands. Even the dim green light was left behind. *Not another tunnel,* Maeve moaned to herself. Only it was not a tunnel, for it was not human-made. The messengers' tunnel at least had been the same height and breadth throughout its length, but this natural fissure or lava-tube in the hillside sometimes became so narrow that she felt she was being crushed, and only the thought of the monster waiting below enabled Maeve to force herself onward. *What,* she wondered, *would this tunnel lead them to? Some dark and dreary cavern in the mountain's heart? A lair with another monster in it?* At least with the messenger's tunnel one knew that there would be daylight at the end.

After what felt like hours, she realized that the fissure had begun to slant slowly upward. That was encouraging, and she pressed on with renewed strength. A few more metres and she was aware of a warmth on her face. Her head was out of water, and she was breathing without the aid of the cap. She had left the water level behind! And now that she was in air again, she could see a faint light up ahead. There could be no doubt: it was sunlight, pure and unmuted sunlight, pouring into the tunnel.

"There's an opening up ahead," she called to Thomas. He too was free of the water now, and was crawling eagerly after her.

A rough-edged cave mouth opened before them, and they struggled on through it to find themselves on the side of a hill, one of several that joined to form a vast, ring-shaped ridge. The circular space within the ring was filled with seawater, a calm lagoon-like expanse. At its centre rose three little islets, smooth sided but irregular in shape.

Hy-Bresail.

"We've made it," said Maeve wonderingly.

They stood, still blinking in the sun, on the dry, stony slope and gazed across the water. This was evidently the volcanic caldera, long ago filled like a cup by the rising sea. At its centre all but a few raised portions of land had been completely submerged. On these small, barren islets were shapes, badly worn by time and weather, yet still plainly not the work of nature. There were columns broken off at uneven heights, fragments of walls, the square outlines of foundations.

The two young people sank to the ground and sat still for a moment, weak with emotion and exertion.

"The sea serpent," Maeve said presently. "That can't have been just bad luck."

"What do you mean?"

"Why would something that big—an animal that hunts *whales*—bother with anything as small as we are? Someone sent it after us."

"The Selkie king, perhaps?"

"Or Domnu."

"Not Domnu, let us hope. That would mean she knows about our quest."

"We can't lose any time. We must cross the water right away." Maeve stood again, looking out towards the islets. She took a step downhill, but Thomas suddenly caught hold of her arm and pulled her towards him. Before she could move or speak, he had planted a kiss on her lips.

This time she did not recoil. There was no awkwardness between them now. They had shared so much, dared mortal dangers together and lived; and now they had arrived at their destination. Whatever happened from this moment on, the triumph of that journey could never be taken from them. She looked into his eyes shyly as he released her, and then she reached out and took him by the hand. "Just a little farther now," she said softly. "Tom, those ruins out there on the little islands—they must be what's left of the old palace and temple. If the Holy Grail is anywhere, it'll be there. Put your cap back on and let's go."

"No need, I think," returned Thomas quietly. "Look down there, at the water's edge!" He pointed.

She stared. A boat drifted there, a boat that might have been sculpted of ice. Indeed, she had taken it for an ice floe at first, seeing only the sun-dazzle on its hull. It was crystal clear from its high, pointed prow to its raised stern; it had no mast, no paddles, no rudder to steer with. "The *Curragh* of

Glass," said Thomas, his thin cheeks flushing with excitement. "The fairy vessel that needs neither sail nor oar, but moves by magic. Old Ned used to tell me tales of it. Someone has sent it to us."

"The fairies, you mean. Then they're not angry that we're here," said Maeve. "Perhaps they will listen to us after all."

They hurried down to the stony shore and examined the curious craft. The glassy substance of which it was made was hard, more like diamond than glass. Maeve marvelled that it could float. Thomas sprang fearlessly into the boat, his eyes alight. "Come! The *curragh* is here to take us to those little islands, I am sure of it."

Then did that mean that the fairies—whoever and whatever they might be—were on their side? Maeve fervently hoped so. She too clambered over the glassy gunwale, and sat down on a smooth thwart.

At once the boat sped away from the shore on its crystal keel. It moved smoothly, soundlessly, raising a glittering wake. They could see through its glass bottom the submerged floor of the crater, with stumps and toppled trunks of ancient trees lying there under the water. The sacred grove of Mannanan mac Lir? And surely those were the remains of a paved road that had once led to the ruins. Maeve's heart lifted—she wanted to laugh or shout.

It's been such a struggle just to get here. Can the end of the quest really be this easy? she wondered.

In less than a minute, the *curragh* had arrived at the shore of the central islet, on which the largest of the ruins lay. They stepped out onto the bare, rocky ground and looked about them warily. Nothing stirred.

After a moment, they approached the broken columns timidly. Maeve guessed from their great girth and ornamentation that this must have been the god's temple. There were the remains of a grand portico and, farther in, a colossal rectangular space heaped with rubble.

"Look," said Thomas, pointing.

She gazed at the shattered fragments of stone and saw a face staring out of the debris. It was a woman's face, carved of white stone and lying on its side. Not far away was a dusty marble torso, and farther on the curved flank of a leaping fish or dolphin. At the northern end of the ruin, a huge head, bearded like a king's, was lying face down, as it must have done for millennia. A severed stone hand a metre away from it still clutched part of a sceptre. The arched neck and head of a horse reared from the rubble beyond.

"The god," said Maeve. "Poseidon, Mannanan mac Lir, or whatever you want to call him. Plato said there was an idol in the temple sanctuary: the sea god riding in a chariot drawn by winged horses—"

"Mannanan mac Lir had an enchanted chariot, with horses that could travel over land or sea."

"And there were golden statues of the first ten kings, and a hundred statues of nymphs—a sort of sea fairy—riding on dolphins. It would all have fallen down, of course, when the side of the volcano burst open. What a shame! It must have been a magnificent place."

They searched the heaps of stone, but found nothing: no Grail of legend lay shining amid the debris.

"It could be buried deep under all this, I suppose," said Thomas reluctantly.

"It's supposed to be in the keeping of the fairies." She pointed to another ruin. "That must be the old palace—the one the god built for Cleito, or whatever her real name was." Maeve started towards the crumbling mass of masonry, its mighty walls and arched doorway still standing.

She had an eerie sense of being watched, of unseen presences lingering in the place. If not inhabited, the islet was surely haunted. She kept wanting to turn her head, although she heard no sound and saw nothing but crumbled stone.

The palace was a roofless ruin, a maze of cracked and broken walls that still formed chambers and passageways. A broken arch of stone stood before it, a gateway that now led nowhere. As they passed under it and approached the ruin, they heard a low rumbling sound from within, like stone grinding against stone. They froze. The sound came again, a grating growl. There was a wide gap in the nearest wall, and as they looked through it they heard heavy footsteps approaching. Thomas drew his sword.

From the gaping hole in the stone wall there strode a lion.

For an instant they stood transfixed, as much by the sheer unexpectedness as by any physical fear. The huge beast stared back at them, its shaggy shoulders nearly filling the gap, its jaws half open to show the yellow fangs. Thomas held the sword out, his hand trembling visibly. The lion's golden eyes narrowed. It came padding towards them, lowered its belly to the ground and sprang with a roar.

Both Thomas and Maeve leapt aside, but the lion was not attacking them. There was an answering roar from behind them. Another beast had been stalking them, and as they whirled they saw it: a reptile, long-bodied and splay-legged and armoured like a crocodile with thick green-brown plates. Its wedge-shaped jaws were open and slavering, its forked tongue darting past snakelike teeth. The lion bounded towards it, cuffed its head with one forepaw and then leaped on the monster's back, clawing and snarling.

The animals spun around in a whirl of green scales and tawny fur, spraying gravel, bellowing with fury.

The two young people ran for the ruin, Maeve looking back at the battling beasts. Suddenly, she stopped. The lion was getting the worst of it: its claws made no dint on the armoured back and flanks of the reptile, while the latter was tearing great gashes in the golden hide. Longer in the neck and legs than a crocodile, it was far more agile and also somewhat larger than the lion. Maeve could not help feeling sorry for the great cat. She was certain that its lunge had been more than a territorial assault on a natural enemy or a quarrel over prey. The reptile had been stealing up on her and Thomas from behind, and the lion, seeing this, had come deliberately to their aid.

Thomas too was regarding the fight thoughtfully. "Such a noble beast," she heard him murmur, "should not fall prey to such an ugly one—"

Before she could stop him he was running towards the two brawling animals. The dragonish creature was on top now, the lion's head almost in its jaws. Thomas leaned forward and stabbed at the softer plates under the reptile's chin.

With a scream the monster reared, releasing its grip on the lion, and collapsed on the bare rock, writhing. The lion stood, blood streaming down its torn flanks, its eyes of liquid amber fixed on the boy and girl. Thomas clutched his sword as it advanced, but it walked on, its great maned head bowed low. Maeve reached out to touch that head as it passed her; she felt thick, coarse fur, warmth, smelled the wild-beast smell. It was real.

Thomas approached the reptilian beast now, his sword still warily out, but it had stopped moving and its eyes were glazed. Blood trickled from its jaws to pool on the dry ground. It was dead.

"Look," said Thomas. He pointed with his sword to a trail of damp clawprints leading from the dragon's body to the shore. "It came out of the sea."

The ring of land around them, Maeve now noticed, was not solid: there were gaps in it where the ocean showed through—entrances through which a boat might come and go; or an unseen sea creature, swimming beneath the surface . . .

When they turned back to the ruin, the lion had vanished from sight—gone back to its lair within the tumbled walls, no doubt. But they were no longer afraid of it. Wiping his sword on a stone, Thomas sheathed it again and led the way into the palace of Mannanan mac Lir. A seemingly endless labyrinth of passageways led them towards the heart of the ruined building. Here they found an empty space where more broken-off pillars, like those of the temple, formed another vast rectangle.

"Look over there," said Maeve.

Several metres away, a small, tawny-furred cat was playing on the piles of fallen masonry, batting bits of stone about with its paws, leaping and dancing in the sun.

Thomas frowned. "Now how did that get here?"

"How did a lion come to be here?" Maeve walked towards the cat, her hand outheld. "Do you suppose he's an illusion, Tom—or something more? Could he be intelligent, a fairy in disguise?"

She was right next to the little animal now. It looked up at her with the lion's eyes.

She halted and stood motionless, watching as the cat calmly returned to its play. Thomas was wandering about the ruin. "This was a great room once, I think. See how large the foundation is, with no walls dividing it. A banquet hall, perhaps, or a throne room."

Maeve was silent, wondering who would have held court here. Morgana's ancestors? A god and his mortal queen? As they both stood in silent contemplation, the little lion-coloured cat mewed at them. Then, having got their attention, it leaped gracefully onto the nearest pillar, which had been reduced to little more than its cracked base. The cat crouched, sprang up onto the neighbouring pillar, and went from there to the next and the next, sometimes jumping up and sometimes down, but always landing neatly atop a stone stump. As they watched, he made a complete circuit of the pillared space. Then he sprang down to the broken pavement again and ran over to a heap of fallen stonework. He climbed this, leaped again. From pile to pile of rubble he sprang, and it seemed to Maeve that he now left a trail of fire behind him like a meteor—a ribbon of golden light that hung upon the air.

Thomas snorted. "What sort of a game is this? Maeve? Maeve, what is it?"

"I'm . . . not sure."

She was gazing about her, wide-eyed. She stood now—or so it seemed—in a grand, high-ceilinged hall, its roof of carved and gilded rafters far above her head. The pillars that supported it were still vaguely recognizable as those that stood in the ruin. She could no longer see the ruin, or Thomas, or the cat; but the strange fiery streamer that the latter trailed behind him was still visible, joining the pillars and weaving through the walls.

A long table in the centre of the hall was laden with a white cloth and lit by candelabra of gold. On platters of fine porcelain and silver lay a feast of exotic dishes. She saw a roasted swan dressed in its feathered skin, and lobsters and whole fish, and a boar's head with a baked apple in its tusked jaws; there were bowls of fresh fruit, flat, round honey cakes and pitchers of a honey-coloured liquor that might be mead. Maeve's nearly empty stomach cramped with hunger. It was like one of those fabulous dream-feasts from which the dreamer always awakes just before the rich array of delicacies can be sampled.

Don't eat of their food, her great-grandmother's voice said in her memory.

She swallowed, stepped back from the table. "Tom, do you see the great hall?"

"Hall? I see only the ruins. Is it the second sight again?"

"I think so."

A moment, then: "The cat has disappeared. He turned to a ball of light, then just faded away," Thomas told her.

The trail of fire had faded too. She spun slowly around. Though there was no one else in the *glamourie* hall, she was certain that she and Thomas were not alone. There were slight suggestions of movement—she could see them out of the corner of her eye, though when she turned there was never anything there.

"Who are you?" she called out. "Who's there?"

There was no answer, but a new light now hovered in the air of the hall, a great misty blur of golden-white luminosity that travelled around the perimeter of the pillared area. And she could hear a faint, sweet singing.

"Who is there?" she cried again.

There were pale, luminous figures moving through the chamber—again she detected them with her peripheral vision, but when she turned there was still nothing there. Like objects seen in near-darkness, they seemed to vanish when she looked directly at them but showed as a pale glimmer when she looked slightly away.

"What do you here, Shadow-child?" came a voice from the air above—a voice neither male nor female, high nor deep. She jumped violently, but could catch no glimpse of the speaker. "This is the place where mortal and immortal come together, where earth and heaven are joined. Why do you come here, to the veil that lies between this world and ours? You are not of either."

"Who are you? *What* are you?" she cried.

"We are the guardians of the Grail."

"The Grail! Then it's here!" she cried.

"It is. We watch over it—we whom you would call the Fallen Ones."

"Fallen Ones," she whispered. Horror filled her. "Then you're . . . devils!"

The voice was clear and tranquil and untouched by any

emotion. "Nay, we are not darkened. You call us that; it is not what we call ourselves. But we took no sides in the Great Conflict, and so we cannot dwell in the Light, but remain in this place of transition until we learn again to be as we once were. Some call us angels, others, gods, still others, fairies. Those of us who dwell in this place have a special task: to guard the Holy Grail, which belongs to neither this world nor yours."

There were figures now, shapes like the walking shades of men and women, though taller and fairer than any mortal. There were nine graceful maidens with hair of gold and two fair youths carrying candles, who walked to either side of the lead maiden.

Angels. She saw the interior of the church again, the plaster angel proferring his basin of holy water. Her hopes rose. Angels were good. They belonged to churches and Christmas; they would surely help her in her desperate need. She stepped forward, her arms outheld in supplication, but the procession ignored her. The unearthly voices sang on, and she saw that the light came from something the lead figure held in both hands, an object shrouded in a square of pale linen.

She followed the half-seen procession, torn between awe and desperation. Angels: messengers of good, of light and hope. She longed simply to gaze at them, to kneel before them in love and humility, to thank them merely for being. But the fate of a world weighed on her, and she could also see the faces of Arawn and Morgana and the families trapped in the *dún*. These beings *must* help her friends.

Then, as though she had spoken the thought aloud, the airy voice answered. It came from the leader of the holy procession, the woman who held the light in her hands. "We do not join in conflicts, child, nor fight upon any side in any battle. We are those spirits who took no part in the heavenly war, yet sympathized with the defenders of the Light. And so we dwell near the boundary of the high realm, the world that is the Light's.

"Once, the Three Worlds were one. We dwelt within a single realm, and the Light shone on all. But two chasms have opened since that time, dividing the higher from the lower realm and both from that one you name Annwn. The rebels chose the lower realm and cut it off from the Light; it became the Shadow-world. My people desired that the Three Worlds be one again, that there be no more conflict and no more divisions; this we sought to do by taking the middle way. But when we set ourselves apart from our brethren of the Light, another chasm was made. In seeking unity, we did but cause more division. The Shining Ones still yearn for reconciliation with us, but the Darkened Ones resist all our efforts. And many mortal creatures choose to be as they are, cutting themselves off from the higher realms, in which they no longer believe."

They had left the palace and were walking through the sacred grove. It was full of dove-white swan-necked birds that flew from tree to tree singing as no earthly bird ever sang. Everything here was as fresh as something newly encountered, and yet at the same time poignant, like a sight, or smell, or sound that carries one back to the earliest days of childhood.

"It is the world of the Light that you see here," the pale figures told her. "We stand upon its very threshold."

"It's . . . it's beautiful." If only Thomas could see it! How alone he must feel, standing and watching helplessly as she wandered about the islet.

Their hair and robes glowed, a hue between whiteness and fire. They did not shine, like something that reflects the light, but *were* light itself. "The greatest among us dwell now amid the stars," said the voice that was and was not a woman's, "which are as stepping-stones to the higher realm. Dana reigns there once more, and Gwydion and Arianrhod. Some of us, though remaining neutral, were very much in sympathy with the Fallen Ones; Cromm Cruach was of that company, and Domnu, and the one you call the Cailleach Bheur. These fell the farthest—not all the way into the Shadow, as did the darkened ones, but to the very deeps of this world that are nearest the Shadow. Cromm Cruach fell into the depths of the earth and that has been his abode ever since; the Cailleach Bheur and Domnu fell into the depths of the sea."

"Domnu was one of you."

"She was. Domnu fell the farthest, into the very abyss of the sea. She lingers now amid the fire-caverns and smouldering vents of the sea's floor, filled with hate for all that belongs to the Light. She wears no face or form, but has become a nothingness, a devouring void."

"She's trying to devour *us*." Maeve raised her arms in an imploring gesture. "We need the power of the Grail in Avalon. Oh, please let us have it, if only for a while. Until the battle's won. We'll give it back, I promise!"

The men and maidens were walking towards a round pillared structure now. Cleito's shrine? Entering behind them, Maeve saw a ceiling of white marble inlaid with precious stones, and beneath it stood a marble altar. The procession halted. The woman-form at its head bowed and placed the veiled and luminous object on it. The two who looked like young men placed their candlesticks on the altar, to either side of the veiled thing. All the figures then stepped back and stood quietly as though waiting for something, some sign or signal that would dismiss them.

Maeve tried again. "I came here with my friend to ask for your help. To ask you for the Grail."

The lead maiden spoke again. "The Grail is not ours to dispose of as we please. We merely watch over it."

"But you must give it to us!" Maeve paused, afraid she had been too bold, and tried a pleading tone. "Please . . . we'll return it, I promise. It's our only hope now."

"Then you must ask the questions," said the maiden.

"I . . . I don't understand."

"Ask and you shall be answered. But only if it is the right question."

Maeve was bewildered. She had read of people on quests having to answer mysterious questions and riddles. But to *ask* a question? How could she possibly know what to ask? *My quest is a question? Is that what I came here for?*

"One question have we answered. Two more you may ask of us," said the voice. "But have a care that they are the right ones, for much rests upon our answers."

No, this was not fair. To have all this rest on *her*, so much responsibility, so many lives—

"Ask!"

With an effort Maeve collected herself. "What . . . what *is* the Grail?" she asked.

The flames of the two candles suddenly stretched taller, as if a draught of fresh air fed them. The linen slipped away from the object on the table, exposing it at last to her view.

Maeve gaped at it. It was a shape of pure light, a glowing golden shape that moved and changed before her eyes like a dancing flame. Now it was broad as a salver, now curved like a bowl, now a goblet as thin-stemmed as a flower. She knew at once what it was. The luminous thing might have worn many guises in many worlds, but this flowing light was its true essence. Even here in Annwn, it flickered as a flame does, wavered on the edge of another, higher, realm.

"Well asked," said the voice in the air. "The Grail is the Feast, the flowing-forth, the cup of renewal and the cauldron of rebirth, the tomb of Death and the womb of Life. It is healing and hope; it is *charitas* that gives all and takes nothing in return."

"I . . . I think I understand."

"One question remains. Ask!"

The Grail balanced on the cusp of two worlds. She racked her brains desperately as it faded in and out of view. Would it pass out of this world altogether?

"Maeve!" Thomas's voice, bodiless as a spirit's, cut into her thoughts. "The sea . . . it has gone wild!"

The temple faded abruptly from her view. She was standing inside the circle of its crumbled foundation, with only the sky above her. Thomas was standing nearby. He waved with his sword at the surface of the crater lagoon. The water was foaming and boiling like a pot on a fire.

"What witchery is this?" he cried.

Maeve's heart thudded aginst her ribs. "It's Domnu," she gasped.

Scattered amid the foam were dark shapes, scaled and finny forms that were neither fish nor dragon but a hideous blend of both. Sometimes a man's pale face rose from the spume, its long dark hair plastered over its forehead like seaweed, then sank out of sight again. They might have been the faces of drowned sailors, lost at sea. But those black, bleak eyes were alive.

Another face arose, was followed by mantled shoulders and a chest coated in mail. Tethra. The king himself was here. He had abandoned the besieged fortress and made for Hy-Bresail, obeying his dark goddess, to keep Maeve and Thomas from finding the Grail.

He was moving rapidly towards them through the waves, and as he drew closer they saw that he was riding on some strange sea beast. They could see only a gleaming, glaucous back covered in lapping scales, and webbed claws thrashing at the surface. The creature's head was concealed beneath the water. Tethra steered his grotesque steed close to the shore, then dismounted and waded through the frothing shallows. "Domnu sees you," said the lifeless voice. "Did you think you could escape her?"

"Come no nearer," shouted Thomas, trying vainly to make it a command. "You cannot come here. It is a . . . a holy place."

The pallid face was as implacable as always. "The Grail will not serve us. But we can keep you from ever coming near it."

He drew a sword from his scabbard, a sword whose hilt was bejewelled and adorned with silver.

Maeve gave a choking cry. "Fragarach—"

"I took it," he said coldly, "from the failing grasp of Arawn, who would be called king."

"Murderer!" howled Thomas.

Into Maeve's mind came an image sent by the second sight: she saw Arawn fighting on the battlements, a plain steel sword in his hand in place of Fragarach. The king's face was grim and his sword arm scarred, but he lived still. At his side, Queen Morgana was fighting, her gold-headed spear seeming to leave a track of flame on the air as she swung it, much like the fire-trail of the cat.

"Tom, it's not true! He's lying!" shouted Maeve. But Thomas's own short sword was already out and up, and he was rushing on Tethra.

"*Tom!*" Unarmed and helpless, she could only watch. Thomas was younger, lighter of build, inexperienced. Only his wild, frantic fury enabled him to meet the Fomori king's defences. Blow after blow he rained on the other's blade. Tethra deflected each one, not troubling to mount an attack himself, his expression unchanging. He was toying with the younger man. And yet there was a joylessness to his cruelty. If only he would laugh or gloat, do anything that was human. But he simply repulsed the blows again and again, without effort, without fear.

Then she saw in terror that he was changing. Whether it was a true transformation or only an illusion was impossible to say, but his frame was growing larger, his shoulders broader. His legs were bowed like an ape's now, the hands that held his sword's hilt were broad and clawed. His pallid skin was tinged sickly green; tusks thrust from his mouth and horns from his matted hair; his eyes were dark no longer but bright red, as though they swam with blood.

"Run!" she screamed. But Thomas would not flee—because she was there, she knew. He could not leave her standing there unprotected, nor would he let himself show fear in front of her. *Oh, Tom, don't be a hero for my sake!* She could not rush to his aid, with no weapon of her own. Maeve whirled, tried to find the pale forms of the Grail guardians in the air about her. "You see what's happening! Help us!"

"It is not for us to intervene. You alone can help him. Ask!"

Sobbing, Maeve stooped to snatch up bits of broken rubble from the ground. She could see the Fomori king's figure within the giant shadow of the illusory ogre: Thomas was striking at limbs that were not real, his blade passing harmlessly through the air. With all her might, she flung the stones at Tethra's form, but most of them went wide and the ones that hit him did not seem either to hurt or to distract him.

"Ask," came the voice again.

Behind her, Thomas cried out in pain.

Maeve leaped back into the circle of the temple foundation and clenched her fists until the nails scored her palms. The question was there in her mind, it was there. What had Tethra said? "The Grail will not serve us. But we can keep you from coming near it."

Will not serve us . . . Is not ours to give . . . Then what use was the Grail?

She straightened, faced the presences that now shimmered at the edge of her vision and cried out with all her

323

might, with all her love and anger and fear: "I want to know what the Grail is for. Whom *does* it serve?"

There, in the desolate ruin, the altar of the Grail reappeared, its candle flames flaring into towering spears of light. "Well asked!" came the cry from the air. "The Grail serves those who seek it. Look, mortal child, on that which is yours!"

Maeve held her breath at what stood now upon the altar.

It was a cup, a tall chalice of beaten gold, its stem studded with precious stones. She had always imagined the Holy Grail thus—though in later years she would smile at herself. As if a poor man, a carpenter, had ever drunk from a golden goblet! But this was Annwn: here things were unshadowed and unobscured. Whatever form it might have worn in her world, the shape it wore here was true.

"You asked us to give you that which we had no right to give," the voice said. "You see now that we withheld nothing from you. Could we give you what was yours already?"

It was in her hands. She felt the cool metal, the gems pressing against her palms. But the radiance had not gone from the Grail. Looking into the cup was like gazing down a bottomless well of light.

Behind her came a shriek, but it was not Thomas's voice. It was a cry full of pain and yet there was no emotion in it, any more than there is in the rasping screech of a seahawk. Swinging around, she saw the Fomori king cowering within his cloud of *glamourie*, shielding his inhuman face from the light. Clutching the cup, she began deliberately to walk towards him; as she did so, Fragarach burst into flame in his hand, its blade a tongue of blue fire that sprang up in answer to the Grail light. The king gave another terrible, soulless scream and dropped the blazing blade. As he backed away, his mantle of illusion faded and fell from him.

Thomas rushed upon the Fomori king, blood still streaming from his shoulder. His arm came up, hovered, thrust forward. Tethra howled again and clutched at the blade now buried in his chest. No blood came forth from the wound, only water: a gushing torrent of water that smelled of the sea. Thomas pulled out the sword and stepped back staring: for the king's form was fading, as his *glamourie* had done. In his place there was only a pulsing, frothing column like the plume of a fountain, and as Maeve and Thomas watched, it subsided as a fountain will when cut off from its source, sinking ever lower and lower, until it was only a trembling pool amid the rocks. The wind abruptly dropped, and the sea was stilled.

Thomas dropped his sword, and his hands went to his shoulder: the rent in his shirt was rimmed with blood, but on the exposed skin there was now neither wound nor scar to be seen. He looked towards Maeve, eyes wide with wonder. And then she was running towards him, still gripping the cup in one hand; he flung his arms about her, and she put hers about him. They stood embracing one another, there in the place of the Grail.

"It is done," said the airy voice behind them. Their heads turned, for both could hear it now, though the speaker remained unseen. "You may take the Grail back with you, child of man, and with it the sword that you have won."

Fragarach lay, gems and silver glinting, in the pool of steaming brine where Tethra had stood. "The *curragh* of glass will convey you and the treasures safely to Avalon."

In that instant, understanding burst upon her, and she saw the whole pattern laid out before her, complete in every detail, like a tapestry. A sound arose from the earth beneath her: a song of power and joy that was death to darkness. She saw in a flash all the things that would come to pass—saw the forces of the dark, hearing the sound as a knell and knowing that their war was lost, falter and fall back from the beleaguered *dún*. Every stone in Avalon roared like the Lia Fail, every tree sang like the silver apple tree.

The Grail was won; it would come again to Avalon.

She and Thomas ran together towards the glass boat, bearing cup and sword with them, their free arms entwined. But the unseen presence followed them, and as Thomas was helping Maeve into the *curragh*, it spoke again.

"Stop! The quest is not completed."

"Not completed?" Thomas straightened, releasing Maeve. "But we have what we came for."

"You have that which you sought, man-child. But the maiden has not yet achieved her quest. One thing more is required of her."

"Required? You said nothing about that before."

Maeve drooped. She had been through so much, suffered through despair and exhaustion and fear. What had she left to give? What price was yet to be paid? Then she remembered the tales of Arthur's court, of the quest for the Holy Grail, and what became of those who achieved the sacred quest.

No, they can't mean that! Horror filled her. She had looked on the living fire that was the Grail in its own world, unlike Thomas, who saw only the form she had given it. But surely they would not exact such a price of her. They could not mean her to die, as the true knights who looked on the Grail had died. . . .

Yet was it so great a price to pay for so many other lives? For the lives of Arawn and Morgana, of Padraig and Branwen and Cordelia? For the return of peace, and for the removal of the dark? "Take what you want," she cried, stepping back from the boat. "I'll give all I have to give. Just let him take the Grail as you promised he could."

Thomas's face was white. "Maeve, *no*—"

"Leave, child of Annwn," the voice commanded. "Carry the holy treasures back with you into Avalon. The Shadowchild goes not with you." A shining, faceless form had appeared in the air, standing between them.

"I'm ready," said Maeve, steeling herself.

Thomas protested again, and she flinched at the grief in his voice. But already his figure was fading, and she knew that she also was vanishing from his sight. His cries were faint now, as though they came to her from across a vast distance. He was sailing away from her, the glass *curragh* was taking him across the sea to Avalon, where she could not now follow.

Darkness fell upon Maeve.

Epilogue

HE STOOD AT THE BACK DOORWAY, feeling awkward. It was a door he knew well, one that he had run into and out of hundreds of times as a child. Now he hesitated before it as though it were a stranger's.

Ellen answered his tentative knock, her familiar face a reassurance, but her smile was troubled. "Oh, Robert. I'm so glad you could come here, on such short notice too. Come in! Why didn't you call? We'd have picked you up at the airport."

"There was no need. I took the bus." He cleared his throat, a nervous habit of his since childhood. "Roy's in, is he?"

"Yes, here he is."

His brother looked so much older, and he wondered bleakly if he looked the same to Roy. Or *was* it age that made Roy's face look so pale, so drawn? He had lost his customary cheery look; his hazel eyes were tired, concerned, showing the lines at their corners. Ellen discreetly left the room so that the two of them could talk alone.

"It was easier than I expected to get a flight," he said

when they were sitting at the kitchen table. "I went on stand-by." The truth was, he hadn't been sorry to get away. The stress in the house had been palpable—ever since Maeve left, he thought.

Roy seemed as uncomfortable as he was. "I just thought you should know, Rob. It wasn't really necessary to come all the way out here. . . ."

Yes, it was, his brother wanted to say. *It was necessary for me*, because *it gave me a reason to leave*. He cleared his throat again, glanced out the window at the bay. Under the overcast sky, the water was leaden grey. "You said you were worried about Maeve."

"I just thought she needed her parents. Rob, I don't want to interfere with family matters, but it's been so hard to watch her. She just seemed listless at first, but lately she's appeared to be . . . almost frightened. She won't open up and talk about it, though. Whatever's going on with you and Maureen, I think she needs to hear about it from you directly."

"She will," he said dully. "I guess I've been putting it off." He continued to stare out the window. There was a long pause before he spoke again. "You know, Roy, I just couldn't wait to get out of here as a kid, get to the mainland and the big cities. I thought you were a real stick-in-the-mud not to leave. And you're here still. Imagine."

Roy also gazed out at the meadow and the stony beach, at the small wooden houses scattered along the bay. "I couldn't bear to leave this place," he said quietly.

His brother looked him in the eyes. "Exactly! That's because this place is *real*. Things that matter in the wealthy provinces don't matter here. But Newfoundland never changes—thank God. How I've come to yearn for a place without progress, a place where the countryside isn't being devoured by housing developments and strip malls, a place no one's trying to *improve*. I'm so sick of the urban jungle— the drive to get ahead, to flaunt and impress, to beat everyone else down. Did you hear about that Toronto stockbroker who committed suicide last week by jumping off a skyscraper? People don't do things like that here."

"Possibly due to the shortage of skyscrapers."

"You know what I mean. These people have every reason to give in to despair—more reason—but they don't. Why?"

"Search me."

"You know the answer, though." His gaze returned to the window. "Early in life, Roy, we approach the world with joy and wonder. That experience is still inside some of us—the way the young tree is still inside the old one, deep at the centre of its growth rings. But most of us lose that ability to connect with the world, and then we're like a tree that has rotted away inside. We have no centre, no inner life. We accumulate possessions for others to admire—big houses, fancy cars—because our life is all on the outside, and we don't really exist *inside* ourselves any more. Then we throw ourselves off skyscrapers. That's what I'm really afraid of, for Brandon and Maeve."

"Oh, I don't know," Roy said pensively. "I can't speak for Brandon, but your Maeve will never jump off any building, I can tell you that. She's in love."

He looked up sharply. "In love—with *whom*?"

"Not who—what. She's in love with life. She'll always love it, even when it hurts her. Mum was the same—how else do you think she survived the Great Depression, the war, the loss of a brother? She endured, she continued, she wove her pretty tales. She loved life right to her last breath—even when she was dying, there was a kind of radiance about her face."

Robert nodded. "I remember," he said softly.

"Maeve reminds me of her, somehow. She won't give in to pain, she'll use it. She'll take it onto the stage, where she can make other people cry and find release. I'm not worried about her in the long run, Rob, it's her short-term unhappiness I can't take."

What about my unhappiness? But Robert did not say this. He rose with a sigh and went to the door. "Where is she now?" he asked.

"She went for a walk. She does that a lot: goes off on her own, wandering aimlessly. There's nothing for her to do here, she's too much alone with her thoughts."

"I'll go look for her." But his voice was heavy.

Outside, the surroundings were poignantly familiar. He had abandoned this place for the mainland with a feeling of superiority, almost of contempt. Now the harbour, the hill, the forest, the rows of saltbox houses, all were a comfort and a reaffirmation. He was Robert Andrew O'Connor here, not some faceless failure in an urban wasteland.

There was no sign of Maeve. He searched along the shore for a time, then slowly climbed the hill, which seemed not to have changed since his boyhood days. He had come up here often, long ago, to see "everything"—by which he had meant the village, the forest, and the sea—spread out before him. Later, the word had amused him, and the village seemed to shrink in size and importance on each return visit. It still seemed small, but he laughed at it no longer. It was true that Mary's Bay did not contain everything. It only contained everything that mattered.

The city was not at fault for the hollow life he had lived there. He had chosen to seek wealth, had chosen his wife for her looks. He had not married for love, but for status and the desire to be envied. And so, cheated of real affection, she too had become twisted and sickly, like a malnourished child, hungering for other things to fill her emptiness. How could it have been otherwise? A real love would have been strengthened by adversity. He thought of his parents and grandparents, who had weathered worse trials, yet given shelter to one another and survived.

He suddenly felt his mother's presence, as strongly as if she stood at his side.

Wishful thinking, said the mainland part of him. But the old-timers down in the village, he thought, would have no trouble believing in lingering spirits.

He was nearly at the top of the hill when he noticed something lying a few metres away: a human figure sprawled motionless on the rough scree. His heart began to race. Its beats became almost painful as the figure grew recognizable on approach. His selfish concerns evaporated. He ran forward, shouting. The figure did not stir. He dropped to his knees in the gravel, shaking her by the shoulders and calling her name. But Maeve did not respond.

She lay suspended in an in-between place, like the tidal zone that belongs to neither land nor sea. Annwn had fallen away, receded like the tide. But like the tide, it had left some traces of itself behind. That flotsam still floated through her mind: a strain of unearthly music, eyes that looked into hers with tenderness, a cup . . .

A voice spoke to her from somewhere near at hand.

"It is not to the Light that I take you, child, but into darkness. You must be brave, and carry what you can of the Light with you into that darkness. But first I will show you what you have won for the worlds."

A vision formed before her in the darkness. She saw a grey standing stone under a blue, cloud-swept sky with two flights of wooden steps leading to its top. Two crowned figures were climbing those steps: a dark-haired man in royal robes and a tall woman whose black hair flew on the wind like the clouds. In Arawn's right hand gleamed the sword Fragarach, while Morgana held aloft the golden Grail; all about the base of the stone, people had gathered. There were finely clad courtiers there, and monks and villagers, and the ochred faces of the Beothuks. Maeve saw Padraig standing near the front, a scar on his broad brow, his arms about his wife and daughter. Not far from them Thomas stood, with pride and sorrow blended in his face, holding upright in his hands the shaft of a golden-headed spear. Above the people's heads banners blew and music played, but despite the sunlight and the fresh colours, it all seemed far away from her.

The king and the queen had reached the top of the stone, and they stood upon it together. In that instant a sound went up from the Lia Fail, a rejoicing voice as deep as the earth itself. Hearing the song of the stone, and feeling the ground beneath them pulse with its power, the people raised their own voices in a joyous roar. Then Arawn put his free arm about Morgana, and she placed hers about him, and as the crowd watched and cheered, they kissed, long and tenderly. The sun shone on their crowns, on the sword and on the spear head; but the Grail burned with its own golden light.

The colours dimmed, the vision grew faint. Only the Grail continued to shine through the wall of darkness that separated her from Annwn.

Remember the Light, said the voice within her thoughts. *Remember* . . .

"Maeve!" called a voice from somewhere above her—not the otherworldly voice, but another. "Maeve, what is wrong? Are you all right?"

Her eyes opened, cleared. She was gazing into the Grail's round rim again, down into the light that had no end . . . But no, that was the sun above her, emerging from the clouds, shining down on her. There was a face above her too. A man's face, with green eyes and hair greying at the temples. "Daddy?" she murmured, peering into the face.

His heart leaped strangely. She had not called him that in years. "Are you all right, Maeve?" he urged. Somehow there was more to the question than he had thought. It resounded in the clear air as though, by uttering it, he had broken a spell. "What happened?" he was asking her as she sat up, shaking off loose bits of gravel.

Maeve blinked. What *had* happened? It had been clear a moment ago, but already the pictures in her head were fading. Something about light and darkness . . . a cup. "I . . . I just lay down. And I dreamed—"

"You were *asleep* up here? I thought you had fainted or . . . or something." She could hear the relief in his voice. He bent to help her to her feet. "I guess you're surprised to see me here," he began awkwardly. "But I was—you know—wondering how you were getting on, and when Roy phoned—"

"Everything's fine." Maeve smiled up at him as she scrambled to her feet. There was still a light within her mind, the rumour of a song. "It's so beautiful," she began, trying to explain.

"Yes, it is," he agreed. "I'd forgotten how beautiful it was. I used to come up here as a boy. You can see so clearly—"

Suddenly she gasped and put a hand to her sweater, over her heart. "It's gone! Oh, it's gone! I've lost it!" she cried.

"What, Maeve?" he queried.

"Grandma's brooch. I've lost it," she repeated dully.

Somehow he knew she meant more than just the brooch. He himself felt a passing sadness, a feeling of something grasped and recognized, then lost once more. . . . No, not lost after all, but found. It was there inside, held safe at the centre. He *had* a centre again. "Don't cry, Maeve," her father soothed, holding her. "I'm here. I've come to take you home. Everything will be all right, I promise. I'll make it right." How could he say that, as though with certainty?

But she too had a look of certainty; a new confidence was in her hazel eyes as they looked up into his. "Yes," she said slowly. "Yes, it will be all right."

He tightened his arm about her shoulders, and together they went back down the hill.